# Adrift

Ellie Pond

MOUNTAIN KEEP
PUBLISHING

# Chapter 1

## *Launch*

Haley

I clutch my duffle bag over my shoulder. It's digging into my skin, while my suitcase thumps with each deck plank it rolls over. Eight a.m., but this marina is bustling. Crew are pulling carts of trash past me; birds squawk and circle above them. I've seen a lot of marinas, and this dwarfs them. It's twice as big as the dock of my last yacht, back in Fort Lauderdale. And the yachts here aren't like at home. *Good Boy*, to my right, is a mega yacht over 80 meters long. The next one, *A Good Deal*, is even bigger. The vessels here make the ones back in Lauderdale look like something you'd put in your bathtub.

My arm aches. Why did I bring so much? I know better. It's just that, after breaking up with Steven, I packed most of my things in the back of my mother's Honda to die a slow mildewed death in her Maryland garage. I've only got essentials with me—at least, that's what I told myself when I hopped on the plane.

I give a nod to a bosun on the next mega yacht. He's scrubbing the side of *Day Trader*, port of call Macao. He waves back. Damn, the muscles bulging out of his crew shirt have me walking a crooked line.

*Focus, Haley.* Having a boyfriend right now isn't what I want. Or need. And I've promised myself I will never, ever have another shipboard romance. And this time, I mean it.

Slip sixty-nine is at the end of the dock. I pray the slip number is a funny accident and not the mentality of the ship's owner. I leave my suitcase at the bottom of the gangplank, take my shoes off, and board. It's a massive boat, 85 meters long. I studied its plan on the plane on the way over.

The deck's empty and a bit of a mess. The deckchair covers are half off, and a bucket full of water sits beside the large outdoor dining table. Inside the main salon, it's not much better. The pillows on the sofa have tight plastic wrapped around them, and a tower of them are threatening to tip over.

"Hello." A deep, warm voice fills the space. "You must be Haley. I'm Captain Samuel. Call me Sam." He puts his hand out for me.

The jet lag is getting to me. I didn't sleep at all on the plane. And with the twelve-hour time difference, I'm in for a world of pain. I need to get a grip on myself. Because I'm staring at my boss like he's some sort of lollipop I want to lick.

Of course, I knew he was going to be good-looking. His brother Charlie—the first officer on my last boat and the reason I got this job —is handsome in that I'm-a-rugged-guy-who-likes-dogs-and-hiking kind of way. But Captain Sam . . . Damn. Thick dark hair, his crew monogrammed polo stretched tight over his chest. Deep blue eyes, with light laugh lines around them. If Charlie is handsome, Sam is traffic-stopping gorgeous. Is that even a thing for guys? If it's not, it should be.

I shake myself out of my daze. Charlie sent my CV to him, and Sam hired me a few days later. A godsend really. Getting out of Florida and away from Steven were my two highest priorities. And this is about as far away from Florida as you can get.

"Haley. Nice to meet you, Captain." I shake his hand firmly, like my grandfather taught me.

He laughs. Sam's got a touch of gray at his temples, wide shoulders, and his arms are those of a captain who does more than steer a ship and sit in the wheelhouse all day. I've never been interested in older men, and that isn't going to change now. I bite my molars together—I'm going to focus on the job, the primaries, and my staff. Being the best chief stewardess out there is my only task. I love being a stew. And I'm darn good at it.

I shake his hand, and that stupid spark of desire rolls around in me like one of my granddad's old pinball games. The captain's blue eyes land on me, and my face has to be turning five shades deeper red than the pillows lying on the floor.

I let go of his hand that I've been holding for too long. "Wow, this place is a wreck." I pause. Captains can be super defensive of their ships. "I mean, she's beautiful but a mess."

"You're correct on both counts. The owner, whom I've known for a few years, insisted they rush delivery from the boatyard, and the company obliged. They finished the interior mechanicals and built-ins, but we took possession on the day some of the furniture arrived from Singapore."

I do a one-eighty in the salon. Everything is in place, if you consider covered in plastic and cardboard "in place." A lot of the finishes that would normally be completed by now are taped down for rough seas or are in boxes on the floor. "My team will take care of it." We can make this place shine.

The captain looks away. His barrel chest lets out a huff, and he turns back. "Well, that's the thing, Haley. I understand I signed you on as chief stew of eleven."

The air in my lungs chokes me. I need the money of the chief stew position to afford to live on my own after the season's finished. I've put down a deposit on a nice apartment for myself.

"But things have changed a bit since you got on the plane to come here." He picks up a box off a chair and motions for me to sit. That's not a good thing. I don't want to sit.

Fuck.

I sit.

And he pulls up the chair across from me. "The owner of the boat has decided not to allow rentals this season. They want to take it all for themselves."

My chest relaxes. Owner-occupied means the tips won't be as great, but it also means not as much work. Unless they're the kind to bring a never-ending rotation of guests through. "That's no problem, Captain. Sam."

"Right, owners can be a pain. I've known this one for a long time. He's good. A daughter in her twenties and a son. I've never met him. Easton Rockwell, the Olympic swimmer. He's always too busy training to come out with his dad and sister. The thing is that this boat was to have ten stews."

"Eleven with me."

He nods. "Right? We're supposed to have a lot of stews. And it definitely calls for it. But the new fiancée doesn't want too many. She called yesterday, when they moved up their boarding again, and told me to knock the interior team down."

"All . . . right. Why?"

"All I could get was that they might be a distraction." The captain clears his throat. "Candy is a lot. I've captained boats for Rocky for years. His last wife was demanding but reasonable. She knew what she liked and how she wanted it."

"Demanding is normal. I can handle demanding." Pretty clever how he told me the fiancée isn't reasonable. "We can work with what we have. And how many do we have now?"

"Three." He shakes his head. "I'm sorry. I really wish there was something I could do."

"Three and me." What the hell? The jealous bitch. What does she think we'll be doing? Not the owner but his laundry.

"Three with you." He purses his lips.

"Did you find any male stews? Maybe she would be okay with some guys." Not that I want to take more jobs away from women in yachting. It's already such a male-dominated industry.

"One of the original ten was, but he hadn't left home yet. And if I had to make cuts, I didn't want it to be on the line of gender. That's not who I am. Your second stewardess, Shayla, is already on board. She was with me and the owners last season aboard the owner's old boat, the *Mermaid's Tale*. Shayla's been unpacking and working the primary cabin for the last two days. Your third stew will be here tomorrow."

I nod. That's yachting—you do what you do with the time you have. Providing the level of service I demand of myself and my team is going to be difficult. But I'll do my best. I need to brace myself for three months of no sleep. Hopefully, the new fiancée enjoys shopping and we can get her off board in a lot of ports.

"I've gotten a raise for your two stews. And I convinced the owner to double your salary." His blue eyes flash, and I want to see him do that again. They're so blue, if you saw a photo of him, you'd think it was a filter. But no, they're all him.

But double damn. I can do three months with no sleep for double my salary.

"I know it's great to have more cash, but I can assure you there will be more than one time this season you'll wish you had more stews and less money."

"I can already tell you I know that's going to be true. But I'm tough, and we can get it done." I wish he'd told me this twenty hours ago. Because if he let eight of them go . . . I studied their CVs over the last few days while I travelled. And I have definite preferences for which two I want. There's one that—as hard as I tried not to—I have already labeled as my problem child. A stew can only be as good as the chief, but sometimes you can't train stupid. Something about that one CV made me cringe. "Who is the other stew?" *Don't say Brianna, don't say—*

"Brianna."

My stew smile slips onto my face. The one I use when guests ask for six espresso martinis while I'm trying to pack for a beach picnic and deal with a belligerent chef. "Oh, I've read her CV."

The captain laughs. His rich tone pulses over me. What should I do? I cross my arms over my chest.

"Is that a problem?" He raises his perfectly arched eyebrow.

"No, not a problem. I might have preferred someone with a little more experience, if it's only the three of us. Her CV is lacking a lot of things." Like everything from bar skills to laundry, and forget about service and tablescapes. "What made you pick her?" I hope I don't come off too condescending.

"Right. She's a niece of the—"

"—new fiancée." It blurts out of me.

His nod and a faint smile make me shiver. Why? I'll have to unpack that when I put my clothes in my bunk. I'm not attracted to my boss. That's going to be my mantra for the next three months.

"Don't let that get around. If you're as clever as my brother says, you'll have figured that out, anyway. I'm going to ask you to try to keep the rest of the crew in order around her."

"You want us to keep things from her?"

"Negative. But don't let things get out of control. Or let any crew talk about the surrounding owners."

"Yes, Captain."

His smile lights up his face. "I'm glad you can abide by my rules. Do you want me to show you around?"

"No, I've got it. Unless there's anything special you want to point out."

"I can do that at dinner. It wouldn't be bad for the deck to hear it too."

I nod and stand in the doorway. I've worked on boats before where the deck hands helped a lot with dishes and serving. Never on a yacht this size. My breath catches.

"Do you have questions?"

"I suppose. Did the fiancée limit the deck crew too?"

"No, we're running a full deck. I detest compromising service, but I won't let safety be an issue. Not ever. They've already pushed us to launch earlier."

"Good."

"I'm happy to have you on board, Haley. Seriously, my brother Charlie spoke so highly of you. He made it sound like you didn't need any stews."

"Thank you. And tell him thank you again for the reference."

"Will do. Although you're liable to see him before me. That's the way it goes with a seafaring family."

I nod. I wouldn't know jack about family, seafaring or not.

"Oh, here. You'll need your radio. My cabin's that door there." He pulls a radio from the top of the chart stand in the back of the wheelhouse and points to the door next to the stand. "Open it up and look. You should know every inch of this vessel."

I clip the radio to my belt. I don't think too hard about how knowing every inch of this vessel starts with the captain's quarters. He's not flirting with me, is he? He gives me the most brilliant smile, his blue eyes shining in the early evening light. I have to look away. I duck my head into his room, a good-sized cabin. Even for a captain. I'm not going to hold out hope that the crew quarters in the belly are as good, though.

I have to get out of his room. The scent is amazing. Whatever his cologne is, it's definitely better than two charter seasons ago when the captain thought being at sea meant not taking showers.

A little wave and I run down the interior stairs. Leaving his space makes me feel empty. It's cozy with the dark tones.

Now for the fun part of exploring the yacht. I open the first door.

*I'm not attracted to my captain. I'm not attracted to my captain.*

Damn, I'm so attracted to my captain.

My body whips around the corner to what I assume will be the main salon or a hallway to the main galley, but instead I run smack into a hard surface. A hard surface that towers over me.

"I'm Haley," I stammer at him as his hand circles my waist to keep us both from tumbling over.

# Chapter 2

## *Bosun*

Zane

**D**amn. The sexiest girl I've ever held in my arms is looking up at me. Never mind that she practically knocked me down the stairs to the galley. Her feet settle and I let go. But I don't want to.

*Don't shit where you eat.* I play the words over and over in my head. It never ends well. Like never. Boat romances are awesome for keeping you busy and happy . . . until they're not. And this is going to be one weird season. A huge boat for an owners-only tour.

Yeah, I lift my hands off her. "You good?"

"Yeah. Shit, I'm sorry. I guess I'm excited about touring the boat. I'm Haley." She holds out her hand and I shake it, my cock twitching like a bastard at touching her again.

"Yup, you already said." A smile crosses my lips. Damn this girl. She's going to kill me. From her eyes to her shape. I really like girls with curves. "Zane Morris. Bosun." I finally let go of her hand, but her other one is still on my arm from where I caught her. Neither one of us has moved our feet, and the scent of her coconut shampoo is still swirling around me.

"Haley Brewster, chief stew." Her lip's between her teeth, and her cheeks are flushed.

Shit, Haley might get me to forget my rules this season.

*Bank over banging.* Not eloquent, but a memorable rule. It's rule number three. "I guess we're going to be working together a lot this season."

"I guess so." She lets go of my arm, and already I want to pull her back to me.

"Oh, for fuck's sake, don't start screwing yet. At least wait until the guests have arrived." Waldo keeps his barking laugh going.

Haley and I explode apart. I'd scowl at my secondary deckhand, but he's too clueless to even pick up on it. "Waldo Wiseman, meet Haley Brewster." I motion to the chief stew like a game show host.

"Charmed." He grabs her hand and gives it an over-the-top kiss.He's been living in Maine, though he said he's from Ohio.

A giggle bursts from Haley, setting my cock on fire. Shit, this is going to last forever.

"Nice to meet you, Waldo." Her eyes twinkle at him. And I want to cut his hand off or call dibs on her like my sister did with the front seat of my mom's car as kids. But we're adults now. So I'm totally telling him later she's off-limits. Because, well . . . I'll think of something. The poor interior crew is going to have a lot of work to do this season. And fuck me, we're going to have to help.

Waldo gives her one of his I'm-super-charming smirks.

"Oh, you're one to watch out for, aren't you?" Haley's laugh hits me in the gut.

Fuck, the last thing I need is a boat crush, and on the chief stew too. Heads of departments hooking up never works, with stews and deckhands taking sides like divorced kids figuring out where to go for Christmas when their parents split up.

"Want me to show you around, Haley?" Waldo sidles up to her.

"I'm good; there's a ton to do. But I'm going to take a minute to get my bearings and make some lists." Haley swallows and turns to me. "I need to get moving. This boat won't put itself together."

"Let me know if you could use a hand or two. Right now, it's the five of us who did the crossing from Singapore, but I have more deck crew arriving tomorrow. Three Americans, a Brit, and an Aussie. We're all in this together."

"I'm super excited you feel that way. Normally I like it when the interior can help on deck too if we're caught up on everything. But with the size of the boat and only three of us—"

I have to cut her off. "It's super infuriating that the primary's fiancée is being such a jealous bitch. Seriously, we are here for you. Waldo washes dishes like a pro."

"Just not the crystal!" Waldo grabs a slice of pizza from the crew fridge and waves as he heads to his cabin. We're taking a twenty-minute break, the first we've taken in eight hours. "I need to text my girl."

The door to our cabin clicks shut, leaving me staring at Haley. "How'd you get this gig?"

"I ran an 80 and a 75 last season. And I worked with the captain's brother out of Aruba. It was strictly one- or two-week guest charters for most of the season. The owner came on for the last three weeks. Super nice older couple. They were in bed by nine. They'd given up drinking. So other than a breakfast smoothie and keeping their waters full, it was a total vacation. Guess I'm paying for it with these owners. No good deed and all that." She waves her hand at the mess of boxes in the hall.

"True." I give a nod, my eyes turning away from the curves of her hips. Shit, I'm done for. I should say okay, see you around, but instead I say, "Let me show you where the primary cabin is. Shayla's in there. She's been at it straight for a few days. Opening boxes and putting things away."

"Right, the captain mentioned that too. A few days in one cabin?"

Showing her is the only way she'll understand. I guide her up the stairs to the primary deck. "Here's one of the larger secondary suites." I open the cabin door and shake my head. "I've helped deliver a bunch of other yachts before, and they never looked like this."

Haley darts in around me, and her mouth opens in an O. "What the heck." She runs her hands over the plastic-covered furniture. "Everything is shrink-wrapped."

It's worse than that—the shrink-wrapped boxes are piled high in the room's corner, leaving no space to even tackle unpacking.

"Every room is like this?"

"Yeah, it took us a few days to get the exterior fit for sailing. And we had to get out of the harbor. It's too busy to safely anchor." The two nights we had a local marina were barely enough.

"Every room," she repeats and shakes her head. "Well, it is what it is."

"That's one way of thinking about it."

She squeezes in between the boxes, and I follow her. "It's the only way to get through yachting with your sanity intact." Haley pats my arm again. Normally, I don't like it when people touch me. But her touch has me wanting to rub up against her like the captain's goldendoodle.

"I guess you're right." I'm leaning on the side of the bed frame, and shit if she doesn't look even better in the unlit cabin.

"I'm off to find Shayla and the primary bedroom." She charges out of the room, turning intuitively in the correct direction, but she walks by the stairs.

"There are six suites on this level. The primary is up the stairs."

"Six suites? Well, all right then." She turns to go up. And we shimmy around each other. Do I need to follow her? No. But I do. "Wow."

The grand staircase is something. "Shayla started in here before moving to the primary suite. There were boxes filling the entire space. I love the marble inlay." I run my fingers over the edge of a credenza with a bookshelf above it. There are a lot of horse paintings and sculptures. "It's not over the top, gaudy like some of the mega yachts." Not that I care what the interior looks like. But I know she will.

"It's actually kind of perfect. Not traditional but not super modern either. I guess I expected with a yacht named *Rock Candy* it would look like—"

"A strip-club?"

She laughs. "Exactly!" Haley's laugh makes me smile.

"After you." I wave her through into the owner's suite. Shayla isn't in here, but a six-foot stack of boxes is teetering next to a perfectly made bed. "Shayla?"

"What?" Shayla's muffled voice comes from the bathroom.

"She's in the bathroom."

Haley and I both turn toward Shayla's voice. The place is enormous: two sinks on either end of the room, a make-up table and a massive shower with enough jets to wash an entire football team at once. Not that I played club football past year ten—I had better things to do. Not that I remember what they were now.

"Stop right there." Shayla has her hand up palm-forward, like a policeman telling traffic to stop. "This room is almost done. It's the only part of any cabin I've finished, the only part of anything I've finished. Back the fuck up." She's wearing braids tied up in a bandanna on the top of her head.

Haley laughs again.

Shayla's eyes go wide when she sees her chief stew. "Please tell me you're Haley. And that you are really triplets who are going to trick the owner into thinking you are less people or you're a robot who doesn't need any sleep?" Shayla pushes us out of the bathroom.

"I am Haley. But no to the rest of it. Although, I don't need much sleep. The bathroom looks amazing, and hiring triplets would be a brilliant idea. We'll have to get the captain right on that."

"Shayla Smith, nice to meet you." Shayla peels a rubber glove off, snaps it, and drops it in a bucket of supplies on the floor. I'm not lying when I say Shayla scares me more than a little. "Well, praise the Lord for something." She smiles and taps a stack of boxes. "Maybe you can get the deck crew to finally help me—us—out?" Shayla throws her long arm over my shoulder and squeezes.

I smirk at her. We've worked on a couple of seasons together and have a love-hate relationship. She can be a lot, but so can I. "Let me get those for you, Shay." I take the box and the rest from the floor. "Where to?"

"Main salon," Shayla says.

"I'll see you around, ladies."

The two of them are chatting up a storm. Shayla either loves her chief stews or is planning their demise. And if the tables turn, I'm going to take her out. Even knowing Haley less than a few minutes, I can tell she won't see the sort of underhanded lengths that Shayla will go to. Shayla and I have history. I don't trust her at all.

I push the boxes up against the outside of the wall and grab my radio. "Hey Waldo, where are you?" Which I love saying because, well, one, it's his real name. And two, every time I've checked up on him, he's been working. So I don't really need to know, I just kind of like saying it.

"Hell if I know," comes back over the radio waves. I'm staring at the radio when he squawks back into it, "Just kidding. I'm in the storage compartment on the swim deck aft doing a water toy inventory. Can't let the owner's son, the golden boy, not have fun in the water."

"Copy. Let me know if you need me. I'm heading for the dumpster."

"Will do."

Shit, I hope this season is a good one. Last one sucked balls for me. But then again, who enjoys watching their ex get it on with their roommate? No on-board sex, no more stews. But damn, Haley is someone I need to watch over.

# Chapter 3

## *Propulsion*

### Calvin

It smells amazing in here. I love a fresh engine room. The new equipment hasn't picked up the high-octane scent of an older boat yet, and I love every second. I'm weird in that boat fuel is practically my cologne of choice.

A bell rings, and the ship-wide announcement comes over. "Captain Sam here. All hands, meeting in the crew mess."

The wipes in my pocket almost take care of the grease on my hands. "Let's go." I slap my second engineer on his back. There's four of us sewer rats down here.

In the mess, Captain Sam sits on one of the benches still wrapped in plastic.

"This place is looking better," I say, which isn't saying much because the entire ship is a freakin' disaster. Packing supplies and stacked boxes everywhere. When the captain told me we were taking possession early, I got excited. Because while I enjoyed the first week of staying in the hotel in Singapore, waiting for the Rock Candy to be ready. The second week was utter hell. The shipyard was running behind on the soft-scape of the yacht—the mattresses, pillows, curtains and extras. And the owner—prick that he is—told us to take delivery of the yacht as it is with things still boxed up. And what rich shits want, rich shits get.

"Thanks," says the girl sitting next to Shayla.

"I'm Calvin Green, engineer. Those are my minions." I jerk my head at the three of them.

"Hey, Calvin and minions. I'm Haley Brewster. Chief stew. I guess you've met the extraordinary Shayla already?"

"We've met." I ignore the shit out of Shayla. Four Med seasons ago, I passed out drunk on deck in between charters and she pulled my cock out and sucked it. Which normally I wouldn't mind, but then she went and told everyone I touched her first—which was total bullshit—just because I didn't want to date her or hook up more. I almost got fired. But the captain reviewed the tapes after I told him my version. I didn't exactly want my old captain watching her going down on me, but being fired didn't sound like a great idea either. The security camera proved I hadn't moved or opened my mouth before Shayla showed up to play Where's the Puppet.

Heavy steps down the stairs announce the rest of *Rock Candy*'s crew arriving for the meeting.

"All right. We're missing three crew members who are all coming in tomorrow: chef, third stew, and another deckie. For those of you who just got here, I won't lie. This is going to be a different season. If you haven't done owner-occupied before, it's a different beast. And on top of this, with the vessel being new . . . they've spent a hell of a lot of money and they are going to expect everything to be perfect." The captain waves around the room. "Two days. We can do it. As soon as the deck crew has things tidied up with the water toys, I need you to help with the interior. Anyone ever worked in the galley before? Because I'm going to need someone to help Chef get his galley ready." Both the stews raise their hands. "You've got enough going on, interior. Any deckhands?"

Good thing he doesn't glance our way. My department has enough checks and tests to run to last a month.

"Right, well, we'll figure it out. Who's cooking tonight?"

We've been talking about what it will be like when we get a proper chef on board since we left Singapore. But one more night won't kill us.

I raise my hand. "Waldo and I will cook tonight."

"Good. Hopefully Chef will make us something other than pasta tomorrow. Any questions?"

The chief stew waves her hand at the captain. "Any word on which of the owner's family will be with him? Shayla has a brilliant plan that we focus on those few rooms. The primary he's going to use first and then the other cabins as we get time." Haley folds her hands in her lap, her eyebrows raised.

"That's an excellent idea. Pick the rooms you're going to perfect and mark the others. The deck crew can work on those and at least get the cardboard and plastic in the dumpster before we set sail."

Shayla sits beaming at the captain. Should I let Sam know to keep his fly locked up? Maybe not.

Haley is clever. I doubt Shayla actually had the idea about the cabins herself. But now she's feeling like a queen bee from Haley talking her up in front of Captain Sam. *Well played, Haley.*

"That's it for tonight. Make sure you get enough sleep. Safety is always my most important rule. Falling asleep on the job and making poor decisions won't help anyone. Got it?" He points around the room at each one of us. A chorus of "got it," "copy," and "yup" rings through the crew mess, and people head back to their own disaster areas to work on.

The stairs to Engineering are a brief trip down the hall. "Hang tight," I say to my guys, whom I'm trying not to see as one-eyed minions. But so far, I haven't been impressed by any of the geniuses. I've got a lot of training ahead this season. And I need a schedule for these guys. Mitch, my second, isn't bad. But honestly, he's a little lazy. Then again, Thing One and Thing Two . . . Yeah, the captain used a yachting service to find two engineers this fast, since we weren't supposed to leave the shipyard for another two weeks. The two guys I had the captain hire first are still on a transatlantic repositioning cruise for a mega yacht. So I'm stuck with the warm bodies that I can hopefully train in time.

The whole galley is clear except for us. I pull out an info pack on the engines with a quiz on it. Unconventional by yachting standards, but I want to know if they've retained anything I've taught them in the last ten days.

I push pencils to each of them. "Do the best you can. I just want to know where and what we have to work on."

"Can't we do this in the engine room? I'll do better if I can see the stuff." Thing One looks like he might cry.

"Hey, do your best. I don't want you to see the equipment and read the gauges. I want to make sure you know the stuff. That you could explain it to someone else if you had to. Not guess at it." I stand up and rummage through the pantry. The first officer did the provisioning, and he's a health food nut. There's absolutely no junk food on board, and I'm going bonkers. I might have to break down and bake something. I used to bake when I was a kid. I don't have to worry about putting on extra weight, with all the lifting down in Engineering and sweating from the heat. My body stays fit without working out in a gym.

I'm just laying my hands on one last pack of peanut butter crackers when I hear Haley and Shayla laughing. I glance at my guys. My second is flying through the test, thank fuck. The other two are moving slowly. Thing Two's lips move while he reads. Doesn't mean he won't become a brilliant engineer. But might mean he'd make a better deckhand.

I grunt and step into the crew cabin hallway. Haley's laugh draws me in. It's deep and throaty.

"And then I said, 'Would you like another espresso martini?'" Haley says.

Shayla cackles like Haley's on a comedy special.

"Oh, hey . . . Calvin. I'm just telling Shayla about my last boat. She's worked with a bunch of stews I know." She puts a stack of shirts in a drawer.

I nod and put my hands on the top of the doorframe, leaning into her room. You're bound to work with some people over and over. And others you'll never see again. It's a minor industry. Perhaps not the Asian market for Americans and Brits, but the Med and the Caribbean . . . Hell, yeah, you'll work with the same people every once in a while.

"I'm across the hall," I tell her. "Unless you want to move people around?" It's customary for the chief stew to assign cabins. But a lot of the deck and all of the engineers moved on board weeks ago, bringing her in from Singapore.

"Oh, no. None of us have time for that. Plus, with the interior crew so small, we have a lot of extra cabins."

"Great. I'm down the hall. Give me a heads up if you need anything." I actually moved into my room after Shayla came on board. She picked the room farthest away from the crew mess. I had the one across the hall. They are the quietest cabins, but after she stood in my door talking to me while I was trying to go to sleep two nights ago, I packed up my one duffle and moved to the end. It had already occurred to me we'd have a lot of spare cabins. And Mitch was thrilled to have his own bunk.

Haley picks up her hard-shell suitcase and shoves it in under the bunk.

"Fancy," Shayla says.

"This old thing?" She taps the aluminum case with her foot. "Two, no, three seasons ago, the primary left it on board. She'd insisted on packing herself. And when the captain called her asking her where to send it, she told him don't worry about it, give it to Hallalahie, which was what she called me the entire trip. It was full of designer clothes five sizes too small for me. I sold them on Designer Beotch dot com and made a ton. I almost sold this thing too. Waterproof, and on their website they have an elephant standing on it, and it looks brand new. As far as I can tell, they don't go down in value. I'm going to use it until I'm done being a yachtie and trade it for an old VW bug."

I laugh. "You'll probably get some money back too."

"Exactly, you understand. Steven, my ex, wanted me to give it to him. But I snagged it before he moved out." She pushes the dresser drawer shut with her lush ass, then gives it a little extra tap, and my dick hardens.

Shayla clears her throat. "Your ex sounds like a real douche."

"Indeed." It might be the only thing I agree with Shayla on. I would have kept Haley and the suitcase. I tap the top of her door-frame. "I'm here if you need anything."

"Thanks." She's twisting her long light brown hair into a bun. And now I'm staring like a creep.

Right, the minions.

Back at the table, Thing One is stirring a cup of coffee. His test is face-down on the table. Thing Two might have sweat running down his neck. I definitely do, but for a whole different reason. This is going to be one hell of a long season if I don't get my cock under control.

# Chapter 4

## *Swamped*

Haley

"Oh, Shayla, never in my life have I been this tired. Wait, that's a lie. I had a twin have a twenty-first birthday on board once. Ten twenty-one-year-olds. The provisioner had to come out three times with more Moët 1942 and Grey Goose." I shiver at the memory and stare at my plate. I've given up on eating the cold, bland pasta. Instead, Shayla and I have melted into a lump on the bench in the crew mess booth. Shayla's head is in my lap, and I'm petting her hair like a dog.

"I'm pretty sure my soul left my body a long time ago," Shayla moans.

She's a lot. But so far, she's been absolutely fantastic at her job. And even better yet, she's taken every direction I've given her—even if she disagrees with it—without talking back. I just hope it continues. Having a strong second can be a blessing and a curse. Big time. But that's not something I can make a list for.

I push the cold spaghetti around the plate. It wasn't worth eating when it was warm. But I didn't have to make it, so I'm not complaining.

"Ladies, I hope you're about to go to bed." Captain Sam's deep voice shakes me awake, and my feet land on the floor.

Shayla bounces and jerks up, bumping her head on the underside of the table. "Shit."

"Are you okay there?" He's on her in a second, his fingers running through Shay's long blonde strands. And I want it to be me. *What in the hell is wrong with me?*

She turns her head and gives me a wink. "Oh, right there? Am I bleeding, Captain Sam?"

"No blood. You'll live." He pats her head and steps away.

But Shayla clings to him. I can't quite see—did she grab his ass? I might be down to one stew in the morning.

The captain turns to fill his coffee cup, and I give her my best death stare.

She laughs and slides off the bench. "Well, goodnight all. Or I guess I should say good morning."

The captain raises his mug at me. "You too! Get some sleep."

"When do you sleep?" It's a silly question. Good captains don't sleep. And if he's anything like his brother, he's a great captain. I just asked it to keep him from making his escape.

"I don't." His cheeks round up, and his eyes get a mischievous twinkle.

And now I'm wondering what his ass feels like.

"Get to bed, Haley," he growls.

I hold up my trusty notebook. "I will. I just have a few more things to write down before I forget them."

He laughs. "I get it. I'm the same way. Thanks for going the extra mile. But don't forget you need sleep too."

"Yes . . . I won't." I've had other captains with whom I've had a good rapport and would have joked, "Yes, Dad." But Captain Sam is more of a Daddy. Heat rises to my cheeks. I don't need to check a mirror to know there's a blush spreading over my face. I'm sure my chest is blotchy all the way up my neck. "I'm twenty minutes out from hitting the sheets." And now I'm blushing harder, thinking about him in my sheets.

Captain gives me a nod, and his eyes land on the floor. He's leaning on the edge of the counter with his ankles crossed, sipping coffee. Not moving, like he's waiting for me to finish.

I take a long sip from my water bottle. Captain Sam makes one heck of a thirst trap just standing there with his *Mermaid's Tale* mug.

I flip the notepad open to the primary cabin, but the words float on the page. What were Shay and I talking about before? Is it his presence that's keeping me from thinking? Or the jet lag and lack of sleep and food? Or quite frankly, all of it?

I circle a few things on the page and write "must do" down next to the primary closet. But I've totally forgotten the rest of the stuff Shay and I were discussing. Staying a moment longer, I hope it makes it look like I wasn't just daydreaming about the captain's ass. Oh, shit, now I'm truly thinking about his ass.

I glance up. He's staring at me, and I can't stop wondering what's going on behind his blue eyes. "All done." I raise the notebook and head out of the crew galley. "Have a good night, Captain." Then I remember the plate on the table. I turn to get it.

He's already scraped it and is washing it.

I rush to his side. "Oh, Captain. I'm sorry. I didn't mean for you to have to do that."

"It's fine, Haley. You've been working awfully hard, and it's not going to get easier . . ." He trails off and nods. Like in a horror movie when the main character tells the clerk at the convenience store outside of town they've just inherited the mansion on the hill.

I clasp my notebook tightly to me, hugging it like a shield. It pushes my breasts up to an obscene level under my chin.

His eyes drop to my chest, then quickly flick up. I drop the notebook to my side. "Well. Thank you. I won't forget in the future." I turn to flee for the hallway to the crew quarters—mine is the first room on the starboard side—but then I spin around again and give the captain a quick wave.

He nods back. "I know you won't."

"Goodnight." Racing to my cabin, I drop the notebook on the empty top bunk and collapse in my little bathroom. Small spaces have always made me feel secure. I did a transatlantic repositioning cruise from the Caribbean to the Med with no guests a few years ago —and as the only stew. I could have slept in an empty guest cabin. I did for one night. But I never fell asleep. I prefer my little bunk. I'm not crazy, though. I did use the palatial primary bathroom. As the person responsible for keeping it clean, my old captain let me decide.

That's the thing with yachting. There are rules. And a lot of them are the same on each boat. But a lot of them depend on the personality of the captain. I'm getting good vibes from Sam. He cares about his crew.

I pull on my pajamas, which are yoga pants and an oversized crew T-shirt. It's so big it would fit Calvin. After crawling into my bunk, I stare at the underside of the top bunk. It still has manufacturing stickers on it. My eyes close, but three a.m. means nothing to my buzzing brain. I'm so overtired. But I can't stop cycling through everything we have left to do. And when the chef comes tomorrow, he's going to flip out. The upstairs galley—the one he uses for the owners—is a shit show. Boxes stacked everywhere. The microwave isn't even installed. One of the giant walk-in fridges is still off. And . . . chefs are always the craziest out of all the crew. They're also the main reason for a big tip or no tip at all.

Anyway, I can help him. I will. I just hope he's normal crazy, not over-the-top psycho. The pictures on his Instagram account look amazing. But not everything you see on Insta is real.

I have to turn my brain off. One hundred, ninety-nine, ninety-eight . . .

Screw counting. I slide my hand down my stomach and into my

underwear. BOB is in my suitcase under my bed. I wish for the hundredth time that I could get off without having to think of someone, but my brain doesn't work that way. As my finger circles my clit, I picture it being Captain Sam's hand.

My legs spread farther apart, and I push my yoga pants out of the way. His other hand is behind my head, those blue eyes of his locked onto mine. He kisses me.

I dip my index finger between my lips and spread the release around my clit, working it harder. When the captain pulls back, it's Zane. It's better not to think of the captain. I picture Zane kissing down my chest, his tongue circling my clit. When he lifts his head, it's Calvin, the engineer who has to be a former linebacker. He picks me up and holds me against the bathroom door. It bangs with each of his thrusts. I hold on to his neck, clinging to his massive shoulders. Until I come.

My chest is heaving, and I pull up my pants, hoping my little activity didn't make too much noise. I get up and wash my hands and, with the softest crew wash cloth I've ever touched, between my legs.

There's a soft knock on my door. Crap. I pull my pants up and answer it. "Hey."

Calvin stands in the doorframe. Like the whole thing. The man is massive. And while my little self-help session was, well, helpful, I'm betting this man in front of me could have made it better.

"I was just wondering," he says, "is the electrical in your room flashing?"

"I don't know. I was just going to sleep. I turned them off, like, twenty minutes ago."

"Shit, sorry to wake you up. I'm chasing these circuits. Nothing's labelled right. I'm trying to install the microwave."

I glance back at my battery-powered clock. It's running, but the one on the nightstand that's built into the wall is dark. "That one is off."

"Perfect." Calvin flicks the dead switch on the wall. "Thanks.

Sorry for waking you up. I heard you in the crew galley a few minutes ago and didn't think you'd be asleep yet."

"No, not asleep." *Just thinking of screwing you and half the boat.* I pull my lips into my mouth.

"Okay, well, get some sleep." He turns and heads back to the crew mess.

My feet shuffle after him on their own.

"Haley?"

My eyes are hooded. All I can think of is a nice cup of herbal tea. On land, I might have been tempted to take one of my mother's old sleeping pills, but I never bring any of them on board with me. That's a quick way to get fired. "Just looking for some tea." I rummage through a cabinet near the coffee maker and come up with nothing.

"Tea?" Calvin asks.

"Herbal tea. Something to help me fall asleep."

"You're practically sleepwalking."

"Maybe, but I can't turn my brain off."

"Well, you need to try." Calvin sounds like the captain now.

"I'm not going to be able to."

"Not with that attitude, you're not." His smile fills his face with blindingly white, straight teeth. He inclines his square jawline to the cabins. "Anders did the provisioning for the initial ride here, and he's more into vitamin water. I'm more than sure he didn't order any herbal tea. Lots of protein powder, though."

"Right." I nod, my eyes closed.

"I have something for you." He takes my shoulders in his massive hands and guides me back to my cabin. "Climb in bed." I do, and he pulls the covers up to my chin. "Stay there. I'll be right back." I close my eyes, but my to-do list dances at the speed of a Russian ballet behind my eyelids.

"Here." He lifts the blanket and tucks something in with me. It's soft and worn.

"What is this?"

"It's my teddy bear. Works like a charm. And you can make fun of me if you want—I'm man enough to not care. Goodnight, Haley." Calvin's hair brushes the ceiling of my cabin.

"Thanks, Calvin." I hug the bear to my chest, and it smells like him: man, a bit of diesel, and a cologne I can't quite name. My brain is still trying to figure it out when I drift off to sleep.

# Chapter 5

---

## *Moored*

Captain Sam

Four hours of sleep is all I can get. Ever. This whole thing has taken a turn for Shitsville. I've never let an owner pressure me into doing something unsafe before. I told Rocky—Winston J. Rockwell, Rocky to everyone who knows him—I'd do my best, but if I at any point thought *Rock Candy*—the fucking name of the yacht—wasn't ready for the water, I'd keep her docked.

Then she, or rather the Candy of *Rock Candy*, wanted to go shopping before they departed. Changing the port.

It didn't help that the shipyard was running behind. But so far, *Rock Candy* has handled every test we've run her through. I don't have any reason to think she's not ready. It's just more of a feeling. But I've gone over the specs and all the data that the computers send out from our little scoot over here. They're all fine. Perfect, in fact. But I don't like being rushed. Never have.

I've plotted out the first week of the trip with Anders, my first officer. Rocky likes deep-water fishing, but we're keeping these first few weeks near a shoreline and harbor-hopping. He's been waiting to take possession of the *Rock Candy* for almost three years. And the future Mrs. Rockwell has been pressuring for it to be ready faster, since his old yacht the *Mermaid's Tale* was outfitted by the last Mrs. Rockwell. Last season when we were in the Mediterranean, she complained nonstop about how outdated the *Mermaid's Tale* was. It drove the crew batshit. It's the main reason my former chief stew didn't return for this season. I don't blame her. She's working on a smaller ship with fewer staff under her now, but I bet she's ten times happier there.

Last night I ended up holding the microwave up as Calvin finished installing it. I have been going ever since. It was an amazing sunrise, though.

I pick up my empty coffee cup and stare at it. I don't remember drinking it. Right, normally I train the stews to bring me a fresh cup of coffee every couple of hours. But I'm not going to do that this season. Haley and her team are going to have enough to keep them busy. They don't need to serve me.

No one has unpacked the coffee machine in the butler's next to the chef's galley, so I jog down the stairs, but the grip strip on one of the stairs catches my attention. It's peeling back. I set my mug down and muck with the step. As captain, I have to do everything. Especially on a new boat.

"Okay, who do you think is the hottest?" Shayla's voice carries up the stairwell.

"I'm here to work, not hook up," Haley responds.

"Right, sure, me too. But the two are not mutually independent of each other." Shay laughs. "Come on, Haley. Who should I keep my hands off so I don't piss off my boss?"

"I don't know. For me, it's not only about looks. I have to like the guy's personality to think he's hot."

Shayla drones, "Boring. Seriously, there are some hot guys on board."

"True." Haley hesitates.

"There you go. I knew I could drag it out of you. On a scale of one to ten—"

"No." Haley is keeping it professional. Charlie was right about her. I might even tell him.

I pull the strip back on the stair and reposition it. And I miss what Shayla says next.

"Fine," Haley continues. "Ten."

"Seriously? I've had that shit, and you can keep it. Four."

I'm not a teenager, and I shouldn't be listening to them. *And I'm not*, I lie to myself, *I'm fixing the steps.*

"Zane?"

"Ten," Haley says.

"Really. I'd say eight, but I also wouldn't say no." Shayla laughs. What about Waldo?"

"Pass."

"No fair, you can't pass. "

"I told you I need to have a feeling about a guy first. Or at least have had a conversation with him."

"Okay, I can accept that. I'd actually give Waldo an eight." A spoon clicks, and Shayla continues. "What about the captain?"

"Ten," Haley answers quickly.

"Okay, okay, I'm liking the rapid-fire answer. I'm going to go wide open ten."

"Wide open? Shay?"

"I'd suck him off. Wide open."

I cringe. I've officially lost it. The step is fixed. My coffee cup is back in my hand. What the hell am I doing hiding on the stairs? I stomp the last six steps around the corner.

"Ladies," I say without making eye contact. I head straight to the fresh pot of coffee and pour myself a cup. I take a sip. It's better than I've had on board since we launched. "This is good. Did one of you make it?"

"I did, Captain." Haley's face is bright red when I turn around. She's obviously wondering if I heard their conversation. And embarrassed. It's adorable. And while having sex with either of them won't ever be happening—they're a good ten years younger than me and I'm their boss—Haley is exactly the kind of woman I liked when I was her age. Until my ex-wife convinced me otherwise.

I glance at Shayla. That's it. I hadn't seen the similarity before, but Shayla looks a lot like Jenifer—my former wife. The girl I should have left alone.

"Well, it's perfect. Thanks." I lean on the counter. I should head back to the bridge, but watching them both squirm in discomfort is way too much fun. "How are the cabins coming?"

Haley looks up from her notebook, where she's been studying something underlined in thick blue pen. "Uh, good. I think after we finish our yogurt, we're moving on to the main salon and the back sundeck."

"Excellent. Brianna should be here early afternoon. Around the same time as Chef."

"Oh, that's good. But I was really hoping to get some of the boxes of dishes out of the galley before he showed up." Haley scribbles something else on her pad.

"We can get it done." Shayla gives Haley a tap with her elbow and gets up, taking both their dishes to the sink. "Ready, boss?"

"Yup."

The two of them head up the stairs I just came down.

I find some bread and plop it in the toaster. Haley's notebook catches my eye, and I spin it around to take a look. The Snooping Union is going to track me down and send me a union dues slip anytime now. What did she underline? I skim the page to where her pen has dug a canal in the paper. It reads: *Focus on safety and the guest experience—the rest is temporary.*

Damn, now I'm getting hard. I pivot the notebook back in the direction I found it, grab my dry toast and coffee, and head back to the bridge to finish my own bridge checklist.

Hours go by. I hear movement in the main salon. It backs up to my cabin behind the bridge. The first officer's cabin is next to mine, but he's down with Calvin and the engineers running a test on the engines.

My phone dings. It's Marjory. She's like the headhunter for the boat, but more like a casting director, making sure that all the personalities and talents dovetail together for the ship's crew. I get the last word, but she finds the talent. She's also responsible for the crew until they find their way on board.

"Howdy, Captain Sam." The line's got a ton of static on it.

"Marjory. How are things?"

"Well, canceling half the *Rock Candy* crew wasn't fun. But it's done. I've got an issue. Chef missed his connection at LAX and is delayed by 24 hours."

"Well, fuck. Sorry Marjory. I appreciate you doing the dirty work."

She laughs and inhales, most likely through a cigarette. "You're funny, Sam. I've heard a lot worse. Right now, he's scheduled in five hours from when you gave the owner's arrival."

"Right. Well, thanks for letting me know."

"Look at it this way, Sam. It can't get worse."

My jaw ticks. I'm not superstitious, but I don't ask for things to get worse. "Right. Have a good one."

"You too."

I hang up. Damn it. The future Mrs. Rockwell is super picky about her food, which is why I have a new chef coming in. Last week, I suggested to Rocky they stay in the city and do some more shopping. But Candy wasn't having any of it. And now the chef is going to be delayed. And the fanciest thing we've made since we left Singapore was a quesadilla with canned salsa.

I pick up my radio. "Haley, can you come to the bridge?"

"Copy, on my way," squawks back over. She appears before my radio's back on the charger. "Hey, Captain. What can I do for you?"

*Not be so adorable.* I make a mental note to do the sexual harassment training myself again. "Have a seat." I incline my head to the raised bench in the back of the wheelhouse and sit in my captain's chair. "So, you raised your hand at the crew meeting about cooking."

"Crew food I can handle, but I've never cooked for guests, and certainly never for owners." The tips of her ears are red.

"Right? Chef missed his connection at LAX. He's going to be here tomorrow shortly before the owners come on board. I'm going to start unpacking the kitchen." I make the decision on the spot. When I called her in here, I thought I'd have her do it. But holy hell, I've already swamped the girl with ten times the amount of work she can handle. Calvin and Anders can work this through. Right now, I'm watching the control panel. A trained dog could do what I'm doing. I swivel in my chair and grab the radio. "Captain for Anders."

"Copy," Anders replies.

"We're going to have to do a lot more than help the chef. We're going to have to set things up for him."

"Copy," my first officer says.

"Anders, send Waldo to the bridge to help out. I have to go work on the galley."

"Copy." He hesitates, and I don't blame him. But they can walk Waldo through the steps.

Haley sits patiently, but I can see the clock ticking in her eyes. "What do you want me to do, Captain?"

Damn, I really need to at least read over the policy again. Because having her on her knees in front of me flashes before my eyes. "Piloting a boat, running a crew—I've got that down pat. But I could burn water, and I'd sooner have chicken breast and broccoli every day than French cuisine. I'm going to start unpacking the galley. And I need you to at least give me some idea of where I should put things so the chef doesn't have to move everything."

"Oh, yeah. I can do that. I mean—"

"If he moves it when he gets here, that's fine. Every chef is unique." Which is my way of saying batshit crazy. But yeah.

Waldo and Anders arrive on the bridge a few seconds later. I nod at them and follow Haley into the galley, which is right behind my quarters. Boxes are stacked two tall on the counters and three and four tall on some of the floor.

"All right." My jaw is locked. And I'm wishing I'd given this assignment to one of the deck crew a week ago. But we've been straight out with mechanicals. Haley's staring, waiting for me. "What would your plan of attack be, Haley?"

"Oh, yeah. Well, I guess I'd take all the dishes and carry them out to the dining room. Same thing with serving pieces. Shayla and I are finding boxes of glasses in the main salon. But there's got to be more. I've seen the chef set up a section for savory and for pastry." She's rattling off what each cabinet might be used for, and my eyes are glazing over when she stops. "You know what? Let me get my sticky notes and I'll label things. Unless you want me to do it." She glances back to the main salon where Shayla has just let off a string of obscenities.

"No, I've got this. The sticky notes are a great idea. What's another good idea is getting Zane up here to help me move some things around." I flash a quick smile at Haley when I push the mic on my radio. "Zane."

"Go for Zane."

"I need your help for a few minutes in the galley."

"Copy," he sings. Damn, I haven't decided if he's chronically happy or lacking a little between the ears.

"Captain, I can move the boxes." Haley has pulled her head out of the cabinet.

"Oh, I know you're strong enough. But you've got a lot on your plate. Stop by in a little while. I'm sure I'll have questions for you." I wiggle my eyebrows at her. Overhearing her and Shayla last night is having a lasting effect on how she's reacting to me. Or she's overtired. Which we all are.

"I am. I'm super strong." She shows me her tiny biceps, and we both laugh.

"Thanks."

"Any time, Captain." She sashays out of the galley. And damn, I have to rip my eyes off of her.

Box cutter in hand, I open a dozen boxes. I know what most of the things are. The new chef ordered the majority of supplies. A double-long box marked "stress reduction" is baffling, though. I slice down the tape and stare at the contents, then push the button on my radio mic. "Zane. Where the hell are you?"

# Chapter 6

## *Heave To*

Zane

"Coming, Captain." Running up the stairs, I don't know what he wants me for, but it has to be better than what I was already doing. We were testing all the sea toys: the wave runners and outboards. Which sounds like a lot more fun than it is. It just means getting wet, drying off, and getting wet again. Fun with the right girl, not so fun with saltwater, Asian humidity, and a to-do list as long as the boats. Not that I normally make lists, but watching Haley at supper last night, I got some inspiration and started off writing down a few things.

The galley is on the top interior deck. I climb up from sea level, hustling just shy of running. You don't run on a boat unless it's an emergency. I have no idea why the captain is in the galley. I did a season with him in the Med a few years back, and I never saw him do anything in the galley. Actually, I don't know if he can even make a cup of coffee.

"Cap?" I call. All the cabinets are open, boxes scattered about.

He stands from behind a pile of boxes. "Look at that box over there and tell me what the hell it is."

My brow furrows as I pull back the lip of the box. And laugh. "Fuck, I was wondering where that had got to." It's bright yellow, not exactly what I thought it would be.

"What in the hell is it?"

I smile at him. "You gave me the spec sheets for the season. One of them was a raunchy birthday party for the owner's daughter. I figured what's raunchier than a ride on an inflatable floating penis toy?"

Captain Sam has his hands on his hips. He purses his lips and glares. "They'll love it. But get it out of the galley before the chef turns up and stabs it."

I pick up the phallic plastic floater in its oversize box. Damn, it's heavy.

"Wait. Last I saw, the swim platform is looking halfway decent. Can you spare an hour to help me get the galley in order?"

"Sure. What do you want me to do?" Normally I hate when a captain asks a question when they mean to give an order, but Sam really is asking. That's one of the reasons I said yes to a season in Asia. I usually like sticking in the Med—it makes the trip home to the Midlands a hell of a lot easier.

An hour and a half later, I'm finishing up emptying what feels like the hundredth box of plates. They're stacked in the cabinets and we'll have to wash them later, but at least it's a few more pounds of cardboard gone. Haley and Shayla are working in the main salon, and I can see flashes of Shayla's red bandana and Haley's blonde hair when I'm not on my knees putting plates in the cupboard.

"Zane?" It's Waldo on the radio.

"Go for Zane."

"What do you want me to do next?"

"I'll be right down." I've made a good dent in the boxes, and I can do more tonight. But getting the swim deck done now with the remaining daylight is a priority.

I duck my head into the galley, but the captain is gone, and damn, he's gotten more than half of the boxes put away, and the rest sit stacked along the long wall, where on most boats extra provisions would go. I thunder down the stairs to talk to Waldo. A short blonde with waist-length hair and claw-like nails is standing on the deck next to the gangplank. She has two suitcases, almost as tall as her, a backpack, and an oversized tote. Or the normal amount of luggage a guest brings for one week.

"Yoohoo." She waves her long nails at me.

"Me?" Fuck, she better have the wrong yacht. We aren't ready for guests.

"Yes, you, silly. Come get my bags." The white skirt she has on wraps around her ass but not much else. Her blue and white striped crop top plunges to a single little button, and that button is working overtime. The white beret cocked on her head holds back a mass of blonde hair. She waves at me again.

"Are you sure you're looking for the *Rock Candy*?" Against my better judgment, I make my way to the back deck and the gangplank. My face comes flush with the top of her head.

She gives me an upward look through her fake lashes, one that tells me how exasperated she is with me. "Yes, I'm looking for the Candy Rock. Are you going to take my luggage?" She puts her hand on her hip and all but taps her toe at me.

"One second." I grab my radio. "Captain, Zane."

"Go ahead Zane."

"I have someone here who is looking to come aboard the *Rock Candy*." I might emphasize the correct name of the boat a little. "What's your name?" I ask, not on the radio.

"Brianna Snodgrass." She cocks her head, her lips puffed out.

The radio squawks static. I need to remember to talk to Calvin about adjusting the antennas. We need to have good communication to run a smooth team. "Her name is Brianna Snodgrass," I repeat to the captain.

The mic clicks on. "Bring her on board. That's our third stew. Let her know I'm up in the wheelhouse. Have her come up and talk to me first, before getting settled."

"Copy that, Captain." I hook the radio onto my belt. "You heard that, I take it?" I raise my eyebrows at the sassy over-packer in front of me.

"Yes, I heard that." She drops her purse and her backpack in a pile next to her suitcases on the dock and saunters down the gangplank.

"Hey, excuse me?" I call to her barely covered backside. "You're going to need to help bring your own luggage on board."

Her eyes flip down to my bare toes and up to my sunglasses resting on the top of my head. "Isn't that your job?" She pivots back to the boat.

"Yeah, for passengers. I'm more than happy to help you, but at least grab a couple of things." My arms are flailing around the bags like a silent movie actor.

She doesn't stop, not a pause. Just heads right into the boat. It crosses my mind to push the bags into the ocean. But I'm an environmentalist, and they would sink to the bottom of the harbor. With my luck, we'd hit them and I'd have to dig a Gucci belt out of the propeller.

I pick the two bigger bags, push them onto the gangplank, and manhandle them on board, leaving the two smaller bags on the dock because she can come back and get those herself. There's pretty good security here in the marina. The more expensive boats and mega yachts are down a long, gated dock. The bags are safe, most likely. Part of me hopes they aren't.

I wrangle the two large bags up a flight of stairs just to have to take them down three to the crew mess. The bags bounce down there with me. Am I careful not to scratch the walls? Yes. Am I careful with the bags? Hell no. I treat them like a baggage handler at LaGuardia who's working his third overtime shift in a week.

When I push them into the galley, Haley has her never-ending list spread across the table. Her hair is twisted up into a messy bun with a pencil sticking out of it. Something else too. The seat next to her beckons me, and I slide into it.

"What ya up to?" I cock my head, dropping it almost onto her shoulder. Damn, she smells good. If it wasn't creepy, I could just follow her around and sniff her. Shit, I need to get laid.

"Lists, but they're almost pointless. There's that much to do. But I've prioritized the most important things." There's an untouched sandwich sitting in front of her.

Shayla comes down the hallway singing some Broadway song I don't know. She plops down next to me, pushing me into Haley. I might have to pay Shayla as a wingman if she keeps it up. "Oh my gosh. Haley, eat your sandwich," she yells in my ear.

Haley glances up from her list, then gathers up the paper and takes a bite of her sandwich. "Fine," she says with her mouth full. "It's delicious." She chews half the sandwich, finishing it in three bites.

Watching her eat shouldn't turn me on.

Shayla pours a glass of milk and puts it in front of Haley. "You ready to get back to work?" She wiggles her hips. "What the heck are those?" She points at the gigantic bags both of the stews hadn't noticed before.

"Those little babies belong to third stew, Miss Brianna Snodgrass." I whistle because if I say what I want to, I'll come off as a dick. "She's up with the captain now."

"Ooh, what's she like?" Shayla asks.

"She's something you're gonna have to experience for yourself. This is just part of her luggage, by the way. There's a few more on the dock, but she can get those herself. I've got to get back to the deck." I push out of the bench, reluctantly leaving. But shit, I've got a lot to do. Hopefully, after we've gotten this boat, well, ship-shape, we'll have more time to get to know each other.

"If you see her, can you tell her to come find me? Because yeah. Oh, lord." Haley stares at the massive bags. And back at Shayla.

Shayla points. "If she thinks she can steal a single inch of my closet, she's going to have another think coming." Shayla tosses back an energy drink and shoots the empty can in a perfect arc into the bin.

"I'm going back to work." I smile at Haley and nod to Shayla.

"Since when do you work, mate?" Shayla mocks me.

I pat her on the back and do the same to Haley. Damn, touching her sends sparks through my body.

I climb the stairs. Even though she's two decks away, I can hear Brianna's voice. She's loud. Like a mom-rooting-for-her-son-at-a-friendly-Saturday-afternoon-match-when-she's-had-a-few-too-many-drinks loud. Come to think of it, she smelled like alcohol too.

# Chapter 7

## *Mess*

Haley

I try not to watch Zane's perfect ass go up the stairs.

"It's a good one, isn't it?" Shayla's looking too.

I wrap up the rest of my sandwich and put it in the fridge. Shayla is one of those people whom you love or want to strangle, depending on the minute. I know after only a day with her I'm going to be friends with her forever. When she suggested we come down for lunch, I wasn't going to eat. But then she made me a sandwich. How could I pass it up?

Shockingly, I never finished my complete tour of the ship. Shayla and I got wrapped up finishing the owner's suite yesterday and today. We've gone from the back portico straight through to the main salon.

"You want to head back to the main salon? I'm going to go up to the wheelhouse and introduce myself to Brianna."

"Will do, boss." Shayla salutes me and heads up the stairs.

I gather my notes and stare at the luggage. Brianna really thinks she's a guest. Why in the world would she need two giant bags and more? And where the heck is she going to put it all? I spent a few minutes yesterday during lunch checking out her social media, and after two minutes I closed it. And I shouldn't be shocked by the giant bags.

In the wheelhouse, Brianna is sitting on the bench on the far wheel. She's swinging her legs, but a flash of beige and bright orange on the far side of the captain's chair catches my attention. A step forward reveals a goldendoodle wearing an orange life vest. The dog is glaring at Brianna.

"Oh, who is this—"

"I'm Brianna." She cocks her head at me.

But I'm after the furry goodness next to the chair.

"Oh, that's my best mate," the captain says.

"Thanks," Anders, the first officer, pipes up from the corner of the bridge. I didn't see him either. His head has popped up from under the control panel, his feet sticking out into the middle of the room. I bite at my lip, wondering why the first officer is under the control panel of a brand new mega yacht. It doesn't build confidence in the *Rock Candy* for me.

"I'm going to have to get my vision checked," I say. "I didn't see the dog at first."

"That's Penny, ranking of first dog." Anders laughs.

Dropping to my knees, I hold out my hand to let Penny have a sniff. She licks the side of my hand, and I scratch her behind her ears. "It's nice to meet you," I whisper into her fluffy curls.

The captain folds his arms over his chest, and his forehead scrunches up. Penny gives me an odd look too. "Wow. She likes you."

Penny lies on her side.

"The feeling is mutual. It's so awesome to have a dog on board. Dogs relieve so much stress for their owners." I scratch her behind her ear, and her back leg thumps. "I bet she's such a good girl." I glance over at Captain Sam and Anders. Interesting, they're looking at me like I've grown a second head. "What?"

Anders cocks his head. "It's just Penny is particular about who she likes and who she doesn't."

"Yeah, dogs like me. All animals, actually." I shrug it off and try not to think about my own dog. Well, she was Steven's dog, but with us both working on ships so much, he gave her to his parents and then they moved back to New Jersey. He never really liked Ginger, said she wasn't a real dog. Just because she was a mutt. I should have known then what an ass Steven was. Luckily, I like Barbara, his mom, enough not to worry about Ginger. I still miss her, though.

"I don't like dogs." Brianna is cowering on the bench. "One bit me when I was little."

"I also used to be scared of dogs. You just need to get to know the right dog." I scratch Penny again.

"Penny's safe," says Captain Sam. "She's never been aggressive to anyone. I wouldn't allow that kind of dog on my vessel."

I extend my hand to Brianna. "Haley Brewster, chief stew. Nice to meet you."

Brianna shakes my hand in a delicate grasp before pulling it back. "It's nice to meet you. I was just talking to the captain about how excited I am to be working on the Candy Rock."

"*Rock Candy*," the captain corrects her.

"Right." She gives a little smirk. "And I was saying how draining traveling is. So if you can just show me to my room, I'm going to take a nap."

"A nap." My eyebrows shoot up. "I see. We have a lot to get done before the owners come on board. Shayla, the second stew, and I have been working since we boarded."

"That's nice. But I'm tired, and trust me, I'm not good when I'm tired. I just need a good eight hours and I'll be ready to go."

"Eight hours is a nap?"

"Yes, I'm a terrible napper, so I need eight hours."

I glance at the captain; his arms sit crossed over his wide chest, his lips firm, and I get it. He's saying it's my department, my call, without saying anything.

I take a big breath in and out. "Brianna, the interior is a team, one that works together. And I know you've got jet lag. I've got wicked bad jet lag too. But the way through it is to stay up. If you go to sleep now, you're going to be up all night."

"That's fine, you can put me on nights."

"Well, you're the third stew, so you're going to be doing mostly laundry and housekeeping. And that's a position I need awake on mids. Let's go find your cabin, get you changed, and I can show you the laundry room." The middle of the day is the busiest on a yacht.

"Laundry room?"

"Let me at her." Shayla's arms and legs are flailing about like a windmill, but she's not actually moving, so I'm almost certain Brianna isn't in any physical danger.

I want to train her, have her be an asset to the small team we have, but other than locking her in the laundry room and praying she actually does something, I don't see how I'm going to get any work out of her. And worse, she's hurting Shayla's productivity already.

"Go take a nap, Brianna," Shayla mocks.

Brianna cocks her head and heads down the main stairs. I spent almost an hour getting her into her cabin with Shayla. Which clearly isn't going to work. Tonight I'm going to ask Shayla if she wants to move in with me. I was looking forward to having my own space, but it's not going to be worth it if I have to work so much harder during the day to make up for Shayla's frustration from rooming with Briana.

Seriously, it's a super good thing the captain already told me about her being related to the owners, or I would have put her up for dismissal already. Less than three hours after she's come onto the boat and I want her gone already. And it isn't ever going to happen.

Shayla drops her hands at her sides and huffs, "You need to do something about her, boss lady."

I nod. "I know."

Shayla is glaring at me.

"Do you want to work on one of the smaller suites? We have to have two of them ready by tomorrow. And if you happen to take a little rest . . ." I shrug.

"I'm going to do the aft portside one. But I'm not resting. Though I am going to lock the door. Radio me if you need me." Shayla nods and takes two steps toward the stairs, then pivots, grabs the large tote of cleaning supplies, and heads to the aft cabins.

The main salon is almost done. Really, there are a dozen more things I want to do. But most of them I can finish when the owners are on board. First, I need to let the captain know what's going on.

Fresh cup of coffee in hand, I knock on the bridge door. "Captain?"

"Come in." His tone is deep and vibrates through me.

"I thought you might be out of coffee. I haven't seen you come down the stairs."

"You're an angel. Thank you." He lifts the mug to his lips. "But you've got enough on your plate."

"Shayla and I are making great progress. I'm moving on to the dining room next, and Shayla is taking on the junior suites."

"It's really looking good." He holds his coffee mug to his lips.

"Thanks." I want to run my fingers through the ends of my long ponytail. It's a stress thing I've almost cured myself of, but my last chief stew told me it's the biggest tell for when I'm uncomfortable and feeling insecure. I never want the captain to know I'm not in control of my department. That I can't handle all two of my staff. But he needs to understand that Brianna isn't here to work. At least, I don't think she is.

Anders' head is still under the main control panel. He and Calvin have moved their radio communication to another channel.

"What's up? That's the face of a department head who wants to have a chat if I've ever seen one."

Anders wiggles his legs. "Calvin, try now. Anything?"

"Nothing," Calvin says over the radio.

"Right, try the next breaker."

The captain is staring at Anders' feet.

"It's okay. I'll come back later." I cross my arms over my chest to keep from pulling on my ponytail.

"I was just about to take Penny O-U-T. If you can spare ten minutes, why don't you join me and we can talk and W-A-L-K."

His dog is at his side in the next second.

"That sounds great. Can she spell?" I laugh.

"No, she thinks anything I spell has something to do with her. Which is fine until I'm spelling out call signs on the radio."

I laugh again. Dang, I need to reel it back in because it's not that funny.

He clips Penny into her harness. "I'll meet you on the dock. I have to get my shoes."

"Let's go, Penny," I say. She trots ahead of me, her ears flopping to the side. "What a good girl you are." She sits and waits while I pull my outdoor shoes out of the crew bin by the gangplank.

We're waiting for Sam when he appears out of the side door. I can't help but lose my train of thought regarding what I was going to talk to him about. The man is amazing. Most captains have slumped postures. They're tired and broken, but not Sam. The way his crew polo shirt pulls over his shoulders, I'd love to see him in one of the swim shirts the deck crew wears. But why would he ever have to wear that?

"There's the girls." He pats Penny on the head when he joins us on the dock, and I've never been so jealous of a dog before.

"So, I need to—"

"Let's walk first. We'll put some distance between us and the *Rock Candy*, and you can really speak your mind."

"Okay." The wind is blowing at our faces, and the sun is dipping down into the afternoon sky. And if I didn't have a list of three thousand things to do, I'd be enjoying it. "I've never been to Asia before, have you?" I glance up at the captain. He has the most stunning profile: square jaw, perfectly sloped nose, like an Adonis statue cut from marble. Geez, I need to get a hold of this crush before he picks up on it.

A slow smile spreads over his face, and he nods. His eyes catch mine, and he snaps his head away. He focuses on Penny leading us down the long private dock. A crew of a mega yacht named *Payback* is serving guests on their back deck. A woman with long raven hair flowing in the breeze raises her champagne flute to us—to the captain, really.

He doesn't even glance at the bombshell. "A few times."

"Right."

We reach the end of the dock, and the captain holds the gate for me. "Ladies first."

"Thanks." It's weird how that expression normally makes me want to run screaming in the other direction, away from whatever misogynist said it, but I don't get those vibes from Sam—the captain—at all.

*All right, Haley, get yourself together and stop thinking of him as anything but your boss. Your extremely hot, sexy boss.* I smile at him and wait as he locks the gate. During the day, there's a guard in the little box at the end of the dock that separates the big boats from the little ones.

We pass the day cruisers and some fishing boats on the way to land. Penny jumps on the captain the second her paws touch the ground.

"Wait a second, little girl." He snaps off her vest, and she trots a few feet away and, well, does what dogs do.

A shiver runs through me when he says "little girl." I reflexively bite my lip and look away from them. The temperature has dropped enough to make the evening bearable, but the breeze from the harbor brings goosebumps to my bare arms. The sun has dipped below the skyline, and the sky is an amazing orange and red.

"Haley, let's sit while Penny runs around a bit." There's a small chunk of land that's next to the dockmaster's office, and a tiny bench.

"Sure." I perch on the edge of the bench, and when the captain sits down, it feels intimate. His bare knee is inches away from mine.

And I've suddenly forgotten everything I wanted to say to him. Instead, we both watch Penny running crazy loops around the yard. With the dog sprinting and the sun setting over the water, this feels more like a date than me conferencing with the captain. I don't want to talk about Brianna. I don't want to think about her. The captain is watching his dog. She's chasing a bug, and it's hysterical. When I turn to him to ask about her, I pause. His blue eyes are twinkling at me, his lips open like he wants to say something but has forgotten what. He holds my gaze and then turns away.

"How old?" I ask about Penny.

"Thirty-nine."

I lean forward, turning my attention away from the dog to focus on the captain. "In dog years?"

# Chapter 8

## *Provisions*

Dante

The cab swerves to avoid hitting a moped again. This one carries a whole family. The wife has a large cardboard box on the top of her head and a baby strapped to her back. You'd think my heart would miss a beat. But I live for this shit. If we end up hanging around port long enough this season, I'll buy one of those scooters and check out the local street food scene. Bring on the fried crickets and pig's testicles.

The driver stops in front of the marina.

"*Xie Xie*." My dialect is off. But I get an A for effort. I pull my backpack out and sling it over my shoulder, then make my way through the maze of golf carts and supplies by the harbormaster's office. It's late and they're bound to be closed. Calling the captain and letting him know I found an earlier flight would have made sense. But my last two captains didn't even know how to text message, and I hate talking on the phone. So not worth the effort. The *Rock Candy* is a new 85-meter mega yacht. I'll find her.

One of those popular poodle mixes barks at me as I come around the side of the building. Damn rich people and their fucking dogs. But this one is cute, and she lands on my feet.

"Hey there, puppy." I scratch behind her ears, and her hind foot thumps.

"Penny," a man calls.

And my new friend flies back around the building. I follow. Two yachties sit on the world's smallest bench—it's definitely some sort of date. The way they are looking at each other, they're about a minute from fucking on the tiny bench. And I wouldn't mind watching because, shit, they're both hot as fuck. The girl's toned legs are crossed, and her flip-flops lie on the ground in front of her. She has really delicate feet, and the rest of her is superb too. Curves, but in the right places. The guy is older. First officer material for sure, but enough muscle on him that it hasn't been too long since he was a bosun. The dog is doing acrobatics by the guy's feet.

"Hey." I wave. "Do you know where the *Rock Candy* is docked?"

"Slip 69." The girl laughs.

"What?" says the guy. "I didn't pick it. It's what the yacht needed for her size."

"Sure, thing, Captain."

I glance back at the two of them. "Captain?"

"Captain Samuel Miller of the *Rock Candy*." He gives a nod, but then he turns back to the beauty next to him. "Haley Brewster, chief stew." When he looks back at me, I see it. It's a moment of frustration. I've definitely interrupted something.

"Dante Evans. I'm your chef." I cross my arms over my chest.

"Hallelujah!" Haley exclaims, and now my mind is wandering to all the ways I'd like to see her cry out in celebration. "You're early. We thought you weren't going to be here until tomorrow."

"Yeah, well, I found an airport employee who was able to think outside of the box. She saved me a good eighteen hours. But they lost my luggage. She warned me that my bag might not make it. They said they'd send it to the port tomorrow when it catches up to me. But you know, like shit. I'm ordering new knives from the provisioner and charging it to the boat." I don't care if Captain Sam likes it or not.

"That sounds great to me, as long as I don't have to cook for the guests." The captain holds a life vest out to his dog, who dutifully sits while he puts it on her.

"That's horrible," says Haley. "I'd offer to go shopping for you, but . . . you'll understand when you see the boat."

"How bad can it be? I thought she was brand new?"

The captain snaps Penny into her lead. "She is, but with the shipyard running behind schedule, so were the outfitters. They barely had time to put the furniture in the cabins before she had to sail away to make it here in time. I captained the owner's last boat, and I explained to him it would be better to let the outfitters finish, but he was insistent that we couldn't wait. That we'd have to make do. After the season, I'm taking her back for finishing touches."

"Rich can do what rich wants to do." I hold my fist out to give Haley a fist bump. Which she reciprocates. "I'll just go ahead and board. I didn't mean to interrupt your meeting."

"It's fine." Haley's voice trails up, telling me it's anything but fine. "I can show you around the boat. I know the captain has a ton of things to do." She glances at him and whispers, "I'm sure."

"Great, I'd love to have a guide." I smile. And the half-second death glare from the captain tells me my first reaction is right. Usually is. I've got a knack for being able to tell by the end of my first or second day who will hook up during the season.

I don't do on-board romances, because they always go wrong. Always. An internal shudder travels through me. But the captain has some amazing taste. Captains don't usually partake in the cabin-hopping of yachties, but I can't blame him if he does.

"Come find me later and we can discuss the rest of what you wanted to talk about," he says to Haley.

The captain's dog leads us to the ship, and the captain takes off for the bridge.

"She's pretty." The *Rock Candy*—dual motor, sleek design—is state-of-the art. I haven't looked, but I'm guessing a heck of a lot. "I'm just hoping they didn't skimp on the galley." Now my heart is thumping like a chain smoker running a marathon.

"I'm sorry," Haley says. "The captain and the bosun tried to unpack, get things going for you. Everywhere looked like a dump before they started. Shoot, that was just yesterday." She's sucking on her lip.

"It's not your fault these rich bastards couldn't wait to take possession of a boat that wasn't finished. And trust me, this isn't bad. I've taken over so many galleys where there are layers of grease and expired food. Not here. So I'll be able to cook them something when they come on board. When?"

"Tomorrow lunch." Nerves bounce off of her.

"Listen, we've got this. You, me, and your team. Who needs an elaborate team? Just brings more drama."

"True. I hate the drama. And I don't have much of a team."

"Love the ship. Hate the drama. And with so few of us, how can we have any drama?"

"I put the number for the provisioner here." She points to the board where the owner's preferences sheets are pinned to the wall. "I also ordered some things because I thought you weren't going to be in until tomorrow. Basics. But I printed out the list." She's taped it to the wall.

"Perfect, great." I run my finger down the list of things she's ordered. All the normal stuff. "That's a shit ton of chicken." Normally I leave it off the list of things I buy. It's common, and who comes on a ship like this to eat common food?

"Yeah, but on the provision sheets, the owner's son eats mostly chicken and broccoli."

"Oh, for fuck's sake, why the hell even come on a cruise if you're going to eat like an overgrown douchebag?" I pull his preference sheet off the wall and circle his well-groomed face with a pen from my fanny pack. "Easton—it even sounds like a frat boy."

"You've never heard of Easton Rockwell?" Her lips jut out in question.

"No." I slap the party boy's sheet back on the board. "Why? Is he more than a party boy spending daddy's money?"

Her eyebrows rise. "He's a three-time gold medalist in swimming. He's about to take over Rockwell Harding financial group from Mr. Rockwell."

"His father."

"He's an Olympian. He has to eat a certain way." She points to the paper.

"Not anymore. He's on a mega yacht throwing down preferences —that makes him a diva." I didn't yell, but I might have raised my voice a little. Either way, Haley cringes like I've smacked her across the face. I bow my head and take a cleansing breath. "My therapist tells me I'm too rigid. I suppose it doesn't matter what the little twat won't eat. His loss." I randomly open cabinet doors. Things are almost where I want them. Fixing it later is the better plan, if my OCD will let me. "I'm going to make some eggs. Want some?"

Haley sucks her lips in; I feel her glare on my back as I find the few things I'll need.

"How long have you been a chief stew?"

"Three years. I was a second on a 70-meter for a few years before that."

I get the sauté pan hot and some butter melting. Damn, this is a nice stove. Actually, the fridge is top-notch too. I do the one-hand egg crack. Am I trying to impress her? Maybe. Not that she isn't overly smitten with the captain already. I do a quick chop on some of the basic herbs I find in the fridge. I'm impressed they're put away the right way: plastic bag with a damp towel to keep them fresh. I tip the bag up to her in question. "Well done on the fridge provisioning. I'm a firm believer that the chief stew is the second most important person on the boat."

"Is that right? And who is the first?" Her cheeks are like apples. She's expecting me to say I am, and she'd be right.

"The third stew in the laundry room. The ship can't work without clean laundry. If they don't have their shit together, then we're all looking like shit." I flip the eggs onto a plate.

She laughs.

"You sure you don't want some?"

"I'm good. I've got a lot to do. I should get back to work."

"I don't know about you, but I can't think when I'm hungry. You know how temperamental us chefs are. You're not going to turn down the first thing I offer you, are you?"

"No, I guess not." She finds a fork from the butler's pantry and takes a delicate bite. "Wow, this is amazing." The second bite is a larger one. "Mmm. So good. I use all the same stuff, and mine never tastes this good."

"It's in the care and the control of the heat."

She takes another bite off the plate. I made enough for two, but this sassy woman is going to eat all of it, and I could watch her all day. "Aren't you going to have some?"

"I was testing out the stove. You take them all. A peace offering for ranting about diva boy earlier."

"It's fine. I'm used to . . ."

I don't want to supply the answer for her, but "crazy chefs" is one of the normal things people mutter about my profession. In the end, I couldn't care less if they call me crazy, as long as they call me talented. My eyebrows rise with my smile. I turn my cheek to her.

". . . dealing with intense chefs," she finally finishes.

"Well, I have a feeling we're going to work out together just fine."

She finishes the eggs and washes the plate.

"How long have you known the captain?" Damn it, why can't I keep anything locked down?

Haley's at the entrance to the dining room. "Um, this is my first season working with him. Why do you ask?"

"No reason." I shake my head. "You were deep in conversation when I interrupted."

"Yeah." She stares above my head. "I had something to talk out with him."

"And did it go well?"

"Actually, we never got to it."

"I guess you'll have to take another walk."

Her apple cheeks are back. "I suppose I will." She leaves the kitchen.

I roll up my sleeves and try not to think what the captain and Haley do behind closed doors. Then I laugh because I sure as hell am going to be picturing it later.

# Chapter 9

## *Manifest*

Easton

The hangover throbs behind my eyes. Why in the hell did I think drinking with Yichen Zhao, the former swim champion from China, wouldn't completely suck today? Last night I had more fun than I've had in years, but then I had to wake up and face seeing my father and his fiancée. Making today a new low.

The cab hits another bump. I hope to hell I can remember to never do it again. I don't drink for a reason.

I suck at it.

My body isn't used to being poisoned the way it was last night. Dad told me to wait at the hotel for them until tomorrow. But if I can sneak into my cabin, I might be able to keep Candy from pinching my ass. One more night without Candy is a gift. I'd do anything to not have to spend one extra minute with that gold digger.

This whole thing is ridiculous, but my sister Emily and I are hoping to pull Dad aside and get some alone time with him. We'll go fishing. There's nothing Rocky likes better than deep sea fishing. We'll take the tender out and get him away from the bitch. The last thing Candy would ever do is go fishing. She's molded him into a completely different person.

He's a changed man since he kicked Susan to the curb. He wears low-rise jeans and form-fitting T-shirts at home. He's stopped going to the club's poker game on the weekends. I know because the organizer called me, trying to get him to come back. Rocky is shit at cards, but he throws chips into the pot like he's a World Series of Poker main event winner. Which is fine. My dad has worked hard his entire life. He's run two marriages into the ground by staying in the office 24/7. When they remodeled the offices a few years back, he put a small sleeping room off to the side. The same room where I caught Candy going down on him last week. She'd known I was coming in because Dad's administrative assistant told me they were waiting for me.

Fuck, it's not something I can burn out of my retinas. I hope to hell we can talk him out of marrying her. I never would have thought that Susan—Dad's second wife after Mom died—would seem reasonable. But seriously, Susan seems downright conservative with her spending habits after watching Candy. But my dad is thinking with his dick. And Candy is thinking with diamonds in her eyes.

I anchor my feet on the floor of the cab to keep from flying across to the door. We've taken enough turns to screw into the earth's crust. But this guy assures me with his not-half-bad English that he knows where he's going. The car stops in front of a rundown harbor house. From the parking lot, all I can make out are fishing charters and smaller boats. But if this marina is like others, the mega yachts are farther out, under lock. I give the driver a tip. It's not customary here, but damn, I'm alive, and there were a few times I didn't think I was going to be.

The harbormaster's house is locked up. Past a little strip of land, I follow the dock. The boats turn more expensive the farther out I go, until there's an empty guard shed and a closed gate. I jump it. Finding my dad's boat can't be that tough. Especially not since Candy helped design it. It's huge and gaudy like her. That's what I'm expecting. Hell, I don't even know the name of the vessel. I should have thought this through. But scanning the bigger boats at the end of the dock, there's only a handful it could be.

I make my way down the pier, taking in each yacht. The first two aren't quite large enough. The third is too old. The next one is too small and too old. I stop and glare at the one after that. *Holy Mackroll.* That's the name of the boat. It's new. And big. And far too classy to be anything Candy was involved with. But I should make sure.

There's a deckhand washing down the side of the boat. They're always washing something, whether it needs it or not. Not that I've been on board one of my dad's yachts in years. He enjoys going out and spending too much time there. When I was training professionally, I couldn't be away from the pool for that long. And no, swimming in the ocean is a completely different thing.

"Hey, excuse me. Odd question: is this yacht owned by Rocky Rockwell?" My dad's real first name is Winston. But the last person to call him that—that I know of—tucked me into bed when I was eight and I never saw her again.

"Rocky? No. Are you thinking of the *Rock Candy*? She's in the second-to-last slip."

"Yeah, that will be the one. Thanks." I try to keep the irritation out of my voice.

"Hey, aren't you that American swimmer?"

"I used to be." I raise my hand in a goodbye and saunter to the end of the dock, to the slip he pointed out. I have to check the back of the yacht. This can't be the right boat. It's sleek and good-looking. I figured it would at least have a pink racing stripe or a lion sculpture on the bow. Candy has a thing for lions and horses.

There's another deckhand polishing the back chrome of the boat.

"Hey!" I call.

He looks down at me.

"I'm Rocky's son, Easton. I know I'm early. Any chance I can crash here tonight?"

"Tonight?" His voice cracks. "Um, let me see." He turns away from me as I wait on the dock, but it wasn't hard to read his shock.

I cross my arms over my chest, stretching out my biceps. It's a habit I'll never get over. But it is what it is. I glance at my watch. It's late. Like, you shouldn't show up at someone's house this late. But this is my dad's place. It will be mine someday.

Emily has a trust fund. It's not huge, not by Rockwell standards, but that was what she requested. She doesn't want any inheritance from Dad and only agreed to the trust fund to shut him up. Last Christmas, she told me the second he's gone she's giving most of it away to charities and political candidates she thinks Mom would have liked. It's up to her. My sister doesn't need Dad's money. She's a top-ranked editor for the second biggest publisher, and she gets to work from home. Not exactly a job that will land you on the Forbes 500, but Emily isn't out for money. A lot like Mom.

"The captain told me to bring you on board." The crewman is standing there glaring at me. My bag is small, but he doesn't offer to take it and I don't hand it to him.

"I'm Waldo, lead deckhand. I'm on night watch. But we're docked. The captain is getting up; he'll be out to meet you in a minute."

I follow him; we're moving through the decks to the top. "Easton." I shake his hand. "Right, Waldo, I don't need a lot of formalities. I don't need the whole crew coming out."

"Good." His mouth cocks to the side. I guess I deserve that.

Waldo slides open a door and there's the captain. I've seen pictures of Captain Sam. Emily loves him, says he's a wonderful influence on Dad. But I call bullshit because Candy was on the *Mermaid's Tale* last year and the captain's wonderful influence didn't get Candy's claws out of Rocky.

"Easton," the captain says as if I didn't haul his ass out of bed.

"Captain Sam. It's nice to finally meet you."

"Same. Your father thinks the world of you."

"My dad also likes Spam, so I wouldn't put too much stock in that endorsement."

"You must be tired. Our chief stew, Haley Brewster, will show you to your cabin."

I glance up, and the most beautiful angel is standing at the entrance to the bridge, her hair pulled back into a ponytail. She's got curves for days, and I'm becoming a lech because I can't stop staring at her. She nods to the captain and then shakes her head as if she's trying to wake up.

"I'm sorry to wake you. Easton Rockwell." I put my hand out. I hope she shakes it.

"It's no bother. I haven't been to bed yet." She shakes my hand, and I end up staring into her blue eyes. "If you follow me, I'll take you to your cabin. I'll give you a full tour tomorrow." She stops in the doorway of the bridge. "Unless you want one tonight."

"No, that's fine, Haley. Tomorrow will be great." I like the way her name rolls off my tongue.

"Okay then. Goodnight, Captain." She smiles.

"Goodnight, Haley. Nice to meet you finally, Easton."

I turn back to the captain and incline my head. He's staring but not at me.

"This deck has the owner's suite, the main salon, and the dining deck," says Haley. "The junior suites are one deck down."

"A junior suite for a junior." I laugh. *Damn, Rockwell, get your shit together.* I sound like an ass. I've had a supermodel hit on me, but this steward is making me act like a teenager. Down the spiral stairs, I try not to stare at her ass. But it's hard to do, because it's big and juicy like a peach. I've become a complete asshole because I'm hoping the short shorts she's wearing are her uniform shorts and not something she sleeps in.

Shit, I got laid last night in a club bathroom. I shouldn't be this horny.

The hallway is full of boxes. Come to think of it, there were several stacks of boxes we walked by coming out of the bridge. "How's the new ship? Are you liking it?"

She shoots me a glance over her shoulder, one she carefully and quickly schools. "The *Rock Candy* is going to be a great boat."

"Interesting choice of words." I smile at her, but she quickly turns away and stops in front of two doors.

"So, here's where you have a choice to make." She points to a door with a brass label that reads *Fortune*, Rockwell Harding's premier product, and then one that's labeled *Emily*. "Fortune is ready, but the door jams and Shayla, the second stew, was stuck in there for an hour earlier today. The engineer is going to work on it tomorrow. Or you can sleep in the Emily suite. The bed's made up, and the bathroom is ready to go, but we haven't hung up curtains or, well, finished it."

"Which is less work for you?"

"Your sister is Emily?"

"Yes."

"I'm guessing she's going to want to sleep in the Emily suite."

"I suppose so. I'll stay in Fortune."

"Excellent." Haley leans into the door, twists the handle, and opens it.

"Wow. This is remarkably nice." There are a few decorations but nothing over the top. Not like how Candy has changed the main house and the house in Florida. They both look like they threw up an accessory store. The curtains are slate gray with a ribbon of gold around the edges. And the bed has the correct number of pillows. Did Candy even have anything to do with the boat?

"Thanks. We're trying to figure out what to do with all the extra stuff in the boxes."

*Aw, there it is.* "Oh, didn't you hear? Candy ordered extra. I'm supposed to take everything you don't want to the women's shelter."

"Really?" Haley's brow jumps up.

"Yeah, you know, she's eccentric and likes to give control to people who know better. You know what they say: surround yourself with smart people and you'll never appear dumb." Damn, I hope I don't get this girl fired. I've got friends with yachts. I'll get her a job if need be. "You better get some rest. We'll need to get the rest of the things you and your staff don't need off the boat early." As in before Candy shows up. I give Haley a smile.

# Chapter 10

## *Stow*

Haley

"Shayla, I'm not lying to you. That's what Easton said."

"Well, girl, it doesn't make sense."

"No, I'm with you there." I eat the rest of my toast over the sink. Making one less dish to wash.

"Well, I've been labelling the extra stuff. We don't know what to do with all the question mark boxes."

"Thank you for stopping writing WTF on them."

Calvin's smells of motor oil or grease and I kind of like it. "How are you doing?"

"I'm—"

Shayla cuts me off. And smiles from Calvin to me. "We're fantastic."

Calvin scowls and pours himself a cup of coffee. "Where's what's-her-name?"

"Brianna." Shayla's eye roll might cause permanent damage to her vision. "She's sleeping in. Has a migraine is what she told me.

Screamed at me loud enough when the light from the bathroom hit her bunk. But I'm not going to not take a shower."

"Gotcha." Calvin leans his butt on the counter, his ankles crossed. Thank goodness he doesn't ask if I've mentioned it to the captain yet. Because I haven't. But I will when I get a second.

"Calvin, Haley has a question for you." Shayla's eyes widen like if I don't ask him, she's going to whine about it for the rest of the day.

"I do. I do. We're getting ready to move a bunch of extra boxes out of the rooms into the dining room."

"I'd love to help." Calvin downs his coffee and washes the mug, setting it in the drying rack.

Shayla races up the stairs, and we follow her. She's not wrong in her assessment that something more pressing would have come up if she'd asked Calvin. She told me what happened between the two of them. It's one of the reasons she doesn't drink on crew nights off anymore. Not that we're likely to have any nights off.

I want to gather the extra things together in the dining room, even though it will make the salon look like a community sale on Nantucket. But we don't have the room for all this stuff anywhere else.

Calvin stares at the boxes in the junior suite, *Candy Cane.* "There's ten if not fifteen boxes in here."

"Yup." Shayla picks up one and tries to hand it to him.

He puts up his hand. "Hold up." He pulls out his radio. "All crew. If you're not doing something urgent, come meet us at the bow junior suites."

A chorus of "copy"s comes over the radio.

I bite my lip and nod. "You're right."

"Everything the room needs has been unpacked?"

"Yes, and spares are stowed. It's enough for two yachts."

"Three," Shayla adds.

"You mind if I go talk to the captain? I'll be right back," I say.

"Should we wait?" Shayla asks.

"No, we have to do something with all of it, anyway." I hustle up the stairs and catch the captain as he's coming out of the bridge. "Hey Captain, can I talk to you?" He looks as handsome as ever. If he smelled like Calvin and sounded like Zane, I wouldn't be able to form a sentence in front of him.

"I was just on my way to help Calvin."

"Yeah, it's about that—Calvin is helping me."

"I see, and what's the problem?"

"No problem with Calvin, he's great. It's all the stuff on the yacht. Shayla and I finished outfitting all the cabins and guest spaces late last night. But you wouldn't be able to tell it from all the boxes of decorations that are left."

"How many?"

I point to the salon, where at least twenty boxes sit stacked in the corner.

"Those are all extra?"

"Yeah, let me show you." I open the first box. There are nine golden horses, and the next four hold throw pillows, but there are so many pillows on the sofa as it is you would have to throw half of them on the floor to sit.

"That's a lot of pillows."

"And there's more." I touch the boxes containing pillows. "Which isn't that big of a deal. I could order storage bags and suck the air out and put them in a coat closet or in the bilge of the boat. But it's all the other stuff, the heavy stuff."

"These were all marked for the salon?"

"Yes." I shift onto my toes.

"I tell you what, let's take them all out and just try it."

"Okay." I cringe inside because Shayla and I already tried it in one of the bedrooms. The bed disappeared in pillows, and the dressers and night stands didn't have an inch of usable space left.

I turn around, and the captain is holding two brass horses. He wanders around the room, like a small child looking for Easter eggs after the teenagers have scooped them all up. "Well, this is blasted nuts. There are nine of these damn things in the box and I can't find a spot for one that won't kill someone if we hit a rogue wave."

"So last night, Easton . . ." I hesitate. Easton is the owner's son.

"What did he do?" The captain's voice rumbles through me.

"He didn't do anything. He told me that Candy wanted the crew to pick what decor to use and donate the rest."

"That sounds like a load of trash. Why would she buy all this shit and tell us to donate it?"

"It wasn't some mistake at the shipyard?"

"No. The deck crew had to check off the content of each box as they brought it on board." Sam looks the boxes up and down. And he cocks a smile. "Is the younger Rockwell up?"

"Yes, Dante tried to make him breakfast, but he wouldn't let him. He's on the sun platform, working out. That's what Shay said. She went up to see if he needed anything, and he said he was good, that he knew he was early and he would come find someone if he needed anything."

"Let's go see Easton."

"You want me to come with you, sir?" I swallow. I'm not sure I want to be part of this conversation. I'm not one for conflict when I see it coming.

"Yes, I'm sure you can get the real answer out of him."

"Okay." I follow the captain up the stairs, at the exact rate that keeps my eyes off his ass.

The sundeck is gorgeous. I've hardly spent any time up here at all yet. There are a couple of exercise machines, a hot tub, and a bar. Shayla and I both came to the conclusion we could outfit the bar and bring up towels as we needed them.

Easton pounds the pedals of the elliptical. His skin glistens in the sun, and I try to not drool. He looks like an Olympian, well, because he *is* an Olympian.

Easton smiles and waves, reaching for his phone to silence his headphones. He brings the machine to a stop.

"Sorry to interrupt your workout." The captain cocks his head back to me. "Haley tells me that Candy is being charitable and wants to donate the extra decor."

"That's Candy—she loves being helpful."

"I know her, that's why I want to confirm with you that the extra supplies are to be donated? We don't have space for many of them, and they will end up being a safety hazard."

"Safety hazard." Easton smiles and then nods. "Of course, they would be too much weight." He dries himself with a towel. A towel that he must've gotten for himself.

"More the flying objects. It's a boat, not a house."

"Yes, I would imagine Candy has forgotten that. The shipyard designers were more than happy to let her order as much as she wanted, I'm sure."

The captain nods. "I'm going to be honest with you. I might be wrong, and maybe Candy has turned over a charitable leaf, but when we give away all this extra—"

"—decor," I interject. "Decor. It's just a lot."

"You want to make sure it comes back to me and not you or Haley or Shayla?"

"Yes." The captain nods.

"My dad likes you. He's had a boat forever, each one a little bigger. But you're the first captain he doesn't complain about. If you want the shit gone, I'll take the fall. I'd love to see the look on Candy's face when all her five million horses are gone. Fun fact, she doesn't know how to ride a horse. My dad surprised her by having a stable put in at the main house when they were in the city last winter. She hates live horses. She won't even go down to feed them a damn carrot." His phone flashes. "It's Rocky. I'll break it to him now." He taps the screen. "Hello."

"Easton, where the hell are you, son? They said you checked out of the hotel early. Candy and I are going to lunch with Brick and Emily."

"I did. I'm at the boat, Dad. I'm talking to Captain Sam. There's a little issue."

"What is it? They said things were coming along but picking it up early made for some additional preparations. Why the fuck didn't they—"

"Dad, you're on speaker with Captain Sam and head stew Haley."

"Well, why in fuck didn't you lead with that? Hello Captain, Miss Haley."

"Hello," I say, wishing to hell I wasn't involved in this.

"Right, Dad, there's so much extra shit ordered for the boat that the captain says it's a safety issue. They gave me a full tour, and it's so much that you can't walk into some cabins."

"Is that right?" Mr. Rockwell doesn't sound like he's buying it.

"Dad, in my cabin there are five horse statues and six anchor lamps. And that's just what's out. There are boxes of stuff too. If we hit a rogue wave, we're going to be buried alive in horses and pillows."

"Is this true, Captain Sam?"

"I'm afraid so, Rocky. It's too much stuff and more."

"Fine, get rid of it. Do you need more time to get the ship ready?"

"Another day would make things a lot more presentable."

"Done. You coming back to the hotel, then, Easton?"

"No, there's a lot to do here, Dad. I'm going to stay and help." Easton smiles at me, and all I wonder is how much does he pay to get his teeth that white.

"You sure? Candy is going to take Emily shopping."

"That sounds like hell. I'll pass."

"All right, we'll see you tomorrow at breakfast." Mr. Rockwell disconnects, with no goodbye or I love you. My mom's been gone for four years, and I can't imagine not telling her I love you.

"That's awesome." I clap.

"Do you want to tell the crew?" Captain Sam is beaming at me.

I grab my radio. "All crew, all crew. Mr. Rockwell and guests are now arriving tomorrow morning. And the extra boxes are going to be donated. Please take them to the dock." The calls that come back are equally as excited as I am.

"That's amazing," says Dante over the radio. "I've got some gourmet lunch going down to the crew mess in an hour, but I'll take the extra day. Woo-hoo!"

"I'm done with my workout. How can I help you, Haley?" Easton takes a long drink from his water bottle.

The captain clears his throat. "That's really kind of you, Easton, and normally we'd say no, due to liability. But as the owner's son, you can certainly help all you want. Shayla is down by your room. Haley and I need to talk."

I glance at the captain, wondering how I've gotten myself in trouble, because by the way the captain's glaring at me, I've done something I've forgotten about.

"I'll see you down there." I wave.

"She's going to be busy most of the day. But I'm sure you'll catch up during dinner service." The captain's gruff, like he's drawing a line in the sand.

"I meant what I said," replies Easton. "I'll find something to eat near the dock. No need to do anything special for me."

I squint, remembering Easton's preference sheet. Then I follow the captain down the stairs to what I hope isn't my dismissal.

"Anders, I need the bridge."

Anders gets up off the floor and points to me. "You don't want me to stay?" It's protocol on most yachts to have two officers issue a correction.

"She's not in trouble." His tone is still gruff. "Close the door," he says to his first officer.

Anders gives me a look of pity and questioning. And I have to say I wonder what the heck this is too.

# Chapter 11

## *Batten Down the Hatches*

Sam

I've officially lost my mind. Bringing the girl—woman—I keep thinking about to the bridge to talk to her alone. But I can't help myself. Watching her look at the owner's son like he was a piece of meat made me want to gouge the kid's eyes out. His, not hers. And killing the owner's son isn't a way to get recommendations for another boat.

I'm holding my breath, and the air in my lungs burns to come out. "Have a seat," I huff. I honestly have no idea what I'm going to say to her, because I'm crossing a line. She needs to do her job. And that is going to involve talking to the men. Even Rocky's son, who, contrary to Rocky's opinion, doesn't walk on water.

Right. I turn to her. She's keeping her eyes down, but then she looks up at me. I can't tell if she's upset, angry, or confused. And that's worrisome to me. I decide to forgo mentioning my opinions on what happened on the sundeck. I stare at her. I can't talk. Calming down first is my only option.

"Good news, isn't it?" She breaks the silence, scooting back onto the large bench that takes up the whole back of the wheelhouse.

I have no idea how long I let the silence linger. But it's still not enough time to let me cool off about the way he looked at her. I want to snap Easton Rockwell into a pile of driftwood. Which might take a bit of effort because this kid is built. But . . . "It is good news. The extra time will help both Calvin and Anders finish up the rest of the electrical. And it's certainly good news for your department too."

"Just getting those boxes out of our way is half the battle. Shayla is amazing. She's working her ass off."

"I'm glad to hear it. You're both doing a great job." I nod like I'm talking to a neighbor over a fence, not the girl I'm obsessing over. It's not healthy, but I can't stop.

"Where's Penny?" She jumps up and peeks around the side of the captain's chair.

"She's in my cabin. She's a good listener, but when someone lies on the floor, she wants to lie on them too. With Anders camped out under the control panel, she's been a pest."

A triple knock, Anders' signature. Shit. I know Haley wants to talk about Brianna, and I want to talk to her about the playboy down on the sundeck. "Come in."

"Hey Cap. Sorry, I wasn't sure if you were done. We're still trying to sort it out. I can come back."

"No, it's fine. We'll move to my office." My office, cabin, and bedroom are all the same thing. We walk the few steps down the corridor to my cabin, and I hold the door open for Haley. Her hair brushes my arm as she walks in. The lock clicks shut behind her.

Haley perks up. "These are nice captain's quarters. I still haven't seen every room on the yacht yet. It's so not how I like to do things." Penny jumps off her bed and runs to Haley. Penny's head leans against Haley's leg. "Well, hello there. It's nice to see you too."

"Lie down." My tone is firm, and Haley's cheeks seem to redden. But Penny trots off to the corner of the room between the bed and the wall. She flops to the ground, her head resting on her paws.

"She's such a good girl." Haley crosses the room to the porthole.

"I had them change the layout of the cabin when they were outfitting it. With Rocky's permission, of course."

She turns from the window and nods. "It works."

"I've never liked having my bed in the corner of the room—it's too hard to make it—but on rocky moorings, I like having the wall." I've had my bed shoved into the alcove made for the desk. And my desk is anchored on the other side of the room. There was a huge horse painting labeled to go in my room, but I hung it in the main salon before we even left Singapore.

"The best of both worlds. And it gives Penny a little nest next to your bed. She must like that."

"She does."

Haley is the first crew member I've had come into my cabin for a chat. I imagined myself sitting behind my desk and the stew or deckhand sitting in the chair across from me, but I don't want to put any distance between the two of us. The idea is crazy.

Penny has wandered over. She leans against Haley's leg.

"Have a seat." I move the chair closer to Haley so as not to disturb Penny. I sit on the edge of the bed. I should get up—this feels far too intimate.

And I'm the one close to crossing a line.

"How is Brianna working out?" I clasp my hands together, resting my elbows on my knees. It is the pose I do to let my dog understand my hands are not available for petting. It also happens to be somewhat intimidating. I unclasp them and sit with my hands on my legs.

"I wouldn't know. She hasn't been out of her cabin. She told me yesterday that she had jet lag. Today she told Shayla she had to sleep off a migraine."

"Oh, those can be bad. Do you want to find out if she needs a doctor?"

Haley frowns at me. "I can do that."

Such a good sailor. "What do you really want to say?"

"I don't want to say anything bad about her. I've only met her for a few seconds. But that's the problem. She's lazy, and even when she does come out of her cabin, I'm sure Shayla and I would do a better job without her. I can't let her stay in there. It's going to drive Shayla crazy. And I understand why. But I'm going to try to train her."

"I know you will. Charlie said you turned around one of the worst stews on board." Seriously, my brother wouldn't shut up about Haley. He told me if I didn't hire her, he'd tell our mother about what happened to her heirloom Christmas tablecloth, and that's a story that doesn't ever need to be told.

"If she never comes out of her cabin, how can I train her?"

"If she never comes out of her cabin, how can she cause any problems?" I half laugh. It's not appropriate, but it makes Haley smile at me again. Fuck, this is messed up. I'm going to have to find a way to pull back these inappropriate feelings for her. "I'm afraid we are going to have to ride it out. If tensions between Shayla and Brianna get overblown and you can't handle it on your own . . ." I raise my eyebrows.

"Maybe Easton could talk to his dad?" She shifts slightly in her chair, coming closer to me.

I tighten my stomach muscles. "I don't think that will be necessary. If it becomes—"

This time she giggles. A soft nervous giggle traveling straight to my cock. "You should see your expression. I'm sorry, Captain. I didn't know Easton would tell his dad."

"I understand. I don't feel stepped on. And I was there too. I could have stopped him. But the real question is why did he do it? Why do you think Easton was willing to challenge his dad and stick himself out there?" I raise my chin to her. I know why he did it. He wants in her pants like almost all the crew. Like me.

"He's not a fan of his soon-to-be stepmother. One more day without her makes him happy. They might be at a five-star hotel with killer views, but she's not here. And on top of that, doing something to make Candy angry will give him a deep-seated, childish thrill."

Shit, that's a good answer. The thickening of my cock has

knocked a good decade off my age and forty points off my IQ. "Possibly there might be another reason." Because I'm sure the SOB was eyeing her like a trophy.

"What? I don't get your . . . Are you saying he did it for me?"

I cock my head and give a small shrug.

"Captain. He's an Olympian and a billionaire and soon to be the new CEO of his family's business. He's not interested in me."

"I think he is. I can tell you're a professional. You know what to do."

Her shoulders square. "I would never lead a guest on." She leans forward, her feet fidgeting.

I've made her uncomfortable. She squirms in the chair, and in doing so, she's squeezed her incredible breasts together. The V-neck crew uniform is something that I need to look away from, but I don't.

"Yes, I understand." I hold her gaze. I see the moment it clicks for her. At least, I think I do. She can tell I'm attracted to her. And I'm fucked. As long as I don't do anything that can be construed as something crossing that line all the way . . . But I'm hovering, man, I'm hovering awfully close.

"Captain Sam, just so you know, I've never had a relationship with a guest. I once dated a bosun on the boat, but that ended. And it ended poorly. He broke my heart. Broke me, really. I'm not going to do anything to embarrass you or this ship. It wasn't my plan to have a boat romance again. Or any romance."

"I never thought you would. Your resumé is impeccable, your references are perfect, and Charlie raved about you—and the only thing my brother raves about is himself. So no, Haley, I don't think you would do anything to embarrass me or the ship. I was more concerned about what the junior might want to do to you."

"If you trust me, why are you worried about what Easton might or might not do?" She drops her arms to the seat and leans back. It's hard to not notice how nicely her uniform hugs her chest. Is she doing this on purpose? Her eyes flit to the floor and then up at me.

"Men like him like using their position to get what they want."

They want her in a certain position: her ass in the air or on the bed. Again, I'm not any better than them.

She smiles. "Well, you don't have to worry about me. I get where the line is between flirting for a tip and staying in bed after turndown service, and I don't cross it with passengers. Not that anyone has ever tried." She nods and stands.

"I find that hard to believe." I stand too. But Penny's long body corrals us together.

"I would never cross it." She shakes her head.

"No, Haley. I find it hard to believe that no one has ever tried to make you." Fuck, I find so much about her hard.

A nervous laugh bursts out of her. "Well, I'm not lying. I guess I don't see it. We'll have to agree to disagree." Her smile is slight and shy.

But something simmers in her as a spark pulls me in. How? How can she not see it? "I really enjoyed talking to you last night. You're witty, funny, and compassionate when it comes to your coworkers." I'm drifting into rough waters without a motor. "And there are men who will take advantage of your age."

"I'm not a child, Sam." She smooths down her shorts. I feel the indecision in her step when she moves forward. "I liked getting to know you last night too."

Her bare toes are inches away from me. There's a bit of a game of chicken going down, and the music of my erratic beating heart isn't letting me walk away from the damn challenge.

Penny wanders off. There's nothing keeping Haley from saying goodbye. Even with the extra day, we both have a lot of work to do. Her big toe touches mine, and her coconut scent swirls around me, hardening my cock against the zipper of my pants.

"You have something on you, just there." Her hand reaches for me.

# Chapter 12

## *Skylarking*

Haley

The touch of stubble on his square jaw is softer than I imagined. And a twitch of his neck muscle catches my attention.

Am I really going to do this?

Dante said he thinks Sam has a thing for me. But I felt it too. Last night, sitting on the bench, neither one of us was talking about the yacht. I thought after he'd told me how old he was and we laughed together, the feelings would pass. But they haven't. I've always dated guys my age. Actually, Steven was younger than me at twenty-five. Which might explain why he has my dog and I have a smashed heart.

This has got to be the dumbest thing I've ever done in my life. I reach for Sam's cheek. My thumb runs along his lower jaw.

Who am I? But I can't stop myself. I don't know what I expected. I've never touched someone like this. My heart is racing, and I can't catch my breath. He's still. Too still, like he's trying to figure out what to do about this. Then he places his hand over mine. His eyes are wide.

"I'm your boss, Haley." His tone is low and rumbles through me.

"I know. I'm the one initiating this. I read the handbook." Actually, I lost a lot of sleep reading and rereading it in the handbook.

"I'm ten years older than you."

"I don't see a problem with that." I push up onto my tippy toes.

"And you're sure you know what you're doing?"

"I always know what I'm doing. And I quote, Section eight, paragraph 2: 'a crew member of lesser rank may establish a relationship with a high-ranking officer as long as it's approved by the captain.' End quote. So is it approved?"

His head lowers, and his lips hover near my ear. "I'm quite sure you have no idea what you're getting yourself into, Miss Haley Brewster."

His hand grabs the back of my head; his fingers thread through my hair. And when his mouth hits mine, my world explodes. It's not butterflies, no—I'm not nervous at all to have his arm around me. It's right. My feet don't move.

A guy like Sam doesn't come around often, not in yachting, where all the men are looking for someone to keep their bed warm. I want to do so much more than kiss this man. Our bodies are flush against each other, and my bare feet are alongside his. I find the edge of his crew shirt and inch my hand up. Touching his firm abs makes me wild, and as I scrape my fingers along their ridges, he groans my name.

I've never wanted a man as much as I want Sam. I widen my stance, bringing our bodies even closer. His cock hits me at my core. I'm the one who presses into him. When I do, he pulls my leg up, and I jump onto him. But I don't stay there for long. He turns, lowering me to the bed. Sam stands between my knees. I know what I want. He's unsure he's doing the right thing.

"You are so beautiful." His fingers trail down my body. Shock waves pulse through me. He lifts my shirt an inch, showing my stomach. I push that from my thoughts. He drops to his knees. He's kissing my belly, his fingers teasing at my waistband. I lift my hips, and he eases my shorts off. He tugs them down.

I'm frozen in time. His smile takes my breath away. His hands grasp either side of my thighs, and his head nudges my legs wider. We lock eyes for a moment, and then his tongue swirls around my clit as he grasps my hips, pulling me closer to the edge of the bed, closer to his mouth. I whimper. At least, I hope it's a whimper.

He lifts his head. "Shh, Haley. We can't have anyone hearing you. Don't make me get out a gag."

His mouth is back and driving me crazy. The tension has my back lifting off the mattress. I've only had a few guys go down on me before, but never like this, never without me asking and never with such . . . Shit, he pushes a finger into me. It's tight. It's been a while since I've had sex. But nothing will ever compare to this. Sam's in complete control, and each of his movements is perfectly timed. It's making thinking hard.

The world falls away. It's only him and me. He adds another finger, the rhythm timed with his tongue to send me even nearer to the edge. I'm so close. My back arches, and I grind into his face. I'm so wet, so close. He adds another finger. I'm going to explode. And when he sucks hard on my clit, he reaches up his hand and covers my mouth. Sam's holding me down, his head on my hips, and my body doesn't know what to do. I try not to scream my release into his hand, but I can't help it. I can't be quiet—it's too good. Convulsions wrack my body, one after the other.

Only when I'm still does he let go of my mouth. Limp and relaxed, I close my eyes. I let myself not think for a whole two seconds before I worry about what I've done. What we've done.

I reach for the captain. But I know the reality of it is we can't snuggle. Heck, we might never do anything again—not until the season is over or maybe not ever. This is going to be the longest two months of my entire life.

I close my eyes for a moment and Sam's disappeared. Water runs in the bathroom. A minute later, he's back with a warm cloth. I move to take it, but he shakes his head. He holds my hand while he cleans me. I let my head drop to the bed. The reality of what I've started is sinking in. He's found my shorts and pulls them on.

I'm enough of myself now to pull them up the rest of the way. Glancing at him, I expect to see my layer of worry or regret, but he's all smiles. He shakes his head.

"We're going to need a plan," I say.

"We're both adults." His fingers trail up my leg.

I bite my lip. "But during the actual season, this could be complicated."

"You are the most amazing woman."

I kiss him, tasting myself on his lips. I want nothing more than to go down on him, but . . . "I've been here too long."

He nods. "Anders won't say anything, but you're right. We both have to get back to work. Our reprieve from Rocky and his family is short-lived."

I stand, and his fingers run through my hair. "I meant it when I said you are one of the most intoxicating women I've ever met. We—"

"—have a job to do. And forming a new relationship during a season when we both are going to have so much work . . . It's going to be impossible."

He pulls me to his chest and presses a kiss on the top of my head. "You're something else. I'm going to Thailand after the season is over, before we reposition the yacht. A month—you should come with me."

I take in his smell, the firmness of his chest. He sends a fire of longing through me. Just last week, I told myself I couldn't have a relationship, not until I got myself under control, learned to love my body and where I am in my life. Being a stewardess wasn't my plan. Or Sam. He's not a landlubber. And jumping into a month-long trip? "I'll think about it."

His laugh resonates through him. "I'm glad one of us is mature enough. All right, Haley. We better get back to work. I hear your boss is a real ass."

He pinches my chin and tilts his mouth to mine. His grip is

strong. And while I'm the one who started this, whatever it is, Sam is clearly the one in charge. I kind of love it and hate it at the same time. The kiss is blistering, and there is no doubt my lips will be swollen. He's claiming me.

Sam pulls back first. He holds my shoulders. "Think about Thailand."

I turn to leave. I'm dizzy. My world is rocking more than a boat during rough waters. I glance in the mirror by his door and smooth my hair.

"Haley?"

I glance back at Sam. He's tucking the comforter tight. "You might need this." He scoops up my radio from the floor and tosses it at me.

I catch it. "Thanks."

"And—"

I know what he's going to say. "I won't tell anyone. You don't have to worry."

"Actually, section eight, paragraph three, I was going to say. It's up to you if you want to tell people. Just let me know if you do. So I'm not blindsided. But you're right, we both have jobs to do. We should slow this—whatever it is—down."

"Yes, sir." But I say *sir* with a sexy twist.

"Fuck, Haley."

I wiggle my eyebrows and get out of there. My nipples are hard, and I'm getting wet just looking at him. And I have a hell of a lot to do.

I leave Sam, the captain, without glancing back at Anders on the bridge. I don't want to know if he heard me. How could he not? I've never come so hard in my life. Actually, all of my other orgasms no longer count. They were meager scraps of what sex should be.

"Shayla, Shayla, Haley," I say into the radio. "What's your location?"

"I'm having a margarita on the pool deck." No way would she

drink on charter. While we aren't underway, we still have a guest on board.

I laugh.

"I was taking a little nap, but I'm getting up now," she says a second later. "I'll be in the crew mess."

"Copy, I'll meet you there."

I step down onto the second landing, and Zane is coming up. We meet in the same spot where we collided two days ago.

"We've got to stop running into each other like this."

I smile at his cheesy line. He's cute, and his tousled hair is sexy in a don't-care way. "Wow, you're in a good mood."

"What?"

"I've just never seen you smile like that. I'm glad. You're doing such an amazing job with the ship. You and Shayla. The third is . . . well, you need to meet her, and judge for yourself."

"She's here. I'm going to go wake Sleeping Beauty up now."

"Sleeping Beauty?" Easton has come out of his room. He's got a shirt on now, covering up his Olympian body. Which is good because he'd be a total distraction for Shayla. And we don't need two distracted stews.

"Hey, thanks for your help." Zane pats Easton on the back.

"No worries, man. Cardio and strength at the same time is a bonus. And we got the boxes off before the wildebeest arrives." Easton holds running shoes in his hand. "I'm going to go for a run now. But let me know if you need anything else." He winks at me and strolls to the gangplank off the rear deck.

I turn to Zane after Easton is out of earshot. "You guys are done?"

"Yeah, in fact, I'm just coming back from taking the last load of boxes to the dock. The harbor master is donating them to a charity shop that supports the local hospital."

"Well, that's cool. I'm going to go find Shayla. Thanks for your help."

"We're all a team. Especially this season, with the owner's new wife being such a jealous weirdo."

"Thanks Zane, I really appreciate it."

He takes off, and I just stop for a minute. Have I ended up not on the other side of the world but in an alternate universe where most of the men are not only good-looking but reasonable? This didn't happen in the Caribbean, did it?

I take the spiral steps slowly down to the crew mess. No, I distinctly remember a bosun from two seasons ago telling me if he wanted to be a dishwasher, he would have applied to be a low-ass stew. There's something in the water here.

I round the corner. And Shayla stands above Brianna with a knife in her hand.

"What's going on?" I scream.

# Chapter 13

## *Melee*

Calvin

I am running toward the crew mess. Brianna screams and then Shayla. Their voices blur together. Someone screeches like a monkey, and I pick up speed. Things have been tense the whole season, and we haven't even gotten truly underway yet. But Brianna isn't helping things, that's for sure.

Haley blurts something out on the radio, but I'm so darn close it just echoes with a high pitch between her set and my ears.

Haley holds Shayla's wrist, and a knife spins on the floor. It flashes with reflections of the lights as it spins. Brianna has backed herself into the corner of the bench.

"What's going on?" I flick my gaze between the three stews.

"Calvin, secure Shayla," Haley grunts out.

"I'm not going to hurt the cunt. I just wanted to scare her. She fucking cut my braid off," Shayla yells in my ear. "Who does that? Cuts someone's hair off? You're mental!" She thrusts her index finger at Brianna.

The tension in the room spins like a storm. "It's a wig. And it was in my bed space." Brianna shakes her head at Shayla. There was talk amongst the exterior team today about some kind of disagreement between them, but I didn't expect things to go this far. Who would?

"It's not a wig, it was my damn hair! You're a psycho." Shayla throws her hands up in the air. "She needs to go, Haley, or I'm going." Shayla takes a breath, and I think she's calmed down, but then she lurches for Brianna, her hands flailing about.

Haley nods at me, but I've already grabbed Shayla's wrist. "Calm down." Shayla has a temper. Everyone knows it. I don't want to be around her. Not after what happened a couple of seasons ago. But cutting someone's hair because it was flopping over the edge of the bed? Shayla's not wrong; Brianna is far out of line. "Are you good?" I look into Shayla's brown eyes. The girl is cuckoo for Cocoa Puffs, but she wouldn't stab anyone. But if someone cut my hair off while I was taking a well-deserved nap? I get it.

Time seems to slow. She nods once. And I let go. My arms are flexed, and I'm ready to jump if Shayla goes to attack again. Or Brianna. I exhale, my heart racing. Girl drama—I'm not sure why some guys think it's so hot.

"Go with Haley to see the captain." I position myself between Brianna and Shayla.

"Come on, let's get you up to the bridge." Haley puts her hand on Shayla's back.

"I'm not going to work with her. She assaulted me." Shayla huffs.

"Yup. Let's go." Haley's voice is calm enough that I stop and watch them leave. Brianna slides out of the bench. But Shayla runs up the stairs toward the bridge.

Haley and I glare at Brianna, her eyes darting between us in apprehension.

"Move." Haley nods at her remaining stews, her voice laced with an air of authority, like she knows how to take on tough situations.

Brianna has barely moved. Even with the death stare Haley gives her. Brianna rounds to the other side of the crew galley, away from us.

"Brianna can't just walk away after pulling something like that," Haley whispers to me.

I shake my head, my eyes never leaving Brianna. "She won't. Captain will handle it."

Haley nods and retreats, leaving me alone with the sulking Brianna. But then Haley stops on the stairs, her eyes meeting mine. Brianna is still in the crew mess. "Calvin," she starts, uncertainty seeping into her voice. "Do you . . . do you think Shayla's okay?"

The question catches me off-guard. It's not that Haley's not caring—she is—but so far, she's seemed more about the rules, the structure. "Yeah, Haley, I think she'll be fine."

She gives me a brief nod, her face unreadable, before climbing the stairs after Shayla. Man, I wouldn't want to be Haley now. They are already so undersized as a team. And to lose Brianna? Even if she's not worth anything, she's still a warm body. A crazy one, but at least she's something. I just hope Captain doesn't let them both go. The less stew work I have to do, the happier I am. Oh, I'll help out as much as I can, for sure. But spending the day in the laundry room is my own personal torture. No, I take that back. Having to serve drunk guests until the wee hours of the morning—that's got to be the worst.

I catch a last glimpse of her retreating figure and turn my attention back to Brianna, steeling myself for the confrontation that's about to come. Brianna is making her way back to the crew cabins. "Stop right there."

"I'm going back to my cabin." She stands defiantly, her head cocked, her arms crossed over her chest.

"No, you're not, Brianna. You assaulted another crew member. You'll be lucky if you don't go to jail."

Her eyes widen, and tears pool on her lashes. Crying women bring me to my knees, but not this one. She cut off Shayla's hair.

"Come. We're going to see the captain."

"Calvin, Calvin, Captain. I need you to bring Brianna to the bridge. Now."

"Copy, Captain. I'm working on it." I snap the radio back onto my belt. "You heard him. Move."

She doesn't move.

"You can't hide from your actions, Brianna. They always come back to find you."

"She was being so loud, and my head hurt."

"Yeah, well, if you let Shayla get at you, a lot more is going to hurt. Move. I don't want to drag you up there, but I will." I give her the look, the one my old captain used to use. But I guess I have yet to perfect it.

She takes a step forward and stops. The scowl on her face is repulsive. She's acting like I did something wrong. But damn. I follow her up the stairs, and on the first deck she tries to make a run for the gangplank off the rear deck. But I catch her forearm, and she yanks herself to a halt. Where does she think she's going? If this is how this season is starting . . . I hate to be superstitious, but it doesn't look good for the rest of it.

"The bridge is one more deck up." There's a hint of sternness in my voice. I don't let go of her arm this time. A quick knock on the side of the bridge wall and I push Brianna in. "Captain."

He's sitting in his chair. Anders is looking at the security camera, and Haley is holding Shayla's hand.

Anders turns to the captain. Anders is the same age as the captain. I like him—he's solid. "What Shayla says checks out. She came into the crew mess, pulled things out of the fridge, took a cutting board and a knife out to cut a tomato. Brianna says something. Shayla pulls her hair to one side—looks at her hair. And screams. Shayla has the knife in her hand when she turns around. Then Haley runs into the kitchen and Shayla drops the knife."

All eyes turn to Brianna, whose face scrunches up tight. "She threatened me."

"I didn't. I was holding a damn knife when you pointed the fuck out that you cut my fucking hair off," Shayla yells again. Haley has a firm grasp on her hand.

"Everyone, sit down," Captain orders.

Shayla squints at Brianna. She raises her head. Damn, even I'm scared. If the cap doesn't fire Brianna, she better sleep with one eye open.

"Shayla, Calvin, if you can wait outside, I'm going to talk to Brianna. Hayley and Anders, please stay." I close the door behind us. Glancing back, I see the captain motion for Brianna to sit on the back bench of the wheelhouse. My eyes find Haley and the captain. They're standing close. I can't see either Anders or Brianna through the window.

Outside, the bustle of the dock continues. I notice a flock of seagulls circling above, a brief distraction from what's going on onboard. A bosun from the next slip over echoes through the open sliders. It's a normal day, but it's not.

I follow Shayla out to the main salon. "You okay?"

Shayla storms to the sofa, cursing under her breath. She bounces on the velvet sofa, pulling a horse pillow into her lap.

In any other circumstances, the absurdity of our surroundings, from the luxurious sofas to the decorative pillows, is laughable.

Something shifts in my gut as I watch the captain and Haley so close. It's not jealousy; that's a futile emotion in our line of work. It's more of a pang of concern, a faint alarm bell ringing in my head. Haley and the captain are both seasoned seafarers, but the look they shared is one I associate with particularly heavy storms.

I need to get back to work, but I can't help but check on Shayla. We have our rocky past, but she's good at her job. And we've worked things out. At least, I hope we have.

I sit on the edge of the sofa. I don't touch her to comfort her. "I'm sorry it happened to you."

"Thanks. It's just hair. But still. I paid a lot for these extensions. They're the good kind, and she even cut off some of my own hair."

I'm not sure what I'm supposed to say now, so I nod.

"If I lose my job over that cunt, I'm going to really stab her."

Shayla is fuming, taking off the braid she has left on the other side, and comparing it to the cut half of her hair.

I laugh. I shouldn't, but I do. "I'd keep the threats down. But I don't think you're going to lose your job. Anders says the camera covers you."

Shayla plays with the end of her hair. It's still long, but nowhere near as long as it was before. Unbraided, it hits her in the middle of her back.

"Sorry about your hair."

"It's not all my hair, but that's not the point. She's a looney, and the captain needs to give her the ax."

"What's all the commotion going on?" Easton has poked himself out from around the bar.

"Nothing," I say. Because you don't let the guest know about any of the difficulties that are going on with the crew.

"The third stew is a crazy bitch. Brianna." Shayla shows him her mismatched hair.

Easton takes a deep breath, his gaze fixed, brows furrowed. "Brianna Snodgrass?" He shakes his head.

Shayla and I both turn to him.

"Yeah," I say. "How do you know her surname? She's been in her cabin the whole time."

# Chapter 14

## *Brig*

Easton

The yelling is loud enough I can hear it from three boats away. My run has been cut short by the heat and the thought of food. Food never means much to me while I'm in training mode. It's fuel and nothing more than that. But I had a burger the chef made at lunch, and shit if I don't want another one. Or twelve.

"How do I know Brianna Snodgrass?" That's a question I don't want to answer. She's Candy's niece, and three years ago, I thought she was a sweet girl who might help me decompress after training. It was during a weekend meet, and she had been laughing, her eyes sparkling with mischief. It's not mischief; it's full-on crazy. Did I ever intend on her being a girlfriend? No, I thought it was clear. But I thought wrong. Dad told me she was going to be on the yacht, and I said I'd have to pass, that I wouldn't come if she was a guest. So Candy found a workaround.

"We dated once or twice," is what I say to keep things simple.

"Man, do you always like them crazy?" Shayla's eyebrows shoot up, and I have to wonder if she is dissing me or propositioning me.

"Shayla," Calvin growls at her.

She shrugs and sits on the arm of the sofa. Her casual demeanor is a stark contrast to the tension in the room.

"Why? What happened?" I have a feeling that I'm going to regret asking the question.

"What happened?" Shayla holds out her hair, waving it at me. "The bitch got chop-happy with some shears."

"Shayla," Calvin repeats himself. I suppose the crew isn't supposed to air their dirty laundry, but after helping for the day, I don't feel like the owner's son now. I feel more like one of them, part of the team. It's refreshing. And I like it. Swimming is an individual sport—that's how I received most of my medals—but I'm most proud of the ones I got from the relays.

"Oh, she's crazy," I agree. "And I'm afraid I'm the reason she's part of your crew." The two of them snap their attention to me. "She's Candy's niece, and Candy hasn't given up on the idea of her being part of the Rockwell family too."

"Is that why she's been hiding?" Calvin turns to Shayla, and her eyebrows shoot up.

"I have no idea. Crazy does what crazy wants. You saved yourself a doozy by not letting her blonde ass hypnotize you."

"I'm more of a light-brown-brunette kind of guy." I smile. "I'm sorry she's caused you any stress. Is the captain on the bridge with her now?" I point toward the bridge.

"Yeah." Shayla rolls her eyes. She leans back, and the resentment on her face is clear. I don't blame her. I'm taking long steps to the bridge. I've got to come clean to the captain.

The door is closed, and they ignore my knock. I knock again. "Captain, this is Easton. I have some information about Brianna."

Through the door I can hear her say, "Don't open it up."

"Come in," the captain calls.

Brianna's cowering next to Haley.

"Hey Captain. I see you've met Candy's niece. Just for the record, I told my dad that Miss Snodgrass wasn't permitted on the yacht as a guest."

"I see. And why is that?"

"Because I have a restraining order against her. But I didn't tell my dad that—I thought to save the woman some dignity."

"This isn't America." Brianna ducks her head out from behind the beautiful stew. "Your order is no good here."

"No, no, it's not. But what you did to Shayla in any country is going to be considered an assault." The captain stands and paces in front of Haley and Brianna.

"She was so loud, and her braid was flapping over the edge of the bed." Brianna's eyes widen.

"You cut her hair off because she was loud and her hair was dangling off her bed?" I ask, turning to the captain.

He gives me a nod. "Indeed."

"Well, whatever you and Shayla decide has to happen to her, I want her off this boat. No way in hell are we leaving the dock with her on board." I put my hands behind my back.

The captain's face is stone. "Agreed."

"But Easter Bunny, don't you remember how much fun we had together?" Brianna grabs at my arm.

I hear a snicker behind me. The first officer. But the captain holds it together and clears his throat.

"You're delusional, Brianna. I've made myself clear. You're off the boat whether it's the police taking you or a derelict cab. I never want to see you again. I don't know how much clearer I can be. Do you understand?" She nods, tears streaming down her face. I don't feel sorry for her, not now, not ever. "The money for your therapy is still in the account. Use it. Get some help, Brianna." It pisses me off that the captain and Haley had to put up with Brianna because of me. Not to mention what she did to Shayla.

"Anything else you need from me?" I ask.

"No. Thank you for the clarification." The captain glares at Brianna.

"Watch her," I say to the two crewmen left on the bridge. I give a cock of my head at the first officer because Brianna's not stable. She's likely to bolt. The captain walks me to the door, and we step out into the hallway. Shayla and Calvin are still there.

"Depending on what Shayla decides, would you be willing to talk to local law enforcement?" the captain asks.

"For sure." I glance over at Shayla.

"I don't want her in jail. I just want her gone." Shayla crosses her arms over her chest.

"You're sure?" the captain asks.

"We do not have time to deal with a crazy person like her. We have a boat to clean. If I go talk to the cops? No. She cut my hair. She's wackier than a clown at an adult birthday party. And I want nothing more to do with her. I wanted her gone before she went all nutso. Let's cut our losses and move on. That's what I say." Shayla looks the captain up and down and nods at Calvin and me.

"All right, then, it's done. I'll give her thirty minutes to clear her stuff out. I need to order her plane ticket." The captain disappears into the bridge. Calvin wanders off too.

Shayla turns to me, a calm mask slipping into place. "What time would you like dinner?"

"You don't have to serve me. I'll go check out what the chef is doing in the kitchen in a little while."

"Okay. Can I make you a cocktail?"

"Thanks, but I'm fine." It's horrible—I know I said for them to not fuss over me today, but I was kind of hoping it would be Haley to ask me these same questions. I could tactfully say no, and she'd see what a down-to-earth guy I am. Instead, she saw that I once had horrible taste in women. And I led her to them, causing a whole layer of hell. "I have some work to do. I'll come out later and go talk to the chef."

Back in my cabin, it's really not too bad. I've taken away six different horse accessories and put them in the closet. And now it's nice. I pull out my computer. My inbox is bursting. I'm a long way from taking over from my dad. But while my dad has horrible taste in second and third wives, his associates and board members are top-notch. The team isn't changing, and as far as we can tell, there isn't anyone remotely unhappy with Dad passing the baton to me. And I'm not happy about digging into a hundred-page report from a factory in Burma. But I do.

I've made a good dent in what needs to be done and skipped most of the busy work, when there's a knock at my door.

"Come in." I don't look until I've finished the last few words on the email I was working on. Mostly because I figure whoever is at the door is going to have a hard time opening it like I do each time I leave the room.

I'm a little shocked to see that Haley is standing there when I look up, her hands behind her back, her eyes flitting about the room. "I'm sorry to bother you," she says.

"No bother at all. Sit down." Shit, I just told the chief stew to sit.

"I'm good, but thanks. Shayla said you were going to go down and talk to the chef. I'd be happy to do that for you."

"It's no big deal. I know you're busy." I shut my computer. I want her to know I can focus on her.

She tucks a hunk of golden-brown hair behind her ear. "It's no problem at all. With your help clearing out the boxes and getting them donated, plus getting us another day, we're ready for the rest of your family to join you."

"No one is ever ready for Candy." And I'm hoping that she doesn't become family. But I don't say that out loud.

Haley laughs. "I'm sure she's a lovely lady who just likes horses and to shop. Speaking of which, what happened to your room decor?"

"It's in the closet." I point to the enormous wardrobe by the bathroom.

"Not a fan of horses?" She opens it and eyes the pieces. I wrapped them in a towel I stole from my sister's bathroom. But I'm not going to tell Haley that. Which I suppose is kind of a dick move, because Emily will have to ask Haley for more towels. But my sister would never yell at anyone for anything. She's not a fan of a private yacht. But she's not going to not come, because she is a big fan of water and of family. She loves my dad, and I suppose she loves me too.

"Horses are wonderful." I flick my eyes to her and back to the closet.

"I see. But you're not a fan of them in such high quantities?"

"I'm not a fan of them anywhere but in a barn or a pasture."

"I like horses. But it's a lot." She smiles at me. "So, what would you like?"

I know she means for dinner, but my cock jumps because what I want is her on the bed with her screaming out my name. "I'd like to go talk to the chef."

"Okay, I'll take you to the galley." She smiles at me, and I pull my stateroom door shut and follow her down the stairs. She smells of coconut and sunshine.

"I like your perfume."

She laughs. "I don't wear perfume. Maybe it's my shampoo or cleaning solution. The mop bucket smells pretty good."

"Whatever it is, it smells great. It's definitely not from the mop bucket." I need to back up—the last thing I need to do is hit on Haley.

"What did the diva say he wants? Raw chicken and overcooked broccoli?" A pot slams on the stove.

"Dante," Haley calls out to him. He's wearing earphones, and he's got his back to us.

"I don't care what his preference sheet says. I'm going to cook him real food. What a prick." He throws his hands up in the air. "A little pork chop or some salmon. Avocados are healthy. But this is ridiculous." He waves a paper in the air.

"Dante!" she calls out and thuds her hand on the counter. The vibration makes the chef turn around. He pulls his headphones off, and death metal blares out of them.

# Chapter 15

## *Hardtack*

Dante

"What the fuck, Haley? Let me know when you're going to bring someone into the galley." I reach for my phone in my back pocket to turn the music off. I slap the paper in my hand back on the wall.

"I told you before I went upstairs that he might come back with me."

I grit my teeth because I told her to leave the pretty boy upstairs and she knows I did.

"Don't yell at her." Pretty Boy is smitten with her too. *Well, get in line.* But I bet he's used to moving to the front of the line, with his father's money moving him there.

The atmosphere in the galley has an added tension now, more than just between me and Haley. There's a vibe that resonates, likely the result of money and privilege entering our little world.

I slam my spatula down on the counter. "She is the chief stew. I'm a chef. That's how we communicate. She yells at me, and I yell back." I point to Haley.

Pretty Boy turns to her.

She cocks her head. "He's kind of right. But I tend to be on the less yelling side. But chefs expect it."

"Really?" Pretty Boy is stunned.

"She's not lying to you. What do you want?" I rip the preference sheet off the wall. I can feel a mix of anger and curiosity bubble up inside me. Why does this guy, with all his money, even care about the minutiae of yacht etiquette? I'm stepping way out of bounds here and slam his paper down on the counter. From what everyone has told me, the guy has been really useful today, and I'm treating him like a normal wanker who rents a yacht for a week, not the son of the owner. I'm not sure why.

Pretty Boy reads down the sheet. "Who gave this to you?"

Haley steps in. "It's from the preference sheet packet that was given to the captain."

"This is what I told Candy I ate last year because she wanted me to go out to eat with her and her friends at the country club. They don't do simple food at the club. I mean, they might if I asked. But I'm not an a-hole who orders things not on the menu." This time it's Pretty Boy slapping the counter. His statement surprises me. Despite his background, he seems to understand the world and its unwritten rules better than most.

"Good." That's all I can muster up. Because I'm the champion of never backing the fuck down.

"What did you make the crew for dinner?" he asks.

"Pasta Alfredo with scallops, garlic bread, and salad."

"I'll have that too."

"Good." I glare at him. I think I won this round, but I'm not sure.

"Fine. Whatever you have, I have. I'm not picky." He crumples the paper into a ball and shoots it into the bin. He misses by a good six inches. "My gold is in swimming, not basketball."

"I can tell. I'll have your food out for you in twenty minutes."

He glances out at the main salon and back at Haley. "I can eat with all of you tonight."

It's a statement. Not a request. Pretty Boy knows how to command a room without raising his voice. And I wait for the chief stew to shoot him down with her grace.

"We'd love to have you," she says.

My mouth drops open.

"What time?" Pretty Boy smiles at her.

"When we're getting ready, we don't all eat together. But I imagine in an hour. Is that good with you, Dante?"

I glance back at Pretty Boy and then Haley. "Yes."

I wait for him to make his way up the stairs.

"I know," she says before I can get a word in. "I know. It's not ideal, and no one wants to eat with the guests. We need downtime. But he's been through a lot today. He's helped us out. But most of all, we don't say no to the owner or guests unless it's a safety issue. And this clearly isn't a safety issue. In fact, it makes dinner service easier for you."

"I'm not plating things up fancy," I growl.

"I wouldn't expect you to." She smiles at me.

"I'm not making him dessert." I hate baking. With more than a passion. I can make a twelve-course tasting menu fit for kings. But my cake looks like a kindergartener slaughtered a store-bought cake with a butter knife. And I only wish I was exaggerating.

"He didn't ask for one, and he doesn't look like he eats them too often." Haley's back with a reasonable response and that stunning smile. She knows how to diffuse every tense situation, making it all feel so normal. It pisses me off because I want to complain about something else. "I'm free if you would like me to wash some of your pots." She gives a little shrug, and I just wish it wasn't only the pots she wanted to wash.

"You know, Haley, you're not a typical stew." I nod at her like I've said something earth-shattering. The girl has to know how special she is. Few chief stews who are running a boat that needs ten stewardesses would take the time to do something that is a chef's job.

She's running water into the big kitchen sink, filling it to wash without me asking her to.

"Oh really? Why is that?" Her shoulders go up in an adorable shrug.

"Because you're so damn agreeable." Another fact she has to already know.

"Well, good. Because I like it when I get along with my chef." She's got the big pasta pot in the water and is squirting it down.

"As well as you get along with the captain?"

Water sprays over my shoes. She turned to look at me, and the sprayer came with her hand when she did. It's dripping over the counter and puddling around my feet.

"Oh my goodness. I'm so sorry." Haley's running for the butler's pantry on the other side of the kitchen, then she's mopping the floor around my feet.

Unlike the rest of the crew who go barefoot, I wear plastic clogs onboard. Mine don't have ventilation holes like theirs for safety in the galley—can't risk burning my feet while cooking over hot stoves. The clogs let me focus on the job instead of having unprotected feet around scalding equipment.

I kick them off. And the next thing I know, she's drying my clogs with a clean rag. Her on the floor looking up at me with soulful eyes . . . Fuck me. I'm getting hard in my chef pants. Luckily, they're loose.

"It's fine, Haley, you don't have to dry my feet." But when she sits up on her knees and wipes the water off the cabinets, her face is inches away from my growing cock.

She sucks her lips in.

I'm blessed in the sausage area. Well, packing, as they say. And I could be a gentleman and step back. But I don't. And now I really want to know how she's getting along with the captain.

"Why did you say that?"

"Say what?" I give her a wink. A wink that would send her to my cabin door tonight if she wasn't already entangled with someone else. But chefs and chief stews are never a good mix, I remind myself.

It's four a.m. and I pull myself out of my bunk, feeling the effects of yesterday's long shift. I've managed to get a solo room, which feels like a luxury aboard this ship, since we're missing so many stews. Another one since the captain sent Brianna packing on a jet plane. Brianna, with her too-loud laugh and endless chatter.

I have muffins to bake, golden-brown tops waiting to emerge from the oven, pastry dough to roll out and a bunch of other shit. I'm not a breakfast fan. I'm not a fan of baking, I even say I'm terrible at it. But I'm good at it. I just fucking hate it and try to do it as little as possible. Baking takes way more time and effort than any guest understands. No one remembers the baked goods, and they don't bring in a bigger tip. It's the glamorous dinners and sunlit lunches that get all the praise. I'd much rather have them eat a croissant, flaky and buttery, and have a cup of coffee. But no. It's three lobster egg benny's and two egg white omelets, this one with cheese, that one with no tomatoes. And the timing of everything is atrocious. Trying to get everything perfect, down to the last sprinkle of parsley, is a dance I'm constantly perfecting.

So I'm in a rip-roaring mood when I get to the galley. The owner, Pretty Boy's dad, is going to be on board at eight. But Easton says that when Candy the fiancée is in play, eight means ten. Late starts are a chef's worst nightmare. Which is another thing I hate. I can understand why last year's chef didn't come back. This isn't a restaurant. I don't have a team of cooks to cook your meal over if you don't show up on time. Or an unlimited supply of ingredients. Hello, we're in the middle of the ocean—there's no chance for a quick run to the store. So no, I'm not a fan of guests showing up late.

Somewhere around six, Haley's up, her hair pulled back in a tight pony. The early light catches the glint of her eyes. She's wearing her white uniform for our official greeting of the owner. And she looks so damn perfect I want to rub a chocolate scone over her, just to break that pristine image.

"Good morning," she sings, as in actual notes. And it's infuriatingly good.

"Wow, you have a voice."

"I like to sing, but not songs. And not in front of people. But thanks. What can I do to help?"

I guess I don't count as people. *Interesting.* I'll have to do something about that.

I give her a smirk and whisk my sauce some more. The aroma fills the air, a teasing hint of spices and cream. "I've got it under control. Wait, taste this." I dip a teaspoon into the pot. "What do you think?"

"Wow, that's amazing." She licks the back end of the spoon and I'm totally going to hell like my Catholic grandma always told me I would. Because I knew the sauce was fantastic; I just wanted to watch her lick the spoon.

"All crew, all crew. Meet on the back deck for the official welcome in five minutes," the captain says over the radio.

"Looks like Easton was wrong. They're early."

"Are you ready to meet them?" Haley's face scrunches up in question, her eyes searching mine for any sign of apprehension.

I've got this. I've always got this. Owners love me. They're in awe of my food because it's absolutely perfect. I could have my own restaurant, but why would I want to? Being a yacht chef, I take the contracts I want and spend the rest of my time on beaches around the world, eating and strolling my way through Europe and Asia between jobs. My life is perfect. Who wouldn't want to be me? One picky owner—that's nothing.

"Everyone's talking Candy up like she's some sort of terror," I say. "I should be fine with her. Her food preference sheet reads like a dream."

On the back deck, we're all lined up ready to receive the owners. Easton isn't here. Captain straightens the lapels of a kid from Engineering. The morning sun makes his brass buttons shine. I've met him, but I don't remember his name.

"Make sure you get your shirt to the laundry room so it's pressed next time," the captain tells the kid. Then he strolls to the end of the line to be the first to greet the owner.

# Chapter 16

## *Salt Water*

Sam

Anders is next to me. Separating me from her. Two months of not touching her is going to kill me.

"You ready for this?" I ask her over the top of Anders' head. He's got the new control pad for the ship pulled up on his phone. A meteor could fall out of the sky—so long as all systems on the boat were in the green, Anders wouldn't even look up.

Haley's holding a tray of rolled towels, and Shayla next to her has a tray of champagne. Normally, the chief stew wouldn't have to hold anything. But there is nothing normal about this season. I spent the wee hours of this morning on the phone, hoping we could get a replacement out for Brianna. But no such luck. I found a stew, but Rocky wants to go out far, so it will be two weeks before we can swing into a port and pick her up.

I haven't told Haley yet. We haven't been alone since yesterday. And it's a good idea if it stays that way. Her coconut scent is drifting on the breeze straight to my cock.

"We're ready. Right, Shayla?" Haley says, a twinkle in her eye.

"We're going to rock this shit." Shayla holds the tray like a pro, her hand loosely over the base of the glasses.

Four silhouettes approach from down the dock. The driver called me ten minutes ago, letting us know they were almost here.

"Rocky." I grab his wrist and shake his hand. He pulls me into a hug. I knew he would. The big man is a hugger. My ribs groan from his pressure.

"Good to see you. How's the little dinghy holding up?" He slaps my back.

"She's a beauty."

"She is! Can't wait to get her out on the water." He pulls his fiancée next to him.

"Candy, it's lovely to see you." I try not to cough from the cloud of perfume surrounding her. She kisses each of my cheeks like the Frenchwoman she wishes she was. "Let me introduce my department heads. Anders was with us last season on the *Mermaid's Tale*. And this is Haley Brewster, our new chief stew. Dante, your chef, Zane the bosun, and Calvin, head of Engineering. Also, we have our stew Shayla, Waldo secondary deckhand, and Mitch the secondary engineer." I catch Calvin shoving his phone into his pocket. I know it's the new systems he's looking at, but the guests don't. I shoot him a raised eyebrow, and he looks away.

"Lovely to meet you, Mr. Rockwell." Haley puts out her hand.

Candy steps in front of her fiancé, blocking Haley's handshake.

Rocky laughs. "My Mrs-to-be is a little territorial."

Haley shakes Candy's hand instead. Candy gives one of those limp-wristed handshakes that give me the shivers.

"Hey, Captain Sam. This is my boyfriend, Brick Hanover." Emily shakes my hand. She's a ray of sunshine, and you couldn't get more different from Candy if you tried. She's wearing cutoff jeans, cheap flip-flops, and a white T-shirt with a hand-painted design.

"Nice to meet you." Brick stops and shakes my hand. He looks like a dudebro straight from a movie. But then again, we are on a yacht. He completely clashes with Emily's vibe.

"Haley's going to show you the boat. She'll give you a complete tour." I nod at the four of them.

"Where's my brother?" Emily spins in a circle.

"He told me to say this exactly." Haley clears her throat. "'Tell the rug rat I'm working and can't listen to her babbling until dinner.'"

"Oh, hell no he didn't." Emily places her empty champagne glass on the tray. "Thank you." She smiles at Shayla. "Where is his lazy ass?"

"Down one flight in the Fortune suite." Haley smiles.

Candy gasps. "He's not supposed to stay in there. He's supposed to be in the Golden Tire." Candy snaps her fingers for Shayla to fill her empty glass. I'm not sure it's possible to dislike a person more. "Why is he in there? I sent specific instructions. I don't care what the shrew wanted in the past. I want him in the Golden Tire suite."

I have no idea what she's going on about, but I'm guessing it has something to do with Rocky's ex, Susan. I turn to Anders, and he shakes his head. He was the one who gave the preference sheets to the heads of the departments. But I read them.

"I'm sorry, Candy. I didn't see any instructions on cabin assignments." Haley's smile is demure.

Candy snorts. "Typical."

The whole "the owner is always right" philosophy doesn't always float with me, not when they are being dicks for no reason. "Candy." My tone drops. "Haley wasn't part of the boat provisioning team. Anders and I received the preference sheets."

Candy shakes her finger. "He needs to be in the Golden Tire room. That's his suite."

"We can prepare that suite for him, and he can move if he wants." Haley smiles. "Now if you'll follow me, I can show you your glorious owner's suite. I know you're going to love it. It's the prettiest one I've ever seen." Haley ignores Rocky, putting all her attention on Candy. "If you'll follow me."

"I think I'll tag along." I give a quick nod to Anders, who looks at me like I'm crazy. The rest of the crew has scurried off to change out of their formal uniforms and get ready for launch. Normally I would go to the bridge too, but I'd bet all of our tip money that Candy is going to have kittens when she discovers that three quarters of her decor is gone. I texted with Rocky about it, and also about Brianna. But if things go true to last season, he didn't tell her.

The main salon looks amazing. It's a lot easier to appreciate all the woodwork when it's not hidden behind boxes.

"It looks good." Candy touches the base of one of the largest horse statues. The thing took three men at the shipyard to carry on board. It's specially mounted on the frame of the ship to keep it from tipping over if we lose stabilizers. Which is bound to happen at some point. Last year's model of this ship had actual issues with the air-conditioning stealing all the power and knocking the stabilizers off. The shipyard promises they fixed the issue. Stabilizers are important, especially on a top-heavy boat like this one. "But I ordered more horse statues. Little ones to surround the big one on the floor. Where are they?"

"On the floor?" Haley's got her stew face on. "I see. Well, boating standards don't allow for things on the floor. If the boat tips, they become projectiles."

"That's what the builders said. And I told them I don't care. I want more horses."

"It could endanger the safety of the passengers and crew," Haley repeats in a more direct way.

"Where did you put them? Where's Brianna? Why wasn't she out on that stupid receiving line?" Candy, finishing her second glass of champagne in a gulp, puts the glass on the bookshelf and turns to Rocky. But he's abandoned the tour. Actually, both Emily and Brick have too. It's just Haley and me following the raging lunatic around.

So Rocky hasn't told her about her niece or the donation. But then, I didn't expect he would. I hoped he had.

"Candy, your niece assaulted another crew member. I have let her go." I don't bring up the restraining order. Easton can do that if he wants to. Which I'm guessing he doesn't, or he already would have.

"Assault? That's absurd. I'm sure the other girl started it." She waves her arms about.

"I didn't say it was a girl." I stare down at her. As far as trophies go, Candy isn't much of one. She's not much to look at and has the personality of a rusted jack hammer. But even though the man has made billions, he's not willing to stand up to her.

"Didn't you? Of course it has to be a girl. Men love Brianna."

Haley's nodding away.

"She's not welcome on board. I'm sure Rocky can give you the details when you ask him about it." I cross my arms over my chest.

"I'll do that. You know, you're not the only captain of yachts. Where's my cabin?" She glowers at Haley.

I stand there and cock my head slightly. Then I give her a quick nod. She's right. They have other options. Few would put up with her. And while I believe you should never talk badly about a former employer, I'll make sure no one I know ends up with this commission. Right now, I'm counting, because my mother taught me never to swear at a lady. And she's the owner's soon-to-be wife.

But Anders was right. He suggested we look for a new boat. I suspect he's been looking for a new one for a while now, on his own. Which is the way of yachting. I didn't expect him to be my first officer forever. He's more than ready for his own boat.

I lucked out getting in with Rocky five years ago. This is my third new boat with Rocky but the first that was new from the shipyard. I can find a new position on another yacht next season, if it comes down to that. Because I'm not going to be her punching bag. I've got a great resumé, and nowhere on it does it include "yes-man."

"This way." Haley is motioning when Shayla magically appears with an espresso martini.

"Oh. Now this is what I'm talking about. I like this one." She smiles at Shayla, whose hair is curled up short with a white headband that matches the shimmering paint of the *Rock Candy*.

Shayla smiles and zips back to the butler's pantry before Candy can draw her into a conversation.

I can leave them alone now. Candy seems like she's not going to cause any permanent harm to any of the crew, and especially not to Haley. I reach for my phone to fake a getaway when Candy gasps.

*Don't say it, don't say it.*

"What's wrong?" Haley responds out of reflex, and I can see her kicking herself for reacting.

"Oh, nothing. The bedroom—I mean the cabin—it's lovely. Without any of that stuff that Susan picked out." Candy spits out the name of the woman she replaced. The cabin is stunning, and the stews have fresh flowers matching Candy's preference sheet in multiple places around the room. The bed faces the bow of the ship, and it has a 180-degree view.

Candy lies down on top of the ivory comforter. Multiple layers of horse pillows engulf her head. Her drink sloshes over onto the comforter, but she doesn't pay any attention.

Haley is there with a towel, immediately dabbing at the large spot.

"Oh, leave it, Kaley. I'm going to sit here and watch the ocean." She takes a big sip of her drink and puts the glass on the nightstand. "Unpack my bags for me and press everything."

"Yes, ma'am." Haley smiles and doesn't say a thing about Candy getting her name wrong.

"I'm not old enough to be a ma'am," she yells. "Call me Candy."

"Anything else you need, Candy?"

"Yes, tell your captain to get the boat moving. I'm waiting."

How drunk was she coming on board that she forgot I'm in the room? "We'll be underway shortly." I leave the stateroom and follow Haley out. We march in silence to the butler's pantry.

"Wow," Haley says. "Just so you know, Shayla and I reached out to your chief stew from last year. I hope you don't mind. I DM'd her. She said our only hope is to keep Candy's glass filled up with espresso martinis. They put Candy to sleep. And to order more sheets."

"Good plan. I asked Kerri to come back, but she said she'd rather die from a thousand paper cuts than set eyes on Candy again." We head up the stairs to the main salon deck where the bridge and kitchen are.

Haley laughs. "I guess you're glad you didn't lead with that when you interviewed me." She cocked her head.

I'm not a dishonest guy. I don't lie. But I might not have described the owners in great detail. I wanted Haley to take the job. Plus, Kerri, while a professional stew, takes everything too personally. She spent a good amount of time hiding, crying over things Candy said to her.

"No, I'm glad I didn't either." My eyes rake over Haley's body.

The butler's pantry is first, then the kitchen. I can hear Shayla talking to Rocky and Brick on the aft deck. Maybe there is a benefit to not having so many stews. I nudge Haley into the butler's pantry and shut the door. It's seven feet long and wide enough for cabinets on both sides and not much more. A long closet, a long closet with no cameras. I shut the door and flick the lock. It's meant to keep the door from banging on rough seas. It won't keep anyone out. But with Haley pushed against it . . .

# Chapter 17

## *Rigging Snob*

Haley

My back hits the door of the butler's pantry, and Sam grabs the base of my chin and tilts it up.

"Sam?"

"You know you're amazing, right?"

I try to nod, unable to form words. Not with his hand on my chin. I lay in my bunk last night from two a.m. until six this morning. I'm not sure I slept at all between my to-do lists and thinking about Sam. My hand goes to the smooth skin on his cheek. He must have shaved right before the owners arrived.

His lips touch mine quickly and softly. Unlike yesterday, our kiss is tender. The tension builds in my toes and zips energy through me. I want to climb him or drop to my knees and reciprocate yesterday. But he pulls away.

"You're amazing. I think that, and so do the rest of the crew. Keep up your good job." He steps back and lets me back away from him. How the hell am I going to focus on what I need to do now?

"I'm going to need a minute."

My eyes flick to the bulge in his pants, and I nod.

"Open the door and show me how to use this absurdly fancy coffee maker." He clears his throat.

I crack the door open, and Dante is staring at me. He looks away from me to the captain with a smirk on his face.

I reach around Sam for the large carafe that's conveniently inaccessible behind him. "Are you sure you don't want me to refill your coffee cup? Honestly, I don't mind." Mostly because I know the carafe is empty.

Dante has moved around the edge of the hall into the kitchen.

Sam blinks at me. "Maybe bring my coffee up to me just this one time. I'll have to figure that machine out later."

"Sure." I put the empty carafe on the counter, and when he scoots past me, I step back, making sure my hand brushes against his length.

"Thank you, Haley." His smile lights up the dark pantry.

"Anything for you, Captain."

He steps out of the pantry. I have to take a few seconds to get my head back in the game. The first thing I do is pull out my phone and order a new bedspread from the provisioner. I might have been able to get out that stain if she'd let me finish. But by tomorrow morning or even tonight, when we get in there, it's never coming out. We have one spare. But we're going to need more. We gave away a lot of things but not a useful linen.

I head into the kitchen and expect an earful from Dante.

"Breakfast can go whenever the guests are ready," he says. Not a word about me being in the pantry with the captain with the door closed.

"Haley, Haley, Shayla."

"Go for Haley." I hold the radio to my face.

"Can you meet me in the main salon?" Shayla's a great communicator. I love that about her.

She's behind the bar mixing a cocktail. There's a neat scotch on her tray already. It's nine a.m.

"Hey girly. Chef says breakfast is ready. By the way, your tablescape is amazing. I know they're going to love it."

"Well, maybe if they love it for dinner. Rocky says Candy made them eat at the hotel for breakfast. He's stuffed. They're not planning on eating."

"Right." We share a look. I pivot back to the galley and brace myself waiting for him to blow up about the guests not eating his meal.

But he shrugs it off. "You want to take it down for the crew?" He cocks his head to the spread he's made.

"I'll be right back, let me check on the guests first." I go through the dining room to the bar area in the main salon, just as Emily's coming in from the back deck.

"Hey ladies, can I get a glass of water, no ice?" Emily asks.

"Coming right up." Shayla pours a bottle of water into a glass.

"Tap is fine next time." Emily lifts her water in a cheers motion. "Thanks. Easton told me all about the Brianna drama. I'm really sorry about what happened."

"Thanks." Shayla pours the blender drink into the glass and puts it on her tray.

But Emily sits up at the bar and looks at me. "So, tell me about yourself."

"I'm twenty-nine. I like to read. I like dogs and long walks on the beach." I wiggle my eyebrows at her. "How about you?"

"I'm twenty-six, the daughter of a billionaire. I couldn't give a shit about money, but that's easy to say because I've never been without it. I love plain vanilla cupcakes, and I was born in Maine and mostly raised in Boston. Until Dad's second wife, Susan, didn't like the snow and moved us to Florida."

"I feel like we could be besties now." I refill her water glass.

"I'd like that. Last summer was horrible. The first year I haven't enjoyed being on the boat with Dad. He mostly turns work off and we talk. But then Susan used to go to bed early. Not Candy. She doesn't let him out of her sight after dinner."

"So, do you still live in Florida?"

"Yeah, in the same house with my dad and Candy. I still miss New England. Although, the move to Florida turned out okay for Easton."

"How's that?"

"We had an Olympic-sized pool in the mansion Dad bought, and Easton realized how much he loved it. Everyone thinks my dad made the pool for Easton. The pool made Easton." She laughs and takes a drink of her water. "Are you single?"

I have to consider it carefully. "Yes, I'm just coming out of a long relationship. It ended, well, messy."

"Don't they always? Brick and I have been together for ten months."

"Nice." I wipe the bar. Emily smiles, but I'm not sure she's happy. Instead, she nods at me.

Normally for a charter, the guests have decided what they want for dinners and the chef adapts the menu. But for owners, there's a lot more catering to their wants. And instead of waking up the kraken in the primary suite, I turn to Emily. "What do you want for dinner?"

"Oh, Dad will want steak. Candy will want something fancy that she can push around on the plate."

"No, what do you want?"

"You know what?" She stands on the footrest of the bar stool, leans across the counter, and whispers in my ear. "I would love something local."

"I'll see to it."

She gives me a high five as I head for the kitchen to tell Dante.

"All right then, now we are talking." Dante's smile is infectious. He bounces around the kitchen in his plastic crocks, singing at the top of his lungs.

Well, at least I've made two people happy today. I think back to Sam in the pantry. Make that three.

I find Shayla cleaning the crew mess. "I'm not sure what to do with myself," she says. "They are all napping now. Other than Emily —she's reading a book in the main salon. Laundry is done."

"Take a twenty-minute break. I'll hang around on deck and make sure everyone is good if they get up."

"Sure." Shayla shrugs. "I didn't think we'd have any downtime."

"Right?"

I head back to the aft of the ship and watch the water. We're getting out there; there's no land in sight. Most yachts don't leave the shoreline. But this one is big and designed for the open ocean. Apparently, Rocky's got a thing for being far out at sea. We're really high-tailing it, hitting some gigantic waves as we go.

"Anders, Anders, Calvin," comes over the radio.

"Go for Calvin."

"Turn to the other channel."

"Copy," Calvin says, and the line goes silent.

I take a deep breath. I don't like to think about what the bridge and Engineering are talking about. This isn't the first time they've brought the ship through deep water.

"Hey." Zane comes up on the railing.

"Hey back at you." I bump his shoulder. "We're really moving."

"Yeah, we're heading for a shelf a few hours away so we have someplace safe to anchor."

"Oh, that makes sense." I guess I should have asked Sam myself, but I was a little preoccupied. "Do you know where we're going after that?"

"Rocky is in the wheelhouse talking to Captain Sam right now."

"Gotcha."

"How are things going for you guys so far?" Zane motions back to where Emily is sitting inside.

"Not to jinx us, but pretty smoothly. Although, Candy came on board and basically went right to sleep."

"Yeah, Easton implied Candy medicates herself." Zane mimes popping a pill.

I raise my eyebrows because any kind of illegal drugs on board could make Sam and the rest of us lose our licenses.

"No, all doctor-prescribed. We're good, she's good. And when she's asleep, we're all good."

"How many years have you been with Rocky?"

"This is my fourth. I started green here. I was on a few other boats when the *Mermaid's Tale* was docked. I still miss her. I saw her before I left Fort Lauderdale. The new owners renamed her *Caribbean Orchid.*"

"Really? Don't they know that's bad luck?"

"I guess they don't care. You pay almost twenty million dollars and you want to call it what you want to call it. But 'the Caribbean Orchid?' They could have come up with a different name."

Zane and I stand watching the ocean. Until we both feel like we need to be doing something. I wave goodbye and get ready for dinner by changing into my black evening uniform.

Shayla's already set the table—a beautiful red Asian-inspired table. It's so pretty.

I squeeze her shoulders. "Darn girl, you are talented."

She waves her hand at herself. "I know."

Candy is the last one to arrive at the table. She's wearing a silk kimono, and I wonder if Emily told her what the menu is.

"You look lovely, Candy," I say, holding her chair for her.

She rolls her eyes at me, and I smile back. I'm going to win this woman over.

"That color looks great on you," Brick says.

"Why, thank you." She reaches in front of Emily and squeezes Brick's hand.

Shayla is standing behind the table, waiting to pour the wine. I can pick out the little flare of Emily's nostrils as she reacts to Candy touching Brick.

I step to the table. "Tonight, the chef has prepared for you a selection of traditional dishes from the region—"

"I don't want General Tso's Chicken." Candy lifts a scowl to me.

"It's not American Chinese food he's made—"

"I want something French," Candy interrupts.

I glance at Rocky, who is staring at Easton.

"Candy, if you could quit interrupting Haley, I'm sure you'll like the meal," Easton says.

"Do you hear how he's talking to me?" Candy bangs on the table to get Rocky's attention.

"Would you shut up, Candy? Thank you for getting the food I asked for, Haley. I know it will be lovely." Emily smiles at me.

"You shouldn't order food for us, Emily. You don't know what I like." Candy is pointing her finger.

"Don't point your finger at my sister." Easton crosses his arms over his chest and glares at his dad, waiting for something I think we all know won't come.

"Babe. I don't like Chinese food," Boyfriend Brick complains.

"I hate it," Candy says.

"Oh my God." Emily pushes back from the table. "I'm sorry, Haley. I can't eat with these two. When you get a chance, would you bring me my food in my cabin?" She's talking to me, but she's glaring at her dad.

I nod.

"Babe?" Brick doesn't stand to go after her.

Candy storms off in a competitive way. Rocky goes after her, while Easton stares at Brick until he leaves too. Only, Brick doesn't head for the cabins but rather the top deck. I saw him puffing on his vape up there earlier.

Shayla fills Easton's glass. "Do you want dinner?"

"I would love it, if it's not too much trouble. I'd say I'll take it in my cabin too, but this table is far too nice." Easton taps the paper lanterns over the table.

"We'll bring it right out."

Shayla and I wash up in the kitchen. We put away the tables as the clock turns eight.

"This is batshit crazy," she grumbles.

"I know. You go to sleep. I'll take the late shift in case any of them get back up." I head upstairs and finish the last of the dishes. The digits on the butler's pantry clock flip over to eleven. I might as well make the rounds and see what cabins have light or sound coming out of them.

The owner's cabin is dark, but it's also huge. They might have lights on in the back that I can't see. I go down a level to where Emily, Brick, and Easton are. It's quiet in Emily's cabin, but Easton's door is shaking.

I knock. "Easton, do you want some help?"

# Chapter 18

## *Confined to Quarters*

Haley

"Easton?" Candy had a fit earlier and we moved him from the Golden Tire suite to Fortune.

"Yes, please, some help."

I pick up the handle, lean, let it open a little, and then push down. I don't know what it's doing, but it works. The door pops open. And I stumble into Easton.

He catches me before I go tumbling into his room. "Are you okay?"

"Fine, thanks."

He lets my arm go, and I swallow hard. Why is it when you're not looking for a guy, they're all around?

"Thanks for helping with the door. It's like a child safety lock—easy to open from the outside, but a bitch from the inside."

"I'll get an engineer to come fix it."

"No, don't worry. It's late. Tomorrow is fine."

"Are you sure? I can call—"

"I'm good."

"Do you want anything? Something to drink or more to eat?"

"Nope. I was going to take a stroll around the deck, but I'm good now."

"Okay, pleasant dreams." I wave.

"You too." He leaves his door open a crack, and I head down to my cabin.

My alarm goes off. Six a.m. Shayla has already brought breakfast to the five passengers in their rooms. Which isn't normal. Even Candy's up, but then time-zone changes do weird things to guests. Kerri, the chief stew from last year, said that sometimes Candy would sleep all day and want drinks prepared for her all night. But today she's up and dressed and reading a thick fashion magazine like a kid at Christmas time making a list. Every once in a while, she holds the magazine out for Emily to look. Emily rolls her eyes, but Brick responds, "How pretty," every time. I watch from the corner of the butler's pantry. Easton is in his cabin, but the four of them in the main salon look like they all need some serious therapy.

Shayla pops up from doing laundry.

"Do you want to do service or housekeeping?" I ask her.

"Do I want to hang out with the Addams family? Are you kidding? I'll take scrubbing toilets any day over them." Shayla's whispering in my ear, but Emily looks up from her book, scrunches her forehead, and smiles at us. We both smile back.

I follow Shayla down the stairs. I can help her for a little bit and then pop back up and check on them. Plus, I should check on Easton too. Make sure he's not stuck.

"Emily totally heard you," I whisper to Shayla when we hit the landing.

"I don't care. She's the only normal one of the lot."

We decide to do Emily's room first. It isn't too bad. I'm finishing up the bathroom when Shayla moves on to Candy's cabin.

"Haley, Haley, Shayla. Can you come to the owner's suite?" She doesn't wait for me to respond. This won't be good.

"Be right up." I race up the stairs and into the room. "Holy . . ."

"It's like a hurricane came through here."

"We can do this." I nod. I know my eyes are wide. But we can do this. I pick up clothes. Shayla is right there with me.

"But every day?" Shay is mad.

I don't blame her; I am too.

"She did this on purpose. She didn't like us defending Emily."

"Yeah, well, I'll talk to the captain later."

"You do that. Because this is bullshit. I'm not cleaning up after a child. I pressed every damn one of these yesterday." Shayla holds up a pile of clothes in her fist.

The rest of the day isn't much better. The waves are enormous. We're moving to some place where there's a ledge or something that Rocky wants to fish on. Candy is getting worse, not better. She sends back three drinks. By the fourth one, she's so out of it she doesn't remember what she ordered.

Emily is sulking. Not that I know her at all, but you can just tell that some people are peppy and kind, and she just feels off. She hardly talks to her boyfriend, although she talks to her brother twice between breakfast and lunch.

It's early afternoon when I set out a charcuterie board for them. I mean, who doesn't love a board of meat and cheese? Most guests go nuts over my boards. It's something I do as a stew, but never too close to dinner or the guests won't eat and the chef will be all furious at me. But maybe not Dante. He's the happiest chef I've ever met. Even if he keeps giving me weird side glances.

"Thank you." Emily takes a small bite of cheese and goes back to her book. I feel horrible. I want to make this better for her . . . and then I remember. She loves cupcakes.

"Dante? Do you love me?" I cock my head sideways.

"I don't know you well enough to love you, Sassy, but I think I could. What do you want?"

"Cupcakes. Not for me, for Emily. She's so bummed out, I just want to give her a little joy, and the cheese didn't work."

"If cheese doesn't work, there is no hope." He laughs. "Actually, I'm personally meh about cheese. Don't tell anyone—I'll lose my chef's card. But I have sad news for you, Sassy. I don't bake. I mean, I can, but not today I have too much to rearrange." He motions to the ten open kitchen cabinets. "What about crème brûlée or honey-glazed boozy pears?"

"I'm great at baking, and I'd love to make it up to Emily, since it was my idea she pick dinner yesterday. There isn't much laundry yet. And Shayla is down for a nap. This will most definitely be the only time this season I can bake anything. There will be more laundry, so . . . And I love baking. Unless you're one of those chefs who's all 'it's my kitchen, and no one can use it.' If you are, I can make it in the crew mess."

"No, Haley. I share really well." His voice is gruff, and I have to hold in a shudder. What the hell is going on on this boat?

"Great." I pull myself out of my little Dante trance and gather the ingredients I'll need. I'm careful to stay out of his way, using the smallest amount of counterspace I need.

"You really know what you're doing."

If you had told me I'd have time to bake, clean up, and have a half-hour break, I'd have told you you were crazy. But here I am, icing up the last of two dozen cupcakes.

Dinner comes and goes. The guests barely talk to each other when we step into the room. They're eating in the inside dining area as it's a little extra windy.

I'm out to top off their water glasses when Candy turns to Emily. "Why do you always dress like a hobo?"

"A what now?" Emily sits up in her chair.

"A hobo. You know, one of those people who followed the trains."

Candy is wearing a black evening gown with a plunging neckline. It's Gucci. I know because I hung it back up this afternoon. But it looks like a potato sack on her. Emily, however, is wearing a white and gold sundress and looks like a Grecian goddess.

Easton stands. "You need to apologize to Emily. And now. Dad, this is insane." Easton slams his hand on the table. "I know I told you I'd give you two weeks, that I'd stay with you. I'd be on the boat; we'd be together as a family. But I can't do this. Not with Candy's big mouth. Not with her here. I have things I need to talk to you about. I've been asking you to come to my cabin so we can discuss them. This is it, Dad. We have to talk."

Rocky looks up at Candy and then back to his son. "I'll talk to you about these things tomorrow."

Easton shakes his head. "I'm done. I'm just done." He stares over at me. "Haley, please give my compliments to the chef. Everything was delicious. Just like it was last night." He growls out the words. He puts his chair back under the table and walks out of the room.

I'm paralyzed. I've seen guests fight but not like this. Usually, it's drunken nonsense they don't remember in the morning. I turn and see Shayla ask Easton a question. I'm sure she's asking him if he wants his dessert brought to his cabin. He shakes his head no.

Emily's looking back and forth between her father and Candy. Her lips are firm. "I can't with any of you." She pushes her chair back, drops her napkin on her chair, and leaves the room.

The interesting thing is her boyfriend doesn't move. He sits there awkwardly with his girlfriend's parents. Then he looks up at me. "Can I have another drink?"

"Sure." I clear the half-eaten meals and take them to the kitchen. I drop them off next to the sink.

Dante's hands are in the air. "They're done already? Didn't they like it? Something wrong with the food? There's nothing wrong with my food," he answers himself.

"No, it's not your food, Dante. Your food is perfect." And it really is perfect. He's a master.

"They're just—they're fucking weird is what they are. All of them. All five of them. They're fucking weird, weird, rich people, filthy rich people. They're just fucked in the brain."

We both turn to see Easton standing there.

"He didn't mean it," I blurt.

Dante is locked in a staring contest with Easton.

"Oh, he means it, and he's not wrong." Easton cocks his head. "I was just wondering if you could make up another bedroom. Emily caught me in the hall, and she said she doesn't want to sleep in the same room as Brick anymore."

"Oh, yeah, sure. That's not a problem. It's already made up, since last night when she asked. I can freshen it up for her."

"Oh, not for her. She's kicking him out." Easton smiles. "Are these cupcakes for anyone?"

"Yeah, I made them for Emily. She seemed depressed earlier."

Easton's grin widens. "Thanks. That's the nicest thing that anyone's done for my sister in a long time. She loves cupcakes. My mom used to make them when she was a little girl. You don't happen to have pink sprinkles, do you?"

"Afraid not, love." Dante tosses his towel over his shoulder.

"I'll make sure she gets them," I say. "I'll bring them down in a little bit."

"Thanks." Easton touches my shoulder and nods to Dante. "Thanks again for the food. It's great." And he thumps down the back stairs.

"Oh fuck, there goes our tip," Dante says. "Unless you can keep flirting with him, Haley. He seems to really like you. You've got the whole boat wrapped around your finger."

We have to finish the service before I can take Emily a cupcake. I grab Brick his drink and head back out. But they're all gone.

I grab two cupcakes. Emily is a kind soul. I can see it. She didn't deserve what Candy said. Well, no one deserves anything Candy says. I rap on the door of her suite.

"Go away."

"Emily, it's Haley. I'm just checking on you." She opens the door. "I bring a gift."

"You had chef make me cupcakes?"

"No, I made them. Chef isn't a baker."

"You're kidding! Oh my. Thank you so much." She throws her arms around me and hugs me. "You are the kindest person ever."

"Oh, you're welcome." I balance the plate as she tackles me. "Well, I'm glad to help in some small way. Is there anything I can get you before I go to bed?"

"No. Thanks for making up a room for Brick." Emily smiles.

"Not a problem. If you need to talk, let me know."

"I will. Things will be a lot better after we take Dad fishing."

I smile and nod because Dante is right: rich people say the oddest things. From what I've seen, there will be no talking any sense into Rocky.

I head back to the butler's pantry where Shayla is washing glasses. "Shayla, I've got the rest. Head to bed."

"You're sure, boss? It's early."

"This is easy peasy." I motion my hand around the dining room table. "Thanks for doing the turndown service for Brick so quickly."

"Easy peasy, boss." She dries three more glasses and closes the cabinet door. "Goodnight."

"Goodnight, you beautiful goddess of a second stew."

I'm collecting the rest of the decorative blue and white sea glass pieces from Shayla's amazing table when the ship stabilizer clicks off and we lunge starboard and then back to an even keel. The wind picked up sometime between cocktails and our own episode of Housewives of Fort Lauderdale. The boat lists starboard. Shit, I've been on boats that have lost their stabilizers before, and it's not a fun ride. But this? This feels different. We whip the other way.

Anders clicks on the radio. "All crew, we lost stabilizers, but we're good now."

I run down to both floors to see if any of the passengers have gotten up to see what's the matter. But Rocky and Candy aren't in the hall and their lights are off. The same thing with the next floor down.

Rich people.

I head off to bed. I change into my leggings and a huge shirt. I always sleep in a sports bra, so I put a clean one on. My eyes flutter shut. I've got Calvin's stuffed animal against my chest, and I drift off.

Then the system-wide intercom clicks on. "Attention all on board. Abandon ship. Abandon ship."

# Chapter 19

## *Abandon Ship*

Haley

My heart is thudding, but I've trained for this for a decade. I grab my water shoes and my crew sweatshirt and toss it on. I glance back at my little cabin and grab Calvin's stuffed animal. I shove it inside my crew jacket.

I open Shayla's door. She's sound asleep with an eye mask on. "Shayla, wake up."

The alarm is still blasting. She goes from asleep to turbo in an instant, jumping down from her bunk, grabbing shoes and a jacket.

I race to the bench in the galley. It's open already. I grab a vest for myself and one for Shayla, then two more for the primaries, because that's where I'm heading next.

Everyone has an assigned zone. When we practiced two days ago, taking time from all I had to do, I was a little upset. Now I'm moving to the primary's cabin, where I'm assigned to make sure they are up and on their way to the life rafts. Normally we would go by levels, but Rocky is older, and the captain said he sleeps like the dead. *Not dead. Not dead.*

I knock on the door out of habit but then turn the handle. They're both still asleep. "Rocky, Candy! Wake up."

That's all it takes, and Candy is screaming.

"Shh, Candy, breathe. Panicking won't help you," Rocky says. He's up and he's pulling on a shirt and a pair of suit trousers, but whatever.

I hand him the life vest and round the bed to the other side. I'm not sure what the heck Candy is sleeping in, but she needs more. I open the dresser and pull out a T-shirt and yoga pants, and a sweatshirt with a horse on it. I shove it all in the laundry bag she's never used next to the dresser.

"Candy, stop!"

She's flailing around picking up jewelry and shit.

"Drop it, all of it," I order.

She looks at me like I'm mad.

"Now," I say.

Rocky is zipping up his jacket. "Now," he yells.

She drops them.

"Put this on." I put her arms through her life jacket and hand her the bag. "Let's go."

In the foyer, Emily and Brick are ready. They both have on sensible clothes and life vests, and Emily is carrying water shoes. "I can't get Easton's door open, and neither can Brick." Her eyes are searching, but she's remarkably calm.

"I've got it. Take them to the port aft side. That's where we launch the life rafts."

"The what?" Candy says.

"Driver's side back," I yell at them. The ocean is loud, and the boat shifts back and forth. Things are flying off shelves in the main salon. I skirt down the stairs by sliding along the wall.

Easton is banging on the door.

"Hold on, I've got you." I do the normal thing: push down, lean on the door, lift. It doesn't work. The boat lists to the other side, and I stumble away from it. I should have had Calvin fix the door. Damn.

"Haley, get back from the door. I'm going to kick it," Easton says through the door.

"That's not going to work." But I hear a thud anyway.

I take a deep breath. *Slow down to go fast*, I remind myself. Focus. I push on the door latch, lean on it, and lift, and the door clicks open.

Easton's more shocked than I am, but he's wearing a life vest.

"Follow me," I yell. We climb the steps, but the angle is wrong. Steep. He grabs my hips, helping me climb. "This way." I haven't seen Shayla since she went to check the rest of the crew cabins.

This is wrong, so wrong. They launched the tender. We're not supposed to use the tender in an emergency—it's too tippy. There are two rafts inflated too, but the tender is pulling away.

"What's going on?" Easton holds my arm. The wind is blustering, and the waves are crashing over where the swim platform would be. I'm holding on to the sidebar. Most of the crew is already in the other raft. Shayla, the engineers, Emily, Brick, and all the deckhands but bosun Zane. Anders is in the tender with Rocky and Candy.

"She wouldn't get in the raft. Rocky made us launch the tender." Zane is scowling at the tender. "Let me help you into the raft."

"Where's the captain?"

"Captain's on the bridge," says Zane. "The radio's down, electrical too. No one knows where we are. Get in the life raft, Haley."

Sam. I can't go without Sam. I spin to head to the bridge. "What about Dante?"

"Shit, I don't know." Zane picks up his radio. "Dante, Dante." But it's clear the system is down. He tosses it in the raft. "Get in, Haley. I'll go get Dante."

"No, you help Easton in." I take off before Zane can stop me.

The boat is really rocking now, and going up the stairs is like a fun house gone wrong. I hit the top step near the butler's pantry. The light coming in is from the small emergency power lights and a little sliver of twilight. There at the end of the counter, his crocks are sticking out.

"Oh, no. Dante."

Ellie Pond

He's unconscious on the floor. There's blood on the corner of the counter and some near his head. I drop to my knees.

# Chapter 20

## *Mayday*

Calvin

The emergency power is on, but I had to rig it to get it going. It's powering only a few of the systems at that, and the intercom to the bridge isn't working. The last thing the captain used it for was to order all of us to the life rafts. Fucking hell. I sent my guys up to the raft already, but I had one more thing I wanted to do. It didn't work, but I had to try.

I fight my way through the crew mess. Plates and tins lie scattered and broken about the floor. I run up the back stairs to the bridge. The power's gone dead to all the vital systems, including the radio and positioning beacon. Captain's working on it on the bridge. But when I get there, the door from the hallway is flapping open. Sam is under the control panel, his damn dog on his feet.

"Captain, I couldn't get it running."

"I haven't got shit here either." He ducks his head out to me for a second.

"Let's go." I give him the look my father used to give me.

"No. Get in the boats. We're not sinking too fast. I'm going to get the beacon going at least. There's too much ocean for a rescue party to cover. We're not due into port for a week. Take Penny and go!"

"Fuck." I rake my hand over my face. But he's right. Without that beacon, we're all dead. This isn't a shipping lane. No one's going to find our little rafts floating in the ocean.

I grab the dog, throw her over my shoulder. She's not having it; she wants Sam. My legs are long and my strides sure. Working on cargo ships for years has taught me how to walk through some tough rolling water. I race to the rafts in the aft.

"What the fuck?" I say into the wind. The tender's in the ocean being tossed around. One raft is away; the other is still tied to the rail.

I pull the dog down from my shoulder and try to pass her to the owner's son, the swimmer, whatever the fuck his name is. But the dog kicks out her hind legs and takes off for the open bridge door.

"Damn, she's a stubborn dog. She would never want to leave the captain, anyway." I'm not risking my life for her twice. "Everyone accounted for?" I say to Zane. He's lashing down a supply bin and sun cover in the raft.

"Haley went back in to look for Dante. I tried to stop her."

Fucking hell. I'm running—well, more staggering—up the stairs to the kitchen. I don't blame Zane for not going after her. He couldn't leave a passenger alone in the raft.

Haley's already in the main salon. She's dragging Dante by the armpits, kitchen towels draped over his head. "Calvin, help me."

I grab Dante by the waist and throw him over my shoulder. "Is he dead?"

"No."

I can barely hear her. The wind howls. She stumbles into the wall, but I grab her with my free arm.

"You good?" I hold her blue eyes for a moment.

She nods. I'm hoping I can look back on this as the most ridiculous thing I ever said to anyone. I hope to hell I'm not carrying a dead man. We're swaying more and more. *Rock Candy* is taking on water, but we're still floating. It's hard to tell what's going to happen—*Rock Candy* might still be afloat in the morning, or a wave could have her on her side. Captain made the right call.

"Can you catch this one, Swimmer Boy?"

"I'm ready."

Haley helps me, and we pass Dante to them. They lay the unconscious man onto the raft floor.

"Haley, get in," Zane says, reaching for her.

"Not without Captain." She takes off running, and damn, she's fast. She scurries up the outside steps, holding on to the rope.

I don't catch her before she wrenches open the side door. And then Captain Sam is there. He's saying something to her, but it's lost in the wind. "Go," he shouts.

She shakes her head. "No."

He glares at her and kisses her cheek. "Don't let this one come back," he says to me. "Keep her safe."

"Yes." The storm rages in my ears.

Captain pulls the door closed. He must have locked it, because Haley is yanking on it with all her might. She's screaming and furious. Her fists are clenched around the handle as she pulls.

"Haley, we need to go," I yell into her ear.

The boat lists, and she sways, her feet lifting off the deck. I grab her around her waist and hoist her over my shoulder. She's wailing, her fists slapping at my back.

But I'm off, pulling away from the wheelhouse, leaving the captain to his doom. To our doom. I want to be positive and say he's going to make the beacon work, but it's a long shot.

I've turned and am making my way back to the aft. Haley stops struggling. She's limper than Dante, but I can feel her chest heaving. And the water on my shoulder isn't sea spray.

"Put me down, Calvin." The way she says it, I know she won't run, and the stairs are safer with two hands on the railing.

I ease her to the ground. "Let me go first." If she falls, I can catch us both. The stairs are a lot steeper than normal.

The life raft is waiting. Swimmer Boy is doing something to Dante. We need to get out of here, launch the raft. If the boat tips while we're still tethered, it won't end well. The other raft is away, its reflective lights showing when it tips toward swells. But the tender, I can't see. I'm holding on to the side of Haley's lifejacket. If she slides and I can't stop it, we're going together.

But Zane is standing on the rail of the boat. "Come on, Haley. Get in," he shouts into the wind, beckoning to her. This time she takes his hand, and he helps her into the raft. The sea is really churning. The raft and boat slam together before moving apart.

She climbs in and immediately slides over to Dante. I've been through some shit in my time on the ocean: pirates twice, a dumb fuck captain who ran us onto a sandbar and had us stuck for a week while news helicopters circled. But this? I'm a positive guy, and when we get out of this . . . I'm going to find a nice girl and become a landlubber.

I step into the raft and turn to give Zane a hand, but he's gone. A second later, he tosses a load of three beach towels into the raft, a half dozen bottles of water, and two cushions from the back deck.

"Get in the damn raft, Zane," I growl.

He's already untied us and slides off the deck into the raft.

I glare at the cushions. But the raft's designed for nine and there's only five of us. It won't hurt the weight.

Haley is helping Swimmer Boy do something. That's when I see she's not clipped in. "Hale—" I'm about to read her the riot act for not attaching herself to the raft.

"What?" She turns. She's holding a bloody towel to Dante's head. I reach around her to clip her into the raft. There are ropes on the bottom of the raft to tuck your feet under and ropes on the side. Using those is actually safer; if the raft flips, you aren't trapped under it. But it's only safer if you're paying attention, which she isn't. The heavy-duty plastic carabiner clicks into the side of her life vest. She can take it off if she wants to. I'm not some prick who will tell her what she has to do.

Zane is attaching the cover to the side wall across from me. The sides and bottom of the raft are triple-lined inflated plastic. The floor has ropes and clip-in rings to keep us from sliding around. And the sidewalls have clips for the roof to hook into and a rope for us to hold on to. There's a hand pump in the kit to top it off as needed, along with other supplies.

"Zane, let's paddle to the other raft. Then we can put the sides up." Water sloshes in on rogue waves, but not enough to sink us. We need to get on our way before we lose the other raft. There's safety in numbers.

"We're not going to catch them. The currents are pulling in different directions already. But we can try."

I could order him to do it. As the lead engineer, I'm third in command on board the *Rock Candy* and the highest ranking on the raft.

"We need to get to my sister. I'll help paddle." Swimmer Boy takes the plastic paddle from Zane's hands.

"We also need to conserve our strength, Easton." Zane looks at me.

"For what? They'll send help to us. We'll be out here . . . what, a day at most? But if we get separated from the other raft, that's going to cause problems." Easton leans over the edge and starts paddling. He's got the gist, but not quite.

Zane reaches over and clips the paddle to his wrist.

"Thanks."

"We'll try for a while." I put my paddle in and pull. It's hard. Rafts aren't meant to be paddled. Steering is possible, but paddling is rough. It's work—you have to really lean in and pull. I'm not a weakling. My football days, and working on the cargo ship, left me with muscles. But working on engines that are now more computer than mechanical has left me not as built.

Zane taps me on my shoulder. "Let me take a turn, then you can spell Easton."

"Give him a break first."

"That's what he said. Just hand over the paddle. This isn't a He-Man competition." Zane puts his hand out.

"Fine." I give him the paddle. We're not making any progress on catching the other raft. The *Rock Candy* is still behind us. She's listing more violently, but she's above water. We've got another half hour of dusky light. From the plastic toolbox, I take out the flashlight and signal the other raft with short on and off until I get a response from their light.

I start with my Morse code, which I'm praying one of the deckhands is good enough to understand because I have zero faith in my second and third engineer. It's gone over in the classes to get your certifications for deckhand, but it's no longer on the test. I'm just hoping someone over there knows more than SOS. Because we're both in the same shit situation already. I'm a pro at Morse code, though. I loved it as a kid. Also, after the first pirate attack on the cargo ship, I decided I was going to be the best at everything to do with my job.

I signal five on the raft. A simple first message to see if they get it.

Easton turns to me. "What are you doing?"

"Morse code."

"Ask them if my sister is okay," he asks, like I'm just going to pick up my useless phone.

"I need to make sure they understand me first." I wait, watching their raft. They are going in and out of view as we catch waves.

Their light flashes. It's hard to get all of it. Long-long-short. "G," I say. Long-long-long. "O. Shit." A wave has them obscured, but I catch the next letter. "D."

"They spelled out god?" Easton's still paddling but looking at me.

"I'm guessing good." They signal again. "E, L, E, V, E, N," I call out.

"Eleven? Waldo and my three other deckhands, Shayla, two engineers, Emily, and Brick. That's who I saw in the raft. That's nine."

"Anders, Rock, and Candy were in the tender. Before I left to find Dante." Haley tries to hand me a bottle of water, but I don't take it. It's one from the deck, not from the emergency stores in the raft kit. We won't touch those until tomorrow.

# Chapter 21

## *S O S*

Easton

My arms are on fire. It feels worse than a marathon training session. I pull as much water on the paddle as I can get, but the ocean doesn't want us to make any progress. The other raft is flashing now. The raft that has two more people in it than it's supposed to. It's horrible, but I don't care if my dad's in the raft or not. As long as Emily is. She's got to be okay. "Can you ask them—" I stop when the flashing from the other raft returns.

Calvin calls out, "C, A, N, D, Y." The light stops. "It's got to be Anders doing the Morse code."

Zane doesn't stop paddling, so I don't either.

"L, O, S, T."

"What?" I keep paddling. A light hand lands on my leg and gives me a squeeze.

"Let me take a turn." Haley's palm is open and up at me.

But I can't give it to her. The burning in my arms is helping me process. I turn around. "Lost as in missing?"

Calvin flashes the light, and I wish I'd taken the boy scout unit on

Morse Code more seriously. Long-short-short. Is that a D or a G? I don't remember. I stop watching.

The other raft replies.

"I'm sorry, Easton. It says Candy's dead."

I nod. Damn, I don't know how to feel about that. It's horrible, but so was she. The whole absurdity of this situation is crazy. Am I heartless because I feel nothing for the loss of her life? She was tricking my dad into marrying her, but still. I take a breath in. This is a stressful time, and there is no way my emotions are going to match what's going on around me.

"Let me paddle." Haley takes the paddle from me, and I let her. I check on the chef. He's breathing. I have a degree in sports medicine. I know more about concussions, torn tendons, and how to rehab, but I've bandaged him up the best I could. Hopefully, his brain doesn't swell. I take my phone out of my pocket. I use the flashlight feature to check his pupils. They're not dilated, and his heartrate is fine. He's cold. I pull some towels around him.

"Is he okay?" Calvin is pointing the light back at the boat, one tiny prick of light out in the night in that direction.

"The towels should help." But the sea spray is getting worse. There's a bailing bucket attached to the toolkit. I take it and get to work. There's not much water getting in, but there's some. And with each larger wave we ride, we get more.

Calvin stops flashing at the tiny speck of light behind us. "We're not making any progress. Catching them." He flashes a long sequence at the other raft. "They're paddling to us too." Calvin puts the lamp down.

"Fuck." Zane stops paddling, and Haley does too. "What do you want to do?"

They all seem to act like Calvin is in charge. "We're not making any headway. It's getting dark. And it's going to be a lot harder to get the top up in the pitch black. With the storm kicking up, we're going to get rain soon, and then we're going to be bailing all night."

"So call the paddling off?" I look at Calvin.

"Yes." Calvin looks away from me. "I think we need to put the sun enclosure up and call it a night."

I stare at the other raft. They're tiny specks on the water, a mile or more away. Fuck, I hate the ocean. But if Candy is dead, my dad's going to lose it for sure.

A hand lands on my leg. "You're not thinking of swimming to them, are you?" Haley's blue eyes are dark, reminding me of how dark it is right now. Maybe if I'd jumped sooner . . . but pool swimming and ocean swimming are completely different.

"No." I totally was. "What can I do to help?"

Calvin unrolls a large plastic covering. "Move next to Zane."

Haley comes to me. We stretch the covering over the top of the chef while sitting in the windows. Zane zips one side and passes the zipper to Haley. Calvin does the same to me. Then we crawl inside, and Zane uses a small hand pump to blow up supports on both sides. A heavy Velcro seals the top to the raft, and we zip the windows shut.

It's warm in the raft. But with no more water flopping in, we all bail out the areas around where we are sitting. It's nowhere near dry, but it's not too bad.

"If anyone has anything they don't want to lose, I'll put it in the sack the tube was in and clip it in." Calvin passes the bag around. He starts the bag by putting in his hat. Zane puts nothing in it. I take off my shoes; I'd put them on when I heard the alarm. I was asleep, and it was a force of habit. All the years living in boarding schools with pulled fire alarms. I never wanted to be waiting in the snow in slippers or bare feet. I add the running shoes and pass it to Haley.

"I have nothing. I think I'm going to keep my shoes on. I just wish I had a hair tie."

"Oh, I don't have a hair tie, but what about a bandana?" I pull my bandana out. It's purple and green and has the company logo on it.

"What, are you in a gang?" Calvin is fiddling with the equipment box.

"No." I manage a laugh. "Rockwell Harding gives them out at events. I stuffed it in my pocket last night. I was going to show Emily the design. She drew it. But then, well . . ." I don't need to talk about what happened at dinner. Now that Candy's gone, I suppose I never need to tell Dad about what she was doing. But that's up to Emily. "You can have it, Haley. I'm pretty sure you deserve more for saving my life."

"Of course. How could I not have come back for you?"

I laugh. She's so pure at heart. "I hate to say it, but most of the people I know wouldn't have rushed back onto a sinking boat for someone, let alone gone twice. You're a hero—all of you are heroes." I can't see their faces, but I'm pretty sure Calvin growls and Zane scoffs. Interesting. None of them enjoyed being called heroes.

"Oh, that's so much better. Having my wet hair off my face and neck. Thank you." She leans over and goes for a kiss on what I assume she thinks is my cheek but hits my lips. It's a quick smack, but it sends chills through my body.

Raindrops hit the top canvas slowly, and then they build. The wind pulses at us, tossing us more than before. Or maybe it's the darkness. With the top up, I can just make out bodies around me: Haley is on one side of me, Zane is next to her, and Calvin across from me. Dante's head is next to me.

"I'm going to turn my phone light on for a second to check on the chef," I say.

"Good idea," says Calvin. "I'll take the first watch. Someone should be awake at all times in case we hear a plane or a boat. We can pass off the signal gun."

I want to dislike Calvin and his "I'm in charge" attitude, but someone needs to be in charge. And he was right about the paddling: we never got an inch closer to the other raft.

The light of my iPhone shows Dante's chest moving up and down. The rest of the crew members move in from the edge of the raft to watch.

"Are you a doctor?" Zane's leaning over Dante's side to see.

"No. I majored in sports medicine. I thought I might become a physical therapist." Here's where the questions usually start coming about why I would want to do PT when my dad is a billionaire. But thankfully they don't. I check his pupils and they're still good. His pulse is fine. "I wish there was something I could do for him." Haley's close to my side.

"We have to wait," Calvin says. "I'm sure the rescuers will help him."

I catch Calvin's expression before I turn the light off. The big guy doesn't think we're going to be rescued. I take a deep breath.

"All right, settle in," says Calvin. "I'll wake Zane in a few hours, and we can take turns."

Curling up, I try to close my mind off from the reality of what's going on. The guy in charge doesn't believe we are going to be rescued.

Rose-colored light shines through the top of the plastic cover when I wake up. But something is holding down my chest. A certain brown-haired beauty is using it as a pillow. I don't want to move. Cocking my head, I see Calvin giving me a death stare. I shrug. I didn't pull her onto my chest. But I'm sure as hell not going to make her leave.

The raft is heating up, but the ocean feels silent.

Zane moves near my feet. "I'm going to put down the window."

In a hushed tone, I ask, "Any sign of the boat or the other raft?"

"No," Zane fires back. "They were both gone before first light."

That's what I expected, but my positivity coach would tell me to visualize the other raft.

The window on one side is zipped up. It's a clear vinyl covering that keeps the water out.

"You could have woken me for a shift," I say.

"You were doing something." Calvin doesn't look up from the supply box.

"I should take a turn." Haley is really out. We're all talking at a normal level, but she hasn't moved.

"Yeah, well, you needed sleep, and I don't sleep well, anyway," Calvin grunts.

"So true." Zane fiddles with the other window.

"How's Dante?" I can see his chest rising and falling.

"The same," Zane answers. "I didn't lift his eyelids like you did, because I have no idea what you were doing."

"I was checking to see if his pupils were dilated. But just leave him alone at this point."

"Shouldn't we be waking him up if he has a concussion?" Zane cocks his head at me.

"Ideally, but I haven't been able to wake him. And if he wakes up now and is confused and disoriented—what can we do? Nothing really. He's breathing. It's not like I can drill a hole in his skull and release the pressure." If I'd stayed in the program, I would have done a hospital round. Maybe then I'd be more help.

"Ew." Zane scrunches up his nose.

"His brain is probably swelling, numbnut." Calvin's thick fingers tie a knot at the end of the line he's fiddling with.

I glance down at Haley's sleeping frame. Dante has two of the towels covering him, but someone has taken the other and covered Haley. Makes sense—she has the least amount of clothes on, other than her jacket under her life vest.

"Good. I want to try fishing." Calvin is rummaging in the supply box. He pulls out the smallest reel I've ever seen. Fishing is something I know how to do. My dad is a fanatic, and it's one reason he was willing to let wife number two move us to Florida.

I lean up on my elbows. Haley snuggles lower on my belly, grabbing me around my waist. She's inches away from my hardening cock, but I'm not complaining. It's the only good thing that has happened to me since I stepped on the plane in L.A.

Calvin throws the line into the water, and we wait. That's the thing with fishing: it's like meditation except for when it's not. The line goes almost immediately taut. He's caught something.

"Pull it in," Zane yells.

"Wow, you've caught something." I sit up farther, trying to get a better angle of the window, when I realize Haley is moving. She gives me a squeeze, the flap of her life vest covering her head. I don't know how she's sleeping. The heat is rising, and I'm already sweating. She's sliding lower and lower, no doubt to avoid the plastic on my chest. Damn. I'm not sure I've ever had morning wood this hard. And we're fighting for our lives drifting in the middle of the ocean.

"You got it," Zane yells.

Haley jumps up. The sleepiness on her face vanishes.

# Chapter 22

## *Chumming*

Haley

"Oh, I'm so sorry." My heart's slamming in my chest. When Zane screamed, Easton's giant dick jumped into my cheek. I can't believe I left drool on the owner's son. That's a definite line, and I've crossed it. It reminds me of kissing the captain.

My heart squeezes, and I want to vomit. Sam. He can't be dead. Rationally, I understand. I understand why he stayed on the boat. Without the location beacon online, we would drift here forever. I sit up. But we should have stayed tethered, letting him join us when he could. Yes, there was another raft, a raft he could get in the water in five minutes. Less, knowing how talented a captain he is.

The back window and front window are down. A slight breeze is flowing through the raft, but I'm dripping with sweat.

"It's fine, Haley. I'm happy to be some sort of help." Easton adjusts himself, and I look away.

Calvin is pulling on the fishing line, expertly letting line out and reeling it back in. The reel is basic, one you could buy at any box store. But the way the tip is dipping, I'm wondering if what he's caught is too big for the gear. Calvin has it in hand, though. The tug and pull, the fight—I loved fishing when I was little. When I told my grandmom I was going to work on yachts instead of going back to college so many falls ago, she replied, *"Makes sense."*

Weird, I miss her so much, but right now, I'm glad she's gone. She would have been mad with worry.

Dante looks the same as yesterday. He hasn't moved. I brush his hair back from his face, and Easton checks his pulse.

"It's a little better than last night, when I checked it last." He smiles at me.

Calvin and Zane are taking up most of the other window. I shimmy on my butt to them. My skin sticks to the floor. It's not comfortable, but I guess comfort isn't the point—surviving is.

The waves are silent today, but my stomach isn't. When the guys finish fishing, I should get the desalination kit going. It's slow, and we'll need to have it running because the kit only has water for four days.

There's nothing around. No *Rock Candy*, no other life raft. Nothing for us to see. Just the swells of the waves up and down, up and down, taking us wherever it wants to go. I know nothing about the currents here, but off the coast of Florida, there are currents that can carry a small boat in a circle. And a half mile away, you could get stuck in the Gulf Stream and end up zipping up the coast.

"I'm getting it. It's tiring." Calvin's determined. The muscles in his biceps are flexing, like their own Morse code.

"Do you want me to take a turn?" Zane's light brown hair flaps around. It doesn't brush his vest, but it's close.

"No." Calvin juts his jaw out, and he's bracing his arms on his knees. Reel, brace, reel, brace. And as he does, the raft is going zipping along with the creature caught on Calvin's hook. The tip of the rod dips farther, and Calvin releases slack on the line.

"How big is it?" Easton pipes up behind me, and I'm glad it's him and not me asking because I want to know too. But I also know better than to talk to a fisherman while he's reeling something in.

"Damn if I know, Swimmer Boy," Calvin grits out between reeling and releasing.

I'm biting my lips when I glance at Easton. He doesn't seem offended by Calvin. No, we're all invested. But it's the peacemaker in me . . . I want them to get along. Even if we weren't on a raft together, I'd still have the same feelings. I don't want people to argue or fight. I'm more liable to do something I don't want to do just to make others not fight around me. It's why I stayed with Steven for so long, even though I had evidence of him cheating.

Zane sits on his haunches. "Who has their phones with them?"

"I do. Why?" Easton pulls his out.

"I have mine too." It's in my bra, beside Calvin's bear. I turned it off before I fell asleep.

"Damn. Is that one of those long-life battery packs?" Zane motions to Easton's phone.

"Yeah. I hate running out of battery." Easton nods. "I turned my phone off this morning, though."

"Good. Can you turn it on now for just a second? I want to airdrop some charts." Zane motions. "I've only got twenty percent left. The charts might come in handy. I'm a nerd, and at night I like to look at the ocean chart of where we are so I can figure out where to take guests fishing or if there is anything interesting to see. Since Rocky wanted to go deep-sea fishing, I downloaded a bunch."

"Yeah, go for it." Easton turns his phone on.

Calvin grunts. His arms flex holding the reel.

"Got them?" asks Zane.

"Got them." Easton turns off his phone and puts it back inside his vest.

Zane stares at his phone, sighs, and turns it off.

"Girlfriend?" Easton asks.

"What?" Zane runs his fingers through his hair.

"You were sighing at your phone. I thought maybe it was a picture of your girlfriend."

Zane laughs. "I guess, in a way. It's a boat for sale back in Fort Lauderdale. I thought I'd have enough money to buy it after this cruise. And now, well, either we're out of work or we're—"

Easton cuts him off. "Don't say it."

I hold in a shaky breath. "You're upset about a boat when the captain died trying to save our lives?"

"Ho, ho, wait a minute there, Haley. We don't know that the captain died. He might have gotten the system running, and he could be in the third life raft right now. You've got to have some faith. The worst thing doesn't always happen." Zane places his hand on my knee.

And I have to laugh, because really? "We're sitting in a raft in the middle of the ocean."

"Positivity can make a situation a lot different." Zane nods at me. "I don't suppose that's one of those satellite phones?" He cocks his head at Easton.

"No, I'm not a serial upgrader. That's my dad's habit." Easton looks at his phone.

"Could you figure out where we are on the charts?" I raise my eyebrows at Zane. If he wants positivity, I'm not sure I can give it to him. But I can change the subject. I'm a pro at avoidance.

"Not yet. I'm writing our headings every hour, though. I need something to chart off of."

"Where are you writing it down?" I ask.

"There's a small notebook and a waterproof pen in the box." He pulls it out, and there's a list of directions and speed. "Calvin did it overnight."

I'm not sure why this makes me feel better, but it does. He hands the notebook to me. Zane's writing is tiny, messy but legible. The notations overnight, in Calvin's handwriting, are more like a typewriter. They are so precise I find it hard to imagine they came from a human hand. "Are we still going the same direction?"

Zane checks the compass. "Yes. But we're getting there a lot faster with whatever Calvin's got on his line."

"Too bad we didn't find an aquatic horse to tow our line yesterday. We might have caught up with the others." I drape the towel on the support behind me. It's damp from picking up the spray yesterday.

Hours go by. I don't want to talk or think. But nature is calling me and she's not going to wait. I've noticed both Easton and Zane sneaking over to the opposite side of Calvin.

Zane takes the reel from Calvin, and a while later, he passes it back.

Nothing about this is going to be graceful. Or easy. And I'm not sure what I should do.

Zane makes another trip to the window. "Sorry," he says to me when he sits back down.

"I just need to figure out how to do that myself."

"Oh," Zane replies. "I have an idea." We've drunk three bags of water so far, but Zane has carefully folded each one of them. We use them with the desalination kit too. He slices one down the back and opens it. Then he takes an extra support and makes a loop around the bag. It looks like the little practice toilet Steven's niece had. Sort of, kind of. Okay, not really.

"That's awesome. Thank you."

"We can turn around and give you some privacy. Right, Easton?" Zane nods at him.

"For sure." Easton nods. Calvin's busy with Moby Dick on his line.

I do what I have to do, then wiggle my yoga pants back up again.

Somehow, when I thought about what it would be like to be on a life raft—because of course I've thought about it—I never imagined boredom to be the toughest part. I ease over to the other side of the raft and open the toolbox. We have four more hooks. It makes sense why Calvin doesn't want to lose any. But how much longer can the big guy last? The sun in the middle of the sky says noon.

And he's been at it for a long time. How long have I even been awake?

I'm just about to suggest he cut the line and save his muscles when Calvin grunts, "There he is."

"What is it?"

"A tuna. Not legal size, but I think we get a pass. Two feet. She's put up a good fight, but she's almost done. Get the knife, Zane, and don't cut the raft."

It's Zane who growls this time, "Right."

I'm clear of the action and ready to throw a towel over Dante if they get too close.

Zane leans over the edge of the window. Calvin reels, pulls, reels, and pulls some more.

Zane's got most of his body hanging over the edge of the window. "She's a beauty. Just a little more."

Calvin pulls.

"Got her." Zane's ready, and he stabs the fish. The flipping stops. He pulls her on board.

Calvin guts the fish and puts all the pieces into the bailer. Luckily, the sponge cleans up most of the mess. The light gray sponge is now a dull red color, but we each have a large portion of raw tuna to gnaw on. And it's not bad. The flesh is firm and full of flavor, and if I close my eyes and pretend I'm not in a boat . . . well, I'm still not in a sushi restaurant, but I'm not hungry and there is more to eat, at least for the next few hours.

We eat our fill.

"Thank you, Calvin." He's slumped against the side of the wall of the raft, and I kind of want to pull out his bear to show him. But I also don't want the guys to know I have it. And that he gave it to me. I hate secrets, but this is one I should keep for now. It's literally resting on my heart. Or rather, under my vest. "I don't think I could eat any more." I glance at the bucket of blood and guts and skin overflowing one of our two bailing buckets. "What are we going to do with that?"

"We're going to have to chum the water with it at some point. We have to put it somewhere. Now is the best time. The water is silent, and its daytime, so we can at least see the predators as they come to claim their prize. Are you ready?"

My heart is beating at a thousand flutters a minute. Sharks shouldn't scare me so much. It's a big fear from early childhood. In reality, there are a lot of scarier things in the ocean, from killer whales to pirates. But it's the great white shark that's the most terrifying to me.

"Ready?" Calvin picks up the bucket.

I'm not sure I'll ever be ready. "Are you sure we have to dump the bucket?"

The guys turn to me.

"Are you scared of sharks?" asks Zane. "Because there are other things that might go after the remnants of our lunch. Eels and other fish too. Plus, it might be nurse sharks or other non-aggressive ones. And this is going to get stinky." Zane is kind enough to reach for me. But I'm already on a downward spiral. My insides are shaking. I can do this.

"I don't like them."

"They're not going to go into a frenzy. There's not enough chum for them to go into one. Barely a snack," Zane reassures me.

But I don't want to know what's going to happen; I just want it over with. I can imagine the worst: a shark biting the raft. That's ridiculous. They have no reason to bite the raft. This is real life, not a movie I watched in my grandparents' basement on their old video player. I'm not going to let this be what makes me crack. I'm not going to let these guys think of me as anything but tough.

"Ready," I say.

"If it bothers you, we can paddle away from the chumming area." Zane smiles.

"No, that's okay. We should save our energy." The raft is warming up, and if we took the top off, it would be worse. At least now there is a little breeze flowing through the raft.

Calvin leans out of the raft and drops the chum in a quick blast.

Red spreads from it in a much bigger circle than I would have thought.

# Chapter 23

## *Life Boat*

Zane

Out past the arc of red sinking into the ocean, the Savu Sea just seems endless. The sun bounces off the water, making everything shimmer, and the horizon's a blurry line between blue-on-blue. Then, outta nowhere, there's this rumbling sound from below. Before I can even guess what it is, I spot a massive shape moving beneath us. A blue whale!

I can't believe how huge it is. Even from where we are, it makes our raft look like a kiddie pool toy. It's wild to think about, especially when all I usually compare stuff to is my life back in Birmingham. The vastness of the sea and the sheer size of that whale—it's like nothing I've ever experienced. The big guy doesn't get too close, but just seeing it, watching it move about, is nuts. Nature's properly wild out here. I barely notice the sharks gathering close by.

Haley shakes, but she's doing all right. I put my arm around her and pull her into my side. "It's okay, Haley."

"I know. I know sharks aren't what the movies make them out to be. That not all breeds are the same." She's sounding like a tape from an aquarium.

"True." I glance over at the diminishing stain we're floating away from. And while I wish I could tell her there's nothing to look at, that the sharks aren't anywhere near us, a fin has broken the surface. But sharks, like dolphins, have learned that boats mean food. And now there's another fin on the other side of the boat, which means no fishing for us for a while. Not that we would be fishing anytime soon. We've all eaten our fill of raw tuna. I've never understood sushi, but protein is protein, and it's better than the high-calorie bars in the tool-kit. I've eaten one, and that was enough for a while. That's the point of them: to fill you up. While tasting like cardboard. "Why don't you tell me more about yourself?"

"Like what? What do you want to know?" Her voice is a whisper below the waves.

"What's your favorite thing to do at home?" I put my toes on her thigh and give a little poke.

She glances outside the window. It's too hot and still to put them up. She shakes her head, but I've got to get her to calm down. In all the certification classes I've taken, they repeat the importance of not letting tempers fly. And the most dangerous thing after dehydration and hypothermia? Boredom. The mind can start playing tricks on you if you're not careful.

"We should all play. I'll go first. Back home in Birmingham, it's me and the boys. It's a bit, well, typical. We go down to the club and play football. You know, soccer," I say in my best, worst American accent. "And then later we head to the local pub for a pint. That's my favorite Saturday." I look at her, but she's still not with me. Her eyes are wide, and I'm nervous for her. Grabbing her hand, I pull her to my side and wrap my arm around her. "You go next, Calvin." I wave at him.

"Hard pass," he grunts.

"Oh, I was kind of hoping you'd tell me." Haley's glued to my side now. "This is helping."

"I'll go." Easton is hanging next to Dante. The bloke hasn't moved in a while. I've been spending far too much time just staring at his chest.

Fuck me. I don't want him to die, and I also don't want to pitch his body over the side of the raft for the sharks to have more of a feast.

Easton reaches out and squeezes Haley's toes. "My absolute favorite day is when I'm home in Florida. When Dad's not at the estate—house—it's just Emily and me. She has a habit of dating guys who are absolutely shit. But I get all the shitty food I never let myself eat. Burgers, chocolate-covered peanuts. Popcorn. What else? Oh, pizza. And German chocolate cake. I don't know if it's really German, but man."

"Shut up about the food," Calvin snorts.

"Then I get in the pool and swim underwater. Or just goof off."

"For fun you swim?" I'm shocked. I'm not sure why.

"Yeah, why wouldn't I?" Easton leans forward but then scoots around to the other side of Dante. He's pinching part of Haley's foot.

"I guess I figured you'd have had enough of the water with all the training you do."

He laughs. "I love swimming. It's work, but I wouldn't have done it for as long as I have if I didn't love it."

I'm not much of a swimmer. I passed the exam for ratings. Putting the jet skis in and out of the water is fine, but I'm not going to spend extra time in there. "I like being on top of the water better."

Easton nods. "What about you, Haley?"

"I like walking my dog in the park on Saturdays. Not that I have a dog anymore."

"I'm sorry." Yeah, thinking about a dead dog isn't exactly going to cheer her up.

"Oh, the dog is fine. He lives on a farm in New Jersey now."

"Oh." I catch Easton nodding his head. We're all thinking the same thing: someone lied to this girl.

"Seriously! He does. My shitty ex took him back and gave him to his mother. She lives on a farm in New Jersey. He's not dead. She sends me pictures on Insta all the time. When I get a place and stop doing yachting, she told me I could have him back. That she wouldn't even tell her son. I'm not delusional." She pulls her arms around herself.

There are three sharks. Haley's not looking outside, but I can tell she knows they're there because she's buried her head in my shoulder. I glance over at Calvin. A little head nod to Haley. He gets it. I'm saying *Come on, man.*

"Fine. I'll play your stupid game." Calvin huffs. "I like taking apart a small motor and seeing how fast I can put it back together again."

"Wow, that's cool. I mean, not for me. But cool," I say.

"Five minutes, ten seconds."

"That's your best time?" Haley leans around me.

"Yeah." Calvin's breath rushes out of him, and he turns away from her. "World record is four minutes, two seconds by some kid in Peru." Calvin's looking out the window. Two fins now. One massive, the other smaller.

Haley looks too. "I'm sorry," she mutters every few minutes, clinging to me. I'm an ass because I really don't mind. In fact, I hope the damn sharks hang with us for a while. I'm not going to be the one to tell her when they leave.

"Favorite food?" I ask.

"Pizza," Haley says into my chest.

I should have picked a different question. I'm feeling like I'm a walking advert for Birmingham because, honestly, it's fish and chips, with Indian a close second. I pick my third favorite. "Waffles with fried chicken," I say, which wasn't something I'd had until I went to Fort Lauderdale. But it's good—I mean superb. "But not with real maple syrup. The fake stuff is what I grew up with and like best."

"Gross. I only like real maple syrup, not that I've ever put chicken on waffles," Easton says.

Haley snickers into my chest.

"What are you laughing at?" I want to tickle her. I bet I can get her really going.

"It's just Dante went on and on about your preference sheet. How you had to have chicken and how chicken doesn't belong on a mega yacht." Haley lifts her head to Easton.

"What do you think Dante's favorite food is?" I ask her, smoothing the hair sticking out of the purple bandana down her back.

"Something Italian, I bet. He'd make the pasta from scratch. Something solid with meat. Fresh, simple, but delicious." She lifts her head to Easton.

He's pinching different parts of her feet. "One of the best lobster raviolis I've ever had. I just wish I'd had the whole meal now."

I have no idea what the guests were fighting about, but I heard the yelling from the bow of the boat where I was wiping down the railings.

"I like popsicles," Calvin bursts out of nowhere.

I really don't want to think about the tattooed giant sucking on a kids' treat. But Haley's soft laugh vibrates from her chest against my side. "What flavor?"

"Red, orange. None of that green shit."

"I love the green ones." Easton changes his position at her feet.

"You would," Calvin says in a gruff tone. He's watching the sharks out the window. There's only one fin breaking the surface now, and most of the blood slick has vanished.

"That feels really nice, how you're rubbing my feet. Thank you." Haley's head dips into my chest.

"Pressure points." Easton takes her other foot. He removes the water shoe. Her skin is pruned. From behind him, he takes the semi-dry towel hanging on the support beam and dries her toes. I'm mesmerized by what Easton's doing. Drying, rubbing, and then pressing on certain parts. He hands her shoes to Calvin, who silently puts them in our spare gear bag. Calvin scowls at Easton and then me.

Haley's breathing has changed. Deep breaths spaced farther and farther apart. Her neck limply rests against me. When have I ever taken the time to watch someone fall asleep? It's really an amazing thing. Sleep. We can repair ourselves. I glance over at Dante and hope the chef will pull through.

"She's out," Easton whispers after a long time.

"No wonder. Adrenaline will do that to you," I muster back.

"She was overtired." Calvin's voice is deep, and I know there's more that he's not saying, but now's not the time. "She wasn't sleeping on the boat. She had too much to do because the fucking owner wanted to leave early." Calvin frowns at Easton.

"Yeah, well, I don't want to talk about Candy. Since she's dead and all. But that was her idea. She wanted my dad to retire early, and she wanted me and my sister to come on the yacht. I had nothing to do with it, other than having a work schedule that only fits this time. So you can point your finger somewhere else." He wraps his arms around himself. There's something else going on, but it's none of my business.

"Calvin, we don't need to get all worked up about this, not right now." I hush him, not wanting to say anything to wake Haley. The fins are still poking through the surface every so often. And Calvin's right, she hasn't really had any downtime since she boarded the *Rock Candy*. "We can hash this all out when we're back on land." We need to remember to act as a team. All the survival certification trainings run through my head.

"Right, land." Calvin's mopping up the rest of the tuna blood with the sponge, wringing it out into the bucket.

"Yes, land. Because we're going to get out of this." Easton checks on Dante. He lifts Dante's eyelids.

"Well, golden boy. Life isn't always easy." Calvin mops and wrings some more. He's using the mostly clean bucket of sea water to clean up the last bits of fish scales.

"Life doesn't have to be hard." Easton crosses his arms across his chest.

Fuck. I've known Calvin for a year. And if the wrong guy in the right type of bar said that to him, they'd be on the ground. One punch and his massive fist could crack every bone in the Olympian's face. Calvin's life has been shit, from the few stories I've heard.

"Whatever." Calvin dips the bucket into the ocean and rinses it clean.

The rest of the day ticks by. I fall asleep, and when I wake, somehow Haley and I have slipped to the floor of the raft. She's using my belly as a pillow, and I'm holding her to me. I can feel daggers on my skin when I spot Easton giving me a death stare. I turn to Calvin for support, but he's got the same expression on his face. I know it well because it's the same one I gave Easton this morning.

"Comfy?" Calvin's wrestling with the windows. The swell is picking up, and the spray batters the side of the raft.

I give him the finger.

Dante coughs. And his hands twitch.

Calvin and I stare, but Easton's at Dante's side immediately. He turns his head sideways, and Dante dry-heaves.

# Chapter 24

## *Dawn Watch*

Dante

I throw up, but there's nothing there. My stomach convulses. And my head feels like garbage. I'm not going to be able to make dinner, let alone breakfast. I have no idea what time it is. "Where the fuck am I?" The boat is really rocking and my cabin stinks like fish. "Why does it smell so bad?" My throat is sore. Like I've swallowed battery acid or cheap Russian vodka. Which are basically the same thing.

I open my eyes. The deck awning has a pink glow to it. It's not an awning.

Haley's here, a weird purple bandana over her head. Like a babushka, or a crunchy girl. I wouldn't think of her as a crunchy girl. Not when she's going around making out with the captain.

That's when I remember. I got up to make the dough for my morning cinnamon rolls, and the ship listed hard. Hard enough that I had to lunge for the pan.

I push up onto my arms. "What the hell happened?"

"We—" Haley tries to tell me something, but the primary's son stops her. Why is he here?

"For fuck's sake, Sassy, just tell me." The gagging is back, and Zane hands me a bucket. A bucket that on a normal day would make me want to lose my shit anyway. It's like the inside of a clogged sink incinerator. I pull what's left in my body up from my toenails, hurl it into the bucket, and collapse onto a soggy pile of towels.

Whooshing echoes in my ears when I go down. Everything hurts. I grit my molars together and wait for the next bout of nausea.

And it comes. "Fucking hell." The only good thing is Haley's fingers running through my hair. My cock doesn't care what's going on in my stomach or my head. Little asshole.

I hold Haley's eyes as I go in for another round, then clench them closed. Everything clenches.

"I'm glad you're awake. I was really worried." The bucket is gone. She puts her knee under my head.

I'm using her for a pillow, and I smell like the bottom of a seafood restaurant dumpster. But she doesn't. I'd bury my nose all the way into her if I could. She's stroking my hair, and I almost relax. My groggy head has figured it out: we're in a fucking life raft. "I'm guessing there's a lot to worry about?"

"You've got a big bump on your head," says the owner's son as he leans over me from the side opposite Haley. Zane is washing out the bucket, and the engineer is leaning against the side wall. I close my eyes. "We're going to have to wake you with concussion protocols. Do you want some water? Just a few sips to start. I'd like to take a look at the injury. Can you lie flat?"

I want to growl "no" at him. But instead, I move onto a small cushion, one from the *Rock Candy*'s back deck. It's covered in a blue and white striped towel. I lie down and let my head rest on the soggy thing.

"What's your name again?" I squint up at the owner's son. Haley and Zane are hovering over me, too.

"Easton. What month is it?"

"June."

"Good, and where are we?" Easton's eyebrows rise.

"Fuck if I know. But you don't either, so I've got my memory."

"He's fine," the engineer huffs from the other side.

"Calvin! Let Easton do his tests," Haley scolds.

"Who's the president?"

"Sunak, Trudeau, Albanese—which one? Except they're all prime ministers." I know the fucker wants me to say the American president, but I refuse, not because I care about American politics, but just on the principle of Americans thinking the damn world revolves around their axis. Even though I'm from Pennsylvania, I've spent enough time outside of America.

Easton scowls at me. "What's your full name?" He's not giving up.

"Dante Saffron Jones." I close my eyes.

"Your middle name is Saffron?" Haley asks.

"His middle name isn't Saffron—it's a damn joke. He's fine." Calvin's not giving up either.

"I think Calvin's right. You'll be good. But we still have to move into concussion protocol now that you're not unconscious anymore." Easton gives my shoulder a light tap.

"Here, have some water, Dante." Haley holds a small cup to my mouth, and I drink. It's warm and tastes like it's been tossed around under my car seat in a dented water bottle for two years, but I'll take it.

"Where's everyone else?" I hold her gaze because Haley can't lie for shit. I asked her last night—or was it the night before? Whenever. When we were still on a mega yacht, not a kid's blow-up pool. I asked her what the owner's wife said about the lobster bisque I made for lunch, and Haley told me she liked it. Her eye twitched, and her voice rose as if she was asking a question.

"Most are on the other raft. We got separated sometime yesterday. Are you warm enough?" Haley straightens a towel on my legs.

Light skips low across the way, but my head can't figure out if the sun is setting or rising.

"How long?"

"Going on the second day." Calvin shifts in his seat.

I grunt back but close my eyes. It hurts like shit, but I've had worse hangovers. Too bad there's no tequila here. A few shots and I wouldn't feel anything. Instead, I give my grandma's meditation nonsense a try.

Next thing I know, the owner's son shakes me again.

"I'm sleeping. Leave me alone. Fuck me, my head hurts." And that's an understatement.

"You haven't thrown up in a while. We voted, and you can have some of the pain killers."

"Voted? Is this Animal Farm?"

A soft giggle makes me smile. At least someone thinks I'm funny. And I have a pretty good idea who the aspirin police is. The engineer. It's always the grunters. I take the pills from Haley and swallow them down. The water sloshes in my stomach, but I'm not hungry. I'm asleep again.

This time when I wake up, it still hurts, but I'm better. I'd be even better if the buzzing would stop. Haley's in a pile between the engineer and the owner's son. I watch them for a while. She's facing Calvin, her head on his life vest, and Easton is spooning her. Both guys have hands on her sides.

I smack at a bug and end its life. Hopefully, it's the only death for the day. I ease myself upright. Zane's awake. "Are there any rations?" I ask Zane, who is staring out the side window. He tosses me a bar.

The crackling of the wrapper echoes.

Haley

Captain Sam is standing behind me, pulling me to him. We're dancing, swaying to the music. The bulge in his pants grinds on my backside. But then he's in front of me, pulling me to him. The music is beating in my ears.

But the dream lifts, and I'm back on the raft. A wave of grief floats over me. I knew him for less than a week. How am I going to tell Charlie? He talked about his big brother so much last season I feel like I've known Sam forever.

Last night the temperature dropped. We're all wet. It's impossible to get dry wearing a life vest. But I won't take it off. I can swim, but I don't trust a rogue wave not to hit the second I remove it. I'm warm and, as crazy as it sounds, cozy. My left hand is sandwiched between my stomach and someone else's. When my fingers twitch, I realize I'm touching skin. Skin that is covering some rock-hard abs. Calvin—he tugged me to his side when I couldn't stop shivering. My face rests on his vest. His nose is in my hair. My back is equally toasty. And a large cock is nestled between my butt cheeks. Easton's fallen asleep behind me. Lots of hands are on my side.

Calvin pulls me toward him. His head is far above mine, and my bare toes are resting on his calf. I don't want to open my eyes. I'm just going to pretend I'm back in colonial times and I'm sharing a room with strangers in some inn bed. One that doesn't have bedbugs. Because in my imaginary world, I let myself have a little more money than I have now, but of course, not enough to be some sort of fair maiden, like a duchess or a lady. No, I'm a middle-class girl who has to share a bed with people she doesn't know in a room that smells like dead fish.

But when I take another breath, I can smell the sea over it. It's different—something's changed.

I lean back, and Easton pulls me hard against his morning hardness. He's asleep, or at least I think he is. Because he wouldn't pull me against him if he wasn't, would he? Not that he has a lot of other options in a life raft. I pull forward, and Calvin's large hand pins me to him, straightening my legs so my crotch is lined up with his. Well, crap, he's hard too. Easton is pushing me into him.

I should get up, move out from between the two of them. But the friction is so good. Too good. I need to move before I start to grind against Calvin. This is ridiculous with my large vest on. I give a little push into Calvin's chest and a push back against Easton and roll onto my back.

"Why did you smack yourself?" Zane's voice is deep and inches me more awake.

"A bug," Dante says, his voice smooth. I could listen to it every day. I open my eyes.

"A bug? We're too far out to sea to have flies," Zane says.

That's when I push onto my elbows. Easton's emerald eyes are on me. I suck in my lips and turn to Calvin. He's adjusting his crotch.

"Hot damn!" Dante points out the window.

I sit up all the way. "Wow."

# Chapter 25

## *Land, Ho*

Calvin

Haley's awake. I feel the second her breathing changes. Dante and Zane are talking, but I tune them out because Haley's grinding herself on my morning wood and, Lord help me, I'm about five minutes away from losing my load in my pants. She pushes on my chest, and I let my hand loosen from around her waist. She pushes Easton back too. Unlike the entitled little prick, I'm not pretending to sleep.

She sits up. "Wow."

I want to grab her and pull her back to my chest the same way I used to hold my stuffed bear. That is now gone. But I'm a grown fucking man who's lived through war, pirates, and shitty captains. I'm not going to get upset because my fucking stuffed animal is at the bottom of the ocean. Along with one of the best captains I've ever had. No. Fuck no.

I haven't sat up yet. I'm waiting for my wood to soften. Thinking about Captain and my bear is working. "What is it, another whale?" I ask, looking at the ceiling of the raft.

"No. Land." Haley's scooting out from between us.

I sit up and there it is, between Dante and Zane's big heads. An island with a sandy beach, mounds of palms, and nothing but ocean on either side of it. It doesn't look that large from this perspective, but it doesn't really matter. It's all we've got.

"Here, Swimmer Boy." I hand Easton a paddle and head to the opening next to Zane and Dante, sticking my own paddle into the water. "We've got to get over the breakers, or the rip current might slingshot us around the island." It's not ideal to paddle with the top on, but leaning over the edge is going to get it done. I scoop at the water, my muscles on fire with every stroke. I'm leaning hard. My body is parallel with the waves. We're getting closer to it.

"Damn, how far away is it?" Easton's screaming into the wind.

"More than a kilometer. Want me to take a turn?" Zane's hanging next to Easton.

"I got it," Easton says.

Sweat is pouring down my cheeks, every muscle in my arms on fire. I'm pulling as much water as I possibly can with each stroke when Haley screams, "Easton!"

I turn back, and Easton is gone. "What the fuck?"

"He dropped his paddle and jumped in." Haley's leaning over the edge. I grab her leg—not that I think she's going to jump in, but . . . Dante sees what I'm doing and grabs her leg lower down, allowing me to move her away from the edge.

Zane's hanging off the side too.

My eyebrows dart up. "The two of you aren't thinking about jumping in after Swimmer Boy, are you?"

"No," Zane says.

He totally was.

The breakers are coming up, and there's not much we can do now but steer. I get my paddle and use it as a rudder, hopefully guiding us in.

Easton's a few feet away from the paddle when he reaches out and grabs it. Thank fuck. If we need to get off this island on the raft, we're going to need two paddles. He holds it over his head like he's in some sort of movie from the 80s.

Haley's clapping.

Swimmer Boy tosses the paddle into the raft. I reach my arm out to hoist him in, but he shakes his head. Grabbing the rope circling the edge of the raft, he tugs us into the breakers. Which sounds like a good idea but is the exact opposite.

"Get the fuck in here right now." I'm screaming at him over Haley's pleas. Dante has moved over to the other side of the raft. "There could be rocks. Fucking rocks! Dipshit." We so don't need a hero.

He's not listening, and I want to grab him by the earlobe like my Nana used to do to wayward children. Stupid fucker. He's pulling us.

"He's doing it!" Haley clasps her hand over her mouth when I glare at her.

"Don't egg him on. And when he's torn to shit, don't help him." I push the paddle into the water to steer. The current is taking us over the breakers. We're tipped up and down like we're on a whitewater rafting tour.

Easton lets go, or he's ripped off by the current. I don't know. But I'm furious at him. I've got my foot anchored under one of the taut support ropes stretched over the bottom of the raft. Dante is holding on to Haley, but she's not leaning out of the raft anymore and has her arm secure under a wall of rope. We scrape over a shallow reef and bounce into a quieter area before the raft is pushed closer to shore and backward a bit and forward with the waves until we bottom out. I let go of the ropes and jump out. Zane's with me. Haley too.

I point my finger at Dante. "Stay put."

"Yes, sir." He laughs like it's a fucking drill.

I glance back at Swimmer Boy. He's bobbing next to the reef. Hopefully, he's smart enough to not rip up his feet.

"On my mark." I wait for the next wave to almost hit the side of the raft. "Go." We sink into the sandy, pebbled beach and yank the raft all the way to dry sand. Zane drops to the sand, rolling in it like an oversized puppy. Haley's jumping up and down. Dante's out of the raft. He puts a towel on the sand and lies on it. Like this is a crew day out.

Haley grabs my arm. "See, we made it. We made it." She gives me a big hug, and I have to squeeze her back.

She's so happy. I don't want to be reminded that this isn't Singapore. And from the looks of this beach, it's not inhabited. The coral is perfect, and palm fronds litter the beach. If there were humans living here, the mounds of exotic shells would be gone. From our approach, there's not another island in sight. A bird screeches in the distance. That makes me happy. We might get something to eat besides fish.

I walk the perimeter of the raft, and fuck, just as I thought, when we went over the coral, we scraped the bottom. It took a gouge out of the bottom layer of thick plastic. The second layer is sitting there.

Zane comes around the side. His eyes are wide. "Shit."

"We're lucky fuckers to have found the island during good weather and daylight. Help me get the gear out. We need to find water and firewood." My brain is whirling at what we need. I toss my life vest in the pile of the others.

"Copy." Zane gets right to work taking the box and the bailers farther up the beach to the tree line.

My eyes rake over Dante, but I won't tell him what to do. We had the same ranking on the boat, and he's injured. He's peeled off his life vest and is using it as a pillow.

"I'll work. Give me a second," Dante says with closed eyelids.

But that fool in the water, he's floating on his back over the reef. Easton turns over and catches the next wave in. Assholes like this make me furious.

"We made it!" Easton runs the rest of the way to the shore like it's some sort of old Baywatch rerun.

"What the fuck were you doing out there?" I'm in his face, keeping him in the surf and off the dry sand. It's a dick move, but I don't care.

"I dropped the paddle. I went and got it."

"Not that, stupid fuck. Trying to pull the raft. I told you to get in the raft, and you ignored me."

"So what? I'm fine. We're all fine." He taps my arm and rounds me to the upper beach.

"Fine? Fucking fine?"

"Yeah, fine." He's hugging Haley. Like he's won some sort of prize.

"You could have died. Are you trained for deep sea swimming?"

"I've got my scuba cert."

I give him a nod. "From where? A five-star hotel off Oahu?"

"Maui, actually, if you want to know. Dad's last wife had a thing for Hawaii."

"Yeah, well, we aren't that way here. There's a hierarchy in a crew. And you're the fucking bottom. Keeping your fancy ass alive is our job, so pay the fuck attention when I tell you something."

Easton slowly blinks at me and steps away from Haley. "You got a beef with me? Come at me. I know you want to hit me."

"Stop." Haley jumps in between the two of us. Her ponytail's flopping. She's taken off her life vest and her long shirt with it too. She's wearing a purple sports bra and black underwear.

"Move, Haley."

"You have a problem with rich guys or just all men who don't think you know everything?" Easton yells. "Because as far as I can see, there's no fucking boat."

"Cal," Zane barks at me.

"Shut it, Zane. He's right. There's no fucking boat." No boat means I can handle this the way I want to. With my fists. I'll beat some sense into him if I have to. I pull back my arm, but Haley runs in between the two of us. I react fast enough, tilting my hips to avoid hitting her.

She skids to a stop, but a stone in the sand catches her leg and she goes flying forward. It all happens in slow motion. I reach for her at the same time Easton does, and the three of us land in a pile, the waves crashing around us.

Stumbling, I stand, pulling Haley with me. Out of the corner of my eye, I see her bandana floating away near Easton. He's able to snatch it out of the water.

Haley's struggling to stand. No, she's limping.

"Are you okay?" Easton is there by her side.

I try to take her arm.

She shakes me off and then pushes him away, too. "Stay away from me. Both of you." A wave crashes around her ankles, and she collapses forward.

I pick her up. "Where does it hurt?"

"Put me down. I don't want either of you thugs touching me." She pushes at my chest, reminding me how we were on the raft not too long ago. The anger in her touch makes me almost regret trying to hit the prick. But if she's really hurt, I won't forgive myself. "Put me down." She smacks my chest.

I grip her tighter. "I will. Let me get you to the raft. Out of the sun and sand."

She glares but stops struggling. I set her down on a towel Dante has laid out.

Easton drops to his knees in front of her. "Is it your left ankle?"

"Yeah." She's glaring at him too.

"How's this feel?" He moves her ankle around side to side.

Haley winces.

"Watch it." I'm ready to pick him up and throw him in the ocean if he hurts her.

He ignores me and moves her foot, feeling around like he might actually know what he's doing. "It hasn't had time to swell. I don't think it's broken. But since we don't have any ice, put it up."

Zane has the bag of supplies under her leg, and Dante's got the cushion on top of it. I have to admit, I thought throwing the towel and the cushion into the raft was stupid, but they've already come in handy.

Easton sits down next to her on one side, and I'm on the other. Dante's lying on the towel. He's got his hand over his eyes.

I've had two concussions before, neither from football. Fell out of a bunk bed in college and the second time I hit my head on a beam in an engine room. I felt like shit for five days, and that was with drugs. So I get it.

"I'm going to get wood to start a fire," I say. "We'll need it for signaling a plane. And other things." Do I believe a plane is going to see us? Hell no. But I know she does. I hold my breath. "I'm sorry, Haley. I would never want you to get hurt."

"I know, Calvin. But you shouldn't want anyone to get hurt."

"I'm sorry too." Easton is sucking up to her. He doesn't mean it. The rich SOBs never do. "But you should never get in between fighting men."

"I know that now." She's giving him the I-don't-need-to-be-mansplained stare.

"What were you going to do?" I ask.

"I was going to flash both of you."

# Chapter 26

## *Harbor*

Haley

It's not the brightest plan I've ever come up with. But the way the two of them were, well, rubbing on me a couple hours ago . . . "I figured if I flashed my breasts, you would both be so shocked you'd stop." I'd just taken off my life vest, carefully hiding Calvin's soggy bear inside it.

"Lots of men have become stupefied by a lot less. Brilliant plan but poor execution," Dante says, his arm over his eyes. "I don't suppose you'd want to help lift my spirits by doing it now?" He doesn't raise his head, so I know he's joking. Maybe. It's hard to tell. He's had a head injury.

"No." My ankle hurts.

"Do you want one of the painkillers?" Easton asks.

Calvin didn't want Dante to have one. We had to vote, and I had to convince Zane to change his vote to even get Dante some. And Dante was unconscious.

"Do you need some?" Easton asks again.

"No." Yes, I want them. "But Dante should have some more."

All the guys but Dante are glaring at each other.

"Dante, do you want some more pain relievers?" I ask.

"If you don't care if I lie here, I'm fine without them." Dante doesn't move his head.

Calvin stands. "I'm going to get some wood."

"I'll go with you." Easton gets up too.

They march off into the woods—jungle? Whatever it's called. I don't know—leaving me with Dante. "Are you feeling okay?"

"As long as I don't move or talk. It's nice to be on land. Even if the land doesn't have air conditioning, beds, and a kitchen."

"Let me know if you need anything," I whisper.

I think he heard me. Dante's chest moves slowly. I'm watching him even now. Worry is eating me up. We've lost enough already with Candy dying. And Sam . . . I take a big breath in. Easton and Zane are right. We don't know what happened to him. Like Schrödinger's cat. Although, if I'd gotten my hands on Schrödinger, we'd know if the cat was alive. I'm not so sure about the physicist, though.

I'm also not sure where Zane went. I lean over the edge of the raft to pull myself up. I stand mostly on one leg.

"You heard what the golden boy said: no standing." Dante hasn't moved his arm. He's like my grandfather asleep watching baseball. When I tried to change the channel, he'd yell at me.

"Well, I'm bored. And I can be of some help."

"Be some help by not getting injured any further. Sit down. Those two are liable to start tearing each other apart in the woods."

I sink to the sand in a one-legged squat. "You think so?" My heart pounds. I turn around, trying to see where they headed into the jungle.

"No." He stands, bringing his towel over to my makeshift ottoman.

"You should rest too," I say.

"You wanted something to do. I'm giving you something to do. Can you pet my hair?" He raises his eyebrows at me.

"Your hair?"

"Yeah, like, smooth it down like I'm a pet." He lies on the towel and puts his head on my lap, bandage side up, facing my stomach.

"A pet chef. That sounds dangerous." I smooth his hair away from his forehead. It's silky and dark with a wave to it.

"I'm harmless without my knives." His eyes flutter closed. I keep petting him. He's kept his crew shirt on, while all the other guys ripped theirs off the second they got their life vests off. I rub the circle on his back with my other hand. A slow groan hisses out of his lips.

"Sorry." I lift my hand.

"No. Don't stop. Feels good." He's talking like a drunken sailor, and I'm worried again. But I keep the circles slow with even pressure.

"So good. I'm not drooling on you." Dante's lips are open.

"It's okay if you do."

"You're drool-worthy," he stammers out.

I laugh. "Now I know something's really wrong with you."

"Seriously? You have no idea, do you? So sexy." But that's the last thing he says before he falls asleep.

I stop rubbing him but leave my hand on his back. Feeling his back lift with each breath makes me feel a hell of a lot better. We're all here for such a short time, and anything could take us away. Like it did with my mom. Or Candy. I lean back against the raft and close my eyes too. I fall asleep and wake to the sound of Easton and Calvin bossing each other around.

"Just take the end of the log," Easton says. "You wanted it." Their voices are coming from behind the raft, so I can't see what they have.

"Put it down there," Calvin calls out.

Zane bounces around the raft first, his arms laden with dry drift-wood. Calvin and Easton are holding a whole palm tree. I raise my eyebrows at Zane.

"Easton wants to burn it. Cal wants to use it as a support beam for the decking of a shelter. And I am staying the fuck out of it."

"That's a good idea." I put my hand on Dante's back.

Zane glances at him. "How's he doing?"

"Sassy. And good." I leave the hope out of it because I don't want Dante to pick up a bad mindset.

"Good." Zane nods.

Calvin and Easton take off for the woods, but Zane is running around the edges of the beach, grabbing enormous stones, bringing them back to the pile of firewood he's collected. It's backbreaking work, and after a long time, he settles down in the shade near his pile of rocks.

"I wish I could help." My chest is heavy. I put a little pressure on my foot, and pain zings up my leg.

"You will, Haley. And watching over Dante is helping." Zane moves sand and places rocks, making a perfect fire pit.

"That looks amazing. Have you done it before?"

The answer is in his glance. "No. I'm a city kid. I ended up on boats on a lark. A school mate started and got me a job on a day charter ten years ago. I've been working my way up. Saving. My boat. Oh well, there will be another one. And we better be getting paid." He laughs. "Right?"

"There's got to be something about it in the contract," I mumble.

"More like something to screw us over." He hands me his water bottle from his belt. It's full.

My eyes light up.

"There's a stream. And Calvin was all, 'don't drink it until we boil it.' But—"

"You drank some."

"Yeah, it's better than that bagged water."

"But parasites?" I bite my lip.

"How are we going to boil water, Haley? We don't have a pot. I'm not going to wait until Calvin finds clay, makes a pot, makes a kiln to fire the pot, and boils some water. This tastes good. If you want to wait to see if I collapse, I wouldn't blame you."

The moment I have it to my lips, Calvin and Easton are back on the beach.

"Don't." It's Easton yelling. "We found coconuts to drink from while we wait and see what happens to Mister No-Fear."

Zane takes the water bottle back from me. "Toss me one. I'll open it and give it to Haley."

Easton tosses it to Zane. He balances the brown shaggy nut on a flat rock, takes out his pocketknife, and uses the screwdriver blade and a small rock to punch a hole in it. He hands it to me. "Bottoms up."

"I thought you're a city boy?" I drink it down—it's delicious. But the cup of liquid is gone in a few swigs. I tilt my head all the way back to get the last drops.

"A summer bartending at the Tiki lounge." He beckons with his hand for the coconut back. In a few swift strikes, he has the thing opened. He pries the meat loose with his knife, leaving it in the shell, and hands it back to me. Then he repeats the process for himself. A few whacks and we're munching on lunch that's not raw fish or from a packet.

"Cheers." I clink shells with Zane. "Thank you."

"Anytime."

Stretching to reach Zane jostles Dante. I pull the cushion from under my ankle and put it under Dante's head.

Easton and Calvin are arranging palm fronds on the beach. I can definitely make out an S and the O, but the large log Easton wanted to use for the second S is too skinny and the same brown shade as the sand.

"Want to go see the stream?" asks Zane.

"I can't." I wiggle my toes.

"How about a piggyback ride, at least to the closest part?"

I glance at Dante. He's asleep, and the other two are arguing about whether they should use the tree or not. "Let's go. They won't even notice."

Zane's eyebrows shoot up. "Oh, they'll notice. Question is, do you care?"

"Sure, uh, no. It's fine."

He straddles my legs and pulls me up, grabbing me. But now we're chest to chest and my legs are around his hips.

"Last time I checked, piggy backs were on backs." I'm staring into his brown eyes, holding on to his large shoulders.

"Indeed, you're right." His hands are cupping my bottom. And in the next second, he moves me gracefully around his back. I hold him around the top of his shoulders, careful to not strangle him as he strolls to the woods.

It's a different world. The temperature drops, but it's humid. Sticky, even. Birds are chirping, and there's a little trail leading from the beach.

"The stream isn't far. Just up this way." Tall ferns line the path. And the farther into the jungle he walks, the louder the birds sing and chatter.

"There. Stop."

Zane stops.

"Look, it's perfect."

"What's perfect, Haley?"

"That stick. It's got a little Y in it like a crutch. I can use that, then you don't have to carry me."

"I don't mind carrying you," Zane growls.

"But you don't have to carry me for everything. I'm too heavy. You should save your strength."

"You're not heavy, and what is there to save my strength for, anyway?"

"Zane, let me try it. Maybe it's not even the right height." Seriously, why does he want to carry me?

He lowers me to the ground and holds on to my elbow while reaching for the stick—driftwood that's made its way into the jungle. I'm not going to think about how it got this far inland.

I tuck the stick under my arm. "It's a little long, but I think I can make it work." There's a knot around where my hand naturally rests.

Zane shakes his head at me.

"What? I like being independent."

"Just don't independent yourself to a bigger injury." His serious face turns into a bright smile.

"I won't." I stand up straight, taking in where we are and how to get back to the beach. The island didn't look that big as we were crashing through the breakers, but now that I'm standing in the middle of the woods, things are larger than I expected. Ferns brush against our knees. And white butterflies are flitting around. Breathtaking. The exact sort of place I'd want to bring guests for a day excursion.

"The stream is just up there." Zane points between some trees. "Let me know if you want me to carry you."

I nod. He points out every rock and tree branch as we walk along the path. But he's right, it is just up ahead. And if fairies don't live here, it's because they don't know about it. The water meanders in and out of the ferns.

"I didn't go too far when I was gathering wood, but it gets deeper up ahead. I think there might even be a waterfall, but I'm not sure."

I kneel on one leg and wash my face and hands. It feels so decadent to wash the salt off my skin. Round limestone pebbles cover the bottom of the clear stream. I pick one up and put it in my tiny yoga pants pocket. Zane crouches next to me. When I glance back at him, the path is super noticeable.

"Right. Zane?"

"Yeah?" He runs his fingers lightly over my good foot.

"If this island is deserted, why is there a path?"

"That's a good question."

Ferns rustle farther inland. And they're followed by a loud grunt.

Zane hoists me up. My bad leg touches the ground, and pain shoots up my calf. "Ouch."

The grunt is louder and on the move; ferns' tops wiggle out of the way of whatever is coming at us.

And the grunt turns to a squealing oink.

"Wild boar." Zane picks me up. He cradles me to his chest, my stick gripped in my hand, and he runs.

The snorts from the boar are getting louder.

# Chapter 27

## *Skirmish*

Zane

"Tree," Haley screams, her lips next to my ear.

I'm only vaguely looking where my bare feet step. I leap over a log to a large tree. It's at least two feet around, with some low branches. "Grab hold." I toss her at the branch and hope to hell she was good at the monkey bars growing up. She grabs the branch and swings her good leg over to another branch. It's not graceful, but it's effective.

"Use the stick," she says.

I swipe it from the base of the tree where she dropped it and pivot around as the boar bursts through the ferns.

He pauses for a second, then charges. I bring the stick down on his nose. It doesn't stop his charge. No, he's coming for me, his dark tusks aiming for my legs. Fuck, if I had boots on, I'd give him some hard kicks. I smack him with the stick again, and he stops. Another limb lies covered in mud on the path. I pick it up so I have one in each hand. This branch is thicker. It broke when it hit the ground, so it's sharp on the end like a real spear.

"Run, Zane," Haley screams at me. "Go away, pig! Shoo!" And then she does a blood-curdling scream. It's so loud birds flutter from the treetops into the sky and even the boar turns his attention away from me—to Haley. He grunts.

That second is all I need. I ram the boar with the stick, plunging it into his lower chest. I let go, and it's hanging there. The damn boar squeals at me. It steps forward but then turns and runs back into the ferns. My heart is beating through my chest.

"What the fuck is going on?" Calvin runs to us. Scratch that. He's holding his arms up to Haley.

"A wild boar attacked us." Haley slides with caution into Calvin's arms. "But Zane stabbed it with a stick."

Easton shows up behind Calvin. "What happened? Are you okay?" Easton puts his hand on Haley's leg.

"Yeah, Zane saved us. He stabbed the boar."

I hold up her crutch for her. "Haley wanted to see the stream."

Calvin turns, keeping the crutch away from Haley's hand. "Yeah, well, that's fucking stupid. It could have hurt her." He kicks at the leaves. "That's a lot of blood. Did you get a good shot in?"

"Yeah, that's why it left."

"This is too much blood loss for it to survive." Calvin passes Haley to Easton. "Take her back to the beach."

"Here's your crutch, Haley." I walk around Calvin to hand it to her. There's a scratch up the side of her leg from where she clung to the tree. "Are you okay?"

"It's just a scratch. I can walk with my crutch." She pulls back and looks Easton in the eyes.

"Yeah, no. This is one order from Cranky Pants I'm more than willing to obey."

Haley sighs. "Thank you." She's staring at me when she says it.

"No problem," Easton says.

Calvin picks up a stick. "You're with me, Zane."

I use a short, stubby stick to move palm fronds out of the way until I find another good one.

Calvin has already moved down the path. "Let's go."

"Why exactly are we chasing down the beast that tried to kill us?"

"Have you ever hunted?"

"No."

"Right, that's a lot of blood back there." Calvin touches a short fern on the side of the path, a drop of blood smeared at the top of it. "It won't heal from a massive injury like that, and when it dies, I don't want some scavenger taking what's ours."

"Or . . ." I'm practically running after Calvin. I'm tall, but he's what I like to think of as stare-at-me tall. ". . . or we could head back to the beach and wait for a rescue plane to fly overhead."

Calvin stops, and I have to haul back to keep from running into him. "Listen. Good move having the charts and downloading them to Swimmer Boy's phone. Have you looked at them?"

"I have. But—"

"But where you thought we should be, there's no island."

"Yeah. I mean, I didn't leave my phone on long."

"We turned that first night. I was watching the compass. We caught some sort of jet stream that's not on the charts."

My stomach sinks. "They'll be searching the wrong area."

"Exactly. Even if they widen the search, the tuna—"

"It changed our speed. Not much, but enough to make the math of where we are not make sense."

"Yup. If that's the case, this is a big meal we can't pass up."

"Have you seen wild boars before? That thing was huge." I shake my hand.

"Have I seen boars before?" He laughs.

Right, Calvin grew up in the middle of nowhere with nothing and walked to school early to pick up roadkill for dinner. At least, that's what he told the chef last year. But then again, the two of them didn't exactly get along.

The spatters of blood get closer and closer together the longer we walk on the path. The stream widens out too.

"You don't think there are more of them around and the damn thing went off to tell them what an arse I am?"

"They live in groups. They don't normally attack humans. But then again, this bunch probably hasn't seen too many humans. If we get cornered by more of them, we climb trees. Good idea you had."

"It was Haley's idea."

"She's smart. Too bad she wasn't smart enough to not get in the middle of Fuckhead and me."

"She was going to distract you."

"I know." Calvin shakes his head. "That would have worked too. She has a fine—" He pops up a closed fist like military or SWAT do in the movies when they're creeping up on the bad guys. Then he points silently to a small clearing near the water.

I raise my eyebrows because I can't see anything. But then I am not a Viking who's defeated pirates twice—like Calvin. I point.

And he nods. From what I can make out, he's going to circle around and I'm going to stay where I am.

Calvin moves through the brush. He grunts and bends down. I can't see what he's doing, but when he stands up, there's blood on his hands. "Help me carry it back."

The dead beast weighs as much as Calvin and me combined. I glance at the ocean approaching through the palm fronds. I want the stench washed off me, but I also want to sit down. The adrenaline from the landing and then killing the beast is gone, and I want to crawl into a bed. But I'll settle for a spot next to Haley. Watching Easton and Calvin snuggle up against her last night made me jealous, and then waves of guilt settled around me. The girl can do whatever she wants. I just happen to want to be the one she does something with.

When we break through the jungle to the beach, Dante is sitting up and the fire is going in the pit I made.

"Put it down here." Calvin points to a dry patch of sand downwind from the fire.

I drop the tail end with a thud.

"What the fuck, Zane?" He puts his half down gently.

I shrug. "It's dead. I didn't figure it would matter."

I give up on jumping into the ocean when Haley catches my eye, and I wander over and collapse next to her.

"Come with me, Swimmer Boy."

I glare at Calvin. He might have muscles the size of an Italian smart car, but if he called me that, I'd be swinging at him too.

Easton doesn't move. And we all glance between the two of them.

"I need your help, Easton. Please." Calvin shoots the word out like it hurts his throat.

"See, that wasn't so hard." Easton stands and slaps his thighs like he's leaving the pub for the night. "What are we doing?" Easton takes a few steps, and the stench of the boar hits him. He shakes his head but doesn't back down. Which I'm sure as hell happy about because I'm not exactly jumping up and down to volunteer for what I think Calvin wants.

"We need to get some palm fronds to make a clean spot to process the boar."

"Right." Easton shuffles off with Calvin, and I think I've got a moment to myself.

Calvin yells over his shoulder, "We need more firewood."

"Right." I stand and pull off my shorts and my shirt. And for the hell of it, I pull off my knickers too. I don't look back at the fire, but someone whistles—Dante, I assume.

"What's he doing?" Haley says in the wind.

I jump in the water. It's clear. The sand under the breaking waves is light brown, and little fish dart about my feet. I'm in to my waist when I duck underwater. I can swim—I'm not an Olympian, but my mom made sure I learned to swim. The drop-off to the ocean happens slowly, and the waves are calmer. The stench of the pig and the blood coating my hands fades away. I'm floating, arms relaxed, eyes closed, tilted to the setting sun.

I open my eyes and go back to the beach. Easton is standing next to Calvin, who has his hands on his hips and his neck bent talking to Haley, still by the fire. Dante says something, his hands gesticulating to the ocean, then to Easton, and finally resting next to his head. Calvin unfolds himself to upright, then bends down and scoops Haley up. Dante's up too, and Easton is saying something. I'm heading back to the shore, but then Dante's got his clothes off and Easton does too.

Haley's smacking at Calvin's arms, and he lets her down and slides off her leggings. Her long T-shirt is covering her knickers, but then she points at them and they all turn around. I don't, though I should. She seems like the bashful type. She pulls the shirt off, but then Calvin has her up against him again. She gives him another playful smack, and I have to head back into the water because, damn, I didn't know I like watching so much. But the taps she gave Calvin might as well have been on my arm.

From here, the help sign and the unlit pile of brush for the signal fire look good. Even our little cooking fire is going strong, but not strong enough to set anything else on fire. I should swim over to the reef to see if we can catch fish. But I can't stop watching them come into the water. Calvin steps up as his knees hit the waves. He's wearing his underwear, as he calls it, and so is Easton. But Easton is helping Dante into the water, and Dante's going natural.

Haley squeals when the first wave hits them. But soon they are beside me.

"I can swim." Haley has her arms looped around Calvin's neck. She's taken her purple Rockwell bandana off. Her hair is loose and floating around her shoulders.

"I'm sure you can, but how are you going to get out?" Calvin hasn't let her go.

"We'll figure that out when I want to get out. You're right, Easton, the water feels great on my ankle." Haley swims away from Calvin and bobs near Easton. She's like a magnet that draws us all in. I can't leave to go look at the reef now, not by myself.

Haley floats next to me. "Feel better?" I ask.

"Yeah. That was a lot," she says. A large wave swells, and we lift on it. When it puts us back down, we're next to each other. "I'm glad you were there. Thank you. It could have really injured me without you. And I like to save the injuring of me to be done by me." She laughs. The dim light catches her blue eyes, making them sparkle with flecks of green. Another wave pushes her into me.

I grab her. The water douses us both. We come up laughing. She wraps her arms around my neck, and now I'm king of the island. Our eyes are locked. I lean in to kiss her. My pulse thuds in my ears as the water surges around us. I see it then—panic. She turns her head as a wave crashes above us.

# Chapter 28

## *Overboard*

Easton

The water rejuvenates me. I've floated away from the rest of them. I'm calm and at peace with this island here in the ocean. And that's fucking crazy. I'm happier shipwrecked with a bunch of strangers and no food than being back in the boardroom with my dad.

Fuck. I hope he's okay. Emily too. Damn it. I hate that I don't know what's going on with them. That they don't know I'm alive. But I can't control it.

I let it go. I ride the waves with my eyes closed and release my anxiety. I'm not like Calvin. I can make out every pent-up frustration in the strain of his thick neck. Thankfully, Haley's convinced Calvin we'd all fall apart without a break. But I know it's Dante who put the bug in her ear. And thank fuck.

I helped Dante into the water. He told me he was good, so I let him go.

The waves are gentle, and there's no riptide. I for one am glad for the moment to relax. Because I'm no fool—the second we're done with this swim, we're not just gathering palm fronds but skinning a pig. And whatever else Robinson Crusoe shit Calvin has planned.

I start making my way over to Haley. She's clinging to Zane, and they're laughing. Her laugh almost outweighs the weird noise Zane is making. I dive under the water and swim below the waves to where Zane and Haley are. I break the surface but end up getting a good eyeful of Zane's junk first.

A wave crashes over us, separating Haley from Zane. Now I'm laughing, and so are they. Zane's more thrashing in the water than swimming, but he's staying up mostly. I'm not going to criticize his technique; the guy killed a beast with a twig.

I reach out to take Haley's hand, but she reaches past me. "Dante." Her eyes are wide.

A splash behind me makes me turn, and fuck, the chef is sinking like a rock. A big breath, and I dive down. His arms are flailing around, but we're barely in eight feet of water. Hell, if Calvin wanted to stand, he probably could. I pull the water away from me and grasp Dante from behind, hauling him up by his chest. He's stop thrashing, but he is coughing.

"Fucker," Dante spits out. He coughs more, and I swim with him to shore.

I've never had to pull anyone from the water before, but I've seen it. Sometimes they fight the rescuer; Dante doesn't. He's clinging to me but not getting in the way of me getting him to shore.

"I'm good. I'm good. Really." The coughs keep coming while I'm pulling him in. When our feet hit the sand, I don't let him go. Instead, I help him almost all the way back to the fire. He stops a few steps short of it, his hands resting on his knees. Doubled over, he coughs a few more times before we stumble together to the fire.

"You okay?" I'm next to him, waiting to see if he goes down.

Calvin places Haley down next to us. "Next time . . ." He sounds more like my dad than a leader.

"Next time we land on a desert island and decide to go for a swim?" Dante gets out between coughs. "I'm fine. I was laughing at the wave taking out Zane. It was the first good moment I've had in a few days, and I got a mouthful of seawater. Next thing, I'm sinking. But Goldie here saved me."

I shake my head. No way I'm answering to Goldie. Swimmer Boy is bad enough.

"Dante, are you sure you're okay? Sit down over here." Haley hops over to the closest log and brushes the sand off it.

"I'm good, Sassy." And he almost sounds okay.

I take a towel hanging from the side of the raft and wipe my face. "Best thing ever." I'm super grateful for the towel. I toss it to Zane, and he does the same.

"Thanks." Zane hangs it up.

Calvin's made his way back over to Haley, like some oversized shadow. He shakes his hair dry like a dog. A damn dog.

Haley giggles. "Stop."

And now I'm fuming inside. "I'm going to get more wood for the cooking fire," I growl.

"I'm going to keep Haley from causing any more problems." Dante laughs, but Zane and Calvin are squinting at him. I feel the same.

Haley stands up with her crutch under her arm. "Well, I'm going to dry out the inside of the raft. Unless you think we should bed down somewhere else?"

"No. It's better for the bugs and the other things." Calvin gives her a nod. Who the fuck knows what the other things are?

I'm the first to move. "Let me help you into the raft."

She sighs and glances behind me. "Okay. But I'm helping."

"We are all going to have to pull our fair share." Calvin glares first at me and then at Dante.

Dante points the stick he's using to tend the fire at Calvin. "What, I'm injured, and he just saved me. So back down, big guy. We're doing our share." He puts the stick back into the fire, pushing the embers around.

Calvin grunts, but I ignore it. It's only a few steps, but having her in my arms is definitely better than any shit Calvin is about to make me do. I lift her over the edge of the raft. Admittedly, I don't want to let go, even though I know she's stable on her good leg. "Let me get you a towel to wipe down the raft."

She shakes her head. "I'm going to use the water collection sponge. I don't know about you, but I'm glad we didn't have to drink from the sponge." She sighs.

"Damn straight," I agree.

"Ready? We need more wood and fronds." Calvin is standing over the other side of the fire, glaring at me like a damn Russian-born swim coach.

"Yeah." I trudge after him. The wind changes when we enter the jungle. I love the beach—the water—but there's something about the jungle here; it feels safer, even with the murder pigs. There are a ton of palm trees and coconuts along the edge of the woods. But inward, closer to the fresh water, the trees get massive. Smooth bark. Big. They're nothing like the redwoods of California. Big but not that huge.

"We're after palm fronds," Calvin commands. "Not staring at the trees."

"Sure." Saying anything else to the brute is pointless.

Calvin has the hatchet from the emergency kit. He chops off the palm fronds, and I gather them up. But I can't stop staring at the big trees.

He carries twice as many palm fronds as I have when we go back to the beach. It's getting hotter out in the open.

The next hour makes me grateful my dad liked fishing and not hunting. We're back in the woods, and I look up over half of the butchered boar. As bossy as the asshole is, I'm also grateful we have him with us. But that reminds me of Emily, and I shiver. I hope my sister is okay. And as stupid as it was, I'm holding on to Zane's Schrödinger's cat theory. Until I know she's dead, she's alive. And that's what I'm going to go with.

Zane has come and gone a bunch of times with more and more firewood, and now he's back again.

"Stop." Calvin leans against a massive tree.

I'm holding the bunch of bananas Zane handed down from the tree he shimmied up. He drops to the ground with a big stack of leaves under his arm, but he's frowning like he knows what Calvin's going to talk about.

"Haley," Zane says. Like I should understand.

"Exactly." Calvin nods.

"What about her? Her ankle will heal. A day or two of rest. She'll be fine." I'm ready to walk back to the fire now that the boar is dangling from the tree.

"Yes. She's going to be fine. But you like her." Calvin scowls at me.

"Yeah, I like her." If this is some sort of Neanderthal claiming of the damsel, I'm out of here. Not that I can leave.

"We all like her," Calvin says.

"Obviously. What's there not to like?" I agree with the giant. Haley's kind, smart, and has curves I would like to know a heck of a lot better.

"No, we all *like* her, like her. And if any of us go after her to form a relationship, it's going to be an issue." Zane cocks his head to the beach.

I scowl. "How is it an issue? The girl likes who she likes, and that's it."

"Exactly. I'm glad you're on board." Calvin crosses his arms, the hatchet resting on his bicep.

"On board?"

Zane nods. "If she wants to date all of us, or some of us—"

Calvin interrupts, "Or none of us."

"Or none of us, we need to be cool with that. Are you good with that?" Zane continues.

None of us? No way in hell is that going to be a thing. I want her.

And I always work hard for what I want. My heart slams into my stomach. I thought about maybe asking Haley out on a proper date once we were back in Florida. But the word here seems preposterous. Date? "I suppose. As long as it's up to her. Did anyone talk to Dante?"

Calvin laughs. "It was his idea."

"Of course it was," I say.

"Like Swimmer Boy said, it's up to her." Calvin puts another palm frond under the swinging carcass. I can't help thinking it's a lot cooler in the woods.

I glance at the boar in the tree.

"This will work." Calvin cocks his head. And I'm not sure if he's talking about the meat or Haley. I nod, but I'm not sure I mean it.

We trudge our load back to our little camp.

"We need to smoke some of the meat." Dante points to the tree and stands. He moves stiffly but joins us around the fire. "We can roast it in the ground. Hell, we can do that tomorrow, maybe."

"We can dig the hole now, get it started. Tomorrow we work on making jerky." Calvin's got a stripe of boar blood across his chest. He looks like a warrior Viking ready for battle.

"Or we get some rest and then we can smoke the shit out of it tomorrow." I raise my eyebrows.

A few minutes later, Zane and I are on our knees digging a hole. We're down three feet.

"That's good." Dante's standing on the edge of the pit. "I'll get some more fronds."

I look up at Dante, but he's gone. "Awesome. Don't go too far into the woods."

Zane and I neaten the hole up. Calvin's back and forth from the woods with armloads of wood.

"We can do it today. If it works, it works. If it doesn't, what did we lose?" Calvin points at the pit.

"Sleep?" Zane answers.

"We're going to be rescued." I say it the same way I would tell myself I'm going to win the race.

Haley cups her hands around her mouth, yelling at us from the fire. "When you guys are done, wash up. Dinner's ready." She's using her chief stew voice. Like we're about to sit down to a five-course meal.

I've lost track of how much time has gone by or how hungry I am. I scrub as much sand off my hands as I can in the shallow waves. As I wade out of the ocean, the sun is almost down and there's a chill to the air. The wind changes, and something smells delicious from the fire. I find my shirt. Someone has hung it over the edge of the raft. Dante's pushing at the fire where one large stone is sitting on coals. He's got a smaller one on top of it. Around the fire is a mat of fresh palm fronds far enough back to keep embers off. Five large rocks circle the fire, and on top of them are hollowed-out coconut bowls set on banana leaves.

"Bloody lovely, Dante. This smells amazing." Zane plops down next to Haley. "I'm knackered. Thank you for cooking. Both of you." He touches her shoulder, but he does that with everyone. Zane's comfortable with everyone, it seems. Not me. It takes a lot for me to get comfortable with people. It always seems that people have an ulterior motive. They want money or to be attached to the limited amount of fame I have as an Olympian. But then I didn't seem to have any problem getting comfortable last night.

"Yes, it's good. Thank you." I sit next to Dante.

"This isn't half bad." Calvin takes the last spot between Zane and me. He puts the hatchet down next to him, within easy reach. It's become attached to his hand. But I don't blame him. We need to be protected if we get attacked again.

Dante uses two sticks like giant chopsticks to move the top stones from the slice of meat on the rock and replaces them with new ones. "The thicker pieces are almost done. But here's some to start." He passes a thick leaf with small chunks of meat on it to me. I take a few and pass it to Calvin, who takes the smallest one before handing it off to Zane.

"You need more." Zane pushes the leaf back to Calvin.

"I'm good."

"There's tons," Haley says. "Literally." And she laughs.

"Okay, thanks." He puts some more in his bowl.

I hadn't noticed, but there's cooked coconut pieces in the bowl. It's salty, crunchy, and a tad sweet. "Wow, this is delicious." I glance around.

"Thanks." Dante inclines his head. "Our lovely chief stew did a lot of the work."

Haley smiles. "Zane found a couple of bananas. Wild ones are full of seeds, but Dante removed them and some—"

"Don't give away all my secrets, darling, or they'll vote me off the island." Dante laughs.

"It's good." Calvin frowns. His eyes flit along the horizon.

When I haven't been in a deep pit, I've been watching too. Nothing. Not a plane or blip of movement on the ocean horizon.

The food is good, and we eat in silence. Another round of meat is passed between us. We finish off everything we have. I think none of us are confident that what's in the tree will be good tomorrow. But we'll see at first light.

My body is shutting down as the stars start their show. I missed them the last two nights. We had the windows closed up, all but a small part for the person on watch. Which was mostly Calvin. The man's got issues.

"I'll wash up." I take the coconuts from everyone and rinse them out in the shallow waves. The wind is blowing onto the beach, and it's almost high tide. I'm glad we have cover for the night. I scrub the leftover bits out of the cups and bring them back to the fire.

Calvin's sitting by the fire when I get back, but the other three are in the raft. "I'll take first watch." He's gruff as he inclines his head at the raft.

"You sure? I can." As much as Calvin wants to control everything, he is an asset to our team, and I'm not going to let him overwork himself.

"I've got it." It's more of a "*I don't trust the fuck out of you to not fall asleep and let the fire go out."* It took him a long time to make the fire, even with the lighter Dante had in his pocket, one he'd used to light the gas stove on the yacht.

"I can keep the fire going. You sure you don't want to sleep first?"

"I'm good. I hear one thing out of her that sounds like distress, I'm coming in and making you pay. Don't scare her."

"Only good sounds, got it." I try not to smirk.

"Slow is the only way this will work," Calvin grunts at me like I'm going to attack her.

The inside of the raft smells like leftover fish guts and sweat.

"All I'm saying is you could let Haley use the cushion." Zane's pointing to the one cushion we have.

"I'm fine, Zane." Haley has her life vest bundled up as a pillow. "Dante's still injured. Let him use it."

"So are you. And he doesn't need to be a cushion hog." Zane is sitting still; he's laying it on thick.

"Well, I'm staying out of Cushion Gate. You can use me as a pillow if you need, Haley." I lie down between her and Dante. The fool took a cushion over the girl. But I didn't have a chance to talk to Dante alone. Perhaps that's part of the plan.

She laughs. "You're hardly a cushion, Easton. More like steel."

"Man of gold and steel. Just what we need to feed his ego," Dante quips, but he's snoring not long after.

"Well, none of you are squishy like me," Haley whispers.

Dante snores and mumbles something in his sleep. He might look healed, but he's not. He rolls away from us and snores again.

"You're not squishy," I whisper. She's facing away from me. "But maybe I need a pillow, then?" I reach out and pull her to me. I wrap my arm around her waist, pulling her ass to my front. It's presumptive and a bit of an asshole thing to do, but after last night, I don't care. Hell, I may never care. I want her. Right now I want a lot of things I might never get, but I'm a winner—that's what I tell myself.

And when she pushes herself flush with me, I know I am a winner.

# Chapter 29

## *Bearing North*

Haley

I love snuggling. It's odd. I've never met so many guys who like snuggling too. But when Easton tugs me up against him and pulls me even closer, the chill in the evening air is gone. Even my toes, which were on the verge of freezing, are heating up. And my core is more than heating up.

Zane has given up on the cushion and is lying in front of me. "Sweet dreams, Haley."

"You too, Zane. Are you cold?"

"A little."

"Snuggle with us for warmth."

Behind me, Easton stiffens. Odd. I'm not sure why he wouldn't want Zane to be warm too. A guy like Easton couldn't be interested in me. I'm just what's available. His hand is on my stomach. Oh lord, Steven used to complain about my stomach. But Easton's full-out pressing into me. It was different last night—the life vests kept us apart a little—but now there's no doubting what's going on. I should stop it.

"Thanks, Haley."

When Zane pulls in close to me, the raft sways on the sand. But I don't because Easton has a firm grip on my side. And my front is warm. Zane's backside is up against me. I'm a sandwich with some high-end, good-looking bread.

I don't know what to do with my arm, but Zane solves the problem for me. He tucks it between his arm and chest, holding my hand to his stomach. *For warmth*, I repeat over and over in my head. But then Easton moves, and his hard length is nestled between my butt cheeks. I freeze, still not knowing what to do. Nervous butterflies flit around my stomach. This is less than what happened this morning, but half-awake Haley who thinks she might die is a hussy. And right now, while I'm tired, I'm not her. I want to be her. With a shot of tequila, I could be her. But the good girl in me isn't going to let that happen. Being attracted to four guys is wrong. Not that anyone is going to blame me.

I let my breath out slowly. Why do I always think about what other people are going to think?

"Are you comfortable?" Zane rolls over, and he's facing me. While it's dark, it's extra dark from the raft's red canopy. But the moon has come out, casting a light glow around the raft. His eyes are open, and he smiles at me. "You okay, Haley? We're not crowding you?" His eyes flit down to my lips.

Now Easton has his chin nestled into my neck, his fingers spread over my stomach. His breaths are long and warm beneath my ear, but they're not the breaths of someone asleep.

"I'm good."

"Good night, then." Zane smiles at me.

And I hear their breath changing. I'm nuts. I really thought Zane was going to do something. Make a move. Or Easton. More than snuggling. What was I thinking? That two handsome guys would both want me? One maybe, but two? I laugh out loud.

Zane snuggles back into me.

But I'm drifting off to sleep, listening to their sounds and the ocean in the distance. I'm grateful to be alive. I try not to think about all the things I miss. My dog, but he's with Steven's mom. Is it weird I miss Sam too? I try to remember what Zane said. Until we know he's neither alive nor dead, he's alive. I chant it over and over in my head until I wake.

There is a warm body behind me, but it's not Easton. The arm over my waist is Calvin's. I lift my head to make out the tattoo that starts on his wrist. My hair is covering most of it. It's a mermaid with a purple tail. Vines wrap around her like they're pulling her to the bottom of the ocean. But I can't see her face. I brush my hair to the side, and Calvin stirs behind me. A girl could get used to waking up beside a hot guy. His chest rises and falls against my back. He pulls me tighter to his chest like a stuffed animal. And that's when I remember—I left it inside my jacket, stuffed in the life vest.

I lift my head. Somehow, I've missed everyone else getting up. Dante, Zane, and Easton are all moving around outside. It sounds a little like Dante orchestrating the smoking of the leftover meat. I roll over onto my back.

"Good morning, beautiful," Calvin says without opening his eyes.

"Good morning, Calvin. But Easton already went outside." I'm poking the bear, and I don't care. I should, probably.

"Not even. You know I'm talking about you." His voice is gravelly, like he just fell asleep. Which he probably just did. And then he rolls over on top of me in a plank. A wall of muscle. My senses are firing in fear and excitement. I'm wet. It's a permanent situation on this island, and it has nothing to do with the ocean.

I push at his chest. It's too much to take. I want to grind myself against him. But that's too much. And then I remember the stuffed animal, again. He moves reluctantly off me.

"When's your birthday?" I ask.

"Please tell me you're not into that astrology shit?"

"Sort of, but that's not why I'm asking."

He grunts but doesn't roll too far away. I raise my eyebrows at him, waiting for him to respond.

"Fine, July 6th."

"Seriously? That's next week."

"Yup, it's next week."

"Well, I have an early present for you."

His eyes dilate in the red-filtered early morning light. My pulse races. I didn't think he would assume the gift is me. I roll onto my stomach, fiddle with my life vest, and pull out his bear.

"What?" His chin ticks with irritation. That isn't what I expected. I don't know what I expected, but irritation wasn't it.

I hold it out to him, and he just stares. "I thought you'd be happy."

He takes it from me. Holding it, his eyes glaze over. "I am, but I'm mad you endangered yourself by grabbing something unnecessary."

"It was lying on top of my jacket. When I grabbed my jacket, I just shoved it in my bra. Really, he's a bit soggy because he kept me dry."

"He's good like that." Calvin blinks and holds the bear to his chest. "Thank you. I'm glad you didn't do anything stupid to save it. It's bad enough you went back into the boat for Dante."

My jaw drops.

"He can cook, though." Calvin rolls toward me, his large hand holding the side of my head. He leans in and kisses my cheek. It's light and soft and not how I thought Calvin would be.

Butterflies migrate through my body. The excitement of being near him, touching him, echoes through my bones. I want him to kiss me.

But he runs his hand down my cheek instead. "Thank you for this, Haley." He rolls away, and my body longs for his warmth.

"Hey." Zane ducks his head in the flap. "Dante's got breakfast if you want some. Easton caught some crabs, and Dante cooked them up in pig fat. I'm not sure how long I can fight Easton off them if you want some." He laughs.

"I'm coming out. You should get some more sleep." I put my hand on Calvin's shoulder.

"Yeah. And tonight, you should actually wake someone else up to take a turn." Zane points his finger at Calvin.

"What?" I give him my best I'm-not-happy-with-you-young-man face. "I'm getting up. Go to sleep." I crawl to the opening, keeping the pressure off my ankle. It's really not too swollen.

"Let me help you out." Zane reaches for me.

"Thanks."

He lifts me out and carries me to a new log that's next to the fire.

Dante is stirring the coals, but next to our little fire ring is the long pit the guys dug yesterday. Easton is tending another fire, and there's a trellis leaning over it, one side covered in palm fronds.

"While I slept, you guys made a whole meat-smoking setup?"

Zane puts me gently down next to the log.

"Your breakfast, my lady." Dante hands me the coconut bowl. Crab meat, coconut, and a little pork.

"It smells amazing." I pick up a little with my fingers.

"Wait." He hands me a small wooden spoon.

"Where did this come from?"

"Calvin carved a set last night, while he kept watch. Full moon and all." Dante sits down next to me. "How's the leg?"

"Good. I should be perfect by tomorrow." I pat my leg and hope I'm not lying.

"You're perfect now."

I groan.

"What, too much?" He nudges my shoulder.

"How do you feel?"

"I'm getting better, but it's going to take time. You know I can never repay you for coming to get me." He kisses my cheek. "You're something else. I'm going to run these down to the water and wash them out."

I watch him go. Easton and Zane are stringing up little bits of meat using what I think is seaweed? I turn back to the ocean. The wind is blowing softly, and it hasn't heated up too much yet. It's a good breakfast even if we weren't shipwrecked. Moreover, the spoon is perfect. But it makes me wonder: if Calvin is whittling spoons and the rest of the guys are smoking meat, do they really think we are going to get out of here?

I put the bowl on the log next to me. Dante's not back yet. I hobble over to the other fire. "What can I do to help?"

Easton picks me up before he answers. "You, young lady, can stay off this ankle and get better."

Zane hollers at my back. "If you watch the fire over there, we could use Dante's expertise at smoking meat here."

Zane gets me. I need something to do.

Easton lowers me to my feet. "We just need you nice and healthy for when the rescue boat comes." He holds on to my shoulders. "How does your ankle feel today?"

"Good," I answer, but I'm kind of lying because the little trip over to the other fire has it throbbing.

For the next few hours, I keep the cooking fire going until they have a full process set up for the smoking of the meat. It's not long before Calvin joins me. It's not enough sleep, but I get it. We're used to being sleep-deprived in our business.

"I brought you your shirt," he says. "You don't want to get burned."

"Thanks, Dad."

"That's Daddy to you." Calvin's cheeks are red as he says it.

"Yes, Daddy." We share a stare. And then I laugh. Because the zinging in my core is something I don't want to think about right now. "I like the spoon." I hold it up.

"Thanks. If the moon is out tonight, I'm going to try making a fork and something Dante has requested, like a I have a full-blown workshop." He shakes his head. "Can I get you something?"

"I'm good."

"You should put your leg up." He touches my ankle lightly.

"I will." Mostly because the other guys are circling any time I move.

"All right then." Calvin goes over to the other fire and then disappears into the woods.

If we are rescued today, the fire from the smoking will have played a part. Zane and Easton are running to the jungle and back with more and more wood. But all the guys are sweet and check in on me. Lunch is more pig meat, but Calvin isn't back to eat. Not yet. And I've been glancing over my shoulder every few minutes, looking for him.

"How you doing?" Calvin's voice booms and I jump. He appears from behind me and shares the log.

"Where did you come from? I've been watching for you."

"I know. I ran into Zane collecting firewood, and he told me. I'm fine. I was checking out the island a little. The last thing we want is to be stranded here for weeks and there turns out to have been a town on the other side."

"Well?" I lean into him.

"No town. But the island is a lot bigger than I thought it would be. And there's a whole section that's really rocky. I saw some goats."

"Really, goats?" I scrunch up my nose.

"Yeah. What's the face for?"

"Goats are cute."

"And tasty."

"You're the worst." I lean back into him.

"Hey, you two. We're thinking of taking a pre-lunch swim." Easton stands behind both of us. He puts his hand on my shoulder, and a zing of desire zips through me. Calvin gives Easton a look.

"Play nice, you two." I wag my finger.

"That's the plan." Easton smiles. "Now about that swim . . ."

"I'm in." I peel off my yoga pants and shirt, standing on one leg. But when I try to hop to the water with my crutch, Calvin throws me over his shoulder and we run. I'm bouncing, holding him around his waist. I glance up, and the other guys are smiling a lot.

Calvin slides me down his body. "How you doing?" I loop my arms around his neck. He leans forward. "Look out, little fishy. Here comes the audience. But that can be fun."

My core clenches, and I look at Zane and Easton swimming out to meet us. Dante is being more cautious.

Calvin holds me, and his hand eases around to my bottom. "You're doing amazing, Haley. A lot of girls would have folded under the pressure."

"I like pressure," I say. "It gets shit done. It's weird here because there are no rules."

He pulls me closer. "Pressure is useful for a lot of things, and there is one rule: stay alive." He eases away, and I'm not sure if he meant to be sexual or not. "Watch out for them. I'm going to help Dante get dinner going." Calvin calls out to Easton and Zane bobbing nearby. He takes off, swimming the free stroke.

The water is cool and a welcome relief from the sun. The first aid kit from the raft has two big tubes of sunscreen, but even so I'm a little pink. Even with the shade screen Zane made for the fire. But swimming with little fish darting between my feet feels amazing.

Easton strokes over to me, so graceful. "Who knew the big guy had some swimming form?" He nods to Calvin on the beach.

We aren't out long before Dante waves us in for dinner.

The setting sun bursts with color over the ocean as we finish eating. "So pretty."

"Yes," Zane agrees with me. But when I look up, he's staring at me and not the sunset.

"Shut up." I push at his shoulder. He laughs; it's deep and rich and all Zane. He sits next to me on the big log. I yawn. "I'm so tired, and I didn't do a quarter of what you guys did today. Are you tired?"

"I could sleep," Dante says.

"You guys go ahead. I'll take the first watch and clean up here." Calvin jumps up, taking the bowls to the water. A new pile of twigs and branches is already beside his seat.

"Okay, but you should wake up someone else to help with the watch." I take my crutch and make my way to a spot behind the raft to answer the call of nature. And when I'm ready to get in the raft, Zane is waiting to help me in. I dust the sand off my feet and look around the raft.

# Chapter 30

## *Muster*

Haley

I'm using Calvin's bare chest as a pillow. And it feels so domestic, like it's Sunday morning and we're going to lie in bed and read. But this is Calvin, and the only reason he is lying asleep behind me is because he kept the fire and watch going all night.

What would it be like to have Calvin as a boyfriend? He'd probably be an early riser, no pancakes and sleeping in. No, he'd have the garage cleaned and the lawn mown by nine a.m. I laugh out loud. Me with a lawn?

Last night, nestled between Easton and Zane, shoot, I wanted to move. I wanted to rub myself all over both of them. But the sun, wind, and big meal all made me so sleepy I fell asleep before anything happened.

But now I'm not tired.

"Good morning," Calvin says into my ear, close enough to be a kiss. I lift my head, and our lips are inches apart. I don't move away. I want him to kiss me.

"Good morning. How was the night shift?"

He lifts his head, giving a bit of distance. "More of nothing." He squeezes me to him. "How were the sleeping arrangements?" Calvin's hand lands on my bare back, where my shirt has ridden up. His thumb rubs lazy circles on my back, and I know I should get up. But as long as he's rubbing circles, I'm not moving. I'm mesmerized by his touch.

A low moan rumbles, and it takes a minute for me to realize I'm the one making it. This might be the first time I've been comfortable since I left Fort Lauderdale. No, longer, since in Florida I was too busy crying over seeing fucking Steven and his new girl at my favorite diner. Now I can never go there. I laugh, because I can never go there again anyway, or to any other restaurant. Not when I'm stuck on a deserted island with four guys who watch me like they either want to fuck me or tie me up for safety. Or maybe just tie me up. I shouldn't find that so hot, but I do.

I hitch my leg up over Calvin's, and he moves his large leg in between my thighs.

Oh, it feels so good. Not even moving, the pressure my own weight is putting on my clit pushed into his leg is enough to send me almost over the edge.

"Take what you need, little one." His voice rumbles through his chest.

My eyes widen. He can't mean what he's saying, can he?

His teeth scrape along his lip. Our skin is glowing red from the light coming through the raft cover. He lifts his leg, changing the angle against my clit. I let out a moan.

"Take it."

I slide my hand down his chest toward his cock.

But he snags my wrist, holding my hand to his chest. "Take it, Haley." His deep, thick voice has me rock forward. I catch his intense eyes. "That's it. Do it." He says it the way one dares someone to shoot back a shot or stuff three hot dogs into their mouth. He doesn't know it, but I'm not one to leave a dare on the table. I rock forward. The first thrust of my hips has me shaking. I want to run away, but Calvin holds my hand at his stomach. "We all have needs, Haley. You're not going off into the woods to hide behind a tree."

I lift my head, and my body follows. More friction against my clit. "Is that what you do?"

"No." His smile melts me, and at the same time I'm ashamed. "Haley, I don't hide from anyone. Roll over." It's a command, not a request.

I freeze for a second. Am I drawing a line in the sand? Am I picking Calvin above all the other guys?

"Roll over. This is about you, not me. Roll over." His voice is like a rough wave over me. "I'm getting you off, not asking you to go steady."

My insides are shaking at how matter of fact he is. Like it's a task on his list: get firewood, carve utensils, make a boat, and finger Haley. But my body rolls on its own. And his hand slides down my chest. His hand is rough, and when he slides it under the elastic of my panties, I turn away. The doubt shows on my face. His other hand grasps my chin, turning my face to his. He kisses me. His lips pull at mine, his tongue demanding entrance. When I let him in, he circles my clit. I mew into his mouth. My hips lift to his hand.

I want more. His kiss is firm. Demanding. I want to touch him too. When I try, he releases my chin and grabs my hand before I can, pinning it above my head. He breaks the kiss.

"This is about you." His fingers are still stroking my clit. He stares at me. His eyes are purple in the filtered light of the raft's canopy. "Understood?"

I nod, unable to speak. I tilt my pelvis up to him again.

And he laughs. "What do you want, Haley?"

"More."

"More what?"

"Move your finger."

He takes his finger out of my pants. I turn my head. I should get up. Go anywhere and finish myself.

"What should I do with my finger?" he asks.

"Fuck me with it." I bite out the words.

"My pleasure." His hand is back in my underwear, drawing lazy circles around my clit. And then he has two fingers in me, or maybe it's one, his hand is so big. His other hand is on my breast. My eyes are shut. It's too much. Too much sensation everywhere. He pinches my nipple and then leans across my body. He sucks my nipple through my shirt.

I'm trembling. He's everywhere. And something happens that never does: all thoughts stop; it's only his body doing things to mine. My lists of things I need to do are gone, along with plans for the future. I have no longing, no past, no trepidation about the future. It's only this moment, with how he is playing my body, that has any meaning. My body shakes with the rhythm of his hand, and I shoot off, the euphoric sensation unlike any orgasm I've ever had.

I'm sweating from places I didn't know could sweat. The plastic of the raft sticks to my back from where my shirt has ridden up. I'm destroyed and wrung out.

Calvin leans over me, his body blocking the rose-colored light. He's extraordinarily proud, and there's almost a smile on his face. He kisses my nose, wiggles his eyebrows at me, and sticks his fingers in his mouth, licking them.

I suck my lips into my mouth and watch him.

"Feel better?"

I nod. My throat is too dry to speak. He smooths my hair down. I'm reliving the last few minutes. "Did I scream?"

Calvin's pulling up his shorts. "No."

I exhale.

"But if you're asking if the others heard, I say yes. But it's like I said, Haley—everyone has needs. And I'm sure they're all off taking care of theirs." He does smile this time. And it almost makes me reach up and grab him around his neck, pulling him back to me. If they heard, I might as well do it all the way.

But Calvin is too fast. He's already out of the raft. A second later, he sticks his head back in. "You should rest a little more. I'll have Dante bring you some breakfast." And he drops the flap on the door.

I stare at where he disappeared. What the heck have I done to myself now? I could go back to sleep, but I should tend the fire. That's something I can do sitting down. I twist my leg. The silly ankle is still tender, but the swelling is dropping. At least, I think it is. I straighten myself out and crawl to the opening.

Easton's there. "I thought I heard you . . . crawling out."

"Nice save." I purse my lips. His handsome grin has the flutters returning.

He laughs. "Can I help you out?"

"Please."

Easton scoops me out of the raft, and Dante's there with my crutch, placing it under my arm. There's a scowl on his face. "Sleep well?" he asks, sarcasm dripping from his lips.

"I . . ." I settle on one of the sitting rocks around the fire, taking the fire-tending stick from where Dante is sitting.

"Relax, Haley, Dante's being a dick." Easton hands me a cup of water.

"I do have one, you know. We all do. But I think Haley knows that already." Dante tends the coconut on his rock grill.

"Seriously Dante, don't be a douche." Easton looks at me and back at Dante.

Calvin and Zane aren't on the beach, unless they are on the little part of the beach I can't see hidden behind the raft. The ocean is calm today. The sky is light blue with big fluffy white clouds. There's nothing out on the horizon. Just like there's been nothing out on the horizon for the past few days. I focus on the water in the little cup. The cup is only mostly waterproof, and the water drips out, puddling in my hands and dripping down my leg.

"I'm going to get more water from the stream." Easton points at Dante. "Don't be an ass."

"But that's my specialty of the day: coconut, pork, and ass." Dante looks up at me.

Easton pauses, one of the two plastic water pitchers we have in his hand. "I'm going to go. Unless you want me to stay?"

"I'm fine." I give Easton a fraction of a smile. He nods and heads to the opening in the woods. I watch him go and then glance at the ocean. I want to get cleaned up, but it's low tide and the water is far away. My ankle doesn't look as good out in the daylight. And I really want to be healed by the time we're rescued. "How's the smoked meat?"

Dante stands up straighter. His hand goes to his head.

"Whoa. Are you okay?" I reach for him.

"Yeah, my head is still throbbing. And the ringing in my ears is not going away. I'm a little lightheaded. But you tell Easton and . . ." Dante points at me with a large wooden spoon.

I put my hands up in surrender. "I won't. I swear."

"Good." He takes a small bundle of banana leaves from a new log that's behind him. "We're finishing up the rest of the fresh meat today. I want to save the smoked meat for when it's raining or something. But here, try a piece." He places a small sliver of the meat in the middle of my hand. "It's not a beef jerky you get from a convenience store."

I stare at the shriveled piece of meat, but then I pop it into my mouth and chew on it. It's tough but tasty. "It's good."

"You don't have to lie to me, Haley. It's edible. But I know I can do better."

I lean forward with my elbows on my knees. "Thank you. Are you sure you shouldn't have Easton take a look at you again?"

"What's he going to do? I'm not going to take any more of the pain pills. We need to save them. I'll make do."

I nod. If this had happened on the boat, I would have a pocket full of ibuprofen. But it's a sprain; it hurts, but it will get better.

I poke at the fire while Dante scrapes the coconut and some meat into a coconut shell. He holds it out but doesn't let go when I put my hand around the bottom. "Thank you."

He's standing over me. "I know you and I got off on the wrong foot. No pun intended." He glances down at my ankle. "But if something happens that you don't want, I will rip that person apart. I don't care if they're faster than me or built like a truck—I will end them. Do I make myself clear?" His eyes are wide, and when he lets go of the bowl, my insides are shaking. I'm caught completely off-guard and have no idea what to say.

He comes back with a spoon and hands it to me. I take it from him, and he nods. He moves a few pieces of wood next to me, piles coals on top of his cooking rock, and adds a few other logs. "Can you mind the fire? I'll be back in ten minutes." He almost smiles at me. "Probably less."

"Sure. I'm happy to help. I can keep it going if you want to lie down?"

His eyes flash like he wants to ask me something else, but he doesn't. "I'll be right back. Unless you don't need me? Then I might poke around and see if there are any edible plants."

"Oh, I'd love to help you with that." I shrug. "Some other time, though. Have fun." My heart is thudding in my chest. I eat my breakfast slowly. I've got a bit of a headache too. But that's most likely my caffeine addiction smacking me across the head. I find myself reaching for my phone, but it's in the water bag in the raft. Turned off.

I follow a pattern: eat a few bites, watch the horizon. For a second, I think I see something. But it's gone. A log or a whale maybe, but it's gone not long after I look. Fire, bite, watch, over and over.

I'm eating my last bite when Easton comes from the woods, the container of water in one hand and arm full of firewood. He drops the firewood next to the empty smoking racks. "Hey." He gives me a chin nod.

"Hi."

"How was breakfast?" Easton puts the water on the rock and covers it with the little scrap of fabric we've been using to keep bugs out. It's amazing how fast we're developing systems. We're all drinking the water from the stream now, since we don't have a way to boil the amount of water we need. The raft wasn't stocked with supplies for in case you find land.

"Really good." I hold the little cup upside down.

"Good." He reaches for the cup.

I don't give it up. "It's fine. I need something to do."

"It's no problem." The way he says it tells me he's been assigned babysitting duty.

"Right. What's going on? Where are Calvin and Zane?" I shake my head, looking back at the woods, not letting go of my cup. I can wait for the tide to pull the water in.

"They're gathering firewood. They'll be back soon." Easton puts another log on the fire.

"Fine."

Dante's gone most of the morning. Easton bustles around the beach, building the help sign bigger, checking on the mound we have ready if we see something. The flare gun is near me since I'm watching the horizon. But Easton makes a few more grease-dipped fire starters for the cold pile of the signal fire. Around lunch, Zane shows up and Easton disappears.

Zane gives me the same answer. "Nothing, bird, we're just gathering firewood."

I squint at him, and he sits next to me. I've been yachting too long to not know when I'm being left out of something. But asking him if they're in the woods jacking off isn't going to happen.

Calvin trades with Zane, but instead of moving firewood, Calvin catches us two fish. The silly things practically jump onto his hook. He guts them on the rock next to me. He's back to mostly grunting at me.

The sun is dropping out of the sky by the time everyone is back and we're eating the fish and coconut in our little bowls, with a few scraps of pork. The guys are silent.

"What the hell is going on?" I look up from my fish, which is amazing. I'm grateful, but I'm not going to live like this, with them keeping secrets.

"Well, are you going to tell her?" Easton puts his hand on my leg.

"Tell me? Tell me what?" I glare at Calvin.

# Chapter 31

## *Chart*

Calvin

Haley's glaring at me like I'm the only one not telling her. She's not wrong. In fact, I'm currently still trying to figure out a way to not tell her. Because hope is an important thing.

Zane's sitting next to her, and he takes her hand. "We didn't tell Dante either."

"Not until I came across them." Dante pokes at the coals.

"What in the world are you talking about?" Haley turns to me, her blue eyes wide. "Calvin?" Her chest heaves. And the memory of her taste on my lips shakes me.

I shake my head. Going around the circle, each of the guys glares at me. I let out a long breath. "It's better if we just show you, I guess. It's getting dark, but we have a little time. How's your ankle?"

"It's almost healed," she lies.

I turn to Easton, the closest thing we have to a doctor, anyway. "You're not going to climb up to let her see, are you?" he says.

"No," I growl.

"So what does it matter, then?" Easton shrugs his shoulders.

"Let's go, Little Bird." Zane stands up and offers her his back, ending the debate. Haley grips him around his shoulders.

We're off into the woods. It isn't too far down the beaten trail from our frequent trips back here. I stop at the largest tree. Its trunk is too big for even me to fit my arms around. "Put her down."

Zane lets her slowly down to her good leg. We stand around the trunk, one of the two longer ropes we have attached to the lowest limbs.

"Wait, what's that?" Haley wraps her hand around the rope.

"This is what we brought you out to see." Easton's got the same regretful look on his face. Damn this girl; she's going to want to climb up and take a look for herself.

Her eyes are on the trunk, but she hasn't let the rope go.

"We've copied the sea charts onto the trunk of this tree. We don't have enough paper, and paper can get wet. Easton's battery is only going to last so long. Mine's already dead, even though I've been turning it off. So you see, this is where we think we are." Zane points to the little X far up the tree. "But this would be our logical position for anyone to search for us." He taps another spot on the tree.

"And you're sure?" Haley gives a nod, her hand on the tree.

"We are," he says. "When you're better, we can show you."

And I want to muzzle him. "No. You don't need to go up there. It's too dangerous."

"You know climbing a rope is about upper body strength and not ankles, right?" She cocks her head at me, the purple bandana wrapped in her hair. "I can climb a rope. Or at least, I could in high school."

"I have no doubt, Little Bird, but—" Zane begins.

"What Zane means is there's more—" Easton butts in.

"No." I cut him off. She doesn't need to worry about where we might be.

"No what?" She turns to me. Her finger is in the air, and she puts it in the middle of my chest.

"Fuck." I cover my mouth.

She pokes me in the chest. Hard. "Calvin. What are you not telling me?"

I stare down at her. Fucking hell, we didn't even make it two days without telling her. "It's been five nights. But the thing is, no one is coming for us. We're too far off course. The only way we're ever getting off this island is by chance. A container ship sees our fire."

"I kind of thought so." Haley is staring at the rope like she understands there's more and there's also much more.

"And . . . ?" Dante leads, and I want to give him a matching goose egg on the other side of his head.

"And?" Haley glances from him to me.

I nod at Zane.

"We're here." Zane touches the little X.

"Okay?"

"But from the top of the tree, we can see things."

"Zane. Tell me what the heck you're getting at." Her voice shakes. This is exactly what I didn't want to happen: we're scaring her. "What can you see?"

"It's a chain of islands. Small ones. About the size of the one we're on."

"But we couldn't see anything on the way in."

"They're right behind this one. We're in disagreement about whether there's three or four more."

"That's a good thing, isn't it? Maybe there's someone on one of the other islands?"

I take a big breath. "That's the problem, Haley. There's no cooking fire smoke. So no natives. But if Zane's positioning on the map is correct, we think these might be a chain of islands that are known for smuggling. And pirates. Even if a boat sees us calling for help, they're not going to stop—"

"Because they will be scared of us, thinking we're smugglers." Haley hugs herself.

"And if they do stop, we might be in more danger."

"What do we have to steal that they would want?" Haley asks. But I see the moment she figures it out for herself. The moment when she knows—she's the prize.

"I would think the authorities will look for us for three weeks. And after that, I'm not sure we want to be found."

"We have fourteen more days." She's still holding on to the rope hanging from the tree.

"Thirteen," Easton says. "We just have to be hopeful."

"And cautious." I glance up at the tree. "If we built a platform, we could station someone with a flare gun. To stay the night."

"You aren't staying in a tree all night." Haley taps me in the chest again.

"I said on the platform. I'll build it tomorrow." I cock my head back at her, grabbing her finger off my chest. There are things I want her to do with that little hand of hers, but they don't include stabbing me with it. "Careful, Haley, or I'll find something else for that finger to do."

She blinks at me, and I'm not sure if she's turned on or pissed. For a moment, the other guys fade into the forest.

"Be careful there, Calvin. Our little tiger has got big fangs." Dante laughs, and a bird takes off not far from where we stand. "She might eat you."

"She's more of a kitten," Easton says.

Zane shakes his head. "Want a ride back to camp, Haley?"

She glares at him. I know she wants to walk. Damn, right now I know she wants to climb up the rope and ding the invisible bell. Her chin down, she nods. "Please."

We head back. It's quiet, and the sun has sunk below the horizon. I expect they'll all climb into the raft-turned-tent, but Easton sets Haley down by the fire and sits next to her. Zane and Dante crawl into the raft.

Easton's watching me. And while I hate the fucker, I don't hate him when it comes to Haley. And that's confusing as hell. I'm in grind mode. There's a lot to do. And these feelings I'm having, I don't need them.

The three of us stare at each other over the fire, and I wait for them to go to bed. I've collected twenty decent-sized sticks I want to sharpen to start making an enclosure. Dante wants another spoon. But more than that, I want to watch the horizon from the other side of the beach. Where I can let my eyes focus on the darkness. There's no one coming. I know that. But that doesn't stop me from searching. Because if we get off this island later, it's sure to be in a trafficker's ship.

"I'm going to head to bed. Are you coming, Haley?" Easton stands and looks down at her for a minute.

"I'll be there soon. I can manage with my cru—"

"I'll help her." I grit the back of my molars. "Get some sleep. We're going to have a lot to do making the platform."

"Fine. Let me know if you need help, Haley." He crawls into the raft. There's no graceful way to do it, but he makes it look not so bad. He jumps and then scoots at the same time. He and Zane are up to something, and there's no doubt in my mind it has to do with Haley.

"I won't need any help, but thank you." Her voice is firm, and while she's talking to Easton, she's looking right at me.

He nods from inside the raft. It needs the air topped off. I'll pump it up tomorrow morning. "Good night, Cal. And good luck. Don't stay up too late, Haley." Easton drops the flap.

Both Haley and I stare at it. I have to admit I'm holding my breath. Because I'm going to need some luck. I've had one long-term girlfriend, but she wouldn't leave Chicago and I can't leave the ocean. She got all weird and obsessive about me being gone for so long, and finally my brother told me about how she had cheated on me. Over and over. With other guys and then with him. They're married now with two kids, a dog. And I don't go home anymore. I'm not even sure I understand the concept of home.

Haley's back is to the ocean. She's glaring at me, the whites of her eyes glowing in the low light. The moon won't rise for a few hours.

During the darkest part of the night, I watch. If I can find a shipping lane, maybe Zane and I are wrong about where we are.

"You really don't think we're going to be rescued, do you?"

"No." I want to protect her, but I'm not going to lie.

"And you think if we aren't rescued now, what's going to happen?"

"We stay here."

"No, that's not what I meant. What do you think is going to happen?"

I stand and pace behind the cooking station Dante's made. I glance back at her. She's waiting. I had this same talk with Zane earlier today. But I haven't told Easton; he would shut me down. The guy is more Pollyanna than a yoga teacher.

"Calvin?"

I glance back. "I think we'll be okay for a while. But when hurricane season hits in a few months, we're going to have a hard time."

"That makes sense, but we can make a better shelter and hunker down."

"Maybe."

"Don't pussyfoot around me." It's getting darker, but I can make out her scowl from the firelight.

"We'll run out of food, and we're not going to be able to build a good enough shelter."

"We butchered a pig. Or rather, you did. Dante smoked it."

"Yes. Yes, we did, but there are five of us. And how many do you think are on this island?"

"There are goats and fish."

"But there are only so many near the shore. With the cheap reel." It was incredible it didn't break when I caught the tuna on the raft.

"Coconuts."

"We're using four or five a day. And it won't be long before they're all gone." I'll have an answer for everything she brings up. Because they've been running through my head from the first hour we were on land.

"You think we're going to starve to death?"

"All of us? No. Those who make it through the hurricanes and boredom, yes."

She stands and takes my hand. Hers are so tiny in mine. "But we have skills. I think you're not seeing the amount we can do."

Fuck. There's nothing I can do. This isn't how I wanted this to go. My chest expands with each deep breath. "We will do what we can. But the reality isn't easy. We're not getting out of here. We've already had two injuries. And building a shelter? We'll do it, but we have two pocketknives, a fish knife, and a hatchet. Maybe if we had more supplies from the boat."

"Boredom. There are lots of things we can do to fight off boredom." She wraps her hands around my neck. We share a look.

"I'm happy to help you anytime, Haley," I say.

"And I can do the same back." She smiles at me.

Shit, I want to pull her up my body and push my dick into her pussy. But I can't. I'm not sure I can share. Zane and Easton are all for it. But having her be only with me? No fair. Not when she's interested in all of us. I can tell. I shouldn't touch her at all, but I can't stop myself. Not after this morning.

Fuck, she's on her tiptoes, her lips inches from mine. I hold her head in place. Our lips connect, and I devour her. I'm never going to get enough of her. She lifts one luscious leg around mine. But does she understand what I mean? Her core is inches from my cock, and I want to go back on my vow to myself. I can't.

I swing her around so her ass is to my front, pinning her to my chest. Then I ease my hand into her leggings, finding her tight bundle of nerves. I'm not careful. I rub with a fierceness and a need until she's doubled over my arm, mewing. My hard cock is between her butt cheeks. With ease, I could slide into her from behind. Instead, I watch the horizon line for ships. She has to understand who I am.

# Chapter 32

## *Downpour*

Haley

Calvin's hand is still in my pants, but I'm doubled over his arm like a rag doll. A dirty, filthy rag doll. Who wants nothing more than for him to fuck me hard. His fingers are big and ruthless, and I want more. I'm not sure if it's my nerves over being stuck on this island, the guys, or the ocean breeze, but I've never had need build so high in me before. It's like the whole island is an aphrodisiac.

"Give it to me, Haley." His gruff words send goosebumps down my neck and arm. He slides another finger into me, changing the pressure, and I break apart. I shake until my hands fall forward to the sandy log in front of me, my ass high in the air.

Calvin removes his fingers, but a firm grip on my hips keeps me from collapsing. He tugs up my pants and slides his large palm over my ass. I push back into his hand. I want more. I want to touch him, but I know that if I try, he's going to shut me down.

His rough hand helps me up. He's licking me off his index finger. I throw myself at his chest. This close, I have to tilt my chin far up to look him in the eyes. I'm not sure what I'll see there—indifference, disdain?

But it's confusion. "They're waiting in the raft for you." He nods at our makeshift home.

I suck my lip in. This is so confusing. Calvin acts like he wants me. I hug him. His broad shoulders freeze. "Listen, I'm not giving up hope. You've got good points. You're a man of reason. But we can solve each of the problems. You don't throw away a boat engine if it needs new spark plugs."

"You might if no one makes replacements."

"Well then, we'll just have to think outside of the box, because there's already a damn cat in it."

He kisses my nose. "I can try."

"You promise? Not just with your words, but in here and here?" I touch his thick hair and then his heart.

"No. I can't promise that. Because I never make a promise that I can't keep. But I'll try. I'll try really hard."

I smile at the word "hard" and slide my hand down to his cock. But he catches it.

"If you're still bored, I'm sure Zane and Easton can find something for you to do."

I step back from Calvin, my brow furrowed and the confusion pulsing through me.

"Don't you go overthinking now. There aren't any rules here. You said it yourself."

"And you reminded me there is a rule."

"Stay alive." Calvin nods at me. "Yeah, well, if I thought you were in danger, I wouldn't let them anywhere near you." Even in the dim light, I see the sincerity on his face. "Go to bed, Haley. I have work to do."

"I'm not tired yet." I sit down on the same log that Calvin sits on, the one facing the ocean, with the best view for spotting boats and planes. I don't really believe he's given up on being rescued. If he had, why would he try so hard to keep the fire going and stay up all night doing the watch? Unless . . . I glance at the raft. Is he worried about seeing something or hearing something to do with me? No. He doesn't care that much about me, or he'd let me touch him.

He stares at me and the log and then sits down. There isn't room for both of us, so I duck my head under his arm and pull myself as close to him as possible.

"I need to keep watch now." He puts another log on the fire. "You can stay up until the moon rises. It's too dark to use my knife now, anyway." And he lifts me into his lap. It's a small victory, but I'll take it.

The air rushes out of my lungs, and I want to tell him I can stay up until I want to. There are no rules on this island. But then I remember his caveat: stay alive. And I keep my mouth shut.

He reaches behind him and pulls on his shirt. I lean forward and help to smooth the shirt down his rugged abs. The firelight bounces off his skin. He's glowing, and his tan arms flex around me as he periodically pokes at the fire. I'm sure if I wasn't out here, he'd be carving in the dark or pacing the beach getting different angles of the horizon. But I'm cozy and no way am I moving unless he makes me. I'm doing his safety a service by making it impossible for him to hurt himself.

The thud of his heart in one ear and the rushing of the waves in the other makes me drowsy. When he smooths my hair down the back of my head, my eyes close. The wind whips around our beach, but Calvin's got enough heat for the two of us.

I'm almost asleep when he stands with me still in his arms. I've never thought of myself as small, but nuzzled against his chest, I'm like a child. "Let me stay up with you for a little longer."

He looks down at me. "Fine, but the moon is rising and I need to work."

I smile at the pile of sticks next to his seat. That pile of wood isn't for someone who thinks they are going to die. "Good. You work. I'll watch the horizon." I sit on the rock next to the log we shared.

"Haley. I like you, but we're not a thing." He picks up a stick and sharpens the end.

"I get it." I do. My stomach doesn't, but I do. My eyes are on the horizon, but I turn to watch him. He nudges my leg with his foot and points to the water. I turn back to the ocean. "How far can we see, anyway?" I've wondered this before, but I'm not usually on the deck of a yacht, just hanging around. There is always something to do.

"From here, three miles. But from our platform when it's finished, twenty, maybe more."

"Okay. The platform is going to be a good thing." I nod. Watching the horizon, I scan back and forth like back in my high school lifeguarding days. The moon is getting brighter, but then I see a little fleck of light. My heart races and the little speck is gone. I blink and squint, focusing on the spot. Did I imagine it? But it's back.

"Calvin, there." I point. Stumbling up as quickly as possible, I round to the other side of him to get the flare gun. It's on the rock Dante uses as a counter.

But Calvin is quicker; he has it in his hand. "Where?"

"Right there." I take his hand and point where I saw it. "Shoot the gun!" I'm jumping up and down, the pain of my ankle absent with the adrenaline of the light. He's holding it, staring at the water. "Shoot it off, Calvin. What are you waiting for?" I'm staring at him, not the light. I look back and the light is gone. I'm dying inside. "Shoot."

His eyes are focused. I know he's looking in the right spot. A white light appears and then disappears again. It's small, so small. It has to be as far as we could possibly see from here.

"The light is white and there's only one."

"So. Fire the damn gun, Calvin." I want to take the thing out of his hand, but my training told me they're like a regular gun and misfire could kill someone.

"That's the aft light of a small boat. It's after midnight. The chances of someone looking out the rear are next to none."

"But not none, Calvin. Not none."

"We only have four shots."

"But we have four shots. Sometimes good things happen, Calvin. Take a chance. Please." The white dot is gone.

"What's going on?" Zane holds the flap open. He sticks his hand outside, and then his eyes flick to the flare gun that Calvin holds. The fire is going strong, and the moon is rising. Crabs are scurrying around the outside of our fire ring, waves crashing. Time seems to stand still.

"Did you see a boat?" Zane asks loud enough to wake anyone in the raft.

"There's a boat?" Easton echoes from behind Zane.

Calvin stares out into the night. "It's heading away from us," he calls over to Zane.

In an instant, Zane is by my side. "You're sure it's going away from us?"

Now we're four across, shoulder to shoulder, moving away from our fire. I can't see the light anymore. Dante is next to us; only Easton hasn't come out of the raft.

"There," Zane yells. "Damn, it's the white aft light. It must be small." He shakes his head. "It's too bad. It's too bad."

"What, a ship?" The sleep is gone from Easton's voice as he steps out of the raft. His hair tousled, he stares at the four of us. "Fire the damn gun. Use the flare gun, Calvin!" Easton reaches for Calvin's arm, but Zane steps in between the two of them.

"No, man. No, we're not gonna fire the gun. They'll never see it. They're heading away from us. Look at the size of that speck. Do you see it?" Zane points to where the light had been flickering.

"I don't see it."

"Wait for it." Calvin's voice is steady. Two more beats, and the white dot appears. But it's only there for a second. "The seas are rough out there. And they're heading away from us. There's no way they're going to be looking for a flare on their tail. They're smaller than the *Rock Candy*—a yacht, most likely. Hopefully not pirates. If they hadn't gone away from us, they might eventually have come back toward us. But not tonight. Not with the coming storm." The clouds are rolling in, and the moon darts in and out of them. It looks like it might rain.

Dante nods at Easton. "No, they wouldn't see it if we fired the shot. It would waste one of the few we have."

Easton glares at Calvin. I can see the uncertainty in his eyes. He wants to use the flare gun as much as I did before Calvin explained it.

Zane puts his hand on Easton's arm. "They'll never see it. They're too small and too far away. To top it off, they're not looking at us." Zane says the same thing as Calvin and Dante, but now it's sinking in.

"But you never know?" Easton mumbles.

We all stare at the spot the light was in, but it doesn't reappear. None of us move. We watch the dark line of the horizon, the wind blowing the clouds in front of the moon.

Someone throws another log on the fire someone else started. More logs, more fire. "Let's get the fire shade back over it," Zane says, looking at the cloudy night sky. "It's gonna rain."

Calvin grabs one of the loose side windows from the raft, and Zane helps reposition it over the fire. Then thick, large raindrops start falling from the sky, ones and twos to begin with, but they soon flood together in the sand. We gather as much firewood as we can, putting it underneath the edge of the raft to keep it dry. Calvin gathers his tools, shuffling them under the rain cover. It isn't much, just a sort of a tripod of long bamboo covered in palm fronds. We've been lucky so far, with no rain falling on us.

Zane moves containers around to pick up rainwater. We have the stream, but rainwater is even safer.

Drops turn to a downpour. The rain pelts down, hurting my bare shoulders. I pull my shirt up over my head. We all scurry around, picking things up and tucking them away. The jerky Dante made is in the tackle box hanging from the tree. We're still not sure what else is out on the island, so we're keeping food out of the raft as much as possible. No one wants to wake up next to a boar or rat.

We don't have much, so it doesn't take long to gather things. I dive into the raft after dusting my feet, getting as much sand off them as best as I can before Easton and Zane follow behind me. We're all pulling off wet clothing. All the cushions and towels are in the raft. The way the wind shakes the raft cover, there is no way the fire is going to stay lit.

I crawl back over to the door. "Calvin, get in here. There's no reason to be out there. You're not going to be able to keep the fire lit."

"She's right," Dante says over my shoulder.

But Calvin shakes his head.

"Come on, Little Bird. You're letting the rain get in. He's old enough to decide what he wants to do for himself. There's no talking sense into him." Zane lightly touches my shoulder and passes me a towel. "You use it first," he says. "Then Easton and I will take a turn with it."

I look around, and there are three towels. But they've set up one as a bed with a cushion. I'm a little shook up about seeing the boat, our potential rescue gone. But they're right. I let my emotions go and get ahold of myself. If there was one boat, there could be more.

"Remember the rule, Calvin," I say.

He looks at me, water pouring off his hair.

"Don't drown." I pull the flap down, closing myself in with Dante, Easton, and Zane.

# Chapter 33

## *Swells*

Haley

The rain has me drenched. In the area by the door, I wring out my hair and shake some of the water off. In a flash of lightning, I see Dante's asleep already. He doesn't move. He pretended to be okay all day. I imagine the second his skin hit the bottom of the raft, he passed out.

More quick flashes of lightning, and I take a deep breath. I've never liked storms. But at least we're not on the water.

On the other side of our steamy little home, where I've been sleeping, is a nest of life jackets, a cushion, and a towel. The way it's laid out, we should all be able to use it. Or at least Zane, Easton, and I. The cleanest of the towels is in the middle of the cushion too. And I have to admit that sleeping on it instead of the plastic bottom of the raft is darn appealing. Especially with the way the wind is blowing the top covering of the raft around. It's not leaking. Not yet, at least. But it's shaking for sure.

"Ready?" Easton pats the raft next to him, and it echoes. I can't really see him. I'm nervous about what we're going to do. Or not do. It's been building each night. Our snuggling.

I swallow and begin crawling across the raft. It's hard to be normal, let alone sexy, when you're on all fours in what is basically a kids' birthday party bouncy house. I inch to the other side. I don't want to wake up Dante. I catch my foot, and it tweaks my ankle. My breath hitches, and I have to stop for a second to get the throbbing pain under control.

It's raining so hard the moon is almost completely blocked. I've lived in a lot of porthole-less cabins, and I used to think of them as dark. I had no idea what dark was. With the flap now shut, I can't see any of the guys. The last thing I want to do is hit Dante in the head with my leg.

I'm shivering. It's nerves, though. The raft is cooler than outside, with the rain. But not cold, not at all.

Calvin said the other guys heard us this morning. But no one said a word. Not even Dante. And now I'm getting ready to bed down between Easton and Zane, again.

"Can you see us, love?" Zane asks.

"See us? Unless she's superhuman, I'm guessing the answer is no," Easton growls.

"I've got my hand out." Zane's voice drops. "Feel around for it."

I wave my hands around like I'm blindfolded and playing pin the tail on the donkey. We have a marine-grade flashlight. But we've all agreed not to use it unless it's an emergency, and while I don't want to bump into Dante, it's far from an emergency.

I make contact with Zane's hand, and he guides me over. "Feel for the edge of the cushion, Haley."

Tonight, lying between them feels a heck of a lot more deliberate. I snuggle down next to Easton, and Zane puts his head next to mine. "Cushion Gate solved. Dante has one, and you can have the other. Do you want it under your head or your ankle?"

"Oh, really, Dante should have both." I'm worried about him. He acts all tough on the exterior, but he's like a marshmallow on the inside. No, not a marshmallow—Dante would never be something so common—a Tiramisu custard. And now I'm thinking about chocolate and rum.

Zane brings me back to reality. "He's already asleep, love. You don't want to wake him up by giving him another cushion, do you?"

"I suppose not." I pat down the edge of the cushion and brush along a life vest, but my hand slips from it and slides down Easton's chest. Oh, that's not his chest. I pull my hand back. Holy hardness. "Oh, I'm so sorry." I just felt him up. I don't know why I'm so nervous. He clearly doesn't mind. My eyes are open, but it's like I'm wearing a sleep mask in the inky blackness.

"You're fine, Haley." Easton chuckles. "Come on. Lie down. Do you want the cushion for your head or ankle?"

"Head." I ease into position between the two of them. Easton at my backside pulls me to him, and I wasn't imagining what my hand was just on. He covers me with an emergency blanket. It's welcomed. A few long breaths and my shivering subsides.

Easton whispers in my ear, tickling the hairs on my neck. "Comfy?"

"Yes, very." My heart's still racing, but I am comfy. It's remarkable what a one-inch piece of foam under part of your body and a thin emergency blanket can do. But then, maybe it's the two attentive, attractive men staring at me that have me cozy and my heart racing.

Zane gets into position, and I lift the blanket covering his side. He's facing me, his knees skimming along mine. And just that small contact from him has zings of need shooting off through my body.

Easton puts his arm around my waist, pulling me to him, and Zane moves along with the two of us. I'm tired—the sun and salt air do it to me anytime I go to the beach and I'm not working. But with the normal red glow of the raft gone—it's different in the complete black—I'm invigorated and excited. Almost as excited as Easton.

Zane stirs. I make out his features, but just barely. He puts his hand on my hip. The rain thunders down. If I was back at home, I'd have my blanket pulled up over my head. My dog—or rather, my old dog—would have been under the blanket with me. Neither of us like storms.

"Are you doing okay, Little Bird? It's a storm. It'll pass soon." Zane makes little circles on my hip with his thumb. It's comforting, and it's turning me on all at once.

And I realize while I'm telling myself I'm cozy that I'm holding myself up with tension. I take a deep breath and try to relax, but that only makes me more on edge. These two. "I know. I just don't like storms. That's all."

A bolt of lightning lights up the top of the raft, illuminating it in a red glow. In a moment, I can make out Zane's handsome face and see that Dante is still asleep on the other side of the raft.

"Storms and sharks, got it. Anything else we need to protect you from?" Zane's tone is light. He's laughing with me, not at me. And it makes the storm a lot less scary. "Come here. I'll hold you."

I move a fraction of an inch toward him, but it makes all the difference. I'm sinking into his arms. He's a well-built man. Not as large as Calvin—more like a runner. And I bury my head in Zane's chest. My focus is on his heartbeat. The strong thuds cover the crash of another round of thunder. It's a few beats and then more lightning.

"One Mississippi, two Mississippi, three Mississippi." I revert to my youth.

Boom. Something hits close to us.

"Mississippi?" Zane mimics me.

"Half a mile. She's counting the distance." Easton's hand lands on my back. He's rubbing little circles. The wind howls, and I know I should fall asleep, but I can't. I'm too unsettled by the boat sailing away from us. And from the storm and not knowing what's happened to Sam.

"We say, one elephant, two elephant." There's another flash.

"Oh, I've got you, Little Bird. Easton does, too." Zane's voice rumbles through his chest to my ear.

Yesterday, back before dinner, when we were taking a break in the waves, Zane really did want to kiss me. At least, I think he did. I panicked and turned my head, but the wave took us down. Then Dante swallowed water. But now it's me who's underwater. Drowning between these two gorgeous men.

The storm beats down, and I momentarily remember Calvin outside. I turn my head to the door, but it's too dark to see anything.

I feel more than see Zane smile. "Cal can come inside anytime he wants." Zane drops my hand, and his fingers run along the edge of my chin. His thumb rubs over my lip.

My heart quickens. Do I want this? This is absolute madness.

"Can I kiss you?" Zane's voice is low, but not low enough to hide his intentions from Easton or Dante—even asleep.

It's an eternity. I stare at him, frozen. He can't see me. He has no idea I'm panicking. Does he?

I can't answer.

I can't do this.

Can I?

Can I kiss one guy while another one holds me? Can I kiss them when I kissed Calvin this morning?

I want to. There are no rules here. It echoes in the back of my head. I squeeze my legs together.

"Haley?" Easton's voice rumbles in my ear. "It's up to you, sweetheart." His fingers on my belly grip me tighter, his cock heavy on my bottom. And then he lifts his hand.

Easton means it. In a flash of a burst of lightning, I see Zane. This is up to me.

And I break. My lips are on Zane's. Just a brush at first. His lips are full and lush. The nerves in my stomach have turned into a fullout hurricane. I'm soaking wet as Zane controls the kiss. Easton's fingers run around the nape of my neck. Electric currents zip through me.

I want this. I'm going to do more than let it happen; I'm going to make it happen. I'm in the moment. I can be in the moment. This is the moment.

Zane's an amazing kisser. Goosebumps pepper my side.

"Haley," Easton whispers in my ear. "Lift your arm. This wet shirt has to go."

And just like that, Zane pulls back. Easton undresses me. My shirt's gone and then my sports bra too. Zane has his hands on my breasts. "Damn, they're the perfect size."

Perfect? It's not a word I'm used to hearing.

"Tilt your head for me, Haley. I want to taste your beautiful neck." Easton's got his hands around my waist. We're kneeling around each other now.

"Beautiful? You can't even see me."

"I don't need to see you to know it's true, darling." Easton laps up the side of my neck to the tender spot behind my ear. And I'm gasping for breath. It's like he's switched me on.

Zane has his lips around one of my nipples and his hand on my other breast. I'm turning into a noodle. I put my hand on Zane's shoulder to keep from falling over. He lifts his mouth from me. "That's it, Haley. We've got you."

A mewing noise tries to come out of me, but I hold it in. I don't want to wake up Dante. I don't want Calvin to be upset. I . . . I . . . Crap, it's overwhelming. And they're not even touching me below my waist. But I'm panting, trying to hold it together. Everything here is overwhelming: weather, food, water, and these men. They're going to be the death of me, but if I have to die, I suppose it's not a bad way to go.

My head falls backward; Easton's kisses have turned my neck to rubber. He chuckles. "Stay with us, Haley. You are going to be the best meal we have out here."

I can't take it anymore—I slump to my side, and Easton helps me down. My back to his front. Zane trails his tongue between my breasts, back to the underside of my chin. A flash of lightning turns the raft red for a split second.

"Damn, Haley," says Zane. "You're . . . you leave me speechless. And I'm the Shakespeare of words."

Now Easton laughs out a breath. "Shakespeare?"

But Zane doesn't respond. His lips are back on mine. Our bodies are lined up. I'm practically lying on top of Easton.

# Chapter 34

## *Full Sail*

Easton

Zane's kissing her, and it turns me on until I think I want to explode. My fingers grip her stomach, pulling her against my erection. Her lush ass cradles me. But I need her leggings gone. I dip my hand into her waistband. Her skin is velvety richness, and I want to revel in every bit of it. I inch my hands upward. Her breasts are both free from her sports bra and Zane's hands. They're heavy in my palms, and when I press on her nipple, she arches her back into me, breaking her kiss with Zane. A flash lights the raft.

"Fuck me, you're gorgeous." Zane's loud, and I want to smack him. Because we hashed this out. Extensively. For far too long. She's not supposed to know we have a plan. So he needs to be quiet enough that reasonably Dante and Calvin can't hear.

She laughs softly, like she doesn't believe him. And fuck, I throw the plan out too. She rolls onto her back, and I need her pants off her more than I need my next breath. Discretion? That's out the window too. Being quiet with a woman like Haley simply isn't possible. She needs to understand how luscious and amazing she is.

"He's right, Haley." And damn, I'm already thinking about how we can get her to do this during the day. I want to see every look on her face, the flush on her skin, the way her head rocks from side to side when she thinks she can't take any more pleasure.

The raft shakes when I move onto my knees. The bottom is inflated as much as the sides are, like a giant air mattress. There is a little foot pump that we use every day to top off the air. Every movement we make sends quakes through the floor.

Another flash. Haley tips her head up, her gaze on Dante, just as he gives his best fake mumbling breath. Or at least, I think it's fake. When I had my concussion back in boarding school, I wanted to sleep 24/7, so he might really be asleep. But I don't care.

Her laugh was one of disbelief when Zane told her she was gorgeous.

"He's right, you know. You're absolutely stunning." I move between her legs and slide my forefinger and thumbs under her waistband. She lifts her hips, and I tug her leggings from her. I toss them away from Dante, away from the door with the water pooling next to it.

"You don't know that. It's dark." She laughs again, but this one is followed by a gasp because I've sucked her nipple into my mouth and I'm rubbing her other one.

"It could be as dark as the bottom of the ocean, my love. Your beauty is embedded in my soul already," Zane says. But he says it with that damn British accent, so it sounds even better. He kisses her again. I should have moved in when he was taking his shorts off. But I have a better idea.

"Your skin is so soft. Like a cloud." I run my fingers up and down her leg to her mound. Slowly, I move her legs apart. My hands are on the lower part of her stomach, and the vibrations of her chest rising and falling speed up with each touch of my hands, each movement of Zane on her lips.

I kiss her smooth skin below her belly button and slide myself down until my lips land on her clit. I taste the ocean salt on her skin, and I want more. With flicks of my tongue on her, I pulse my fingers in and out of her in unison with my mouth.

She whimpers. "Oh, oh."

I want her. I want to know how good she feels. I want to double her pleasure, triple it. To take away every fear and uncertainty for a while and make her explode with desire. I am obsessed with this girl. I don't even care that I'm sharing her. At least not now, not here. She echoed what Calvin said: There's only one rule. Stay alive.

Zane moves, straddling her around her waist. His ass blocks any view of what's happening on the other side. But it's too dark to see, anyway.

His thrusting vibrates the raft. She's soaking, and I want to see the expression on her face, the flush on her cheeks. I'm relentless with the pace. I suck on her clit, and she explodes. Her moans are muffled, and when I move to her side, I can make out why. Zane has his cock nestled between her breasts. He's holding her head up, and she's sucking on the end of his cock. Fuck if it isn't the most erotic thing I've ever seen. I move to behind her head, putting my knees by her ears, supporting her head with my legs. I figure Zane will slide down, but he leans back, cradling her breasts with both hands now. She sucks him in harder and deeper. The noise of it makes me want to come.

"Fuck," Zane says. "So good, Haley." And he pulls back, spilling over her chest.

I don't know what I expect, but him flipping her onto her stomach when he moves off her isn't it. Her hands are on my cock, and then her mouth hits me. Her lips are warm and wet. She shimmies up until her knees are under her chest.

With more lightning, I see Zane move behind her, letting her use him as a chair. "Lift your beautiful ass, Haley."

She doesn't move, and her lips plunge over my cock.

"Haley. Lift your ass now. I want to taste your pussy," Zane says.

If I'd said it, it would have come off crass. But with his British accent, it sounds like he's inviting her over for tea.

She works my cock and licks the top, holding me in her tight hands. I can see hardly anything, only the top of her light blonde-brown hair.

"It's too much." Her breath is husky and shallow. She sucks me back into her mouth, and my thoughts go white.

"I'll say when you've had enough pleasure. And this isn't it. One orgasm isn't enough, sweetie. You deserve far more, and we're going to give it to you." Zane laughs.

I let my hands travel from her neck down her sides, exploring, seeing with my hands. Her knees are tucked into her chest. Zane's there on her ass. A flash and I catch Zane's smirk. He raises his hand, and the light is gone. A soft smack and she moans around my cock. She didn't expect the tap. But she didn't mind it either.

I grab the sides of her thighs and let my fingers sink into her. She moans again. And I'm gripping harder, and I can only imagine the smirk on my face matches Zane's.

"Slow down, Haley. Torture him a little. Like you did me," Zane huskily whispers to Haley.

"Damn," I hiss out because Haley does exactly as he suggests. Her tongue swirls slower. Her head bobs up and down, but she's moved everything down a gear. Which has upped the intensity ten times. Ten thousand times. "Fuck, Haley. Don't listen to Zane. He's some kind of ass."

She laughs around my cock, and it's enough to make me want to let go.

But not yet. I need to last longer.

I feel my muscles tense. I'm going to explode. "Damn Haley. This is so good." It's going to be a big one. I know it. I need to warn her. But I can't stop her. I'm so hard and so close. I don't want to come, but the orgasm is right there. It's going to happen. She's only concentrating on sucking the top of my cock, but then she takes me deep into her throat.

"Fuck, Haley." I hiss through my teeth. A loud moan rips from her throat, and it's enough to make me want to come harder than I ever have before. "Fuck. Yeah," I say. I'm fighting it. I'm fighting like hell. Trying to stay in my body, trying to fight back the oncoming eruption. I'm losing every battle. Her head bobs up and down faster, and she's using her hands to pump me at the same time. I'm close. So close. I don't know how I'm managing to hold on. More sucking noises. Her moaning and her whimpering—it's going to make me come. "Haley, holy shit." I'm louder than I know I should be. No way Dante can sleep through this. We're bouncing all over the place. Hell, Calvin has to be able to hear us even with the howling wind.

My hands are in her hair, trying to slow her down, trying to control her. But she's too good. I'm not going to survive this at all. "Pull back a sec. I need to . . . I need to pull out." I'm telling her without words. I'm going to come. I'm going to come. I can't stop it. I can't. But she doesn't listen. She's too caught up in what she's doing with her amazing tongue.

And I'm going to come. I'm still fighting it. But it's too late. I'm going to shoot down the back of her throat. "Fuck, Haley. I can't pull out. I'm going to . . ." I groan. I'm so close. I'm holding it back, but just barely. My cock is about to explode. "Fuck!" I'm trying to pull back, trying to stop it, but my control is gone. "Haley, I'm going to come," I say through my teeth.

She lifts her head in time, and I shoot over her knees. Or at least, I think I do. It's too dark to tell. "Damn." The stars are out behind my eyes. Every cell in my body fires at the same time, and I'm shaking. When I settle back to earth, I realize I've left a mess all over Haley. My shirt is nearby. I grab it and reach for her. But she's already missing. And I feel hollow inside. I take care of what is mine. But then, she's not mine, is she? A brief flash of lightning reveals her on the other side of the raft with the bucket and sponge.

I move to go after her, but Zane grabs me around my ankle. "Let her be." It's clear. She's not mine, she's not his, or ours even.

The boom for the last flash is twenty seconds later. We're through the storm.

Zane is rearranging the bed cushions. The rain and wind are slowing, and there is even the slightest bit of light coming from outside.

"Are you doing okay?" I can't let her be. Letting something or someone be isn't in my nature.

"Yes, I'll be right there. I'm mopping up some water that came through the flap."

That's it. I'm beside her. If Dante was asleep before, he's not now. "I'll do it. You go lie down." I put my hand on top of hers.

"It's fine. I've got it." Haley doesn't let go.

"I insist." My face is next to hers, but I can't make anything out.

"Okay." She lets go of the sponge.

"I've got a nice nest for you over here, Haley," Zane says. She makes her way over to him. "You good?"

I imagine him tucking her in. I move the sponge along the side of the raft. There's a lot of water. But it doesn't take too long to get rid of most of it, and I head back to Haley and Zane.

She lifts the cover, and while I'm not cold in the least, I crawl under it. It's not long before the raft vibrates again. I lift my head. Calvin's there, lifting the flap. He's silhouetted in the entryway. I don't blame the ass. I'd want to be in here with her too. Both to be with Haley and to be out of the damn rain.

# Chapter 35

## *Plunder*

Calvin

The fire's out. I tried the best I could to keep it going, but the rain poured through the flimsy fire protection we threw together at the last minute. It didn't stand a chance. The wind was the big issue. We're going to have to start over tomorrow. And there's no reason to keep watch. It's stormy as shit out there, and the visibility is nothing. Any boat out there is going to be busy enough keeping themselves off the coral and sandbars surrounding the island. No one is moving at a leisurely pace tonight. No one is going to be looking for a flare, either.

The only thing that was keeping me outside in the rain was the noise coming from the raft. Fuck me. I told her to have fun. This was the plan. But still. I told her to keep herself alive. I kept her hands from touching me, kept her off me. I'm not ready for a girl like Haley. She's the kind you keep. And I'm not someone who is a keeper. I'm the one who wouldn't let her touch me. But damn it, she was more than willing. The sounds lifting out of the raft, rising above the howling wind and the crashing waves, were more erotic than anything I'd ever heard.

It's quiet now when I crawl over the edge. I'm not gentle. The raft shakes with my landing on the floor. Dante's to one side of the door, asleep—I can make out his shape rolled against the sidewall. The night sky has cleared enough, and somewhere under the cloud cover, the moon is trying to lend some light. On the other side of the raft, the rest of them lie. When the flap closes, it's dark, like pitch black. Cave-like. My eyes are open, but I feel like they're closed. I hear them moving their hands. I thought they were done.

I peel off my wet crew jacket. My shirt is in here somewhere, dry. I leave the flare gun next to the door. It's remarkably dry. I pad over to where I remember leaving my shirt. I need to dry off if I'm going to have any chance of sleeping. At least a little. The raft is humid but warm and smells of sex. I inch along the other side of the wall of the raft, away from Dante.

"Calvin, is that you?" Haley's voice is husky.

"No," I answer because I'm an ass like that.

"It's him. Who else is there?" Zane's quick to reply.

"Don't mind me, I'm just looking for my shirt to dry off." I clear my throat.

"We have a towel. You should take the towel," Haley says. I can hear her moving around, getting the towel. "How's the fire?"

"Dead."

"Sorry, thank you for trying. Here, take the towel."

I move toward her voice, but she's moved too, and she smacks into me. Her chest is bare. Her skin is clammy. She's naked. I'm naked. And I grab her around her waist because the raft is shaking and I don't want her to tip over. Or at least, that's the story I'm going to go with, because it can't be the softness of her skin or the way she smells of coconut and rainwater. My dick is instantly hard, and I want to lick her.

"You've been having fun?" I push my nose into her neck. Her hair is damp with rain and sweat.

She doesn't miss the opportunity to touch me. Her hands trail down my back to my bare ass. I took my underwear off earlier today to keep it dry, for something dry to sleep in. But now I don't care. This girl is driving me mad. I have to have her.

Haley's fingers trail around my bare ass cheeks, causing goosebumps all over my body. I let my hands travel down her sides, exploring every inch of her in the darkness. Zane and Easton are over there. I hear them moving. Are they mad that I've stolen the prize? Are they going to pull her out of my arms? I'm not going to let that happen. They've had their fun; now it's my turn.

I kiss down her neck, just stopping to nibble on her breast. My other hand finds the remaining one. Damn, she's perfect.

I'm hard, my cock standing at attention. If we're going to die, we might as well have some fun before we go.

Her hands are in my hair. Her fingernails scrape along my scalp. I trail my tongue lower, nipping at her waist as I go. I had my fun feeling her body break apart on me not long ago. My cock remembers all too well. I'm hard again. I want to pull her down to the floor of the raft and fuck her. Hard.

Something's different. I twist my ear to the door flap. The rain, it's stopped; the wind is blowing but not as fast. A sliver of moonlight is fighting its way into the raft. I can make out Haley, her gorgeous body in front of me. Her dark nipples, Zane and Easton behind her. Easton is sitting up. Zane is lying on the cushion, both of their heads turned toward our silhouettes. It's an instant, but I break. This goddess belongs to all of us. Just like Zane mentioned before. She's ours.

I lick her clit, and her fingers pull on my hair. I suck her into my mouth, one quick harsh pull, and I move my head away, untangling it from her hands. I pick her up and put her down next to Zane. But I'm on her, between her legs, my cock nestled at the tip of her pussy.

"Fuck yeah." Zane makes it sound like he's at a football match. But his hands are on Haley's breasts. I'm holding my cock, inching it in. I'm not ready to be a dad, and that's what the pull-out method makes you. "Damn, don't stop." Zane's voice is on edge.

"I'm on the shot. And I'm clean," Haley practically whispers.

My balls tighten. I feel like an ass for hesitating.

"I'm clean too," I growl out. I push in. She's tight, despite how often I've had my fingers in her in the last twenty-four hours. "Fuck."

She clamps her legs around my waist, and I have to bite the side of my cheek to keep from coming when her pelvis tips back. Her pussy fires around my cock, and it's heaven. It's so dark I can't see her face. And I want to say fuck it and squander the power to see her. But then the wind picks up the flap and I see her. She's kissing Easton. Zane's head is on her breast. And fuck, it makes me harder. I'm not going to question it. Why the hell should I? It's unbelievable, and I'm going to take it for what it is.

"You're so fucking good." I thrust harder, driving all of us into a rhythm that will leave us on the other side of reality, and the raft.

Muffled cries come from Haley, and there's movement next to me. She's got her hand wrapped around Easton's dick and is yanking him off. I pull her up tighter, giving her arm more room.

"Fuck, Haley." Easton's gritty voice rages over the wind. He sits up. He's let go of her mouth, and I lean in. Zane's got a finger on her clit. He's stroking more than her, and I'm not going to think about how I feel about it. I only know that she's fluttering around me. So wet and tight, so close to losing control of her senses.

I brush my mouth against her puffed lips. They're warm and soft, and when I swipe my tongue into her mouth, she tastes of musk and sunshine. She's more than I could hope for. Zane's moving on her hard with frantic, tight actions. And hell, I'm about to come from it. I grab her hips and tilt them up, my cock and tongue moving in unison.

Her back arches and her pussy flutters around me. I'm a wild animal. Pushing hard into her, each thrust sends her deeper into the raft. The whole thing is shaking, or that might be my insides. I'm sheeting white with pleasure. A galaxy is born behind my eyes.

And I come in her. I might never stop. I reach out and hold her up and off the raft's floor.

Easton screams. Zane isn't far behind. We're one mass of arms and legs shaking.

Haley's low moans pitch sharp. "Oh my, yes." She's screaming as her feet clamp into the back of my butt, and that's it for me.

I set her down slowly, my cock still twitching in her. This whole thing is crazy. The raft is stifling now. It's damp and stinks even more of sex. But when I settle on top of her, holding myself up to keep from squashing her, I have to laugh. I can't help myself, because damn, that was the strangest, most amazing thing I've ever done. And I can't wait to do it again.

Easton moves to the opening and ties it up. It's not raining anymore, and the moon is almost shining. I should go back out there. But instead, I settle into the side where Easton was and roll Haley into the middle. My cock is still in her, and I don't want to let her go.

She tilts her head to mine, and I kiss her nose. I was aiming for her mouth, but when she lets out a giggle, I'm glad I hit her nose. She grabs my chin and gives me a soft kiss before turning over to Zane and kissing him too. I'm not sure how this is going to work. Easton has gone outside, and I don't feel guilty for taking his spot next to Haley. I don't even feel guilty for taking his spot with the cushion. But I do think about getting up and seeing if I can get the fire going again.

The flap smacks the side of the raft. "Where's the flare gun?" Easton yells. "Where's the flare gun? There's a boat. There's a fucking boat. Get out here."

It's a scramble of legs and arms to make it out of the raft. It's fucking pitch black, cloudy, foggy, and zero visibility. There's fucking zero chance he saw a boat. But we're all up, all of us, standing on the wet sand outside the raft, naked. The moon strains through the clouds. I can barely see the tips of the waves as they crash on the shore.

"Where's this ship?" I ask. Because it sure wasn't a boat if he saw it out there. I'm holding the flare gun in my dry shirt.

"There to the north." Easton points.

I bite the inside of my mouth, holding back from calling Easton a privileged prick. Mostly for Haley's sake. Because the whole owner-crew, employer-employee thing? That's over for me.

"That's west, you numbnuts." Dante's up and out of the raft.

"Whatever. West," Easton says.

We stand shoulder to shoulder like we did last night, when we saw the other small boat sail away. Maybe I was wrong? Two boats. Maybe we will find our way off this island in one piece. But I know for sure, we're risking our lives by both firing this gun and not. The traffickers and pirates in this area are dangerous. We're in international waters, with vigilante law in place. It was one of the reasons we wanted an extra week or two to get the damn yacht in shape. And now look at us. Always go with your gut—that's what my brother used to say before he married my girlfriend. I knew something was up then too.

I'm not letting anyone near this gun. The ship we use a flare for has to be close enough that we can tell they're not pirates.

# Chapter 36

## *Unmoored*

Dante

"You know what would be fucking fantastic?" I shove the coconut full of crabmeat and seedy bananas at the golden boy.

He's got his steely blue eyes turned up to me. He's not going to answer me.

"If you'd shut the hell up about the damn boat. What you saw was the Loch Ness monster. It didn't exist. All right? And if it did, it doesn't matter. It's not here anyway."

"I'm telling you; I saw it. A large white boat."

"With no lights on?" Zane adds. "This is good, Dante." He raises his bowl at me.

"Enjoy it. That's the last of the bananas you found. We're out until we find another tree or some more ripen." I scrape the rest of the residue off my rock grill and push coals over it to heat it up for the next meal. All morning, Easton's been going off about the fucking boat. I've had all morning to listen to him gripe about it. Ship this, right there. He needs to shut the fuck up.

"I'll find some more," says Zane. "I'm going to do a scouting mission when I go out to get some more firewood."

"I saw a boat. I'm not imagining it." Easton gathers the dirty coconut bowls and my two prized spoons the lug made for me. He stands there. His glare doesn't affect me. I've worked in some stressful kitchens all over the world with chefs that are two cabbages shy of a coleslaw. Easton crosses his arms over his chest and looks between Zane and the water instead of heading there and being a good dishwasher. Granted, there's really no such thing.

"Right, well, boats don't just vanish." Zane licks the inside of his shell and hands it to Easton.

"It was a post-sex delusion." I push the coals around and put a new log on top. The pile of wood is getting low. If the damn pain in my head would stop, I could walk around for more than a few minutes and actually be useful. Am I salty about not being in the damn Haley pile? Fuck yeah. Am I mad that I woke up just as they were finishing and didn't get to watch? Damn right I am.

Haley joins the kitchen circle.

"How was it?" Zane asks Haley.

"It's a hole with palm fronds around it." I shake my head at Zane. She'd made it clear she wanted to go relieve herself in the new latrine by herself. It's a hundred feet up the beach. Calvin and Zane dug the hole this morning. Shockingly, the two of them are getting along like two peas in a pod. Guess sharing is caring. I huff a laugh and scrape the grill rock with my sharp rock. I've already done it, but it's keeping me busy.

"Dante. It's nice. Better than just going along the trail. I've got some ideas on how we can make it a little better."

"You don't need to worry about that, Haley. Two boats in one night. We won't be here long." Easton squeezes her arm and takes off for the water.

I glance over at Haley. "Ready for some food?"

"Please." She nods.

I hand her her bowl. She's the last to eat, but she definitely has the best of the lot.

I saved her some of the bananas. Did I spend extra time picking her seeds out? Yes. Did I put the seeds from her bowl into Easton's? Also yes. I take the plastic cover off the top. I've got a few small pieces of plastic I'm keeping, all from the emergency supply kit. They were used as dividers to keep the fishing gear separate. Calvin has come up with another system, leaving the bags for me. They're a blessing. There're all kinds of bugs on the beach. Hopefully, we won't have to fall back on bugs for protein. We still have some boar this morning, and the jerky from the first day is holding on okay in the dry bag. Damn, we could use a few more of those. I checked it this morning, and none of it is ruined.

"I'm going to go collect some palm fronds after breakfast." Haley looks up from her bowl.

"Oh." I have to wonder what Calvin and Zane are doing.

"I'm feeling a lot better. Did you notice I didn't use my crutch to cross the beach?" Haley smiles.

I nod and shake my head to the side.

"What? You know, when you don't talk, it makes me anxious. I can go into the jungle and get some fronds."

"Calvin has the hatchet."

"Right." Her shoulders dip.

"But I'm sure you could convince him to give it to you."

Now it's her turn to cock her head and give me a sassy look. "That thing's attached to him."

"So were you last night." Immediately, I know it's the wrong thing to say. Her neck bends, and she's digging in the sand with her toes. "Oh no you don't. Don't you regret what happened. I'm just a jealous bear, wishing it was my hand in your honey—"

"Ew. Stop right there. You . . . You're jealous?" Haley's shoulders rise.

I have to laugh. "You have no idea how much."

"Oh." She nods, not looking up from her food.

"Are you okay?"

She sucks in her lips. "It's a lot, you know. All of this is a lot." She motions around the beach.

"I get it." I want to pick her up, sit down on the big log, and put her in my lap.

"I'm sorry we woke you up last night."

"I'm sorry you didn't wake me up sooner."

"Oh." Her sweet tone rings. "How are you feeling?"

She's changing the subject. But I'm not having it. "Left out."

Her laugh is one that could cut a guy if he didn't have as much confidence as me. Did I set out to share a woman with three other dudes? No. Not something I would have thought I was into. But there's something about Haley. I'm not going to let her go. Hell, I was into her when I thought she and the captain were hooking up.

My stomach thuds. The captain.

I sit on the log next to her, and she turns her blushed cheeks to me. "Left out?"

"Yup."

"Oh."

"'Oh' as in good, you want me in the mix next time, or 'oh, no thank you'?"

"I . . . I like you, Dante."

I wait for the but. It doesn't come.

"I've never done anything like this. I've hardly done anything at all. I've had two long-term boyfriends, a few flings, but nothing like this."

I take the empty bowl from her hand and put it on the log next to me. Her hands are soft, and I pull them onto my leg. "If you don't want me in your gaggle of guys, then I don't have to be in it. But I like you, Haley. I liked you before all this." I wave my hands around. "You're good at your job, which I find sexy as hell. You're smart, brave, you fuckin' saved my life. And Easton's too. Whatever you want, I'm cool with it." I've presented dishes to billionaires, to owners of Michelin Star restaurants, and my heart didn't beat as fast as it does right now. The fact that she's not looking at me has my palms sweating. "You're in charge, if you haven't figured that out yet. Calvin might think he is, but he's not."

She nods and stands. But then she leans over and kisses me on the lips. It's a quick brush. But then her lips part, and I want to consume her like a French pastry. She pulls away all too soon. "You need to get healthy first."

"Got it." I'm still holding her hand. I can feel that she wants to take off. Run and hide. But I'm not letting her hand go. "No gymnastics. I suppose I could say the same for you."

She laughs. "I'm going to go find Calvin."

"I'll come with you. Swimmer Boy, watch the fires," I holler over my shoulder.

Easton waves at me. I'm hoping he heard. But at this point, I don't really care. Haley has a head start on me. I grab one of the sharp sticks that Calvin has in a pile next to the cooking area and follow her. When I catch up, I interlace my fingers with hers.

"Are you sure?" she asks.

"That I want to get speared by a boar's tusk? No. But do I want you to stay out of trouble with the largest bore on the island? Yes." She knows I'm talking about Calvin.

"He's not boring."

I grunt a bunch and shuffle my feet like a wild animal.

"Dante," she laughs. "Stop. Calvin is just concerned for our safety."

"Right." I nod and lead her down the path to the jungle. I've been down here a few times. I take my time, going slowly. The last thing we need is for her to re-injure her ankle. "You doing okay?"

"Picture perfect. Thanks for taking it easy on me."

"Oh, trust me, this is the only time I will take it easy on you." A blush blooms up her neck, and I fucking love it. "Looks like you need some sunscreen." I rub my knuckle over the round of her cheek.

"I'm going to stay out of the sun today. I've got two skin tones:

pasty and red. But I want to save the sunscreen. You never know when you might need it."

I smile at this woman. "Damn, Sassy, have you ever thought about yourself first? It's okay for you to use sunscreen. Calvin, Zane, and Easton spend most of their days in the water. They'll make it through."

"What about you?" Her shoulders go up.

"Oh, my Irish-English ancestors must have spent a little time in the med. I tan up nicely when I'm out in the sun. I'll be fine."

"Fine isn't good enough. I don't want you to get hurt."

"And the only flush I want to see on your cheeks is from what we do to you. Am I clear?"

"Yes, sir." She smirks.

But damn, I like it. I like her following my directions, and I like the "yes, sir" more than I want to admit.

The jungle path is always farther than it looks. Stepping past the tree line on the beach is like stepping into a different world. The humid air sticks to our skin. There are birds making noise on the tops of the trees. And I can't help but wonder where their nests are and if we can find some of their eggs. Zane's able to climb the banana trees. Maybe he can find some eggs for us.

"Palm fronds you're after?" I pull out my knife. To think I almost hadn't put it on when I got out of my bunk that morning. Damn, it feels like yesterday and last year all at the same time. I use it mostly for opening boxes and such. I'm not sure Calvin even knows I have it yet. I hold it up. "I think we can get some of the smaller ones with this." I haven't had a reason to pull it out before. Much like Calvin with the hatchet, I'm a little possessive about it. Knives and women are things I don't usually share. Guess there is a lot changing for me.

"Dante? Where did you get that?"

"It's mine. I've had it all along. Thanks for not dropping it when you dragged me out of the *Rock Candy*."

"You're welcome?" She stops in her tracks.

"It's fine, Sassy; I was joking." I haven't let go of her hand. She twists both of us to face down the path.

"I know. Did you hear that?" Haley tucks her hair behind her ear. "I heard something."

"Hear what?"

She points down the path near the pool where Zane has been getting our water.

"No. I don't hear anything." I pull the knife out of the sheath, pushing Haley behind me. With the way my head feels, I can't carry Haley out of the jungle like Zane did. But I'm not going to let her be gored by a boar either.

# Chapter 37

## *Tack*

Haley

I drop Dante's hand. "It's not a boar. It's smaller. Over there." I move through the ferns off of the path. I'm careful how I place my feet. There are plenty of sharp rocks and coral in the undergrowth. Little shells are all around.

"I don't hear anything."

"Shh, Dante," I whisper. I stand still again and listen.

"What was it?" he whispers back. Well, as low as Dante's volume gets.

"I don't know. It sounds like something small."

He flourishes his hand at the undergrowth, and I take it as a sign to keep looking. I'm not using my crutch really anymore, but I have it with me. I push the ferns and knee-high plants out of the way, clearing a path. But whatever was there is gone. I turn around and shrug. Then it occurs to me. "Do you think it could have been a snake?"

"There are no snakes on the island," Dante says with authority.

"How do you know? There was a boar, and Calvin said he saw some goats when he was looking around the island yesterday."

"Because I fucking hate snakes."

"You're like Indiana Jones, then."

"I suppose I am. Are you ready to go find the Temple of Doom?"

"Not Doom. Hope." I nod.

"Somehow I don't think the Temple of Hope would have been as much of a smash hit in the box office."

I laugh. "Definitely."

"There are some fronds over there we can reach." Dante points to the edge of the stream.

"Perfect."

I'm used to doing a lot of work. Dragging beach chairs up and down castle stairs for extravagant excursion lunches. Cases of wine from the lower decks to the sundeck. Laundry! Don't get me started on how much laundry weighs. So much laundry. I've never had to go to the gym. Palm fronds, you would think they're light, but they're unwieldy. My arms are stacked as high as Dante would allow me. I could have taken more, but I'm glad I didn't, because I'm dropping them as we leave the jungle for the beach. One or two here and there.

"Who knew palm fronds were the new breadcrumbs?" Zane laughs. He has the ones I've dropped in his hands.

"Shoot. Thanks for getting those." I smile.

"No problem. I just have to ask, what were the two of you doing in the jungle?" He arches an eyebrow at me.

"Getting palm fronds for Sassy here." Dante waves his load at me. "Where do you want them?"

"Next to the raft." I drop mine beside the fire ring.

"Do you need more, Little Bird?"

"I'm good. This should be enough. Maybe? I've never made a palm frond mat before. How hard can it be?"

You know when you say something and you know you've made a mistake the second you say it? Yeah, that's me and weaving palm fronds. An hour in and I've got something that almost resembles a mat, along with a half dozen cuts from the edges of the sharp fronds. Two hours in, it doesn't look too bad. Easton and Zane both keep checking in with me in between going in and out of the jungle, bringing ever more wood. It's nonstop, and with each trip, they're gone longer and longer.

"How's it going, Sassy?" Dante gets up from where he's been resting in the shade. After we came back from the jungle, he poked at the fire, complaining about how Easton needs to pay more attention to things, and then fell asleep.

"Okay. I think I'm getting the hang of it."

"Want me to help?"

"I'm good. You rest up. Do you want me to cook tonight?"

His eyes widen. "I'll leave the weaving to you. You leave the cooking to me."

I smile. I knew that was going to be his exact response. I get back at it: in out, in out. I place the next section beside the raft door. A measly ten or twelve more and I'll have most of the area around the front of the raft covered. Sand in the raft is gross, but the next thing I should make is the fire cover. I get to work. Dante's asleep again, and I haven't seen Zane or Easton for maybe half an hour. I don't know. I wish I had my mother's old-fashioned windup watch. My breath hitches. It always hitches when I think about her and how I miss her.

But from there my mind wanders to Sam. As much as I don't want to think of him as dead, that he's not gone, when I think of him as alive, I can't help but sink into guilt. He asked me to go touring after the charter season with him. We weren't an item. There weren't any labels on it. Still, my mind wonders how I would feel if he went off and had a ménage à trois—no, quatre, or is it cinq? I'd be hurt. Mad. No, I'd be disappointed. My stomach sinks when I think of Sam being disappointed in me.

"Hey, Little Bird." Zane puts his hand on my shoulder, and I jump. I didn't even see him coming out of the jungle.

Damn it. I'm crying.

"Hey, hey. It's okay. We're going to be okay." Zane sinks onto the log, his legs facing the opposite direction to mine. He grabs my head and puts it on his chest. "You're okay." He smooths my hair. "We're all going to be okay. We've got lots to eat. And a Michelin Star chef to make it taste fantastic."

I open my eyes, and Dante has woken up. He's kneeling at my feet.

"What's going on?" Easton is here now too. His arms are loaded with wood, which he drops so he can join Dante on his knees in front of me. "Haley, are you crying? Why is she crying? We're going to get out of here. Two boats. Come on." Easton sits on my other side. He pulls my legs into his lap. "No more tears. But if you want to cry, that's okay too."

How do I even tell them I'm not crying about being shipwrecked but because I cheated on Sam when I didn't even have a relationship with him? This is crazy.

"Oh, are you crying about something else? Are you crying about us? You don't need to cry about us." Zane lifts my chin.

But it makes me cry even harder. I inhale. And when I open my eyes, there are now four sets of eyes staring back at me. I don't know where Calvin was, but he's back.

"What in the hell did you do to make her cry?" He glares at them.

"They didn't do anything." I wipe my eyes with the back of my hand. I need to be tough. Tougher than this. I've never cried in front of guests. I've almost never cried while on charter. I say almost because there was a charter last year when I figured out that Steven was cheating on me. But my cabin mate was really good to me. She gave me space and picked up a lot of the slack I dropped. But that was only for a few hours. I'm not one to sit and wallow in self-pity.

"What is it, then? Does your ankle hurt?" Easton runs his hand down the side of my leg.

"It's not her leg," Calvin scoffs, and I get the impression I've disappointed him too. "You know you have nothing to be ashamed of." He hasn't dropped to his knees like the other guys. No, I have to crane my neck to look him in the face. The sun is behind him, outlining him like a superhero.

He's hit the nail on the head. And the other guys, even Dante, turn from Calvin to me.

"No, Little Bird," says Zane. "You're good. Don't go thinking about anything, but you're good. Do you understand?" He lifts my chin to him and kisses me on the lips. He's warm and smells like coconuts and saltwater. I wish I could swim in his words. But I have too much baggage.

Easton touches my elbow. "Haley, we all like you. But we'll all do what you want."

I nod. Because what I want is what happened last night. Still, I can't help but worry.

"Oh." Dante stands up. "Are you worried about what the captain might think? Is that it, Sassy?"

My eyes are wide, and I can't look at any of them. I suck in my lips and dig my toes into the sand in front of me, grateful I haven't made a mat for where I'm sitting yet.

"Dante told us. You think too much." Calvin's voice is gruff.

"She does," Dante agrees. "You have nothing to worry about."

The next second, I'm no longer sitting between Easton and Zane. Calvin has me over his shoulder. His long strides take us away from the fire. My face is at the top of his waist. "Calvin, what in the heck are you doing?" I yell into his skin.

"Making you think less."

"What?" But he's flipped me and has me in his arms.

"Hold on, Haley." He jumps into the water. The waves surround us, and he quickly makes his way with his long legs into the waist-deep water. "Float." He lets go of me but keeps his hand on the underside of my back. He steadies me there. "Now listen. Easton and Zane are coming."

I turn my head to the side to not get a mouthful of water.

"You're right, the captain would be furious. Because he knows quality when he sees it. We all do too."

The air in my lungs freezes. Is he trying to tell me that I shouldn't be with him and the guys?

"Let me finish! Okay?"

I nod.

"Your life isn't his to live. You're doing what you think is right. For right now. That's what you need to do, Haley. Live in the right now. There are no guests to serve. Not even Swimmer Boy. This is about you. Focus on taking care of yourself, and we will too. Because you are more precious than fresh water or food. Got it? If Sam was here, he'd realize how important it is for you to take care of you. He's not, so you need to do it instead. Take care of you. Let us take care of you." Calvin leans over me. His eyes sparkle in the midday sun. "Here they come."

I don't have to lift my head. The splashes of the water announce Zane and Easton. Calvin leans over me, and I can't help it—I loop my arms around his neck and kiss him. Locking my feet around his waist is natural. As he deepens our kiss, I can hear Zane and Easton cheering.

"That's our girl."

"Fuck, you're so sexy, Little Bird."

The waves crash around us, and I can't stop them. I can't stop where I am. I can't stop how I feel. Calvin's right. This is my life. And if I want this, there's no reason why I shouldn't have it.

He breaks our kiss, but I'm not ready for it to be over. Then I realize he's giving me to Zane.

Zane's brown eyes glisten like amber against the sun, reflecting off the waves. "Feeling better, Little Bird?"

"So much." I reach for him and give him the kiss that scared me the other day. His lips are warm and subtle. But I don't have much time before he hands me to Easton. They're all good kissers, but so different. Each one in their own way. Each of them is built of firm muscle but differently. Easton's back is like iron when I grab him around his neck. His lips are firm and commanding. Calvin wants to please me by taking control, while Easton is slow and easy. And

Zane? Can lips convey joy? I think they can, and his do. It makes me wonder what Dante's kiss will be like. Calvin's right, though. I need more in-the-moment thoughts and feelings. I hang on to Easton.

He breaks the kiss. "Are you okay?"

I let my legs drop, although I know he can hold me up. Heck, the way he saved Dante was amazing. That's when I look up and see Dante staring at us from the beach.

"I will be."

# Chapter 38

## *Grounded*

Easton

I hold the towel out for Haley as Zane holds her hand coming out of the water. Calvin's impromptu swim has taken a good hour out of the middle of the day. It made for a nice distraction from what's become our normal routine for the ticking days: work, swim, eat, collect firewood, and do it all again.

It's sunny and warm. A light breeze sweeping across the beach will dry us all off within a few minutes, but there's something I've always liked about having a dry towel ready for me. Zane leads her right to me. Dante's back in his kitchen. I get why he didn't follow us out into the water. Someone has to tend the fire, and after what happened? He's not ready for the water. I think he's putting on a lot of "I'm fine" bravado. The last time I asked to check him out, he swatted me away. I figure if he wants help, he'll ask for it. Not that there's a lot I could do here. Not that there's a lot I could do if we weren't on an island, either. Set a bone? Maybe. Massage a muscle? Definitely.

"Did you enjoy your swim?" I ask.

"Yes." Haley lifts onto her tiptoes and kisses my cheek. "Thank you for getting the towel." She quickly dries herself and hands it to Zane. "I'm going to weave some fronds for the fire-protection cover."

"Want some help?" I ask.

"At some point, but I'm trying to perfect my technique first."

I nod. I can understand wanting space while you're learning something. When I first got into competitive swimming, I liked to practice for hours in the pool by myself. "What you've done looks good to me."

"Thanks, but I want them to be super tight for the fire shelter. Hopefully, it will give us more of a waterproof covering."

I nod and leave Dante and Haley over at the raft. I want to be with her, but smothering someone is never a good idea. I head into the jungle. Down the path to the map tree.

"Anyone up there?" I crane my neck back to look up at the tree. I've passed it a hundred times today getting firewood. We've already exhausted the area around camp keeping the signal fire ready to go for whenever the ship is just right for Calvin. But I'm here at the tree with the smooth bark.

I stare at the tree. There are two maps now: the nautical one that Zane and Calvin showed Haley the other day and a new one of the island. I can make out our beach, the stream, the tree, and a few other marks Calvin made that I don't understand.

"Calvin?" I call out. A bird flies out of a tall tree, away. And twenty feet past the tree, the ferns move. More than they would for the wind. Which isn't blowing hard enough to make its way into the jungle anyway.

Fuck it. I jump, grab the lower branch of the map tree, and pull my legs up until I'm hanging like a sloth. I saw a ship last night. It was moving on the horizon, and the moon caught it for only a second. Light reflected off it. But then nothing. From the top branches, I can watch the other islands and see where the ship went. Maybe. But even I am starting to doubt that I saw anything.

I move to sitting, then standing, on the limb and make my way up, one branch at a time. Until I find the large branch that has scuff marks on it. Calvin's definitely been here. Two more branches up, I poke my head out above the canopy of trees. The tree sways more up this high, and it has branches that extend even higher. I grip the next branch and brace myself between the two.

Calvin's right; there is a chain of islands beyond us to the north. They're not close. It's hard to make them out. I don't know why he said he couldn't see any campfires. I can barely make out the islands themselves. And what I don't see is a boat, a container ship, or a yacht. I don't see anything. Nothing that doesn't belong here: birds, surf, waves. And in the distance, a whale spouts. It's amazing and was very unnerving to see from the raft.

I watch the whale for a while. It comes closer and closer, passing by our beach. I follow it, wait for it as it dives, disappearing for a while before it comes back up.

I reposition my hands. I have no idea how long I've been up here. I suppose it doesn't matter. For as much gung-ho work ethic as Calvin puts out, he's not whipping the lot of us to do the same.

There's nothing to see up here. I turn around, looking at the interior of the island. The canopy is varied, and to the northeast I think it goes up. I can't see any ocean in that direction, at least.

I make my way down the tree, and when I reach the bottom, I shake out my legs and arms. I pick up a loose palm frond or two that I find lying next to the path and make my way back to camp. Dante and Haley are by the raft, and Zane is in the shallows with a pile of sticks.

But Calvin's nowhere around. When I turn, it's like he magically appeared. He's behind me, working on the smoking tent next to the campsite. He gives me a chin up and then turns to Zane and cocks his head at him. We're officially summoned. Zane joins us behind the smoke shelter.

"Where the hell were you all day?" Zane starts, pointing first at Calvin and then at me. "You know we need as much wood as possible for the signal and cooking fires."

"I haven't been gone that long. I was bringing firewood in. But I also climbed the map tree. I wanted to get a good look for myself."

"See anything?" Zane asks.

"A whale, birds. No campfires from the other islands."

"And no boats," Calvin says.

"Where were you? Or did you forget about the massive amount of wood you said we need?" Zane's normal mellow demeanor has vanished and left him turned into a drill sergeant.

"I know, I know." Calvin runs his hand through his hair. "But I've found something. It's a good mile through the jungle on the southeast side of the island. I want you guys to come see."

"What, like now?"

"Yes." Calvin picks up the hatchet from the log he left it in. "We'll be back," he calls to Haley and Dante.

Haley jumps up. "Oh, no you don't. Where are you going? This isn't interior crew and exterior crew anymore. This is all of us."

"Do you want to come?" I ask Haley before Calvin can shut her down.

"It's a long way into the jungle. Is your ankle up to it?" Calvin's staring at her legs.

"What did you find?" Haley moves to him.

"Are you coming or not?" Calvin says.

"You're not going to tell me unless I come?"

"I thought it would be fun to have it be a surprise." Calvin smiles.

"You, sir, are full of surprises. The word 'fun' coming out of your mouth . . . How can I not come now? What about Dante?" Haley wraps her arms around her waist.

"Dante, want to come on a mile-long hike through the jungle when I'm not telling us where we're going?" Calvin barks across the beach at Dante.

"Fuck no. It's been nice knowing you. Well, some of you. Make sure you come back, Sassy. I would miss you."

"I'd miss you too." She stops. "Well, I guess if I'm not back, I would have a hard time missing you."

"Stop," I grunt. I don't want to think about anything bad happening to Haley.

"We'll bring you back something." Haley waves at Dante.

"Excellent. I'd like a coffee, black, none of that macchiato, almond-whip bullshit."

"I'll do my best." She smiles.

"I expect nothing less." Dante goes back to tending the fire.

"Want me to carry you, Haley?" Zane steps forward. And I'm kicking myself for not offering.

"No, I'm good. Two summers ago, a guest wanted a picnic by a tropical waterfall. I had to carry a fully stocked bar kit, a table, and a cooler through the jungle. And I had to get there before the guests to set up."

"That sounds horrible," I grunt.

"It was fun once we got there, but I had to run practically because the primary guest was a retired football player. And former running back. The guy ran the rest of the guests to the waterfall. He also got up every morning and wanted his orange juice fresh squeezed and waiting for him on the treadmill." She glances at me. "But they were totally great. A lot of fun. And super appreciative."

Zane laughs. "But the real question is . . ."

"Oh, the tip was good. At least, I remember it being good."

Calvin shakes his head. "If you can't remember what it was, then it wasn't really that great."

"That's not true."

"Haley, you're trying to be nice because Swimmer Boy is here. You know it's true." Calvin slaps me on my back.

We hit the edge of the jungle, and I have to wonder if I would have requested something like that if I'd been on any of the cruises as an adult. I sure as fuck hope I wouldn't have. Having people haul full-ass tables out into the jungle . . . Candy, yeah, she sure as hell would have. Maybe dad's last wife would have too.

It hits me. I wouldn't have stopped it from happening. And I don't like that, not at all.

Calvin leads the way. We follow the boar's path for a while, but then he turns off it, heading to the ocean. Zane picks up a stick and moves things out of the path.

"Are you going to give us a hint at what it is, Calvin?" Haley's walking right behind him, and if I'm not wrong, I think she pinched his ass.

"Do that again, and we're not going to get there, Haley," Calvin threatens.

She shrugs and glances over her shoulder, smirking at Zane and me. "Come on, a little clue."

The jungle is staying the same. Waist-high foliage, coral and rocks below, with pockets of dirt. It's not an easy hike, but once you get used to what to expect, it's not too bad.

"How about twenty questions?" Haley sings.

"No," Calvin spits back. "You just have to wait."

"You said you wanted this to be fun." Haley steps too wide, and she stumbles forward into Calvin's back. But he twists and picks her up in one fluid motion. He has her on his back.

"Fine. Hang on." Calvin sighs.

She turns and gives us another smile. Oh, we are all in for it. Because I know I'm as wound around her little finger, twice as tight, as Calvin is. I thought he might be the one to be able to say no to her. I guess I'm wrong.

"All right. Zane, you guess first," Haley says with a joyful tone.

"Is it an animal?" he guesses.

"No," Calvin says.

"Easton, your turn."

I think hard about what he might have found. A ship? He would have told us straight out. A village? He already said that he didn't find that yesterday. "Is it plant-based?"

"Fuck, yes, no. I'm not sure how to answer that."

"All right, now we're getting somewhere. Want me to carry Haley, Cal, so you can lead the way?" Damn, I do love a puzzle.

"I can walk. He was just being overprotective." Haley pats his shoulder.

"His specialty," I pipe up. That gets me a glare from Haley. She doesn't like it when Calvin and I go at it. I don't blame her. That's how her leg got hurt. "Your turn, Haley."

"Okay." With Haley on Calvin's back, he's really picked up the pace. We can't be far from whatever it is he wants to show us. "Okay, let me think. It's plant-based but not."

Calvin takes a sharp right to the water through some low scrub. A thorn scratches along my leg, but when we push through the underbrush to the rocks? I can't believe my eyes.

# Chapter 39

## *Derelict*

Zane

"Look at that! It's a bit of a dog's dinner. But damn, we're going to be able to use every last bit of it." My heart beats in my throat. Calvin has found us a first-class proper shipwreck on the rocks. It's a fishing boat. Old, completely wooden. And in her day, she must have been a glorious thing. She's painted in green and red. A broken mast in royal blue hangs over the side of the rail, the tip long lost to the ocean.

I'm making my way out onto the rocks. Everyone else behind me is forgotten.

"Zane, be careful," Haley yells.

I stop in my tracks, her call bringing me back to reality. There's no one around, but the rocks certainly are dangerous. "I will."

It's local or local-ish, maybe from Thailand? And it's proper old. From the 1950s at least, although I'm guessing she was sailing long after. A giant split has the hull open on one side to the ocean during high tide. It's almost low tide now, so we have a few hours before it will turn and start to fill the hull again. I scramble over the rocks, climbing up onto one that's a little taller.

"How's it look?" Easton shouts.

"The top of her looks sound," I holler back. I move to a smaller rock balancing on top of the one I'm standing on. I can see the top deck—it's solid. But the hull? There's not enough for it to ever sail again. On the deck is a wheelhouse. The panels on the side are carved, some painted red, others a light green, all of it peeling. There's so much wood. And the boards touching the rocks are battered and torn up. No way she'll ever even float again.

I climb down and round the bow. And the starboard side is mostly missing. I duck my head into the gaping hole. It's cold. The aft is full of sand, and the bow has a tide pool with small fish darting about it and a few starfish. There's nothing left of whatever the boat hauled. From the size of it, it was definitely a fishing boat. Looking up at the important part—the underside of the deck—it's solid. Oh, there's some seaweed here and there, but it looks usable.

"How is it?" Haley calls. At least, that's what I think she said. It's muffled by the wood and ocean. From here I can't see any of them.

"Great!" I back out and find Easton standing on a rock behind me.

"Think you can boost me up there?" Easton bounces, his eyes full of excitement.

I blink at him. The rocks I'm standing on aren't close enough to get me to the deck. The man is dense. Not that I can't haul my weight and then some in rope. "How about you boost me, Swimmer Boy?" He's got a better chance of getting me up and over the side.

"Fine. I'll let you have all the fun." He locks his fingers together. "Hop up." Easton takes a step toward the side of the ship and braces his legs.

I put my right foot in his hands and reach for the deck, but it's not enough. "Toss me."

"What?"

I glare down. "Toss me like you're a damn Scot throwing the

caber at the Highland games. Don't make me call Calvin over here." And that's enough. I sail through the air like a cannonball. If a cannonball only goes two feet. But it's enough for me to grab the side rail and roll over the edge. My shoulder hits the deck, but I bound right up.

"Are you okay? What's going on?" Haley's got her hands cupped from the other side of the boat and Calvin's scowling at me. But all I can do is smile. This, *this*, is going to make all the difference in the world.

"I'm good." I wave over at her. "The deck is solid." Though I don't stamp my foot down to prove the point. I'm not daft.

"Hey," Easton yells back from the starboard side.

"Hey." I lean over the edge. But that's when I see a little metal ladder. It's eight feet long and hooked under the edge of the rail. I'm moving like a cat, listening for any signs the whole ship's going to tip over. But it feels more solid than a ship tethered to a dock. "Give me a second. Stay there," I say to Easton.

The U-shaped brackets that hold the ladder in place are snug, but with a little prying, I get it out and lower it to the rock below. "Think you can get up here with that?"

"Definitely." Easton spends the time getting the pointy ends of the ladder positioned on the rocks and catapults himself up the ladder. I grab him by the wrist and help him on board. "Damn."

"Spot on."

"What's in there?" Easton points to the wheelhouse as he steps toward it. The boat creaks, and we both freeze.

"Are you guys okay?" Haley yells.

"We're good," I reply. But I know my eyes are as big as Easton's. "Step on the beams. Find the nails," I answer before he asks.

"I know construction. I helped my dad build a barn. Or rather, we helped the contractors." We step more gingerly to the wheelhouse. He pulls the door open. It's damp inside but not wet. The roof has held. "Jackpot."

"Exactly." This is better than winning in Vegas. Not that I've ever been. I've been to Monte Carlo, but not into any of the casinos—too busy washing the boat. But damn. The room is a mess, the contents of the cabinets spilled out over the floor. A tattered bed is along one side of the wall. There are bird feathers all over it, but thank fuck, no current birds. But my eyes flick to the potbelly stove in the corner and then the cooking pots on the floor. I pick up a decent-sized kettle and start filling it with utensils from the floor. Two knives, a ladle, and a frying pan. Hallelujah, this is the absolute jackpot. Dante is going to be chuffed when he sees this. I rub my hands together, almost not knowing where to get started.

From the wall, Easton pulls a beaten orange metal box. "First aid kit. There are scissors, a little knife, and some old gauze."

"Grab it." Then, from underneath the bed, a flick of orange grabs my attention. "What's this?" I push the tattered bedding away. It's a net, and it's solid. The rope in it doesn't show any wear at all. I put the pot down and tug at the net. Easton joins me, and when it's out completely, it dominates the room.

"I'll take it out to Calvin." Easton has his hands overflowing with net.

I nod at him. "Cal's going to want to come up. I don't think the three of us up here at the same time are a good idea, though."

"Agreed." Easton disappears out the door. With Calvin's mass, I'm not sure he should come up here at all.

There's stuff everywhere. When this was an operational ship, I bet every surface was covered and every inch of the wall had something hanging on it, every nook filled. I don't know what I'm specifically looking for. Already the net, stove, and cooking gear are more than we could have hoped for. Behind the door, I find two large plastic water containers. Easton pops back into the room, and I hand the containers to him. "Take these out."

There's a trunk in the corner. With a lock. I pull on it, but it doesn't open. Poking out from a broken crate on the floor is a hammer, and my heart sings. I think about giving the trunk a good whack with the hammer but decide against it. We have more than enough to carry. As soon as we can, I want to come back for the stove. We'll be back for sure.

"Zane." Calvin's voice booms from below. "Get what you can and let's get back to camp. It looks like rain." It's a command, not a request. Rain isn't going to hurt anything here, nothing that hasn't already been damaged.

I gather the pots and cooking gear. And I'm not sure why I do it, but I toss the covers back on the bed. There, in the corner of the bed frame, is a little dark bottle. I uncork it and smell it. "Whoo." It's strong alcohol, whatever it is. I put it in the pan and head out to the deck, making sure to shut the door to the wheelhouse behind me. I give it an extra pull. "We'll be back."

When I turn to the deck, Easton is lowering things off the port side to Calvin. Calvin's got a long wingspan, and they're almost able to hand things directly to each other. The net is down, as well as the water containers. There's a pile next to Calvin of other things Easton must have found on deck. I give Easton the pot, and he passes it down. Cal's right. Angry storm clouds are building behind us. And the wind has picked up significantly since we climbed up here.

Easton's over the starboard side to the ladder. When his feet hit the rock, he holds the ladder for me. I tuck it under my arm and carefully make my way back around to our pile of loot.

Haley's bouncing with excitement. "Dante is going to be so happy."

Calvin has the net managed into a tight pile. His large ass is in the air as he finishes the packing of it.

"Happy?" Easton says. "I thought he had only one emotion: sarcasm."

Haley rolls her eyes and playfully smacks Easton's arm. But we all know he's right. "He's going to be happy, and you know it." She takes the cooking gear under her arm. "What else can I carry?"

"Just keep tending to your ankle, Little Bird." I give her a kiss on her head.

"Let's go," Calvin says in a gruff voice. He takes the massive net and heads into the jungle, leaving us with some of the other small things and a chair. Easton puts the chair over his arm like a bag, and I gather as much of the rest as possible.

Fat warm raindrops begin to fall as I look back at the boat. I can't help but wonder what happened to her. Did she get thrown off-course in a storm? Or was it something more sinister? The slave trade in these parts doesn't only affect women. Hundreds of sailors and fishermen are captured and forced to work on major ships every year. I might have gone down a rabbit hole on Reddit last summer when I learned we were going to Asia, but I'm keeping that to myself.

Looking up, I see the others are already making their way back to the jungle. I gather the rest of the stuff: two books, the first-aid kit, the alcohol, the ladder, and two of the water jugs.

We're toddling at a snail's pace down the trail. Even Calvin is being mindful of Haley's leg, keeping the pace slow. He turns every few meters, looking back at Haley. The muscles on his neck are bulging. The driftnet is at least a hundred pounds.

"It didn't feel this long to get there," Haley says.

The trail is getting wet. The rocks beneath the greenery are muddy and slick. "Let me take the pots." I reposition things and reach for Haley's load.

She frowns. "I've got them." She holds them closer to her chest. "Really, Zane, I do."

"Okay." I walk behind her on the trail, minding her every step. She's limping, and I can't help but throw a look over my shoulder at Easton. He shrugs.

"Let me have the pots, Haley." Easton pushes past me.

"I've got them." Haley smiles back.

"No, come on," Easton growls. "We don't want you to strain your ankle again."

"I'm good." She lurches even as she says it.

I'm with Easton. She needs to pass them over, but being all grabby isn't going to convince her.

"Haley?" Easton's not letting it go.

Calvin drops the net on the side of the path. "Fucking Rockwell. Did you not hear her? She said she's got it." Calvin's in Easton's face.

Easton drops the chair and other things he's carrying. "It was a question, Cal." He emphasizes "Cal."

# Chapter 40

## *Retreat*

Haley

My heart slams against my chest. "Calvin, it's fine. Easton was trying to be kind." The peacemaker in me wants them to get along.

Calvin's tone is low. "I'm fucking sick of it. You're just like my brother." He glares at Easton.

"What, your brother doesn't like you either?" Easton goes chest to chest with Calvin.

My breath hitches. Easton doesn't know about Calvin's brother, but I do. Shayla told me all about him when we were scrubbing the plastic-film residue from the shower in the Fortune suite. "Easton!" I call out, but it's too late. Calvin punches Easton in the jaw. It echoes in the humid air. It is a crunching sound I can't describe. A sound I know I'll hear in my sleep. I'm going to hear it for the rest of my life.

Easton shakes his head and spits out a glob of thick blood. And I'm about to step between the two of them again, but Zane grabs me around my waist. The things he was holding are pitched to the side.

My legs are flying. I can't see Easton or Calvin anymore. Zane's holding me like I'm nothing more than a flopping stuffed animal. The world blurs around me. The green of the jungle and the dark stormy sky are bouncing blobs. Each plodding step he takes on the trail splatters sand up onto his legs and onto the green undergrowth next to the trail.

I twist, trying to see the guys. Even the big droplets of rain splattering the palm leaves don't slow Zane down. He runs fast enough that we really are running between the raindrops. Between his rhythmic breath and the rain, I can't hear anything else. He runs past the stream.

"Put me down." He doesn't slow through the clearing. "Really, Zane." We are almost back at our beach. Another thirty feet and we're home. Home? Whatever. "Put me down." I squeeze on his shoulder. "Please."

Zane makes it to where the beach and jungle blend before he slows. "Right, sorry, Little Bird. I don't want you anywhere near those two knuckleheads. Let them do what they have to do." His grip loosens, and he sets me down. My feet hit the sand, and I resist the urge to go back and see what damage the two of them are doing to each other. I'm more afraid for Easton than Calvin. I'm hoping that Calvin . . . can stop himself. I shake my head and look off into the distance. The ocean and sky are both churning an angry gray.

"Do whatever it is they need to do?" I can't resist, and I turn back to the head of the jungle path. "They could really hurt each other."

"No Haley. If they need to pound on each other, let them do it." Zane turns me back to the raft.

Dante laughs.

And Zane and I stare at him. The wind howls through our encampment, but the rain for now has stopped.

"What, pound? It's funny." Dante's under the small kitchen rain shelter, and he glances between us and the jungle. "What's going on?"

"Those two daft sods are going at it again." Zane throws his thumb at the jungle.

It's only then I remember I'm still clinging to one of the two pots I managed to not drop when Zane picked me up. "We—"

"Holy shit! Fantastic, Sassy." Dante forgets about Calvin and Easton the second he sees the cast-iron pot. He looks back at the jungle. "But where's my coffee?" He laughs.

"I had a second pan, but I dropped it." For a moment, my head clears of the guy's fight. I knew Dante would be over the moon with the pots.

"This is perfect, but let's not wave the metal around in a storm. We'll go back and find the other one tomorrow, love." His laugh rolls with the crashing waves. He tucks the pot under a mat in the makeshift kitchen area. "It's brilliant! Where did you find it?"

"Uh, a derelict fishing boat." I turn back to the jungle. I feel like I can hear them fighting, but I know I can't. Not over the waves crashing, even though the tide is at its lowest.

"You two go get in the raft. I'll go back and see what's going on with them." Zane cocks his head inland.

I'm furious at both Calvin and Easton. We've got enough going against us; we don't need the two of them having a contest for control every other day.

"Let's go get dry, Sassy," Dante says.

The wind shifts and the rain starts up again, pelting the side of the raft. "Dry sounds good."

Dante places a hand on my back, and Zane disappears into the jungle.

The rain is picking up again, but we both take our time getting all the sand off our feet. If I had imagined being stuck on an island, I would never have guessed it would be the sand that drove me the craziest. If I'd spent any time thinking about it, I would have. But I guess when you think about being on a deserted island, it's always about what three things you would bring.

Dante closes the flap to the wind. He's made good use of his time. The raft is tidied, and in the center of it are four bowls of jerky and coconut.

"Are you hungry, Sassy?"

I look out the little slot of the window. "I . . ."

"They're adults. If they want to act like little boys, let them get bloody and wet." He hands me the coconut bowl. "It's not warm, but it's something to eat."

"Thank you." I can't help glancing back at the flap. The coconut is tasty, and he's right: I need to eat. Without him, we'd be chewing on fishbones. I sit facing the flap. I can just see out while not too much rain is getting in.

"We're going to lose light soon." Dante sits across from me.

I nod at him and start eating. Something is different. It tastes better. I look up at him.

His eyebrow arches. "I knew you'd be able to tell."

"It's good."

"I harvested some salt. It's hard with the damn rain. But . . . Okay, enough about that." The way he shuts down the conversation, I have a feeling I don't want to know where he found the salt. And I'm not asking. "What else did you find?"

"Oh, a lot. And I think there's even more that Easton and Zane haven't told us about. It started to rain; we were trying to hurry back here. And then—"

"The fight was about you?"

"Yes." I purse my lips. It's not the first time Dante has shown his intuition. "There's a frying pan somewhere along the trail, and a ladle and a big metal spoon. Easton was carrying a chair, and Calvin had a huge net." The words tumble out like I'm an excited child.

He nods.

"But even better, the ship is made of wood. I'm not a carpenter, but I think we should be able to build a structure. Something more than this raft. But . . ." I stare at the raft wall, wondering what is going on outside.

"That's good. Eat, Haley. They'll be back soon."

I'm eating without thinking about it. Each bite swirls in my stomach. I sway to the left occasionally to get a better line of sight to the jungle. The wind is really blowing the tops of the trees around. And it makes me think of all the mats I made. I inch over to the flap.

"Where do you think you're going, Sassy?"

"I should make sure everything is secure."

"I've already done that. What you need to do is get dry." He holds out a towel, and I take it. I've already forgotten what it is to smell clean. But I'm grateful we have a little reminder of civilization.

"Thank you for the dinner, Dante. It was really good."

"I don't know about it, really. But with what I had to work with, it was fucking fantastic. I'm brilliant."

I have to shake my head. "You're feeling better?"

"So much so." He takes my empty bowl and puts it by the door flap.

"Where are they?" I look outside. I can almost see the trail from where I'm sitting. Angry clouds move across the tops of the trees.

"They'll be here soon enough," Dante says with his normal cocky tone.

I shiver.

"Are you cold, Sassy?" He pulls the flap closed.

"It's crazy right? How can we be cold here?"

"It's a lot—the stupid alpha dog shit, the storm. But we've got pots. This is a gold star day!" He opens his arms. "Come here."

I pause for a second.

"Unless you don't want to." He says it with a smirk and a cocked eyebrow.

"No. I . . ."

"You're worried. I get it. I'm just going to get you warm."

Am I worried? What am I worried about? The storm? The guys fighting? Or being alone with Dante? Which is crazy.

That's crazy, right?

I crawl over to him. I'm about to lean into him, but I realize my zipper jacket is dripping. I pull it off and hook it to the side of the raft. It won't get dry in here, but at least it won't get anyone wet either. "The storm is really picking up." Rain pelts the top of the raft.

Dante moves from my side and pushes at the few places on the ceiling that the water collects, sending it down the outside of the raft's sidewalls. "We're good, Sassy."

I put my head on his shoulder and take in a deep breath. And glare up at him. "How do you smell good? I smell like dead crabs and seaweed."

His laugh fills the raft at the same time the ground shakes from a lightning strike. An unnatural squeal comes out of me.

"You smell like home." He rubs his hand up and down my arm.

"Yes, well, I guess your home stinks of a clogged garbage disposal."

He laughs again. "You do not smell like dead crabs or a garbage disposal. Sassy. Come here." He pulls me around to his front, and I snuggle into his chest. Another flash of lightning and clap of thunder hit somewhere on the island.

"I'm doing okay. I'm doing okay." It's a mantra I keep repeating to myself. I know Calvin doesn't think we're going to be rescued. But I do. I believe it. I just have to say it over and over and make it true. I will manifest the shit out of this. The storm is gone. The guys are getting along. A nice ship takes us off the island—back to dry clothes and pizza.

"You're better than okay." He kisses the top of my head.

And I flatten my hand on his chest. His heart is constant and strong, and I'm trying to focus on it instead of the storm. My stupid fear of storms has come to bite me in the ass more than once. I'm going to get over it.

When I tilt my head up, his eyes darken. I know I shouldn't. It's not the right time, but I can't stop myself. I tilt my chin far back and take in his lips. My heart does sprints inside my chest. His kiss is firm, but while I might have started it, I'm no longer in control. The others might be fighting for top dog position, but Dante knows who he is. It doesn't take long before he's hiked me up to straddle his waist. I'm on top, but I'm as much in control as someone driving an amusement park car ride.

"Sassy." He holds the sides of my cheeks and locks eyes with me in the low light. I'm chained to his gaze. His eyes aren't solid brown. They are amber with flakes of deep blue. He has a square jawline and a dimple on his right cheek that gives him a celebrity chef look. The man is like artwork, artwork that smells of cookies and fresh laundry. It's easy to forget how attractive he is with his mouth continually running.

A wiry smile takes over his handsome face. "What are you thinking, Sassy?" He shifts a bit, and his hard cock hits me in just the right spot. I move back, doing it again. Loving how it feels. I'm chewing on my lower lip. "Damn, Sassy. I'm trying to be a gentleman, but if you do that again—"

I slide up on him, and he full-on growls, leaving a trail of goosebumps down my arms. Then my back is on the bottom of the raft. "You're mine now, Sassy, understood?"

"Yes," I gulp.

# Chapter 41

---

## *Scuttle*

Calvin

My knuckles hurt like hell. I shake my hand out, trying to disperse the sting. Easton's eyes blaze with a mix of anger and something else I can't quite place. He comes at me, his feet tearing up the dirt trail. He's fast, I'll give him that, but not as fast as me. Ever since he stepped onto the *Rock Candy*, smug and self-assured, I've been itching for a reason to wipe that arrogance off his face. His smirks drive me fucking bonkers, like he's flaunting everything he has that I don't. I don't give a shit about his gold medals.

But he's easy to fight. I dodge him, and he goes flying past. "Did Daddy forget to teach you how to fight?"

"Fuck you." He spits out some blood and runs at me headfirst. We're close, and there's no getting around him this time. I brace myself, but we still go sailing backward into the scrub next to the trail. Arms and legs flying, our bodies are snarled up together like two thorns on a bush, pulling at its own branches.

"Get off me, Swimmer Boy." I shove at him, but he's heavier than he looks. He gets up and stumbles back. But I don't move. I need to not kill the fucker. Which right now is going to be one of the toughest things I've ever done. Marring his perfect face makes me fucking happy.

"What? Can't get up? The giant is brought to his knees. How fitting. What's Haley going to think?" He laughs, and killing him doesn't seem like such a bad idea anymore.

I stand. "Fuck you." He's all talk, thinks he can have anything he wants, say anything he wants. But this time, he's crossed a line. Talking about my brother, saying he doesn't like me? Haley's name on his breath is like a dagger to my soul. He doesn't know a damn thing. The rage bubbles up inside me, a fiery torrent I can barely control.

I lunge forward, my fist connecting with his shoulder. I flinch at the impact—not from the pain but from the raw emotion that courses through me. The memory of my brother, his betrayal with my ex-girl-friend, their child—it's all a tangled mess in my head, fueling my fury.

Easton stumbles back, his face contorted in surprise and pain. He's not used to being on the receiving end. But he quickly regains his footing, his eyes narrowing. "Is that all you've got, you dumb oaf?" he sneers, wiping a trickle of blood from his lip.

The taunt hits me like a physical blow. My breath comes in short-sharp gasps. The surrounding jungle seems to close in, the air thick and heavy. I can hear the distant sound of waves crashing against the shore, a stark contrast to the chaos of our fight. But with Haley out of sight, I don't care what I do to this silver-spooned asshole.

I charge again, driven by a mixture of pain and anger. Our bodies crash together, a tangle of limbs and raw emotion. His elbow jabs into my side. It stings even as I move for a better hold. We're both grappling for dominance, but it's about more than just physical strength. It's about hurt, betrayal, and the unspoken words that hang heavy between us.

As we fight, the world fades away. It's just him and me, our grunts and gasps the only sound in the dense jungle. Sweat and dirt build on our skin. We're tromping down the path—the low ferns around us are flattened. The sweet smell of plants, dirt, and rain mix, reminding us of how far away from home we are.

Easton's hand gets wrapped up in my shirt and the seam tears away, leaving my stomach exposed. He stares at it for a second, the cloth hanging down to my side. We're evenly matched. I'm bigger, but he's fucking fast. He weaves to the right. He lands a good punch to my gut. "Fuck." I step back, and he gives me a second. We're no longer trying to kill each other. No, this is now more about trying to get out some of our anger. "Good hit."

"Henrick Schmidt."

"What?" Did I hit him too hard? I'm confused.

"My dad didn't teach me to fight. But mid-weight boxing silver medalist Henrick Schmidt did."

I nod, catching my breath.

"Dad never had time to do anything with me. Henrick and I both had a week after our events were over until the closing ceremonies. I taught him how to control his breathing while swimming, and he gave me some boxing pointers."

I nod again, looking down at my feet, and the next thing I know I'm on my ass, a sharp stump just an inch shy of my chest.

Both Easton and I stare at it. If either of us had landed on that, we'd be dead.

"Fuck." Easton's up, and while I could wrap my leg around his in a wrestling move and bring his face into the mud, I don't. "He taught me about surprise too."

My eyes flick over the muddy billionaire.

"You done?" He wipes his hand on his pants and runs his hand through his hair—smoothing it out of his face.

I stand and grunt at him.

"That's your way of saying yes?" He cocks his head to the side.

"Yes. Fuck you."

"Right." He's blocking the trail back to the beach and doesn't move. His hands on his hips, he looks like a damn disappointed teacher. "No, you know what? I'm not done."

I glare at him, but fuck this. If he wants to be pulverized into the ground, I'll do it.

"Whoa, whoa, big guy. I'm done with my fists." He throws his hands up. One of them smacks a palm frond, and a gallon of water pours over his head. His long bangs drip into his eyes, and it makes me laugh.

"Ha, ha." He gets his hair out of his face again. "What's up with you and your brother?"

"No." I push it out. I don't mean to shout it, but I do.

"No, what?"

"I'm not your friend. I'm not telling you shit." He's going to be lucky if I don't smother his arrogant face with one of the cushions we have tonight. Although I can't help smiling, he's got a nice shiner coming on to match the bruise on his jaw.

"Fine." He's got his shoulders back. The fucker is resilient. I'll give him that. Maybe his life hasn't been as cushy as I thought.

"Good." A loud clap of thunder shakes the surrounding jungle. Our necks swivel to the interior of the island.

"That was close." Easton's eyes are wide.

"It probably hit on the mountain. Up where I saw the goats." I need to get back there and see if I can capture a goat. Haley would like that. What the fuck am I thinking? I need to kill it. We don't have a way of feeding it. She's making my brain go soft. Then I think about Haley and how much she hates storms.

Another smaller crack of lightning hits somewhere farther away. The rain is really coming down now.

"You just don't like him, huh?"

"What the fuck, Rockwell? You're not my friend, and you're sure as fuck not my therapist."

"No, I'm not. But I've got my own shitty family." His lips are pursed, and he's looking at me like I'm his personal project. Which I sure as fuck am not.

"Yeah, I feel really sorry for you. When you cry yourself to sleep at night, do you blow your nose into hundred-dollar bills?"

His chest inflates. His fucking stupid blue eyes blink at me. "I don't know what happened between you and your brother. I'm sure it's shit, but money doesn't make people any different. If anything, it makes them worse." He wipes the blood off the side of his mouth.

"People are just shit." I touch my raw lip and take my hand away. I look back down the trail to the massive net I was carrying.

"Not all people." He says it like he believes it. Like it might be real. It's not.

"Yes, fucking all people. Every last one of us is a shit. If this were the Andes mountains and not an island, you be fucking looking to eat me."

"No thanks, you're not my type." He smirks again, but it doesn't quite reach his eyes. He grabs the chair he had and some other things.

Talking to him is pointless. Hitting him? Hitting him helped a little. I'll deal with the bruises.

I pick up the net, but it pushes on a bruise on my stomach. I was barely able to carry it earlier, before the rain and the fight. "I'll come back for the net tomorrow."

Easton nods. There's an unspoken understanding between us, a ceasefire that's as fragile as the peace the storm has brought us.

I gather the net up and push it under a palm frond. Then I find a few things that Zane dropped. A ladle, a little orange metal box, and some other cooking supplies. A few feet away, I find a small canvas tarp wrapped up with a small amount of rope, a machete handle sticking out between the folds. I tuck it under my arm.

"Right. Are you okay?" Easton has his arm looped through the chair, a bunch of other stuff under his other arm.

"I'll be fine."

"Your lip looks like shit. It's going to swell." I can see his medical background clicking in. Like he's some sort of Florence Nightingale—junior prince of all nurses. He probably doesn't even have basic first aid certification. I don't give a flying fuck. He helped Dante. I mean,

I'm glad Dante's good, but I don't think Easton had much to do with it.

"I'm good. We can't use any of the medical supplies."

"For this? I've had worse injuries from a light practice." He turns and walks down the trail.

Ahead of him, I make out a figure coming at us at a quick pace. It's not Haley, going by the way they're racing toward us. Her leg is healing, but it's not there yet.

"What the hell were you two blokes thinking?" Zane's back. Alone. "Don't answer that. You fucking weren't. You weren't thinking about anything other than your damn selves. Scaring the shit out of Haley?" His eyebrows shoot up. For a second, I think he's going to hit me. "You're supposed to be our bloody leader, Calvin." His chin is up in my face. "Act like it."

Easton pauses up ahead. "She's okay with the storm?"

"I don't know. I was almost to the stream when the ground shook. I took the long way around to keep from being out in the open too long." He eyes us both. "Did you get everything?" He takes the tarp from my hand. In slow motion, the damn machete falls free from the tarp.

I drop the other things and reach for the handle of the machete, but I'm not fast enough. The damn thing slides out of the tarp. It lands tip down in Zane's foot. It vibrates from side to side, like a cartoon. It even takes Zane a second, but then he's screaming.

"Fucking shit," Zane gasps. "Fuck, fuck bloody fuck." He reaches for it, but Easton's there to stop him.

"Don't touch it." Easton looks up at him, and then at me. From the look on his face, it's not good. The chair is still looped through his arm. Easton frees himself from it and kneels at Zane's foot. "Hold still. Let me take it out."

"How the bloody hell do you want me to hold still? There's a rusted cleaver sticking out of my foot."

"Machete," Easton and I say at the same time.

"For fuck's sake. You two should have beaten each other unconscious."

# Chapter 42
## *Refitting*

Dante

When I hear the thundering footsteps of idiots, I know they're on their way back to the raft. As heavenly as it is to hold her, touch her . . . I need to slow things down, anyway. I'm not letting my first time with Haley be when they're bringing their own chaotic energy here.

Haley freezes. I give her another quick kiss before I roll from her sweet embrace. "Don't move." But I know she will. I know whatever bedraggled condition either of them are in, she'll be upset. It's one of the reasons I still have my dick in my pants. It's the reason I haven't unwrapped Sassy like the amazing Christmas present she is. Fuck, I can barely move.

Easton pulls the flap back, and it practically flies off the side of the raft.

"What the hell?" I shout. "Calm yourself the shit down." Then I see past Golden Boy. Calvin is carrying Zane on his back. There's a trail of red blood mixing with rain flowing down Calvin's leg. And it's not the giant's blood. Calvin tosses Zane's shoe to the right of the raft entrance.

"Get out of the way." Easton pushes past me.

"Zane?" Haley's voice rises.

"These fuckers tried to cut off my foot." Zane growls, his arm clenched tight about Calvin's neck.

"He's exaggerating," Easton retorts.

"Piss off." Zane slides off Calvin's back and hops on one foot, then dives into the raft. "Shift over, you bloody idiot."

Haley's by my side. And the second Calvin and Easton see her, their shoulders drop like they've been caught by the police. "Oh Zane. What the heck?"

"How can I help?" With Haley at the entrance too, it's become a bottleneck. Zane's foot is wrapped up with Calvin's shirt and some rag I've never seen before. He rolls onto his side.

Zane smiles at Haley through gritted teeth. "It's fine, Little Bird. It doesn't really hurt that much at all. I'm just going to get the sand out of it. And maybe use one of the sterile wipes if everyone thinks that's okay?"

"Is that okay? Of course it's okay." She gasps. "How did this happen? Did they do this on . . . ?" Haley's mouth hangs open.

Zane grabs the knob of her knee. "No. Haley. They're shitheads but not . . . well, I don't know. They're reckless, but there was no mal-intent. I grabbed a tarp out of Calvin's hands, and the bloody machete fell on my foot."

I want to chime in with my two cents that the testosterone-filled balloons masquerading as men are going to be our doom. But I've got the sense to know that now isn't the right time to bring it up.

"How bad is it?" Haley turns to Easton, who is still standing in the rain.

"It's not too bad. Infection will be the worst thing to worry about. And tetanus."

"To work on the ship, you have to be current with that and all your shots." I glance at him. Am I grateful for what he did for me while we were on the ocean? Sure. But I've got my level certifications, including medical. Two years ago, I just didn't feel like cooking. I thought about moving to being a captain. I took shit tons of classes only to realize I was bored with the boat I was on, not being a chef.

Easton still isn't in the raft. "Let me in."

I move over, and Easton brings his wet ass into the raft. Calvin glares at me but doesn't make his way in even when there is room.

Haley spreads the towel out underneath Zane's foot.

"Maybe we shouldn't use the towel. I might get blood on it."

"It will wash off." Haley smooths the towel and takes Zane's hand while Easton unwraps the bandage around Zane's foot. I brace myself for something extreme, but when Easton pulls back the cloth, it's not bad. Deep. But not bad.

"It's dark in here. Can we use a minute of the flashlight?" Easton asks.

This is exactly why we haven't been using the light. I find it in the pocket by the flap and take it out of one of our precious plastic bags. I glance outside. Calvin has the rain shelter for the fire set, reinforced with a small tarp. And he's crouching next to it tending to the smallest of glowing embers.

"Once the fire is going, I'm going to use the new pot to get some water boiling," Calvin announces.

"Good." I glare at him. Between the wind and the rain, I don't know how he thinks he's going to get it going. But whatever. He needs to get his shit together. If anything is going to kill us, it's going to be splintered morale. I know it. Shit, everyone here knows it. But I've had enough of him for one day, and I wasn't even on their expedition to the fishing boat. "The pan is under the mat." I point it out to him. There are two big water jugs lying next to the fire pit that I hadn't noticed before.

"Thanks, but I've got another one." He points with a stick next to his leg. It's part of a cast iron dutch oven. The half with the handle. It's the most glorious thing I've ever seen. I'll be able to make almost anything now.

"Where's the flashlight?" Easton demands.

I ignore the tone. "Here." I turn it on and shine it on Zane's foot. The puncture wound is a stark, jagged tear against his dark skin, about two inches long, with inflamed edges hinting at a deep, angry red beneath. Beads of blood seep slowly from the wound. Zane's skin is peppered with white sand.

"You doing okay?" Haley holds his hand with her free one. Zane is slow to turn to her.

"Fucking sand is everywhere." Easton brushes at Zane's skin. "How's this feel?" He pushes a few inches around the outside of the wound.

"It doesn't feel good, but I've had worse." Zane nods at Haley.

"Right." Haley has her arm around his shoulder. "You're doing amazing."

Zane has his head turned to her and his bright smile shining. "I'm tough, you know."

"So tough."

"I think I'm going to barf." I wiggle my eyebrows at Zane.

"Right, well, that's nothing we haven't already seen." He laughs. And I don't care if I'm the butt of the joke if it makes him feel better.

I keep the light steady. "Okay. What do you think of your patient here, Golden Boy?"

"I wish I had more than one of these fucking sterile wipes." He's used two so far. There's a half dozen more. A bottle of alcohol would help.

"There was a bottle on board the ship." Zane's voice cracks.

"There was everything on the ship," Easton says.

Zane shakes his head like Easton's nuts. "No. The derelict. I grabbed it. It's in the orange case."

Easton nods. "We picked it up and brought it back."

"Hey Calvin." I poke my head out of the raft. "Golden Boy says there is an orange box out there?"

He lifts a few mats, and beneath it is a box. And I'm shocked the fire is already going a lot better. "Not bad." I open the case, and nestled next to an unlabeled bottle is a roll of bandages. They're wrapped in a yellowed, thin, crackling cellophane. I hold them up to Calvin. The raft medicine kit had bandages, but they used them on my head. They are rinsed and dried, but no way are they sterile. Then again, I'm not sure bandages from nineteen-whenever-these-were-made are sterile now.

He nods.

"How about these?" I hold them up and toss them to Easton when he puts his hand out.

"It's better than the barely washed ones." Easton hands them to Haley, who delicately unwraps them.

I screw off the cap of the bottle. And give it a gentle whiff. It's hooch of some sort. I take a second whiff.

"Don't drink it. You don't know what it is." Haley's holding the bandage loosely in her palm.

"I'm no spirits sommelier, but I've tried a lot. This is some sort of rice whiskey. The box has Thai writing on it. So it might be Mekhong Whiskey."

"No fucking way you could know that." Easton scowls.

I hold the side of the box. "Yeah, it says right here, 'Easton Rockwell is an asswipe, who is the only person who doesn't know that Thai writing has more fucking curves than a lot of other Asian scripts.'" I take a small swig from the bottle. "It's rice whiskey. It will work for his foot." I hold in a cough; the shit is strong.

Golden Boy has his face twisted up, but he takes the bottle. "Ready?"

I move to the other side of Zane and hold his hand.

"Yeah."

"It's going to sting."

"No bloody shit." Zane squeezes my hand hard enough I'm wondering if he's planning on giving birth. My sister didn't even cut off the blood vessels in my hand when she gave birth to twins. With ten hours of labor and then a C-section.

Fuck, I've done a really good job of thinking only of myself and not my sister. She's got to be flipping out. She always thought something like this could happen. How many times did I tell her that I was more likely to die in a car accident? I'm betting that the entire crew has told their families the same thing. Damn, the whiskey better kill every last germ in that wound.

Easton holds it over the top of the gaping hole. "You're sure that's what it is?"

"Haaaa." I breathe on him.

He coughs. "Right. Smells like my grandfather." Easton raises his eyebrows at Zane.

"Do it," Zane says through gritted teeth.

Easton pours like a spendthrift barkeep. It drips out of the bottle. Zane's nose twitches. The amber liquid pools in the wound, and Zane's grip on my hand turns my fingers white. "You good, man?"

He wordlessly nods.

Easton caps the bottle and covers the wound with one of the last gauze pads we have left; then he wraps it with the bandage from the derelict ship.

"It's not great, but it's clean." Easton nods. The bandage's stretched-out edges make Zane's foot appear like it's wearing an odd paper flower.

"Let's get you comfortable." Haley moves a cushion over for his head. "Maybe you should move to the other side of the raft. It's drier over there." Haley glances at me and Easton for support.

"Sure. Let's get you to the other side, big man," I say, and Zane mercifully lets go of my hand. I can't help but shake it out. Easton tries to help, but Zane pushes him away.

"I've got it. I'm not unconscious." He shimmies over to the other side of the raft, holding his bandaged leg up. Haley takes a long time over there, doing I don't know what. Fluffing his nonexistent pillows. But I don't care. What I care about is turning my attention to Easton and Calvin. I could just leave it alone. I could just let things alone. Only not this time. This isn't a passenger who says they're allergic to onions because they think they don't like them. No. They're going to take us all down. These two asses need to get it together. Or we could just let them beat the shit out of each other. Take a Darwinian approach: let the stupid show itself out.

"Let me get you the bowl of dinner Dante made. It's really good. He made, well, found salt!" Haley's deference tactics might not work, but I can tell he appreciates them.

He takes a bite. "It's good, Dante. But blimey, I'm really feeling it today."

A nod, a "You're welcome," and I turn back to Easton.

His eyes flare. "I'm going to go help Calvin with the fire. See if we can get some of the other bandages sanitary."

I nod. I don't need him to give me a play-by-play. But that happens with narcissists who didn't get enough attention as a child. I should know—I am one.

He slides out of the raft, leaving a trail of sand behind him. Zane, even with an injury, managed to bring less in.

I lie by the door flap, using my arm as a pillow. I fully expect that my solo Haley time is over. But a few minutes later, Zane gives her his empty bowl. Then she's lying next to me, snuggled into my side.

"Hey." I smile. "How is he doing?"

Zane has his eyes closed already. It won't be long before he's asleep. Crashing adrenaline will do that to you. I'm still coming back from smacking my head during the evacuation. Something still isn't right. Every once in a while when I turn, it's like I'm on a damn rollercoaster.

Haley closes her eyes. The raft wiggles. Behind the flap, I'm expecting to see Easton, but it's Calvin.

My gut tenses. "Did you and Easton work things out?"

"No." He turns, lifting his feet to clean them.

"Then stay outside until you do."

It's getting dark, but the narrowing of his eyes isn't hard to pick out. He nods, turns, and leaves.

"Dante!" Haley lifts her head.

"They're behaving like animals. They can sleep outside."

# Chapter 43

## *Supertanker*

Haley

The rain has stopped, and I keep expecting Calvin to come back—or at least for Easton to pop his head in. Neither do. I can't help but listen for voices amongst the crashing of the waves, but there's nothing. No arguing, grunting, or anything but normal ocean noises outside. I didn't speak up when Dante told Calvin and Easton they couldn't come in. Because he's right. The two of them need to come to an agreement. First my ankle. It was my fault —I'll take the blame on that one. Now Zane's foot? What other weird accident is going to happen because the two of them are fighting? I saw Easton's eye, Calvin's lip. They both look like shit. I hate that they're hurting. And that they're hurting each other.

There's nothing but more and more crashing waves. I squirm around on my life vest pillow. I'm wide awake. Like having three cups of coffee and a Red Bull kind of wide awake. But I'm not cold and only slightly damp, which is my new standard for feeling pretty damn good.

My thoughts race. We've been here two weeks—no, eight days. Six? How long have we been here?

"Fifteen days, Sassy."

"Sorry." Now I'm thinking out loud.

"Nothing to be sorry about." Dante rolls onto his back and pulls my head onto his chest. A big step up from the nylon of the life vest. Dante's heart thuds loud.

Zane mumbles something, and then he gives a snort like a snore. Like someone's pressed his off button. It's so reassuring I almost laugh. "He's going to be okay?" I meant to say it as a statement. Five days or twenty, they're changing me. I want to go home. I want us all to go home. In one piece, more than anything. We have to be a unit.

"Sure he is. He's a tough bloke," Dante says with a horrible British accent.

But I laugh. I have to—he does that for me.

"I love hearing you laugh, Sassy." He pulls me closer.

I nuzzle my face into his neck. How the heck does he smell this good? His fingers play with the bottom of my shirt, and then it's gone. An image of Sam flits across my consciousness, but I push it out. I made a choice. This is what I'm doing. I'm not doing it halfway. Dante deserves better.

"Dante." It's a plea and a gasp all at the same time. I lift my neck from his shoulder, and his lips are on mine. Firm. Demanding. His tongue eases into my mouth, while his hands play with my nipples. He moves me onto my back. The rain continues to hold off, but the last bit of the storm has the ocean waves angrily crashing. I shift in Dante's arms, desperate for comfort. My greedy self is hungry for him. I lift my hips, and he pulls my pants away.

"Fuck, Sassy. You're so gorgeous. A work of art. I can't wait to devour you." He nods at me, and he's asking but not asking. I reach for him, and he pulls me closer. Where I want to be.

"Yes," I moan softly, feeling his words caress me as much as his hands do. Our kisses are wild, frantic. "Waiting for you is every bit worth it."

Dante's mouth finds mine again, his tongue probing and demanding. I kiss him, our lips hungrily crashing together. My body craves his touch.

When he stops, his voice is low and gravelly. "You taste so fucking good, Sassy. I can't get enough of you. You're the best thing on the menu." In the low light, he wiggles his eyebrows at me. His head dips low, and I tip my head back and look up at the canopy. There are growing puddles of water in the low spots. Dante's fingers skim lower on my skin. I close my eyes in anticipation. He's taking things slow—so slow.

"I need you."

"Are you ready for the first course, Sassy?"

"Yes," I hiss out.

He licks down the center of my pussy before going back to take a swipe around the outside of my clit. My hips jerk into his powerful hands. He's holding me down, and I love it. I reach for his head, running my fingers through his brown hair. It's never in his face, but at times it covers his ears. It's so silky soft. When he sucks my clit into his mouth, I can't help but pull on his hair.

He groans. Dante likes a little pain. I don't stop the tension.

"Sassy." It's a promise, a threat. It's everything.

"Dante." I don't really want to have a conversation right now. I want him to keep his mouth right where it is. I want him to take my soul from my body. I want to be far away. Warm and safe. And that's how he makes me feel. Safe, honored, cherished. I love it.

He cocks his head, pulling against my grip until I let go. "I told you, Sassy. I'm in charge. You're mine now." He pushes a finger into me. First one and then two. My hips respond on their own. Pulsing and jerking. It's so good.

"Yes." I want to cry. I don't know why this is so overwhelming.

"Say it." There's gravel in his voice, a tone I don't want to deny.

"I'm yours now." I know what he means. At this moment. Not forever. Out of all the guys . . . he's the one who's most into sharing. I'm sure he's done it before. I'm sure he's done—

I shut down my thoughts. I know where I'm going with something like that. I'm going to think about how I don't compare, how I'm sure Dante has shared before. How I'm not enough to handle this. Right now, I am.

I am.

I am.

I'm more than enough to handle all this.

Dante.

Zane.

Easton.

Calvin.

And Sam.

"Sassy." Dante growls, and he grips my hips, tipping me up and back. His fingers thrust with a pace that's going to take me there soon. So soon. He lifts his mouth. "Stay here with me."

I want to be here. With him.

"What a good girl you are."

I whimper, my body reacting to his words as much as his touch. He thrusts deeper, and his tongue doesn't stop. The sounds of the beach fade away, and I'm tipping over the edge. My release is so good. I'm not sure how I'm ever going to stop screaming his name. "Dante." It's loud. It vibrates in my head.

"Did you enjoy the first course, Sassy?" He licks at my belly button and trails kisses up my body. His smile consumes his face.

"Your turn." I grip his shoulders.

"Oh, but that was my turn. Did you think that was for you? No, Sassy, watching you break into a thousand pieces of pleasure? That was for me. Now I'm going to really get things—"

"Cooking?"

He laughs. "You said it, not me." He rubs his thumb hard over my nipple. And I feel my eyes flare. "Now I'm ready for the main course. We've got you good and ready." Dante pulls his clothes off. He's the only of the guys I haven't seen naked yet. Sure, he took his clothes off when we went swimming but I didn't stare and yes, earlier tonight I was straddling him. But there's a difference. My eyes flick to his cock. It's beyond huge.

He takes the one remaining cushion in his hand. "Like I said, Sassy. Take this and lie back. I want to show you how things can go."

"It's not a competition." I put the cushion under my backside, grateful for the protection against the now sticky rubber raft.

"It is for the rest of them." He smiles, and his hand cracks down on the side of my ass. He raises his head in a little nod.

"You are so full of it."

"So are you." Dante pushes into me. And I still. He's big, and even with my last orgasm, I have to hold still and breathe as I adjust to his size. "Fuck, you've got a tight little cunt, don't you, Sassy? Damn." He tilts his head back and then grabs my legs, pulling them around his backside. I lock them behind his ass. He feels so good. He leans forward. "Are you ready to go?"

"Mmm." My head flops to the side.

"I asked you a question." His hand circles around my neck, and he holds it there. Our eyes lock. "I asked you a question, Sassy."

My brain is fuzzing out. "Uh, yes."

"Yes, what?" He glares at me, his amber eyes like dark moons.

"Yes, sir." It's all I can think to say.

He laughs. "That's not what I meant, Sassy. But I like it." Dante starts slow. His thrusts are calculated and rhythmic.

I'm sweating from every pore. Each push takes me higher. I'm becoming addicted to these men. How could I live without them? Any of them? My eyes drift close.

"Look at me, Sassy. Don't you go anywhere. Right now, you are here with me. You like my big dick." He's staring at me, a glint in his eyes. He hasn't moved his hand from around my neck. And I like it. I like it a whole heck of a lot. I grip his wrist with one hand. To keep it there or pull it off, I'm not sure. My other hand is on his shoulder. His pace is relentless. Each thrust follows the last with the exact precision I expect from Dante. His eyes hold mine. And I can't look away. I wouldn't look away if the whole world came crashing down.

There's a sound from behind Dante. But the only thing I'm focusing on is him.

"That's it. Take it. You're such a fucking beauty." He takes his other hand and squeezes my nipple. It hurts but in a way I like. To say I've never done anything like this before is absolutely true. "You have no idea, do you?"

"I . . ." I've never thought of myself that way. Hell, Steven spent years telling me my ass was too flat and I was too fat at the same time. These guys want me, but they only want me because I'm available. I understand the way it is. I'm not dumb.

"Say it. Say 'I'm so fucking beautiful.'" He pauses. And when I don't immediately say it, he stops. He freezes and leans over me. "Say it," he growls into my ear.

I can't say those words. I don't believe them. I . . .

"Say it." His grip on my neck tightens.

"I'm so fucking beautiful." I get it out. And he smiles, but he doesn't loosen his grip. "Sir," I add. And he's beaming. But most importantly, he moves again. Those spectacular brown eyes of his are glowing. The dimple in his cheek is like an exclamation mark on how handsome he is.

"That's right, you are. You're a beautiful girl who's taking my monster dick like a champion."

I tilt my hips up and squeeze. I squeeze harder than I ever have in my life. I want to give him so much.

"Fuck." Dante throws his head back. His motions become feral, but he never moves his hand from my neck. He lets go of my nipple, and when he does, the blood rushing back to it sends a bolt of electricity through my body. Dante reaches between us and rubs my clit.

My body hitches like I've been hit with a bolt of lightning. My back arches, and my shoulders convulse.

Dante lets go of my neck. My arms fly above my head like some sort of weird party game. I find a rope on the wall and hang on to it. My body twitches, and I hang on to that rope like I might float away. I'm completely undone.

"Fuck, Sassy, that was everything." My legs are wrapped tightly around him. I may never be able to unwrap them. I might be stuck this way. But maybe I don't care if I am. They are ruining me for the rest of my life. He thrusts one more time, and my hips jerk, my arms pull forward, and the rope in my hand breaks.

# Chapter 44

## *Blind Sector*

Easton

I don't even try to go into the raft. What the hell would be the point? I stare across the fire at Calvin. We've got the new canvas tarp strung up over the side the wind blows from. It's big enough that we can both be out of the rain. We are silently taking turns bringing wood over from the big pile and keeping it dry. Moving around is helping the swelling of my face. Calvin spits next to the fire. It's hard to tell in the dim light if his mouth is still bleeding. I'm not anymore. In any other situation, I wouldn't care if he was bleeding out his eyes. But keeping the peace for Haley's sake is something I want to do. I glance at the raft. Calvin's neck twists as he looks too.

Dante hasn't had any time alone with her until now. My skin bristles, and I can feel Calvin vibrating. He's doing that shuffle back and forth thing. Maybe he's jealous. I don't know. I'm not. Would I switch with Dante? In a heartbeat. But I'm not jealous, or I don't think I am.

I stare at the side of the raft, then toss another log on and turn to the raft again. Did I hear something? Calvin heads back to the wood pile. The water in the Dutch oven is boiling. The tan bandage floats around in the water. I give it a stir with a stick we've been using for poking at the fire for the last few days. Honestly, I have no idea how long it will take to kill the bacteria in the fabric.

"It should be done." Calvin nods at the fire. The logs are hissing and spitting out water. It's a miracle there are any flames at all.

"It needs more time." I give the pot another stir. I don't really know, but I don't want to agree with him.

"Water needs one minute at a boil to kill anything in it." Calvin crosses his arms over his chest.

"Cloth isn't water," I say, clamping down on the rest I want to say.

"It's been long enough."

"No. It hasn't." Somewhere in the back of my college training is the answer. "If that was the case, hospital linens would be done in five minutes."

He grunts. I guess that's enough for him. Damn, it's weird how much I miss my phone for stupid shit like this. A timer, a camera, the fucking internet. We both stare at the pot and watch it boil. I can hear my mother—a watched pot never boils. Guess she was wrong.

Haley moans, and fuck if my cock doesn't go immediately hard. I can't look at Calvin. I don't want to know if he has the same reaction I do. Instead, I stare at the pot, watching the rolling boil go on.

"Now," Calvin snarls.

"Whatever." I take a stick and fish the cloth out, draping it on the rope Dante is using for his kitchen roof.

Calvin takes the crutch Haley was using and pulls the Dutch oven out of the fire. We're standing across the fire from each other. The rain has completely stopped. Calvin pushes the remaining logs around. I watch the water from the bandage drip onto the sand. It's drilling little holes. Focusing on the dripping water is far better than straining to hear what Dante and Haley are saying and doing.

The crutch drops behind the kitchen, and Calvin takes the other poker. He moves the coals closer together and puts the large flat rock Dante's been using as a griddle on top of the fire. It's how we've saved embers in the rain before.

"Do you want to talk about it?" I ask. "Because Dante's right. And I want to sleep in the raft."

"Tell them we talked about it. I don't fucking care." Calvin drops sand around the rock, leaving little chimneys on either side. He turns and heads into the jungle.

I have to run to keep up with him. "Where the hell are you going?"

He doesn't stop. I should just go back and leave him the fuck alone. Let him run into the wilderness by himself. Dante called him an animal, and he seems to be living up to that. And who am I to tell him anything? He's an adult. An adult who had no qualms about punching me just a few hours ago. But the fact that he hasn't stopped has me running after him like a little kid seeking approval. And maybe I am. Or maybe I'm just curious as to what he's up to. He's the one who found the derelict.

I've been giving him a lot of credit, some of it unwarranted, because he's fucking human. One who is also stuck on a fucking island with not a lot of resources. "Did you find something else? Is that where you're going?"

He stops and looks back at me. "Yeah. I can't listen to Haley with Dante or Zane. And definitely not you, asshole. And I'm tired of getting rained on." Calvin takes off again. At the big map tree, instead of going straight, he takes a left.

"Wait, where are you going?" I figured he was heading to the fishing boat. But that was straight past the stream, the clearing, and along the beach. Calvin takes the trail near the stream. The same one where the boar attacked Zane and Haley. The moon came out back on the beach, but here? Here it's downright dark. "Can you see anything?"

"You can go back if you want." It's the same tone my biggest competitor on the team used with me when he was trying to get me to back out of a swim meet. Or not level up in a new type of stroke. But it only made me try harder, push through the water with more vigor, more determination.

"I'm good." I keep up behind his giant legs, and the deeper we get into the jungle, the more my eyes adjust to the deep shadows.

It smells different here. Oh, I can still pick up traces of the ocean breeze, but there's an unfamiliar scent with the whistling wind above the trees. It's humid and oh so wet; with each palm frond or large leaf that touches my shirt, I'm a little more soaked. I'm starting to wonder if just getting pelted by rain while standing on the beach was a better idea. If I shouldn't just turn and head back to the beach. But then I couldn't help, and where is he heading if not to the derelict or the map tree?

With all the secrets he keeps, I trust him a little less, which isn't much since Calvin has thrown his fist in my face not once but twice.

I'm not on his tail too closely. I'm close enough he knows I'm here, but not close enough the branches that slap back from his passing whip me. He pushes on and on. The stream turns to a dark pool on the side of the trail. Moonbeams now cross the trail, and I swear he's trying to lose me. The pool gets larger as we round it.

I haven't been this far from the beach yet. I've been finding dry driftwood in the scrub brush where the jungle and the beach meet. This pond is getting wider and wider. It's unsettling. Why didn't he mention finding this? I'm watching where I step on the lava rock. One misstep and I'll have matching legs to my fucked-up face. We're climbing up.

Fuck it. "Calvin, where in the hell are you going?"

He stops, and his shoulders drop. "There's a cave. It's really small. But it's dry or almost dry."

Yeah, I sure as fuck don't trust him now. We climb for another ten minutes. It's slow. And when the moon drifts behind storm clouds, it's a lot harder to know where to step. But then I see something. That can't be it. It's not the classic kind of cave you expect a kid to draw. "Is that it?"

He grunts and scampers over to the opening. Even on the way up, there's a path. And I can't help but wonder what we're going to find in it.

"How do you know there's nothing in there?"

"What, like a bear or a sabertooth tiger? The most dangerous thing on this island is me."

"Fuck." The rain picks up. It's a light drizzle to start with, but by the time Calvin backs into the cave, the drops are large. I'm not going back down, not with how much darker it's become. So it's into the devil's mouth with the devil himself. I poke my head inside.

"Come feet first. There's not enough room to turn around," he growls.

When I was in elementary school, I went on a backpacking trip with my dad. It's one of the memories I have that's just him. No phone. No work. No stepmom. We stayed in a small backpacking tent. This reminds me of that. Long enough that Calvin could stretch out completely. Really, if I wanted to, I could turn around or sit up.

"Don't think of sitting up—the roof of this place is like razors."

If anyone had told me three hours ago I'd be lying next to Calvin in a sand-floored cave staring out into the darkness, I would have laughed in their face. "Why didn't you tell anyone about this place?"

He clears his throat. "We can't all fit in here."

There's an emphasis on *all*. And I smirk. "You wanted to show Haley first."

"Shut up and go to sleep, Rockwell."

I roll over onto my side and grumble. It hurts. Not bad, but enough to know I'm bruised.

"You going to make it?"

"Yeah, I'm just peachy." I move around. We're close but not touching. And honestly, I'm grateful he let me in. I watch the shadows of the spikes on the ceiling and try not to think about spiders. "You going to tell me why you hate your brother?" Emily has pissed me off from time to time, but I could never hate her.

Fuck, I hope they made it somewhere. I hope to hell that she and

Dad are having drinks in a port city planning our rescue. That's the only way I can think of my sister. Laughing, giving away her inheritance to charity. Shopping in secondhand shops. Bringing home clothes with somebody else's used tissues in them.

Calvin doesn't answer right away. And I go back to blinking into the darkness.

"I don't hate him. Not really. I hate what he did. I hate what she did."

She, he. I get it. "The she was—"

"My ex. Well, she wasn't my ex when . . . They have two kids. They're cute. I mostly avoid them when I go home. Which is almost never. I suppose it doesn't matter now."

"Don't say that, man. We're going to get rescued. I told you I saw a boat."

"Right, a boat with no lights on."

"Yes."

"Rockwell, a boat with no lights on is a death sentence. Pirates. They find us? They'll kill us. Well, we'll get off easy. Haley, on the other hand . . . Yeah, not such a great way to live. Pretty blonde. That's not what I want for her."

"Yeah, you said that already."

"I'm sorry about your dad's fiancée," shoots out of him.

"Thanks." Candy was a gold-digging bitch. But she didn't deserve death by anything other than a pack of lawyers ripping her away from the money she loved so much.

Memories of Dad and Emily before Candy, before Dad's second wife, float around me. The rain spatters down outside, and eventually I use my arm as a pillow and drift off to sleep.

When I wake, I'm by myself. I'm also covered in little flea bites down the side of my legs. But I'm dry. Honestly, the driest I've been since we landed on this island. I stretch. I reach upward, and fuck, I cut the side of my right hand. Damn, it stings. Blood trickles down my wrist. "Fuck." I pull off my shirt and wrap it around my hand. It's no big deal.

Outside, the jungle is alive with birds. I stand by the opening for a minute and take in the view. The mountain goes up higher. If I hadn't given my hand the little slice, it would be nice to get to the top of it. But it's taller than I imagined. Instead, I make my way down and stop and admire the waterfall. It's amazing.

I crouch and clean the cut. It's nothing. It wouldn't even need stitches if I was back home.

The foliage along the path hasn't lost last night's rain, and by the time I'm to the big map tree, I'm fairly wet. I round the path and come out onto the beach. The first thing I notice is that the raft is missing the canopy. The second is that the furry thing in Haley's arms is moving.

# Chapter 45

## *Limey*

Zane

"Do you want to hold it?" Haley looks up at me. The gray, brown, and white bundle of fur and claws squirms in her arms.

"I'll hold your pussy." I wink at her.

Dante groans from next to the fire. We already had this conversation when I found the tiny thing. I know Americans call a fanny a pussy. And to them a fanny means butt. I'm not daft. We already went a round when I brought the wee thing onto the beach.

"Hey, Easton!" I wave him over. "Where the hell have you been?"

He jogs over. "I was in the . . . Where's Calvin?" He cranes his neck around the beach.

"I've got no clue. I thought he was with you." I'm staring at the little kitten Haley's holding. I'm pretty sure she's never going to let it walk again.

"Um, yeah. He was, but when I woke up, he was gone. I thought he'd have come back here." Easton runs his hand through his hair. That's when I notice the shirt wrapped around his hand.

"You good?" I point at the makeshift bandage.

"I cut my hand on some rocks. But it's nothing like what happened to you. Man, I'm sorry for any part I played in that."

"I'm doing good. It stings, but only when I move it. I'm not even limping. Taking it easy today is the plan. At least as easy as I can while looking for firewood, keeping the fire going, and foraging for food. That's how I found . . ." I wave at Haley holding the kitten. "Found it in the weeds up in the clearing."

"Fluffy? No, Muffin? Do you look like a Muffin?" Haley holds the Siamese-like kitten close to her chest. When she turns it around to show it to Easton, it's crazy how blue the little thing's eyes are, almost as blue as Haley's.

Easton puts his hand on her shoulder. "Oh, it's super cute." He reaches down.

"Don't," Haley calls out, but the tiny little thing hisses and spits at him.

"It's feral. Seems to only like Haley," I tell him.

"That goes for a lot of us around here." Dante looks up from where he is tending the fire.

"Where do you think Calvin could be?" Haley asks.

"I'm guessing he went out exploring again. Maybe at the top of the mountain." Easton looks off to the jungle. You can't see much of the mountain from our beach, but you can make it out really well from the top of the big tree. Not that I'm climbing up to the top of it anytime soon. Not with the stinging in my foot.

"What did you do to your hand?" Haley reaches for me.

"It's no big deal. A little scratch."

I glare at him. "Clean it up. The supplies are over there." I point at the kit near the firepit.

"What happened here?" Easton asks, surveying the raft and the roof hanging over the side of the large log.

Haley looks up from the demonic fuzzball. "Well, I got a little carried away. I pulled on the ropes."

I glance between her and Dante. It made for one complicated night, but we got through it. And it was worth it. Seeing her shatter the way she did was worth it. I woke and Dante had his hand around Little Bird's throat. She liked it. Fuck, I'll remember the look on her face for a really, really long time. Then the water soaking all of us was shocking.

"Is it fixable?" Easton stares at the raft.

"Sure, maybe," I say. "We're keeping the top off to let it dry out. But the thing is, do we want it to be? I don't know about you, but I'm sure as shit tired of living with sand in my butt crack. We need to build something. We have the fishing boat now. But this is almost a sign that it's time to get some proper shelter." I know Calvin will agree with me. He's been down on the chances of being rescued ever since we landed on the island. I'm sure we can get him on board.

"What do you have in mind?" Dante looks up at me.

"Something out of the way of the boars—away from the sand," I add.

"With good airflow." Easton nods. There's something going on with him.

"You didn't get into another fight with Calvin, did you?" I glance at my foot.

"Fuck no. I don't know where he is." Easton shook his head. "Actually, I think we're good now. As good as anyone can be with him. I think?" He takes a step closer to Haley.

"That's great, Easton." She looks up from the kitten. "Where do you think its mother is?" Haley turns to me.

"I'm sure it's around here somewhere." Easton tries to scratch the little demon's head again, and it hisses.

"Shh. Don't do that, Whiskers. Easton is a friend. No, that doesn't feel right, either." Haley rubs it behind its ear.

"Ah, she's finally figured it out about you, Easton. You're not a friend," Dante says

"You shh, both of you. I was talking about Tiger. Nope, not Tiger." She walks away shaking her head, taking the kitten down to the area right before the surf. When she puts it on the sand, it sits next to her, looks up and then plops down between her feet, curling itself into a ball.

"What sort of structure do you want to build?" Easton's eyes follow Haley. Mine too.

"A treehouse," I say. "The bugs are getting to me in the sand. And in the jungle, it gets too hot. But sitting in the top of the map tree, it's almost . . ."

"Pleasant?" Easton suggests.

"I was gonna say not hellish, but pleasant works. I've got ideas." I sit on one of the bigger logs near Dante and stretch out my leg, slowly, ignoring the little twinge in the top of my foot. Subconsciously, I wiggle my toes. Everything still works. "Right, ideas. The map tree is big, but there are two normal-sized large trees."

"Normal-sized large trees?" Easton crouches next to me like a yoga instructor.

"Yeah, you know, like you and Dante are normal tall and Calvin is . . ." I give a shrug.

"I think I know what you're talking about." Easton takes a twig from the woodpile and starts drawing. "This one here. And the other one is a little farther away, over here?" He draws $x$'s next to the large circle. "There's another one over here." He points across the path, and Dante marks it.

"Fuck, I didn't think about it, but you're right. There's no reason why we can't cross the path. We can make a new path, or if it's high enough up, it won't matter," I say.

Dante pulls up next to me and sits. "What about this stove you're so excited about?" What Dante means to say is the stove he's so excited about. He hasn't stopped talking about it all morning. That and smiling, but then again, I get the smiling. Still, it's a bit creepy. At least his sarcasm level has dropped.

"Yeah, well, we can have a kitchen down below. Near the trunk.

If it's cold, we can stay down below around the stove." It sounds good. I can see all the little details we can build. I've even stared at the branches of the trees enough to know we'll be able to connect them. I can envision it down to the last detail. When Easton mentioned the tree across the path, my brain cracked and the drawing in my head shifted over. Some of the new details are blurry, but I know they'll come together. They always do when I draw a sketch. I cup my hands around my mouth. "Haley, can you and the demon watch the fire? I want to take Easton and Dante over to the map tree."

She waves back with a big thumbs-up. "Don't call Snuggles a demon."

I give a thumbs-up back, and we head over to the map tree.

"See that branch? That one is big enough for a small platform, but if we join it to that tree, it will distribute the weight."

"That's a great idea." Easton's nodding right along with me. But Dante's leaning against the big tree.

"What?" I cock my head at him.

"You ever build anything?"

"No." I put my hands on my hips. "No, the kid who grew up in an apartment in the Midlands didn't have a chance to build much but a little dollhouse for his sister. But I've been reading architecture books forever. You think you can do any better?"

"Unfortunately, yes. My dad wasn't around, but my mom's brother owned a construction company. I had to work with him all summer and most days after school. It's fucking why I'm a chef. I got a job as a dishwasher at thirteen. It paid under the table. So much fucking better than having to pick up soda cans and cigarette butts from the construction site."

"What did you learn? You were a fucking thirteen-year-old when you started working in the restaurant. How the hell are you going to know anything about construction?"

"Oh, I didn't stop working with him just because I got another job. Fuck no, that asshole wouldn't take that as an excuse. But I didn't have to go as often because I had a job, even though the asshole took some of my salary from it. We were living in an apartment building he owned. Correction, a rundown piece of shit he owned. Still, he thought he needed to punish his youngest sister for getting knocked up by the wrong guy. Dear old Dad. He had worked for my uncle for a year. Long enough for my mother to end up with my sister and me. She's eleven months younger than me. Then he split with 100k of my uncle's money and his truck. The best thing I ever did was pay my asshole uncle off and move my mom and sister the hell out of the place." Dante scrubs his hand over his face.

I know exactly what he's thinking. Who's going to take care of them now?

He shakes his head and pushes off the trunk. "This will work. We just need to be careful not to kill the trees in the process. Supporting the limbs and keeping the weight balanced is crucial. All without a hell of a lot of supplies."

"I should show you the fishing boat." Easton puts his hand on Dante's shoulder, and Dante stares at it. "Right. Do you want to see it or not?"

"Hell yeah I do." Dante follows Easton down the path.

"You coming?" Easton turns back to trail.

"No, I'll stay and keep an eye on Haley and the fire. Let my foot have a little time to rest."

They wave, and I spend some time staring at the jungle. Fuck, Dante and I aren't that different. He has his sister and his mum. I have my sister and my mum. Granted, my dad wasn't a thief—just in the wrong place at the wrong time.

I should get back.

When I do, Haley has the kitten in the raft. She's drying the rubber creases down with one of the sponges. "Hey, do you want to help me get the roof back on?" she calls to me.

I look over my shoulder at the jungle, but it's still going to be there after we get the raft set back up. I'm a full believer that Easton is right. I don't want to sleep on the plastic anymore, feeling it move every time someone rolls over. Sure, it's like sleeping on an air mattress. An air mattress with a two-year-old and a box of biscuits. "Let's get this done."

"It's not going to be fun." Haley pulls the ropes down over one side as I hold it on the other, and it pops off like it's the wrong size lid on a takeaway container. The plastic of the raft is showing some age. Just like we all are.

"We need a new plan of attack." I'm practically growling the third time the roof comes unseated.

"Yeah, we do. You go on the inside." Haley points.

"With the demon kitten?"

"You're my big strong man. I think you'll survive, my love."

Fuck, I roll over the entrance into the raft with the little fuzzball who is running around and bounding off the sidewalls. It sees me and gives a hiss but then turns back to bat at the tassels of one of the cushions. I can't help but smile. It's such a normal cat thing, a normal home thing. Cats chasing tassels. My heart squeezes.

"Do you have it?" Haley asks.

"One minute." I pull the plastic roofing taut. "Yeah."

"Great, that worked. Let's do the other sides." She lifts the unconnected bit of the roof and smiles at me. "How's Mr. Nibbles?"

"Well, he's a she, and I don't think that's a good name to give a demon kitten. She might take it to heart and nibble us to death in the middle of the night."

"She would never." Haley gives her best shocked voice. "She's a good kitten."

"You're a good kitten."

She clears her throat, and I picture the blush on her cheeks I can't see. "Sorry if we woke you up. Well, I know we woke you up when the water flooded the raft. But the before part."

"Never be sorry for waking me up like that, Haley."

She moves down the side of the raft.

"Pull tighter."

"Got it. Two down, two to go. I sound like a football announcer." She laughs.

"An American football announcer."

"What's your favorite team?"

"Which type of football?"

"Both."

"Right, well, I guess the Ravens."

"You're just saying that because you know I'm from Maryland."

"You got me. But my favorite club is Aston Villa. Man, there is nothing better than going to the pitch with all your mates. It's brilliant. I fucking love it. We get tickets in the standing zone. A couple of pints before the match. Damn, I miss them." I tap the side of the roof. "This one's good."

The last one is a lot tougher to get back into position. The sun has tightened it to where it's almost impossible. But twenty minutes, a half dozen curse words, and a bucket of sweat later, it's back in place.

I crawl out of the raft as Calvin comes in sight from down the beach at the edge of the jungle. His arms are loaded with fruit and coconuts.

"Calvin!" Haley jumps up and races after him.

The devil cat jumps but misses the edge of the raft, bouncing back in. "Come here, you monster." It hisses but comes to me and jumps into my arms—claws fully extended. It nestles at the corner of my neck.

"Where were you?" Haley takes a bunch of coconuts from the pile in his arms.

Calvin glares at me as the devil spawn eats my ear, then looks back at Haley. "The island isn't what we thought."

# Chapter 46

## *Fish Weir*

Haley

I unload fruit out of Calvin's arms as fast as I can. It's stacked under his chin, and it's going to drop any second. Pomelos and I think tamarind pods? I don't know what to do with the pods. But Dante will. "This is amazing." I take a good sniff of a deep golden-yellow pomelo. It's like a floral grapefruit. Man, I want to dig into one right now.

"The island is a fucking ton bigger than we believed. I found a shit ton of fruit trees on the other side of the island. Over the mountain. Last time I went to the top, I looked around. But I didn't go any farther . . . and it looked like the land slid right into the sea. When I continued down the mountain's shoulder, the land jutted out to the ocean with another section of island. I thought it was all just cliffs like I had seen before. Those cliffs down to the ocean are so steep; I didn't figure the rest would be different. But man, there are a ton of fruit trees."

"Planted or natural?" My heart speeds up. If someone is going to come here looking to get their fruit, maybe there is a way home.

"Natural. There's no pattern. I thought of that too. There's no sign anyone has been there. Not that I can make out. At least, not in a really long time. Goat tracks are the only thing I found."

My heart drops. I really was hoping someone might come to harvest their fruit. But it's definitive. Calvin's proven he's a good tracker. If he didn't see any tracks, I believe him.

"What is that?" He points at the Siamese kitten nibbling at Zane's ear. I think it's playing and not actually trying to eat him. But I don't know, maybe it is.

"That's the kitten Zane found." We walk back to the raft. "I'll get my basket." I bring the woven thing over to Dante's large stone.

"Where's this basket?" Calvin looks right at it.

"Okay, it's not the best, but it's not flat, and for now, that makes it a basket." I layer the pomelos around the edge of it and take the pods from Calvin. He's not looking at me, his focus on Zane.

"A kitten?" His green eyes flick to me and then back to the kitten. "Where? How?"

I'm holding my breath, waiting for him to go berserk about how we can't keep a kitten, that we can barely feed ourselves. That we're not going to be able to take care of it. All the things I could hear my dad say. *Get a cat at your mother's house. I don't want a dog, too much fur.* But he knew Mom was allergic, while he was just allergic to love. And it creeps in.

I wonder if my dad even knows I'm missing. I don't have him on any of my emergency contact forms, only my college best friend and her husband. I don't have much other than them. I thought about putting Steven's mom on my list. She raised a horrible human being, but she's an angel. Dad didn't pay any attention to me when I was a kid. I doubt he'll give me a second thought now.

"Yeah, a kitten," I say. "It was near the map tree in the clearing. Wandering around in the underbrush. I think Dante and I heard it the other day. But we thought it was something far more horrible. Like a huge rodent. But no, it's just Simba." Simba doesn't sound right either.

"You named it Simba?" Calvin's big hands reach for the little brown thing. "This pretty, pretty princess isn't a Simba. Are you—"

"Calvin, wait!" I try to stop him as he scoops the kitten off Zane's shoulder. It's feral. I'm afraid it will scratch him, but there's not a hiss or screech in the air.

"Why?" He has the kitten in the palm of one hand. His big thumb smooths down the fur that's sticking straight up on the little thing's adorable head. "My cats at home always liked sleeping in my hoody."

"You have cats?" Zane peels one of the pomelos. "Damn, these are good." He holds a segment out for me and pops it in my mouth.

"Omph mmy." The flavor bursts on my tongue. "How many cats do you have?"

"I have no idea. Dozens. I grew up on a farm. Most of them were barn cats. My brother and I each had our own that was allowed in the house. Winter and Summer."

"White and orange?" I shove another slice into my mouth. Calvin has yet to have any. He's too busy playing with the cat.

"No, that would have made sense. They were both tuxedo, black and white short-haired."

"I want to talk to you about a new shelter." Zane eats more of the citrus fruit.

"Did you move the raft?"

"Yeah, but not on purpose." I really, really don't want to talk about it with Calvin.

"We needed to take the top off and let it get some sun. It was really wet in there after the night of rain." Zane stops. "Right. Where did you sleep last night? It really seemed like Easton didn't want to tell us."

"Easton and I stayed in a small cave near a waterfall. If we're going to build a shelter using the wood from the fishing boat, maybe we should just build it by the mountain. There are caves. Or rather, a cave. It's super small. Easton and I barely fit in it together. But I think we should systematically explore the mountain. We might find another one. Bigger. But if we don't, I still think we should move inland for the rainy season."

Zane purses his lips. "Maybe. I've got some ideas." He excitedly told me about them while we were getting the last side of the roof of the raft back on. If we can build it, it will be really nice. But part of me is torn. Moving away from the beach, putting so much effort into a new structure, means we're giving up on getting rescued. I don't know how I feel about that. I don't know if I can let go of the dream of going home again. Indoor plumbing and nachos. I'm a fan of both. Pizza, ice cream. Hell, I'd murder for some roasted Brussels sprouts.

"Zane's plans sound fantastic. Being up in the map tree with the breeze. Think about it, Calvin, no plastic when we roll over at night. It could be fantastic." I blink up at Calvin. He's holding the cat up to his face.

"Okay. We should talk about it. This little guy"—he flips the kitten over—"*gal* has the bluest eyes. Almost the bluest I've ever seen." Calvin gives me a wink. "We can talk about the shelter placement later."

Now I can hear the subtext of the big old fat no, the one I had expected about the kitten. "Calvin, we're going to really talk about it. Make the decision together as a team, as a family."

"Family?" He laughs. "This is one messed up family."

"It doesn't have to be. With some work, it can be great." I rub the kitten behind her ear, and she purrs.

"You're right, Haley, with some work. I'm willing."

That was at least something. A start.

"Where are the others?" Calvin plops down on the log next to the fire. He puts the cat on his lap and plays with its belly. The little thing flashes its paws at him. I'm dying inside from all the cuteness.

I'm pretty sure this is the first time I've ever seen Calvin sit during the day. Normally he's twitching, gathering firewood or plants, whittling us a new something, almost anything. But not sitting.

"Easton and Dante took off for the fishing boat. Dante hasn't seen it yet, and he wanted to take a look."

"Good." It's a quick word, but I see a flicker of relief in Calvin's face. He's as happy as the rest of us that Dante feels good enough to go exploring the island. "And how's your foot?" Calvin turns to Zane.

"I'm going to make it. I haven't changed the bandage yet today. I'll do it when Easton gets back." Zane pokes at the fire.

"Is your ankle doing better, Haley?"

I nod.

"Good. Good. I should show you guys the waterfall. Have you seen it yet, Zane?"

"No. But I think that would be good." Zane picks up a stick from Calvin's pile of straight wood. "What are you doing with these?"

Calvin has kept his pile of straight sticks away from the firewood. Each one is sharpened on the end. We all leave his supplies alone, even without being told to.

"Fishing weir. I have almost enough to make a small one. The posts get stuck in the sand at regular intervals in the tidal area. Fish swim through them, the tide goes out, and they don't."

"Whoa, that's cool. How did you ever learn about that?"

"From an archeology class." Calvin stands and puts the now sleeping kitten in Zane's lap. The groggy thing looks up at Zane but closes its eyes again. "Want to help me set it up, Haley? Low tide is the perfect time."

I want to say no. I want to make him sit back down and be still. "Sure."

Calvin hands me a small pile of the sticks and takes the rest himself. Down at the shoreline, he stops. "Here should be good. Space them out, one every few inches. Push them in at least eight inches. Deep enough the waves won't knock them down. No worries if it does. This is going to take some experimenting."

I slide a few in. "Like this?"

"Yeah, that's perfect." We work together for a while until we have four rows that curve up to where the high tide mark is. It's something to look at, like an incomplete fence protruding out into the ocean. "Here." He hands me the last stick. "Do the honors of finishing it up."

I push it in.

His smile cocks to the side. "About yesterday." I turn and look up at him. He visibly gulps. "I was wrong. I'm sorry."

"You didn't hit me. I also didn't have a machete dropped on my foot. Have you talked to the guys yet?"

"A bit. Easton and I, we have some things to work out. Or at least I do. We talked last night—"

"He told me." The waves drift over our toes.

"All right. I'm glad. I hadn't told anyone about the waterfall or the cave. And that was wrong. I shouldn't keep information from all of you. I wanted to show you first. I wanted it to be a surprise. Just for you."

I wrap my arms around Calvin's neck. "That's really sweet. But I'm happy you understand that we have to be a team. I . . . I'm attracted to all of you, Calvin. It's the weirdest thing ever. I could never have imagined having something like this happen to me. But it is. I have feelings for each of you. I know this has to be hard on you. Especially you."

Calvin twists his face up. I'm pushing him too hard. I get it. We're all our past experiences.

"Are you doing okay?" I ask. "With this arrangement, I mean?"

His forehead furrows this time. "I'm good, Haley." I wonder if anyone has ever asked Calvin how he's doing before. He's the work-horse who never stops. Or that's who he's become.

"Okay, all right. But if you're ever not good, you need to tell me."

"Why?" It's a quick response. One that I can tell he didn't mean to give. "Forget it."

"No, I'm not forgetting it. You have to tell me because your needs and wants are important, Calvin. You get to ask for what you want."

A wicked smile eases over his face. I know what's coming; I brace myself. My feet are in the air, and he's heading for the raft. Past his fine ass and muscular back, I can't see much.

"You're back. Get the towels. Grab Haley's shoes. Bring the cat," Calvin barks at Easton.

# Chapter 47

## *Home Port*

Haley

We're well down the jungle path by the stream. "I can walk now, you know," I whisper into Calvin's ear. Somewhere around the map tree, he slides me onto his back. I'm more than grateful for the blood to stop rushing to my head. I reach for my shoes that Easton is carrying.

"I know," Calvin grunts. "But I need to carry you."

I've given the genie his magic words. Big mistake. So instead, I fight back, kissing Calvin behind his ear. Little nibbles at first. I catch Easton looking and wink at him.

Easton laughs. "She's not going to fight fair when you have something she wants."

"No, she's not, but we'll be there soon. I can manage," Calvin growls out.

"You can do it, man. Be strong," Zane says from behind me.

Oh, this is war. I let go of Calvin's shoulder with one hand and ease it around the front of his chest. I feel around his hard abs. But up or down? I have to decide. Up first, then down. I let my fingers lightly caress his abs, bringing them up to his nipple. I roll it between my fingers until it's a hard point. I pinch it once again. From the side of my cheek against his neck, I feel his jaw tighten and his steps lengthen. I let go and slowly, with thoughts of torture, slide my hand over his abs down to his waistband. I run my thumb under it, which is quite the feat as he's jostling me side to side with each step. I suck his earlobe into my mouth.

"Fuck, Sassy, I don't think that's the way to get him to put you down. Unless down is pressed up against a tree with his cock in you." Dante laughs. And I know he's priming Calvin with ideas he wants to see. I'm pretty sure I wouldn't be upset by it either.

"Mmmm," I say and then lick up the shell of Calvin's ear. I stretch a little lower with my right hand, but with the speed he's walking, I don't think I'll be able to reach his cock. Instead, I lightly play with the skin above it.

"Watch where you're going, Green. Don't drop our girl." Easton comes around the side to me.

Calvin's head snaps in Easton's direction. "Never. We're almost there. It's up ahead."

"It's amazing." Easton runs his hand down the front of my calf. Goosebumps follow. "I'm sure we can find lots to do there."

Calvin stops and slides me to the ground, but I don't get a chance to look around. He's grabbed me by the back of my head. His lips on mine, he pushes his tongue into my mouth. Demanding, tantalizing, possessing. He hitches me up again, this time our fronts together. My core drags over his hardened cock. I'm on fire. My fingers are in his hair. And then I'm back down. I have to blink away the misty haze of my desire.

"Whoa. This is . . ." My words are lost. It's like a fantasy. A waterfall cascades from three stories high to a large pool. The water is clear. It's deep but not so deep I can't see the bottom of the pool. Ferns and plants surround all but an area near the waterfall. A large slab of eroded lava rock is flat and smooth. Dappled sunlight glistens on it. A beacon in the jungle calling to us. "This is unbelievable."

"I know." Calvin reaches down and takes my hand. He kisses the top of it. "I wanted to show you. But I also knew once we knew this was here, we weren't going to want to stay on the beach. I didn't want to take that hope away from you. But . . ."

"I know. I saw the map tree yesterday. Today is three weeks." Three weeks. Twenty-one days. It's the amount of time any government with a budget is going to search for a group of citizens. *Rock Candy* was ported out of the Bahamas. It has to be all over the news. Sensationalized, but then anything about someone with as much money as Mr. Rockwell was going to be in the news over and over again. He owns two large companies. But any search effort past now, one of his companies would be funding. How long would they look? How much longer? Was the other raft found? And if so, what would they do about it?

But no, we are on our own for now. And spending time on the beach hoping for hope when it might not exist—it doesn't make sense.

"Three weeks," Zane repeats, shaking his head. "It doesn't feel that long. But I guess it is."

Dante takes my other hand.

"They think we're dead," I say, looking at him.

Calvin clears his throat. "We're not dead."

"No, we're not." I take Calvin's hand with my other one.

"We're very much alive." Zane steps in front of me, kissing my nose. "And I know you think this place isn't going to provide for us, Calvin. But fuck it. We have to have a little faith in it. In ourselves." He has his crew sweatshirt on backwards, the little kitten nestled into his hood. "We've found friendship. We've found Sandy." He rubs the top of the cat's head.

"No." The rest of us veto the name.

Easton steps behind me, his uninjured hand on my waist. "We've got each other. We can work through the rest."

The rest, it's going to be a lot. The problem solver in me wants to make a list. The rainy season, food, shelter, medical supplies. So much more. The list will get longer and longer, and there's nothing we can do about it.

"Hey, Little Bird. We're okay." Zane cups the side of my cheek. His lips are warm on mine.

Hands surround me. Touching me. Easton strips my shirt off. My pants vanish with Dante's movements.

I'm crying, but I'm not crying because we're wrecked. I'm crying because I feel so loved. So cherished. It's too much. When I glance at their faces, their eyes are dilated with desire.

I duck between Dante and Calvin, slip right out of their hands. I take quick steps and run beside the pool to where the rock calls out my name. I should test the water, know the depth, and check for the Loch Ness monster, but I don't. I jump straight in. My best dives always turn into belly flops. Instead, I cannonball in. The water is warm and clear, like the bougiest of luxury pools. Like one I swam in in Saint Lucia at an owner's mansion. Five underwater strokes, and the water glides over my nude body.

I break through the surface as Zane says, "Let's go." He jumps into the pool, his bandage gone. He swims over to me. "How you doing, you gorgeous Little Bird?" He pulls me closer, and we have that water kiss I missed before. He takes my hand and loops it around his neck. He's keeping us afloat, paddling slowly behind him. I'm not worrying about drowning. The rest of the guys around me wouldn't ever let anything happen.

Protected isn't enough to describe the feeling I have, but I'm not ready to call it anything more than that. Zane is an amazing kisser, and floating doesn't change any of that. I'm on top, but he's controlling everything. I tighten my legs, getting rid of any space between the two of us. His cock hits me in just the right spot. And I close my eyes, letting the sensation take me over.

Easton is right beside me. And when I lift my head, he leans in, takes over kissing me. Dante tows us to the edge of the pool. The three of us cling together like a family of sleeping otters. Only there's nothing sleepy about me right now. I'm more awake than I've ever felt.

There's a loud splash to my side, and when Easton releases my lips, I turn toward the sound. Dante's perched on the edge of the rock. The rock hangs into the water, submerged by a few inches. He spreads his legs, his cock standing out of the water. "Come here." He reaches for me. And I go. I take Dante into my hand, running my fingers over his length. I take him into my mouth.

"Fuck, Haley. That's not what I meant, but don't stop." Dante's breathy. His massive cock stands upright.

Someone has their hands around my waist. Hands big enough they cover my entire rib cage. Calvin—it has to be. "Float your legs back, Haley." Calvin smacks at my ass.

I let my legs drift up, anchoring myself with one hand. The other is wrapped around Dante's cock. My tongue circles his head, running over him. I inhale and take him to the base of my throat. Something's going on down my body. Hands are on my breasts. Calvin is standing between my legs. My ass is floating to the sky while he holds me up. And then I feel it. A tongue on my clit.

It's slow at first, circling. A finger slides into me. A splash of water and Easton comes up next to my waist. And disappears again. I keep working Dante.

"Fuck, Sassy, you're doing such a good job. Don't let Swimmer Boy distract you. Is he making you feel good? With his big old tongue?"

I moan around Dante's cock. Zane's standing close. So close. He's got one hand on my breast. I reach out, and at first I'm bracing myself on his waist. But with each stroke on Dante, I become more stable. I slide my hand down and take Zane in my fist.

"Fuck, Little Bird." He guides my hand up and down his dick.

So many hands, so many sensations. My brain is frazzled taking them all in. From one to the next, to the next. Dante's in my mouth. Zane's hand on my breast, his hand over mine. Easton's tongue on my clit, his fingers pushing in and out of me. And Calvin's hands on my ass. He's keeping me up. But then something else. There's a gentle pressure on my ass. Calvin's pushing slightly on my butthole.

"What do you think of that, Sassy?" My eyes flick up to Dante. "Look at those gorgeous eyes of yours. Watering. Am I too big for you? You can take a break."

I grab on to him tighter. And Dante laughs. I suck harder, hollowing out my cheeks. Dante screams. His come slides down my throat, filling my mouth until it spills down my chin.

I turn to Zane. He takes my hand off him. "Sit in Dante's lap, Little Bird."

I don't have the chance to move myself before Calvin has me flipped and on Dante. Dante whose lips meet mine. When he pulls his head back, he winks at me. "You're fucking amazing." A brief part of me slips and almost believes him. Dante pulls me up out of the water. My legs splay open. I'm aching. Zane pulls the other leg wider onto Dante's lap. And then he stands next to me. His cock bobbing.

I take him in, his full length, and back out. I send my tongue around his tip. His hands are in my wet hair, and he gives what's left of my ponytail a yank back and his cock goes down my throat.

"Easy, Sassy. You can take all of him," Dante grits out in my ear. "Look at your neck. Fuck, it's so sexy." Dante's fingers circle around the backside of my hairline. "Do it, Easton." Dante is conducting this orchestra.

Easton's tongue is back on my clit. Calvin slides a finger inside me. At least, I think it's Calvin. I can't look over. It feels so good, though. So good. Easton sucks hard, and I mimic him on Zane.

"Damn, Little Bird." He comes, jerking out of my mouth. His come spills down the front of my chest. Water sprays over my chest and face when Zane crumbles to his knees.

Dante reaches around and mixes the water and come over my chest. I turn and kiss him.

"Fuck," Calvin growls from the pool.

"What are you waiting for, Swimmer Boy? Sit down," Dante calls to Easton. He lifts me, and Easton takes his place.

Now I'm staring at Calvin between my legs. "Turn around." In typical Calvin style, it's not a request.

"That's a fantastic idea, Sassy. Show us how your pretty cunt takes Swimmer Boy's cock."

I flip over. Easton's blue eyes are glowing. "Damn, girlie, you are so hot."

Dante laughs. "She's more than hot, Harvard. You need to pull out a thesaurus?"

I'm not listening when I straddle Easton. I lower myself onto him. I'm so ready. Ready for so much, as much as they can give me. I'll take it all. I wait, loving how I feel, having him inside me. This is what I need. What I crave. Easton's hands are low on my hips, our pace set so we can do this all day. My head tips back, and my wet hair hangs down my back. My head rolls to the right. Calvin sucks on my neck. Zips of energy slide around my body. I'm not going to last. It's too good. Dante rolls my nipple between his fingers.

Then Calvin's finger is back on my bud. "We're going to have you here. Take you two at a time, Haley. Not today. But soon."

"I'm making a coconut oil cocktail, just for you, Sassy." Dante puts his head between Easton and me, sucking my breast into his mouth.

Calvin removes his finger. He grips my waist, pulling himself close to me. His cock nestles between my butt cheeks. I'm sandwiched between two walls of muscle. Calvin takes over, changing the pace I set. But I don't mind. My head rolls back, leaning against his chest. One hand lifts from my waist, and he wraps it around my neck, tilting my head back. His lips are warm and soft. It's in direct conflict with the assault he leads me in. Completely Calvin. Hard and firm for the world to see, and a warmhearted marshmallow on the inside for me.

Dante's hand travels low between Easton and myself. He rubs my clit, and it's more than I can take. I shatter. I'm screaming, but I have no idea what I'm saying. Easton and Calvin are both swearing and groaning.

"Look at our girl. Fuck, Sassy." I open my eyes. Dante has his hand on his cock, and when I lick my lips, he loses it. Over my stomach. "Damn."

I'm so relaxed I can't hold myself up. I'm reclining on Calvin's chest. Easton's cock is still inside me.

"Come here, Little Bird." Zane takes me in his arms and eases into the water. I put my head on his strong shoulders and close my eyes, enjoying floating without the waves or ocean animals. It's like some dance. The guys come over one at a time, and I float and cuddle with each one. Until Dante pulls me out and dries me with the cleanest of the towels.

"Have a rest, Sassy." He tucks the towel around my middle and puts another one under my head. Lying on the warm rock, I spend a lot of time watching the clouds float in and out of view above the jungle trees. I doze on and off. When I wake, Zane is floating in the middle of the pool. Dante is in the waterfall, taking a shower. And Easton is showing Calvin how to . . . I'm not sure if he's trying to teach him the backstroke or drown him. But they seem to be having a good time. We're a family. Us and our fuzzy little unnamed kitten. A family. Something I didn't think I'd ever have.

Sam

It's fucking raining again. And night. It only ever rains at night. It's driving me crazy. With the clouds, I can't see any damn stars. No stars, no charting. Out of three weeks, I've only seen stars for maybe two or three nights. But standing on the bridge with Penny at my side, I'm pretty sure through the fog and rain clouds I can see fucking land.

Land.

. . .

Want to know what was going on with Sam while the others were on the island? You can find a free Novella, *Lost* at www.elliepond.com/wrecked.

What's going to happen now that Sam has joined the party? Read book two: Uncharted

# Also by Ellie Pond

**Dark Wing Holiday Cruises**

Resisting the Bear

Claiming the Wolf

Courting the Bear

Redeeming the Dragon

Tempting the Bear

Defying the Dragon

Chasing the Wolf

Fighting the Dragon

**Dark Wing Series, Hidden Valley Wolves**

Hidden Heart

Brilliant Heart

Bewildered Heart

Mated (completed series of Hidden Valley Wolves)

**Mermaid Why Choose—Enchanted Elements**

Wicked Water

Rugged Rock

Western Winds

Fire Falls

**Veiled City**

Captured by the Dark Commander

Caged by the Ruthless Thief

Caged by the Ruthless Thief

Bound by the Golden King

**Dark Wing Series, River Divided**

Crafting Love

Fighting Love

**Dark Moon Rising**

Guard

Protect

Honor

**Wrecked**

Adrift

Uncharted

Unmoored

# About the Author

Ellie's had many professions, including costume designer, contract archeologist, organic farmer, fabric store owner, and airline gate agent. She's happy to be a full-time writer now. She lives in New England with her three teenage sons, husband, and father. It's a lot of testosterone. When time allows Ellie likes to travel. You can follow her on social media for her travel adventures, and more.